AN ANGEL'S DEMISE

ALSO BY SUE NYATHI

A Family Affair (2020)
'A contemporary African saga that serves up all the
ingredients: rags and riches, hero women, sex, the megachurch.
And romance – so much romance!'
– KARABO K. KGOLENG, writer, broadcaster, public speaker

'Sue Nyathi is a powerful literary force. *A Family Affair* exquisitely
captures the complexities of family, culture and the societal
constructs that surround women. Eloquent, evocative
and utterly engrossing.'
– DESIREE-ANNE MARTIN, author of *We Don't Talk About It. Ever.*

'This story had me wrapped around its finger. What a warm reading
experience. The authenticity of the characters is what endeared me
the most to this tale. A gem!'
– PHEMELO MOTENE, broadcaster

The GoldDiggers (2018)
This book is a page-turning tale of struggle and triumph.'
– *Sunday World*

'Nyathi's book is rich in detail and never dull. There is inspiration
from her characters for South Africans hoping to rise from humble
beginnings to success against all odds.'
– *Business Day*

'Nyathi has woven a work of fiction which is vividly authentic … in
a lyrical and beautiful way.'
– *Destiny* magazine

'If there was ever an author who could do a book like
The GoldDiggers justice, it would be none other than Sue Nyathi.'
– *Drum* magazine

AN ANGEL'S DEMISE

A Novel

SUE NYATHI

MACMILLAN

First published in 2022
by Pan Macmillan South Africa
Private Bag X19
Northlands
2116
Johannesburg
South Africa

www.panmacmillan.co.za

ISBN 978-1-77010-808-0
e-ISBN 978-1-77010-809-7

*Although the story is based on recognisable historical facts and places, this is
a work of fiction. Any resemblance to actual persons, living or dead, is purely
coincidental.*

Editing by Jane Bowman and Sean Fraser
Proofreading by Sally Hines
Design and typesetting by Nyx Design
Cover design by Ayanda Phasha
Author photograph by Shaun Gregory

MIX
Paper from
responsible sources
FSC® C022948

Printed by **novus print**, a division of Novus Holdings

To my granny, Selina the centenarian, in celebration of your life.
To my aunt Jane, you are a heroine in my eyes, applauding you and all those women who joined the struggle.
To my uncle Johannes, who was swallowed by the struggle.
In memory of you and all those we lost along the way.

PROLOGUE

High Court, Harare, May 2008

Robbed of light, she was unable to discern the transition from day into night, or one day to the next. The hours blended into each other seamlessly. There was no beginning or end. No sense of the passage of time. In solitary confinement she was in complete isolation, with no access to the other prisoners. By virtue of her crimes, which were classed as serious offences, she was assigned to a private cell – an advantage if one considered the overcrowding in prison cells, but it also meant she was isolated, her own thoughts tormenting her. She knew he had deliberately engineered it so that she would go insane. She could no longer vouch for her own sanity because she had now reached a stage of talking to herself. Conversing with people she had conjured up, some from her past, a few from the present. When she could no longer invoke them, she spoke to the cockroaches or spiders that crawled into her cell. At first she had been fearful of a furry spider with long legs that had crept furtively across her face and had screamed before flicking it away and squashing it to death. An action she later regretted as she reflected that it probably meant her no harm. So when another spider made its way into her cell, she had been more welcoming. Even letting it rest on the palm of her hand. The legs tickling her, reminding her of her sensibilities and that she was not completely dead. Now she knew better: those arachnids were harmless. It was people she needed to be wary of – and they were outside, living their lives with careless abandon while she merely existed inside this purgatory.

She heard the footfall of steps. The police were her only conduit to the outside world but even then they only responded to bribes. They brought her food on occasion, lumpy porridge or sadza with a few strands of watery cabbage, but she never partook in any of the meals. She did not drink the water either. Her paranoia would not allow her to. She was fully reliant on her lawyer to bring her dry goods and mineral water on their consultations. Not that she was ever hungry. Oftentimes her lawyer would try to coax her to eat, insisting that she would need her strength to stand trial.

The jangling keys turning in the door made her jump, snapping her back to the dreadful reality of her prison sojourn.

'Missus Ngozi. You have your court appearance today.'

She felt apprehensive about leaving the prison cell, uninhabitable as it was. She was no longer as conscious of the foul odours saturating the air as she had been when she first arrived. The filth had caused her to retch until she was hollow inside. Now she had become acclimatised to it and the smells permeated the pores of her skin. She was as filthy as the uncleaned toilet in her cell. Yet still she found refuge in these unsanitary surroundings. The walls shielded her from the judgement and scathing condemnation. There was no sympathy in the world, only wrath.

She emerged on the outside, welcomed by the blinding light of the day. Instinctively, she shielded her eyes with her hands. She hated that the radiant sun was shining a spotlight on her. The prisoners were piled unceremoniously into the prison van with other inmates. The wire mesh over the windows allowed some shafts of light that illuminated their faces. It also gave prisoners a glimpse of the freedom they yearned for. She was inconspicuous now – you could not set her apart from the rest. As they were transported from the Harare Remand Prison to the city centre, the other inmates chatted among themselves. She remained buried in her own thoughts, jostled in discomfort as the van sped over gaping potholes in the roads.

She was assisted out of the van in leg irons. As a Class-D prisoner they said she was a flight risk. The nerve. The minute she emerged from the van there was a barrage of cameras on her. Foreign media correspondents from Al Jazeera, the BBC and the SABC. They clicked furiously, trying to capture her humiliation and showcase it all over the world.

'We are outside the High Court today where the General's wife appears to be facing charges. Mrs Ngozi is set to take the stand in the most anticipated trial of the year!' spoke another journalist from the state media.

She avoided the cameras, looking ahead as she shuffled towards the court. In the days when she wore long Brazilian hair and Gucci sunglasses she had been able to hide behind them but there was no more hiding; she was exposed to the world. She felt very vulnerable and afraid. Once upon a time she had been fearless. She recalled an incident during the campaign trail when she had lost her cool after being harassed by some journalist. She had slapped him across the head with her Louis Vuitton clutch bag. Her security personnel had to intervene, but the incident had caused a skirmish. In those days she had power, or at least a proximity to it. Today she was powerless, like Samson, her hair shorn like a frightened sheep. Looking away gave no respite from the steely glares so she looked down instead, at her feet. Walking was a struggle and it wasn't the leg irons that made it difficult; it was the beatings she had received. In the middle of the night, she was often woken up to face the assault of police. She knew they had been sent by him. They inflicted the scars where they were not visible. Under her feet, on her back.

'Confess!' they said. 'Confess.'

She had no idea what she was supposed to be confessing to. Even the priest who had been assigned to her urged her to confess her sins.

'Kill me,' she replied, 'just fucking kill me!'

With no confession forthcoming, they beat her till she blacked out. She was comfortable in that space, veering between sanity and insanity.

The reporters accosted her, bombarding her with questions. She responded to none. That had always been her default response. Aloofness. It had not endeared her to the masses then and it further alienated her from them now. She did not want to meet their eyes, those contemptible stares. The disparaging remarks about what she had become. She could hear the gasps of horror her appearance elicited. When her husband was on the campaign trail, it wasn't his speeches that had excited reporters; it was her sense of style that had been fodder for the tabloids. She had always looked fashionably elegant in Chanel and Dior. Now she looked jaded in her green prison frock that hung on her like a hospital gown. On her feet she wore black plastic flip-flops. The ones you found at Bata. Pata Pata they called them. She knew of them because her domestic workers wore them. She had always worn Havaianas, her brand of choice even as a young girl. Her lawyer had offered to buy her a pair. She had declined, of course; it's not like she needed to turn up in prison or for her court appearances in branded flip-flops. She was long past the point of caring about those material comforts that were once the hallmark of her former life. She had fully embraced prison life and its rigours.

As she advanced towards the courtroom, she wondered if this was how Jesus must have felt as he carried his cross with the crowds jeering and heckling in the background. Except, of course, he was pious and sinless and she couldn't claim to be either. Church had rarely even featured in her life. They had celebrated Easter and Christmas ceremoniously, but beyond that there had not been room for religion. Now she thought about God often. The Afterlife. It had all started with that priest who paid her weekly visits. Father Dominic. He said he had come to save her from hell. She had laughed at him. What did he mean she could avoid hell? She was in hell. Every single day of her life was hell. That dirty, damp cell was a hellhole, robbed of sleep between 800-thread-count white cotton Egyptian sheets. Torture was being denied the luxuries and comforts she had been accustomed to. She used to have croissants and salmon for breakfast, not lumpy porridge laced with rat poison. Hell was the torturous beatings she endured, causing her body to swell in pain. The voices in her head tormented her. While hell might have been an abstract place for him, she was living it. Every single fucking day.

The law required that any arrested individual had to be charged within 48 hours and be brought before a court. She had been in custody for 30 days. And the law had not been applied consistently in her case because *he* was above the law. He could change the rules to accommodate himself.

Her lawyer, Beather Mteto, was at the courthouse to meet her. Dressed in a crisp linen suit, high heels and her braids styled neatly, she enveloped her in the scent of For Her by Giorgio Armani. The musky notes of bergamot and mandarin lingered in the air and it had been one of her favourite scents pre-incarceration. Her lawyer immediately took over, fielding questions from the media. She was adept at shielding her from the brutal onslaught. She tried to remain expressionless in the face of more clicking cameras.

'My client has no comments!' said Beather with authority, her voice rising above the chorus of those competing to get a word in.

Beather was a human rights lawyer with a solid reputation and a thriving practice. She had been the only lawyer willing to represent her. Others in the legal fraternity thought it was career suicide. Beather had argued that some cases were not about winning but about justice, as elusive as it was. Some accused her of doing it for the money, to which she argued she was not receiving a cent from Mrs Ngozi, whose assets had all been frozen.

The courtroom was just as noisy. Filled to capacity as though it were a movie premiere and she was the leading actress being led to the dock to face the charges levelled against her. This was Zollywood and she was there to put on an award-winning performance. Her freedom was at stake. She was thankful that no cameras were permitted in the courtroom. Out of the corner of her eye she saw someone furiously sketching her face. There was always someone trying to capture a moment, to sketch her guilt.

I am not a criminal. The real criminals are out there. I am just a scapegoat. The fall girl.

It was only when the presiding judge walked in that the courtroom settled slightly. Judge Rita Rezende was presiding.

She chuckled for the first time, thinking about how they had sent a woman to lynch her. Rita had been a friend once upon a time; they had lunched together on several occasions. Yet today Rita was in her red robe, her head crowned with a white horsehair wig, a vestige of the colonial past that the country still hung onto. She could see Rita sweltering beneath her wig. She wondered whether it was the air-con that wasn't working or if it was just her nerves. The state prosecutor, a thin wiry man in striped black Crimplene, presented his evidence against her. She felt the sweat trickle down from her armpits and between her thighs. She wrung her hands nervously. She no longer sported manicured hands with acrylic nails. She had bitten her own fingernails out of sheer fear and anxiety.

The judge read out the rap sheet of charges. They were like the credits at the end of a movie.

Attempted murder
Assault with the intent to cause grievous bodily harm
Evasion of justice
Fraud
Malicious damage to property
Money laundering and bribery

'How does the accused plead?'

There was a long pause as all eyes settled on her. She opened her mouth but no words emerged. She coughed, clearing her throat.

'How do you plead?' said the judge, repeating the question in a higher octave, as if she hadn't heard it the first time.

'Guilty!' she heard herself spit out.

The courtroom was in uproar. Beather was horrified. This was not the script she had rehearsed with her client in their last four meetings before the hearing.

'Silence!' said the judge, slamming down her gavel.

'Objection, My Lady!' said Beather. 'I would like to confer with my client.'

'Overruled. The accused pleads guilty. The court will sit on 23 September 2008 for mitigation hearings and sentencing. The accused is to remain in state custody until then.'

The prison guards came for her, escorting her to the awaiting van. She could see her lawyer smarting with anger. Beather was trying hard to maintain a neutral facade for the benefit of the journalists who pounced on her like vultures.

She did not care any more. She was ready to die. By the time September rolled around she would be no more. She wanted to be reconciled with her parents. The first question she would ask them was: Why did you bring me into this world only to abandon me?

PART 1 : THE GENESIS

What we call the beginning is often the end. And to make an
end is to make a beginning. The end is where we start from.
TS Eliot

1

An angel's nascence

Like a thief in the night, he ran across the grassy plains as fast as his sturdy legs could carry him. He was agile, like a gazelle, his sinewy frame illuminated by the full moon that cast a doubtful shadow behind him. He was propelled by an urgency that drove him towards the imposing farmhouse that stood elevated and proud, looking down snootily on the rest of the valley. Panting profusely, he leaned against the fence at the foot of the garden that separated him from them. The viciousness of the barking dogs caused him to stumble backwards, collapsing to the ground with a thud. He could feel the hairs on the back of his neck rise. The dogs sprang forth, restrained by the steel fence, but he could see the animosity in their eyes. They snarled menacingly, baring their sharp canines.

'Baas! Baas!' he bellowed in his raspy voice, 'Baaaaaaaaaaaaaas Paul!' The echo of his desperate cries resounded into the night.

At first she heard the loud, insistent calls in her dreams. They were distant and remote, on the fringes of her subconscious. Then they got closer and more persistent. She heard the dogs barking. They were loud and visceral and this jolted her out of her slumber. Her husband had heard them too and he had already clambered out of their king-sized four-poster bed. Through the mosquito net that covered their bed like a bride's veil, she could see him pulling on his cotton striped boxer shorts that had been discarded at the foot of the bed. Sleeping in the nude was the only way to endure the stifling summer nights. The ceiling fan that whirred like a helicopter was more a source of irritation than relief from the heat that left them sticky and wet. Paul reached for his revolver, which he shoved into the waistband of his pants, nestling it against his crotch. The coldness of the steel barrel against the warmth of his skin made him shiver. Ever since the disturbances in the country had started to escalate in the past year or two, he had become more vigilant about their safety. He hoped he wouldn't have to use the gun, but he had no qualms about killing someone if he felt that his family was under threat.

'It's those fucking munts!' he swore in irritation. 'You can't get a peaceful night's rest here without those munts causing chaos.'

By this time, Melanie had swung out of bed and pulled on her silk kimono.

'Stay in bed, Mel!' he cautioned. 'I'll handle it.'

It was more of a command than a request.

'No, Paul. I'm coming with you,' she responded defiantly, tightening the sash of her gown around her waist.

Paul moved swiftly from their bedroom, heading down the length of the passage with great speed. Melanie was not too far behind him, despite his repeated requests that she remain in the safety of their bedroom. As they scurried down the stairs, the shouting had elevated into screaming and the dogs were barking savagely. Paul quickly unbolted and unlocked the solid oak door, unsure of what exactly they were opening themselves to. Armed with bravado and his firearm, he ventured off into the night with Melanie close behind him. The dogs came bounding towards them, alerting them to the perceived danger. Melanie calmed them, patting them reassuringly. They licked her in acquiescence. With the dogs calmer, Paul was able to discern that the voice belonged to Douglas, one of the farm labourers. They strode across the rambling garden that surrounded the double-storey farmhouse like a moat around a castle. Their homestead was cordoned off from the rest of the farm with a high mesh security fence at the bottom of the garden. This is where they found Douglas, panting furiously, trying to calm his anxiety and exhaustion.

'What the fuck's the matter?' growled Paul.

Douglas prefaced his response with an apology as his baas glowered at him with growing impatience. Then he tried to articulate the problem in his limited English.

'Sorry to wake, Baas, but, Baas – we have problem. Big problem. It's Simmy – Simmy have birth pains. Simmy bleed and bleed. Bad, Baas. Very bad!'

From Douglas's disjointed sentences, Paul was able to infer that something had gone awry with Simphiwe's pregnancy. Instinctively, Paul did not want to get involved. He did not understand why these kaffirs insisted on breeding like rats and making their reproductive problems his.

'I'll get some towels,' insisted Melanie, already leaping into action, much to his chagrin.

'Towels for what?' he barked, seemingly more agitated than the dogs.

'We're going to have to take her to the hospital, Paul. Do you want blood all over your truck?'

Paul ran his hands through his jet-black hair and expelled a deep breath in exasperation. He suddenly yearned for his pipe.

The compound was located 5 kilometres from the farmhouse and was accessible via a gravel road. However, the workers had carved a meandering route through the acacia bush and savanna grassland that was much shorter. The owners of Belle Acres had been intentional in the spatial design, creating distance between themselves and the labourers. Approaching the dwelling unit, one of many identical matchbox houses built out of wood that constituted the living quarters, Mel and Paul were greeted by Simphiwe's hoarse screams. A crowd had already gathered around the modest quarters, curious about the ruckus. The settlement was prone to noisy disruptions, like a drunken brawl or a woman being beaten by her husband or lover. The crowd dispersed with the arrival of the baas and his madam, preferring to hang around the periphery of the action. Melanie rushed inside but was stopped by the sight of the heavily pregnant woman, her belly like a ripe watermelon, writhing on the bed. The combination of the pungent smell of blood and festering fear caused the pile of towels to fall from Melanie's hands to the floor. She felt her insides coil with apprehension, forcing bile up into her throat. She quickly ducked out of the room and spewed a torrent of vomit onto the sweet veld grass that grew wild at the doorstep.

'Khiwa, what is going on here?' demanded Paul, unperturbed by his wife's lack of stoicism.

Khiwa was a middle-aged, matronly woman who was sitting next to the bed mopping the young woman's face with a wet towel, trying to subdue her fever and coax her into silence. Another older, frail-looking woman was also in the room, sitting on a chair muttering incoherent incantations, her voice rising and falling like a longitudinal wave.

'Simmy is in labour. There is blood everywhere,' said Khiwa, panicked.

'We need to get her to a doctor right away!' said Paul, urgency in his step as he moved to her side.

His eyes met briefly with Simphiwe's, her pupils dilated in shock. She had stopped screaming, as if she had resigned herself to the pain as the being inside her pushed its way out of her uterus. Then slowly the foam appeared, frothing around her mouth like a witch's brew. As if in some magical dance, she began to shake with almost rhythmic convulsions. Paul moved down and could see the baby's head crowning and he reached for it. He was familiar with the birthing process, having delivered many calves in his lifetime. The baby was quiet when it emerged, smothered with blood and the slimy afterbirth. Paul pinched it to ascertain life and only then did it whimper softly and unconvincingly to signal its arrival in the world. Khiwa received the baby in a towel while Paul swiftly moved to attend to Simphiwe. He lifted her hand to feel for her faltering pulse. He shivered as he felt the spirit of death hovering over them, waiting expectantly to snatch a life. But the spirit of life remained, unmoved, not willing to cede dominion over the living. The line between life and death was fragile.

2

The other side of midnight

Midnight was almost upon them when they pulled up to the hospital, which felt like a deserted outpost. The lighting from the hospital signalled life and movement within. As they made their way onto the sterile premises, their nostrils were assaulted by the cloying smell of disinfectant. Upon presentation, Simphiwe was moribund and dehydrated. Douglas was holding her hand, her pulse wavering, but a flicker of hope still burning in her eyes. A black nurse was manning the nurse's station. It was a peculiar sight because it was uncommon in those days to have black nurses working in white hospitals. They had started recruiting them in the early seventies to relieve the pressure on their European counterparts.

'We can't treat her here,' she said. 'You know the rules.'

Paul ran his hands through his hair in abject frustration. He knew the rules intimately; he was not one to break them either, but what choice did they have?

'She is at death's door. If we drive to Gwelo, she won't make it.'

A 30-kilometre drive would definitely make the difference between life and death. He could tell the nurse was torn between breaking the law and saving the life of a black sister.

'I can't admit her,' replied the nurse, resolute in her stance, while staring down at her feet in shame.

'Nosipho, please,' pleaded Douglas, who had seen her name on her badge.

It was at that moment that a European doctor arrived, demanding to know what was going on.

'We have a situation here,' said Paul, trying to launch into an explanation, but the doctor immediately cut him off and demanded that Nurse Nosipho get a stretcher for the patient. She called out to a male orderly to assist. They wheeled a prostrate Simphiwe down the corridors as life and death wrestled each other, fighting for supremacy.

They sat in silence, watching the clock on the wall as each minute stretched painfully past. A quarter-past his growing unease. Half-past disquiet without an inkling of news. A quarter-to confusion as Douglas paced the room restlessly, unable to sit still. Tick tock. Tick tock. The clock's hands moved slowly, further stretching his apprehension. Eventually, Paul succumbed to sleep in his chair, snoring noisily, breaking the peaceful silence of the night. Two torturous hours later, the doctor finally emerged to brief them on Simphiwe's status. Douglas exhaled noisily when the doctor indicated that she had been stabilised. He gave them sound assurances that she would be fine. Paul thanked the doctor profusely for being so accommodating. It was then that the doctor enunciated the condition for black patients who were admitted to the private hospital: they had to pay cash upfront. Paul was aghast at the significantly higher tariffs, but he still paid. As they headed back to the car, Douglas expressed his profound gratitude. Paul nodded curtly, 'I will dock it from your wages. I don't want you thinking you can make your problems mine.'

Still Douglas thanked him because, even in his reluctance, Paul had been instrumental in saving the lives of Simphiwe and his newborn child.

They drove through the receding darkness as it was overtaken by the light of a new day. Douglas sat on the back of the bakkie on his own, the blustery winds flapping against him as Paul stepped on the accelerator. He had not invited him to sit in the front. Douglas felt the discomfort now that he did not have Simphiwe to distract him. He hugged himself to stave off the early-morning chill. He might have used the towels for warmth had they not been soaked with blood. The stench stayed with him, a rancid reminder of the events of the night. The rising sun lit up the sky and he found it comforting. He was used to being up at this hour and it always calmed him to watch the stars fade into the dawn of a new day.

The Belle Acres signpost, on an arch above the gate, signalled their arrival at the farm. The 'e' had long since fallen off and had not been replaced, but it hardly seemed to matter in the grand scheme of things. Turning off the main road, they had to travel another 6 kilometres on a gravel road. Paul didn't reduce his speed, oblivious to Douglas bouncing up and down as he went careening over bumps. Driving through the farm, the road was flanked by sweet veld grass that grew everywhere uncultivated. Paul drove straight to the milking yard where the cows were milling around, munching on hay while waiting their turn to be milked. The farm workers were already marshalling the cows as part of the first milking shift, which ran from 3am to 7am. They would return for the second shift from 3pm to 7pm. There were two teams of labourers at Belle Acres: the ones who milked and the ones who ran the general farm operations. Douglas belonged to the former. Until his death a few years ago, his father had been a labourer too. It was how Douglas had been initiated into the life.

While milking was a laborious process, it was something he could do in his sleep. They first had to inspect each cow and clean the udders so that the milk would not be contaminated and then each cow was milked manually. The cows would be distracted, feeding on the concentrate used to stimulate milk production. The smell of fresh cow dung infused the air but he was immune to it. It took him on average ten minutes to milk one cow. Any longer and Paul would have certainly whipped him. The milk was collected in stainless steel buckets, which were then pooled into a large refrigerated steel bowser. The milk remained there until the Dairibord trucks came to collect it. As he milked, Douglas considered the plight of his newborn child, who would be unable to breastfeed while Simphiwe was in hospital. His heart constricted in pain as he worried about the baby's sustenance. Instinctively, he knew he had to set aside an urn of milk for his daughter. He thought nothing of his actions until he was stopped by the foreman, Tyrone, and quizzed about it. Their exchange was overheard by Paul, who was immediately drawn to the altercation.

'I just took a few litres of milk for my daughter,' explained Douglas.

Paul eyed him warily. 'A few litres? You think I am running a fucking charity shop here?'

'No, Baas,' quaked Douglas.

'This is theft!' pronounced Tyrone.

All the workers who had been washing up after the first shift stopped what they were doing to see what the hullabaloo was about. To their horror, they watched the scene unfold before them as Paul wrestled the urn from Douglas's hands and it fell to the ground. The white liquid splashed onto the dark red soil, spreading like the tributaries of a river.

'See what you have done?' growled Paul. 'This will not go unpunished. Let this be a warning to all of you!'

Harsh disciplinary action followed as Paul whipped Douglas with a sjambok in front of the other workers. The whip sliced through the air before landing on Douglas's back. Paul flogged him mercilessly till he cut through Douglas's T-shirt. Collectively, the workers felt Douglas's pain. Flinching as the whip landed on his back, lash after lash, they were helpless to stand up to Paul. He was only one man against them all, yet he held sway over their destiny. The foreman finally interceded on Douglas's behalf, insisting it was enough. Douglas could barely straighten his back as he limped his way to the compound.

3

Cry for freedom

Simphiwe found solace in her hospital sojourn. She did not delight in the circumstances that had led her there, but rejoiced in the conditions surrounding her internment. The warm and friendly European doctor had provided her with a prognosis. He explained that she had suffered postpartum haemorrhaging. This was the result of the inability of her uterus to close after expelling the baby and the placenta. He went on to explain that a suture had curtailed the bleeding. He treated her with such empathy, which she found quite disarming. Apart from the Williams men, she had never come into contact with white men, especially calm ones with a peaceful and kind demeanour.

'Where is my baby now?' asked Simphiwe, who had no recollection of the birth.

Placing her hand over her tender belly, she was fully aware that the tenant who had occupied her womb had vacated the premises.

'The baby is fine,' reported Nurse Nosipho. 'Your mother was here yesterday with the baby to see you. She is fine. We inspected her.'

Simphiwe had no recollection of her mother's visit either, but was relieved to hear that her child was okay. While she was keen to be reunited with her baby, she felt weak and frail. She spent the next few days convalescing, and it was during this time that she developed a growing admiration for the nurses. When she was not sleeping, she observed them carry out the seemingly mundane tasks of bandaging wounds, taking temperatures and administering shots. She also admired the way they showed up in starched white uniforms, nursing caps, stockinged legs and shiny brown shoes. Some had bronzed badges that shone when the morning light danced off them and she learnt that the badges denoted different ranks and designations. The nurses also took pride in their work and in the stature that the profession afforded them. She was in awe of them. She loved the sanitary environment they worked in.

In contrast, her own home was cluttered and dusty, filled with a lingering smell of concoctions, herbs and snuff. Her mother and grandmother were always brewing one thing or another. She liked that her grandmother was able to heal people with her assortment of muti, but the nursing profession seemed to command more respect than Gogo did. Simphiwe was aware of the rumours that circulated in the compound. Many people called Gogo a witch, *umthakathi*. Simphiwe wondered whether it was her demeanour that people loathed about Mabusi, because she only ever wore black garments that often went for days without being washed. Mabusi also rarely bathed, claiming it would rinse away her luck.

From a young age, Simphiwe had roamed the rambling bushes with her gogo, identifying herbs by their smell. It was like she was an apprentice as they foraged in the bushes where Mabusi collected her medicine. Khiwa hated their outings and didn't want to be her mother's escort so she was grateful that Simphiwe was.

Through their peregrinations, they developed a close relationship. She was closer to Gogo than she was to her own mother. It had been in those moments that Simphiwe decided that she too wanted to be a healer. Watching the nurses further validated her decision, except she was clear that she wanted to become a sweet-smelling nurse in a uniform. Nurse Nosipho later introduced her to Depo Provera, a contraceptive she told her would prevent her from having more kids. Until then Simphiwe had never been exposed to any discussion about birth control. Nosipho assured her that having the injection would give her time to study and improve herself before she considered having another child. Simphiwe welcomed the intervention. Furthermore, Nosipho whispered to her, no one would know she had had it, unlike the pill that carried such a stigma. Simphiwe had no idea what stigma meant, but she didn't want to have another child before she could achieve her nursing dream.

Simphiwe thoroughly enjoyed being catered for while in hospital. She received daintily prepared meals on a tray. It felt good to be served. In her entire existence, she had no recollection of ever not being of service to someone. As far back as she could remember, she had started serving her grandmother from the minute she could walk. She always had to fetch one thing or the other. As she grew older, she assumed the role of being her grandmother's eyes. Her mother did not spare her the servitude. Even when she couldn't reach the kitchen sink, Khiwa had used a stool to elevate her so that she could be initiated into washing dishes. By the time she was twelve, Simphiwe was able to cook all their meals. Khiwa always complained that after serving the Williams family all day long, she had no energy left to serve her own family. Simphiwe was expected to run around her, serving her every whim. The situation had not improved as she got older; even with the demands of schoolwork, her mother still expected the same attention. Simphiwe was quietly resentful as she served her mother, ensconced in the worn armchair every day.

After she was discharged from the hospital, Simphiwe went home to the reality of being a mother and the rigours of motherhood. She was acquainted with her daughter for the first time. They had named her Velile in her absence as Khiwa was adamant that the baby had appeared from nowhere. The name annoyed Simphiwe because she felt it was Douglas's place to name their child and not her family's.

'He has no rights over this child,' stated Khiwa matter-of-factly. 'None at all.'

Simphiwe felt she had no right to her child either. That she had forfeited it while she was in hospital. Each time she held Velile in her arms the baby cried incessantly. Her cries began as soft whimpers and then graduated to a loud and persistent shrill. At that point, only Gogo could placate her. Simphiwe always marvelled at how Velile would immediately be still in the older woman's arms. It depressed her how her daughter rejected her, refusing to suckle on her full breasts, but soothed herself on her grandmother's breasts, which looked like dried prunes.

'You are restless,' Gogo would say sagely. 'She can sense your anxiety.'

Simphiwe exhaled noisily. She had no idea how to become restful and less worried.

'*Uthwele,*' intoned her grandmother. 'I don't know what they gave you at that hospital but you are carrying spirits that are not yours.'

Simphiwe was baffled by her gogo's words. Apart from the drip that had been administered and the medication she received around the clock, she couldn't fathom where these supposed spirits came from.

'Did they give you blood?' asked Mabusi.

'They did, but only because I lost a lot of blood.'

Mabusi intoned the dangers of blood transfusion, claiming that Simphiwe had taken on certain spirits, thereby polluting her bloodline. Khiwa had been dismissive, saying Gogo was being too superstitious and that it was the blood transfusion that had saved her life. For days Gogo burnt *imphepho,* the wispy fumes curling into the air, forming smoky patterns. Khiwa would immediately open the windows and doors to let the air in to diffuse the stench, cussing as she did so.

'What is this all for?' she screamed. 'You'll choke the baby!'

'It's to chase the bad spirits; I am fighting for Simphiwe's life.'

'Fighting for it? You almost killed her with your muti. I told you to stop it!'

'I wanted to make her birthing experience easier, to allow her uterus to contract. I did that with you, Khiwa, and you didn't even have a single tear!'

Khiwa was visibly agitated. 'That was seventeen years ago, Mama! You could still see then,' she hissed. 'Now you can't.'

'I can see,' replied Mabusi stubbornly. She was settled on the floor, cradling her great-granddaughter, cooing in her ears.

Khiwa merely pursed her lips.

While the issue had not been raised again, it had created a knot of tension in their home, which dissolved every morning when Khiwa left for work and then reformed on her return. Gogo and Simphiwe agreed it was peaceful without her. When Khiwa returned, it felt like the space had become too small for them. Four generations of women heaving, humming, howling and hurting under one roof.

As she lay outstretched on the bed, Simphiwe was thankful that Velile was cosseted in her grandmother's lap in the living room. She relished the quiet without the baby cawing in her ears. While she would not vocalise it, she definitely felt that motherhood was mundane and messy. Lying on the cold cement floor beside her was Douglas. He said it was cooler than lying on the quilted coverlet. Simphiwe knew that was a lie; he was just being respectful by not lying on her grandmother's bed. As Mabusi had aged, she had opted to sleep on the floor as she was prone to falling off the bed in the middle of the night. From where she lay, she had a view of his back, which was engraved with deep welts from the whipping he had received from Paul. The ridges were distended and drew haphazard patterns on his back. Duggie insisted he was no longer in pain, but he flinched when she caressed him gently with her fingertips. That was what she called him. Duggie. Even in the throes of passion, he was still Duggie. Others called him Dug-lass or Dug-lace.

He couldn't even wear a T-shirt because it hurt too much. And she hurt because he hurt. She felt the wound deep in her heart. Simphiwe's eyes welled with tears that wet her face, leaving tracks of despair.

She was glad he couldn't see her weeping; she didn't want to appear mawkish in his presence. Her gogo had done a great job of trying to assuage the pain by mixing a dark ointment that she massaged into his flesh. Every time she did so, Duggie closed his eyes tightly shut.

He was a brave man, and even in his anguish he would still come over during his lunch break and cook for them. Custom dictated that, as a new mother, she was unclean to handle the pots, so he came by every day to cook them lunch. Duggie lived in his own dwelling quarters, which he shared with another farm labourer. Both were unmarried and had to fend for themselves. She had spent a lot of time at Duggie's quarters and it was always her first port of call when she came back from school. He would cook a steaming pot of *isitshwala* for her, served with vegetables in season like the leaves from the spider plant or pumpkin leaves. On rare occasions, there would be rabbit-meat stew immersed in oily tomato gravy. Braised chicken would be served on pay day to reflect his liquidity. On other days, he would fry chicken intestines or boil chicken feet. But most of the time they just ate *isitshwala* with sour milk. Meat was an extravagance he could not often afford. They would eat with relish before devouring each other with equal fervour on the cold cement floor. That had been part of the attraction; he served her. Even when he was wooing her, he would carry her bag, trying to make her load lighter. He would help her with her homework because he had been forced to drop out of high school due to a lack of funding after his father passed on. She would leave his quarters when he headed off for his afternoon milking shift.

'*Uzomitha*,' her gogo would caution as she walked in, satiated and content.

And true to Gogo's word, Simphiwe had conceived. They had tried to keep it a secret from her mother, who eventually discovered it when she was taking a bucket bath one morning. While Khiwa said nothing, her face contorted into a grimace, conveying her disappointment. Crestfallen, Simphiwe confronted her grandmother.

'If you knew I was going to fall pregnant, why didn't you give me something for it?'

'You never asked me,' replied Mabusi nonchalantly. 'You just giggled and walked away like you didn't know what I was talking about. You forget I was a young girl like you. That I had those feelings once upon a time.'

Simphiwe had never imagined Mabusi young, nubile and in love. She couldn't even envision her own mother in the same light. Khiwa was always tired or angry, sometimes both. She wondered about her father, but the mood was never conducive to broach the subject with her mother. On the one occasion she had tried to tease information from Mabusi, her face had become creased with fury and she had responded angrily that there would be 'no talk of that man in our home'. Simphiwe knew from that interaction not to raise the subject again. She was happy that Velile had a father she would know, a father she could form a relationship with.

'We should leave here,' she said to Douglas one afternoon. 'And go somewhere else. I *hate* it here.'

Douglas looked up at her as if evaluating her suggestion, weighing his words carefully.

'It's no better in the cities,' he replied, 'and I don't have my O-levels certificate. What job could I possibly get there?'

'So what's going to happen to us, Duggie? Are we going to grow old and die here? On this wretched farm? Is this it for Velile?'

Douglas let the question hang in the air, unanswered, searching for a concrete response, but the void in his head could not formulate one. He switched on the stereo, wanting to find a diversion from the prickly silence between them. It was an uncomfortable quiet that carried the burden of words unsaid. He was hoping for a musical interlude of sorts, but instead he stumbled on a news broadcast. Simphiwe hoped he would switch it off because the radio was making a scratchy sound as the signal was not so strong.

'*Wozani bantwana benhlabathi, lizolwela inkululeko.*' Come forth, children of the soil, come and fight for your liberation.

The voice on the radio filled the room, even with the crackling in the background.

'I want to sign up,' declared Douglas. 'It's the only way we can change this. Get freedom. It's the only way we can make a better life for us, for Velile.'

Simphiwe sat up in bed; he had caught her attention.

'You're right. We should sign up.'

'What do you mean *we*? What about Velile?'

'Gogo will look after her. If you go, I am going. I don't want to sit here every day wondering where you are or whether you will ever come back to us. It would kill me. I would die, Duggie. Don't kill me while I'm still alive.'

He was unmoving as he measured her response.

'Then we must go together.'

Simphiwe smiled at him. She was filled with excitement at the prospect of enlisting to fight for the liberation of her country. Unwittingly, she was also fighting for her own freedom.

4

A white wedding

Everything that transpired after that conversation was geared towards their flight. Douglas was determined to have his daughter baptised before they departed. They knew they were leaving; they were just not sure of the day, nor the hour. He harboured reservations about leaving his daughter in the hands of Mabusi and Khiwa, but he was resigned to the fact that he had little choice in the matter. Customarily, he had no rights over the child; he had not paid *inhlawulo* for impregnating Simphiwe out of wedlock. Neither had he made any overtures towards paying *ilobola* for her or the child. It wasn't that he didn't aspire to do these things; he simply lacked the financial means. So, while Velile might have been denied legitimacy according to their culture and custom, he wanted his daughter to have legitimacy in the eyes of the Church. A Roman Catholic by faith, he approached the parish priest with his request. Father Silonda eyed him disdainfully before declining.

'Why?' asked Douglas, taken aback.

'I only baptise children born in marriage. I will not sanctify what is not of God.'

'Are you saying my daughter is a curse?' queried Douglas. 'I thought all children were a blessing in the eyes of God.'

'That is not what I said. I merely pointed out that she was born out of wedlock. Born from the sin you committed with *that* girl.'

'I want to be right with God,' responded Douglas. 'How must I come right?'

'You need to marry the girl. Then it will be right.'

On paper, marriage sounded like an easy proposition, but it was difficult in practice. Douglas explained to Father Silonda that he did not have the money to even suggest marriage to Simphiwe's family.

'You knew this but still you gave in to your fleshly desires? Sin has consequences, young man. This child is the product of your immorality.'

Douglas felt affronted. He had expected sympathy, not the harsh reproach being levelled by this man of God. He walked out of the church feeling somewhat discouraged. Nonetheless, he plucked up the courage to approach Khiwa, who laughed so hard it was like she baptised his face with specks of spit.

'You want to marry my daughter? Do you even hear what you are saying?'

As she spoke, her chest heaved, her breasts rising with aggravation. Khiwa was a big, burly woman, stuffed into her maid's uniform that was slowly tearing at the seams.

'Yes,' he replied. 'I want to know who the males are in the family that I can speak to.'

'There are no males in our family. It's just Mama and me. You will address us. We are the ones who raised Simphiwe.'

'I just thought her father might—'

Khiwa cut him off. 'Where have you ever seen her father? Don't insult us. Don't insult me!'

Douglas apologised profusely, afraid that he would sour negotiations even before they had started. He then reiterated his request, much to the bemusement of Khiwa. She beckoned to her mother to hear what Douglas had put forward. Mabusi, from her position on the floor, cradling Velile in her arms, had heard everything that had been said. When she sensed Douglas's presence in the room she had known what he was going to say.

'He has a good heart, Khiwa. He has good intentions. You should let them marry.'

'Never,' replied Khiwa. 'Over my dead body. My daughter is too good for you. I had plans for her life until you ruined them.'

'Mama, I am sorry,' intoned Douglas. 'I just want to make things right here. Let me do this. I will fix the rest.'

'I will not let you marry my daughter. And mark my words, even if you do get married, you will never live with her. Not even for a day. Never. You hear me!'

Simphiwe had heard her mother, pushing her ear against the door so that no word escaped her. She felt glowering resentment towards her mother for trying to quell the only chance she had at happiness.

When Khiwa came to her bedroom to sleep, she found Simphiwe curled on her bed weeping quietly. Khiwa ignored her soft whimpers as she clambered into the bed. The three of them had always lived in close proximity; privacy was unheard of. Yet Khiwa craved it in that moment. The only thing she wanted after a taxing day at work was to succumb to sleep, but now she had Simphiwe crying beside her like the newborn baby.

'*Thula, Simmy. Thula!*' she hissed.

This only made Simphiwe cry louder. Khiwa sat up exasperated.

'Are you crying for that man of yours? *Yi Simmy? Ukhalel' indoda? Yi yi for indoda?*'

Simphiwe cried even harder, triggered by her mother's callousness.

'How could you have done this to me, Simphiwe?'

'Mama, how is this even about you? Why are you making it about you? This is my life and my child's life,' Simphiwe spoke out in anger, knowing her response might invoke a backlash from her mother.

She had been raised to always rein in her emotions and not display them because that would have been sheer insolence. Khiwa got out of bed and turned on the bedside lamp, lightening the room and showing up her own anger. When Khiwa started fishing around in her wardrobe, Simphiwe had a strong sense of foreboding that she was going to receive the beating of her life. Much to her surprise, her mother pulled out a huge stocking filled with money, which she threw on the bed at Simphiwe.

'Can you not see how hard I was fighting for you to be better? To get a better life? To move away from this godforsaken place and make something better for yourself?'

The statistics were stacked against them. For every 1 000 black children in Rhodesia only 750 attended school. Of the 750 that did go to school, less than half finished their primary education. Khiwa was part of the half that never finished her primary education. The system was rigged against them to curtail social mobility and economic liberation. Khiwa understood this and, while not in those exact words, she knew that education was the only way to get them out of this quagmire.

'Here. Take this money, Simphiwe. It's yours. *Ngikuzamile mntanami. Zizame lawe.* You can marry him if you think that is what is best for your life.'

Douglas and Simphiwe married shortly thereafter. It was a hastily sewn-together affair to cover their shame in the eyes of the church folk. Melanie decided to get involved after hearing about the impending nuptials via Khiwa's Monday-morning rant. She gifted Simphiwe a white dress with Chantilly lace that had been hanging stoically in her closet for years, unworn. The dress fitted perfectly and they only had to adjust the hem because Simphiwe was much shorter. Without shoes to match, Simphiwe wore white Bata takkies. She beaded them to make them fancier. Melanie ordered a wedding cake from the famous bakery, Downings: a two-tiered cake with dollops of cream and a figurine of a white couple on top. Khiwa spent the week leading up to the wedding baking scones and biscuits. On the day of the wedding, Melanie arrived at the compound armed with her Kodak camera and a make-up kit to glam up Simphiwe, who emerged looking powdered like a ghost with bright red lips.

They were married on the farm in the shade of a deserted barn that housed a workshop to service old tractors. All the guests settled down on haystacks, which had been set up like pews in a church. There was no organ or harp, only the rhythmic pulsating of African drums. The ladies from church led the singing, their buttocks rising and falling with the tempo of the beating drums. There was ululating and singing as Douglas and Simphiwe made their way down the makeshift aisle, walking hand in hand. Douglas was decked out in his Sunday best, a crisp, white cotton shirt and black trousers turned up at the bottom. They looked like a dashing young couple, deliriously in love, their eyes lit up with hope. Khiwa had cleaned up for the occasion and was wearing a plaid brown skirt and a white blouse that was too tight across her bosom. Mabusi had refused to step out of her black regalia.

Father Silonda preached about love from the Book of Corinthians in a sonorous voice.

'Love is patient, love is kind. It does not envy, it does not boast, it is not proud. It is not rude, it is not self-seeking, it is not easily angered, and it keeps no record of wrongs. Love does not delight in evil but rejoices in the truth. It always protects, always trusts, always hopes, always perseveres. Love never fails.'

'*Uyazini' ngothando lowu?* What does he know about love?' said Mabusi, who sat beside Khiwa, oblivious to the fact that they were in the front row, within earshot of the priest.

'Mama!' chastened Khiwa, elbowing her mother so as not to draw any further attention to themselves, but she was sure they had been heard.

Father Silonda did not hesitate to pick up on Mabusi's comment.

'Judge and you will not be judged. The day of judgement will come and we will all be asked to account for our sins. And so we leave it to our Maker.'

Khiwa was relieved when he finally closed his Bible and performed the marriage rites. They were not regulars in church. On Sundays when other women bathed and dressed in their Sunday best and headed to church, Khiwa brewed her beer.

When the marriage service was concluded they stayed behind to perform the baptism rites. Baby Velile was christened Angela after the Saint Angela Merici, a woman born centuries before in Brescia, Italy. Angela became her first name as Christian names were said to be superior to indigenous ones. Velile became her middle name and she took on Nzima, her father's last name. Angela Velile Nzima.

After the wedding service, those guests who did not shun Khiwa's home returned there to eat. Some came out of sheer curiosity and converged in her living room to marvel at the interior. Being a housemaid meant she was the recipient of anything the madam no longer wanted. So, in contrast to many, Khiwa was able to create a cosy, well-furnished abode. The men occupied the tiny veranda, squatting on the ground because there were not enough chairs. They were not strangers, having often occupied the space as they flocked there to drink, conversing loudly like hadedas. The meal was a simple one of samp, goat stew and tasty 'road runner', or free-range chicken.

Khiwa had risen before the sun to cook the food in three-legged cast-iron pots, fanning the flames and smoke. Everyone applauded her efforts. The men helped themselves to copious amounts of Khiwa's famous home-brewed *umqombothi*, a traditional beer she sold on weekends. She used a combination of sorghum and maize, which was readily available on the farm. She would ferment them together with yeast to create an illicit bootleg that was loved by many. There was something cathartic about mixing all the ingredients together and watching them ferment.

Khiwa had a Supersonic record player she had inherited from the Williams family and on weekends the stereo blared with the sounds of Don Williams, Kenny Rogers or any other albums they could get their hands on. With no access to pubs or beer halls, Khiwa's shebeen was the only place where men could get a slight reprieve after a hectic week at the farm. Very few women came there and the ones who did were called unsavoury names. The rest despised Khiwa for running her shebeen, saying alcohol made their men violent and irresponsible. Then there were those who gossiped that the men didn't come for the beer but to sample Khiwa's fat labia so that they could bury themselves in the thick folds of her cunt. They said the men were fascinated with Khiwa's milky-white complexion and her snow-white pubic hair that was said to grow in tufts. Khiwa never took heed of the dissension or gossip and continued to brew one barrel after another. She had a captive market comprised entirely of farm labourers in the area who flocked to Belle Acres.

Those who did not want to be part of the sin of insobriety drank Mazoe orange juice, a watered-down concentrate supplied by Melanie. The dance floor was opened by Hugh Masekela and Herb Alpert's rendition of 'Skokiaan'. It whipped the guests to their feet, and they danced in the soil, raising plumes of dust with their adept moves. Melanie joined in, having danced to the song at many illicit shebeens in the Transkei. The original song was initially recorded in 1947, the year she was born, but it had become so popular that there were several cover versions done by the likes of Ralph Marterie and Louis Armstrong. This knowledge she had garnered from one of her music history modules at university.

Khiwa was visibly impressed by her madam's ability to dance and how easily she assimilated among them all. In that moment Khiwa related to Melanie as a friend more than a madam. For a brief time the strife and oppression were forgotten as they made merry and danced with abandon. Even Father Silonda loosened his collar and stomped the ground with zeal.

In the midst of all the merrymaking, Douglas approached his mother-in-law and thanked her for all she had done for them. Khiwa was unmoved and pursed her lips tightly.

'I didn't do it for you, I did it for Simphiwe.'

At that moment Melanie appeared, camera in hand, and egged them to move in closer for a picture. Simphiwe jumped in too, flanking her mother on the left. The flash blinded Khiwa and revealed her lingering disdain.

5

The farmer's wife

Being at Simphiwe's wedding made Melanie reflective about her own. It had been a splendid affair at the newly opened, resplendent Carlton Hotel in 1973. Her wedding had been featured in magazines like *Fair Lady* and *Femina* and she was certain those images had stirred ambitions of marriage in many young and impressionable girls. Their nuptials were followed by a two-week honeymoon in Lourenço Marques (before it was called Maputo).

When she had met Paul, three months earlier at his mother's wedding at Claridges, Green Point, she had not even entertained the thought of marriage or even dating him. His mother, Belle Williams, who had been widowed for over a decade, had remarried into the circle of her parents' friends. Uncle Scotty, as they called him, was a former shipping merchant turned wine farmer who had been single for years. He had met Belle at a tenpin bowling contest and left bowled over and in love. Paul and Melanie had both been dateless at Belle and Scotty's wedding. Single, floating about, unhinged. In retrospect, Melanie wondered whether it was by design or coincidence that they were seated together. During the main course he confessed he had recently broken up with his girlfriend of forever. High-school sweethearts, he had said, making her yawn with boredom. She had nodded and kept knocking back drinks to numb the pain because she was reeling from her own heartbreak. Their broken spirits had gravitated towards each other, drawn by the loss each had suffered. It was during the toasts that she decided his jet-black hair, bronzed arms and diminutive stature were quite appealing. So when he asked her for a dance she didn't say no. They literally rebounded into each other's arms. Three months later they announced their wedding. Then she returned with him to Southern Rhodesia to begin a new chapter as the farmer's wife. In the background, the liberation struggle was intensifying. This made her parents nervous and they insisted she return to Johannesburg until things settled.

'I refuse to be separated from my husband,' declared Melanie with an ardent loyalty that fired up Paul.

She had always been stubborn and fiercely independent. It was a trait that was further cultivated when she went to Rhodes University in the sixties to study journalism. She had deliberately chosen Rhodes because she wanted to distance herself from her domineering folks. She had wanted to create room away from them so she could become her own person, beyond their sphere of influence. Up until then, she had been ignorant about the inequality and the injustices of the world she lived in. She had been an uptown girl who had grown up in Saxonwold in Johannesburg, cosseted from police brutality in the townships. The only black people she interacted with were those who came to clean their home. Her father had been a mining magnate and her mother a lady of leisure. She had grown up in the lap of privilege in a lily-white world. Being at Rhodes in the Eastern Cape, she was exposed to anti-apartheid student activism. She fell in love with an African National Congress comrade, Luthando Bam, who was studying towards a teaching degree but militating for freedom after hours. They had it all planned out; they would escape to Zambia, get married and live in exile. The plan never materialised because Luthando had been picked up by the police during an ANC-sponsored riot in East London. He was charged under the Suppression of Communism Act and sentenced to fifteen years on Robben Island for inciting violence and anarchy. This indictment extinguished Melanie's fighting spirit.

She had not been able to attend Luthando's hearings. She had not received closure, nor had the chance to say goodbye. She had deliberately stayed away, knowing that as a white woman at a black court
hearing she would have been highly conspicuous and equally suspicious. Shortly after Luthando's arrest, two stern-looking Afrikaner
policemen descended on her flat in Grahamstown. They insisted on
'a word or two' with her, but proceeded to interrogate her at length.

'Should I call a lawyer?' she asked, wringing her hands nervously.

'It's not necessary,' replied the one officer who introduced himself as Frikkie van der Beek and his partner as Commander Hans Joubert.

'It's relating to this,' cut in Hans, holding up a transparent plastic
bag. Inside was a gleaming gold chain. Melanie recognised it immediately and her heart pulsated in her chest. She was afraid the two
officers would hear the erratic beating of her heart and take her in for
further questioning.

'Do you recognise it?' asked Frikkie, as if reading her mind.

'Yes,' replied Melanie, touching her neck. 'I lost it a few weeks
ago.'

'And you didn't think to file a police report?'

Melanie nervously ran her fingers through her tousled blonde
hair.

'The thing is, I wasn't sure if I had lost it or misplaced it.'

'It's an expensive chain. Pure gold.'

'Yes, 9-carat gold,' she replied. 'It was a gift from my mom for my
twenty-first birthday.'

It had the letters of her name attached as gold trinkets.

'It was one of the things we found in possession of Luthando
Bam. Prisoner 1504.'

She had gasped in horror. She wondered whether she had been
convincing enough.

'Do you know him?' asked Commander Joubert.

'I don't,' replied Melanie candidly. 'And I can't for the life of me imagine how he would have got hold of my chain.'

'We will add theft to his rap sheet then,' said Frikkie swiftly.

They left after that and Melanie sank to the floor in shame. She had betrayed Luthando. Why had she not owned up to the fact that she had gifted him that chain for his twenty-first birthday? Then again, theft was a lesser charge than breaking the Immorality Act. She brushed her hair aside, as if to brush away the memory. A tear glistened in her eye.

The following day, when Paul asked her how the wedding was, she replied that it had been frugal but fun. They were drinking on the porch overlooking the large expanse of the garden where the boys were playing with the Great Danes. Beyond this were the paddocks where the horses grazed. It was a hot Sunday afternoon and Melanie was fanning herself furiously with a straw hat. She was wearing a floral print sundress that left her back and arms scorched by the sun's merciless heat.

'Only my wife would attend a fucking munt's wedding,' remarked Paul, his tone a mixture of wonder and disgust. He was addressing Cheryl and Mark Watson, their neighbours to the west, who were there for lunch. They hardly ever fraternised with the Wittstocks, their neighbours to the east.

'Khiwa is like family,' replied Melanie defensively. 'She raised Bradley and she raised you too!'

'No, she didn't,' said Paul defensively. 'Khiwa grew up with us. She has always been part of this family. Like an honorary member. It was Mabusi who raised us before she went blind as a bat.'

'So it was her daughter who got married?' asked Cheryl, who was trying to piece everything together.

'Granddaughter,' interjected Melanie. 'Simphiwe is Khiwa's daughter. She fell pregnant. Such a shame. She was a bright girl.

Could have gone far.'

'It's a good thing,' added Cheryl. 'Clever blacks are a problem.'

'I have told Paul that we should build a clinic on the farm so that the workers have access to birth control.'

Paul threw his hands up in exasperation, 'If Melanie had it her way, she would be building a fucking spa for them!'

'Paul, you spend more on those cows than you do on the workers.'

'It's called return on investment,' replied Paul. 'It's the government's responsibility to build clinics and schools and everything else you dream up!'

His voice had become raised and belligerent, rousing Adrienne, who was asleep in Melanie's arms but refused to be put down. Melanie patted her gently, stroking her silky blonde hair.

'Is the food ready?' Paul asked, trying to steer the conversation away from social welfare issues.

'I'll check on the roast,' said Melanie standing up, knowing that this was Paul's subtle way of reminding her of her place. As she made her exit, she plonked Adrienne in his lap, gently reminding him of his responsibility as a father.

Cheryl followed her to the kitchen to see what she could help with. Melanie thanked her again for agreeing to babysit the children while she had attended the wedding the previous day. Cheryl and Mark had twin boys who often played with Bradley. Cheryl was expecting her third child and was hoping for a girl.

'You'd do the same for me,' replied Cheryl, who often dropped the boys off on short notice when she wanted to go into town to run errands. 'What can I help with?' she added, trying to be useful.

Melanie asked her to make the salad while she poured more brandy into her sangria. She peeked into the oven. The roast chicken was a golden brown and the potatoes were crisp. It was the one thing she was able to cook without messing it up. She had grown up in a home with both a chef and a sous chef; her mother had never ventured into the kitchen and neither had she. When she had become Paul's wife she swore she would take cooking classes and try to be a bit more domesticated, but she never got round to it.

'This is why I want Khiwa to come back. This week without her has been a nightmare!'

'I thought John was around,' said Cheryl pointedly. 'I would never be able to manage without help.'

John was their houseboy. He cleaned and did a lot of the heavy lifting, but he was not good with the children, which was Khiwa's forte and her Achilles heel. As much as Melanie loved her children, they tired her easily. After an hour or two, they were more an annoyance than a source of pleasure. She had enjoyed both pregnancies, though, and had been yearning for a third child, but Paul insisted that two was enough.

'Are you happy here?' asked Cheryl, the question catching Melanie off guard.

'I was unhappy in the beginning,' she replied. 'Look, I wasn't born to this kind of life, but I'm making the most of it. I see Paul's vision for Belle Acres. I want to be part of it. He is a part of me now.'

Initially, she had been secretly excited that the country she would call home was on the brink of change and she wanted to be part of it. However, after a few weeks of living in Southern Rhodesia, her excitement had waned as the reality of the situation dawned on her. One afternoon, when Paul was hosting a braai to introduce his new wife to the farming community of Somabhula, the conversation had turned to the Bush War. It was the topic on everyone's lips. Paul's brother, Graham, had joined Selous Scouts, a special wing of the Rhodesian army. He was passionate about defending the autonomy of the rogue nation born out of Ian Smith's Unilateral Declaration of Independence in 1965.

'It will be a disaster if the munts take over,' declared one. 'This country will go to the dogs.'

'We're leaving if that happens,' voiced another.

'I think it's a good thing if we have majority rule. For how much longer can you contain the masses?' declared Melanie.

Everyone had turned in her direction, their eyes wide with horror. Paul had quickly interjected, saying his wife did not understand Rhodesian politics.

'Oh, but I do,' she said vociferously.

'Melanie thinks she does,' said Paul, talking over her, holding her by the hand, tightening his grip on her. 'She marched a few times at uni and thinks of herself as somewhat liberal. She was born in the cradle of capitalism. Your daddy made his wealth by exploiting munts, isn't that right, hun?'

There was loud laughter, brazenly mocking her. Melanie could not believe that her own husband was belittling her. He took her by the hand and led her to the kitchen.

'Don't you ever embarrass me like that!' he growled at her.

Melanie's complexion turned beet red like the salad on the table, and she burst into tears. Her eyes were puffy and red like the ice-cold sangria they were drinking. He left her there to regain her composure while he returned to commiserate with his friends as if nothing was amiss. It was in that moment that she realised that, while they shared the same bed and the same surname, they did not share the same ideologies. Melanie quickly learnt to keep her opinions to herself.

6

Choose your battles

Melanie prided herself on being able to discern Khiwa's mood according to the noise coming from the kitchen. That morning it was particularly loud, which indicated it was a bad day. Melanie wondered what the source of her anxiety was, considering that the wedding had gone extremely well.

'I'm stressed because of this!' said Khiwa, pointing to the baby strapped on her back.

Melanie was confused; she didn't understand. Adrienne was jumping excitedly in her arms, ready to migrate into Khiwa's arms.

'They left me with the baby! They just upped and left!'

Melanie stared at Khiwa, still not comprehending the root of her anxiety. It was in that moment that Khiwa pulled out a letter from her apron and slapped it into Melanie's hands. She drew out a chair and sat down and began to read. While immersed in the words, Khiwa brought her a steaming mug of coffee and made one for herself too. She offered Melanie a slice of carrot cake, which she declined, and Khiwa sat while holding Adrienne, who was happily cooing in her arms.

12 April 1977

Dear Mama
This is goodbye. We are going to fight in the war. I know it's

bad to just leave without saying goodbye. I was afraid if I told you, you would have tried to stop me, or us. While we are gone, please take care of Velile. We are fighting for her future.

Bye
Simphiwe

'What nonsense is this?' howled Khiwa.

Melanie decided to keep her thoughts to herself lest she rile Khiwa further. Instead, she silently applauded Simphiwe for her bravery.

'You are going to have a lot of work on your hands, looking after your granddaughter and my children.'

'Mels, I will have to manage!' replied Khiwa.

'I have no issues with it,' replied Melanie. 'I can't say the same for my husband, of course, but I don't see a problem.'

'Thank you, Mels,' replied Khiwa, throwing her arms around her and then quickly withdrawing as she realised she was overstepping her boundaries. That was when Paul walked in, demanding his breakfast. Melanie broke the news to him.

'I don't see how this can work. Adrienne is still a baby – how will she manage both of them?'

'I will manage,' stated Khiwa obstinately.

'No,' replied Paul, throwing his napkin aside. 'If you are unable to come to work without your granddaughter, then don't come at all. There are plenty of women looking for work.'

'I don't want plenty of women,' replied Melanie, coming to Khiwa's defence. 'I want Khiwa to look after my babies.'

'And besides,' added Khiwa, 'you owe us. We have sacrificed ourselves for your family, only to be treated like we're dispensable!'

Paul glowered at Khiwa with contempt. Then he turned to Melanie.

'It's this sense of entitlement that bugs me. I don't owe you shit, Khiwa!'

'My family has served yours for years. It's your turn now.'

Khiwa took the babies with her to get Bradley ready for pre-school. Paul pushed his plate aside in frustration.

'She's right you know. It's the least we can do.'

'I don't owe anybody shit,' replied Paul.

He stood up and stormed off, leaving Melanie to eat alone, in silence.

Life before the children had been routine and predictable. Being a farmer, Paul rose at 3am every day to start his day with a round of vigorous morning sex, which lulled Melanie back to sleep. She would rise at 6am and start her day with a cup of steaming hot coffee and some journalling. As she sat in the dining room, she decided she hated the structure of the farmhouse and started to furiously sketch a design that suited her. At 7am Paul would return to the farmhouse for breakfast and then go back to supervise general farm operations. They rarely breakfasted together, but always sat down to lunch together. Paul would then take his power nap. She would retreat into his office to do some admin, which entailed sorting and filing invoices and chasing up payments. This earned her the right to introduce herself to people as his glorified PA. Post-nap, he'd return to the farm to supervise the afternoon shift. They would reconnect at dinner in the evening. Only on Friday nights did they break from this routine when they headed to the club to socialise with other farmers and their wives.

In the first year of marriage, Melanie had busied herself with renovating the farmhouse. She had found the bungalow boring and Belle's taste in furniture rather gaudy as she had tried to recreate sixteenth-century England in Rhodesia. Melanie had transformed the single-storey home into a double-storey one. She created en-suite bedrooms upstairs, leaving a guest room downstairs and converting one of the bedrooms into an office for Paul, another into a library and TV lounge. Once the renovations had been completed in the first year, she launched into decorating the house in the second year. That was time-consuming too, having to fly back and forth between Rhodesia and South Africa to pick up fabrics and paints she was often unable to source locally. In her third year of marriage she fell pregnant and that year was consumed with preparing herself for motherhood and decorating the nursery. The arrival of Bradley upset Paul's schedule because Melanie was too tired to even twitch for his morning glory. After Khiwa reported for work and relieved her of Bradley, she slept till midday. Unlike her mother-in-law, she was a hands-on mommy and brought Bradley to bed with them, which Paul hated. When he was nine months old, they moved Bradley to his nursery, which was adjacent to their room, but by then she was already pregnant with Adrienne. When he was two, Melanie decided she wanted to send him to nursery school, but soon discovered there were none in the vicinity of Somabhula. Then she started wondering what the workers did with their children and found out that the ones who did go to school had to walk 20 kilometres every day to get there. She insisted that Paul convert one of the abandoned barns into a makeshift school. He was reluctant at first, but eventually gave in, not wanting to upset her. He was well aware that as long as Melanie was preoccupied with a project of sorts she was a much happier person. Melanie established a preschool for children aged three to five, adding a class as her enrolment grew.

While checking on Khiwa, who was off sick, Melanie then discovered the appalling living conditions of the workers. She was determined to make changes in her sphere of influence and so that became her next pet project. Visiting on his week off from the bush, Paul's brother Graham had stumbled upon the school and had not hidden his disgust.

'My brother wasn't lying. You are really invested in these munts who are skinning us alive in the bush.'

'The children have done nothing wrong. And, besides, it's my money.'

Melanie, on turning 21, had gained access to a generous trust fund established by her father.

'You should invest that money by leaving here. The way things are going, the munts might take over.'

'Then, if they are going to take over, we need to ensure they are equipped for the task.'

Melanie was resolute in her stance. She would not be moved by the tide of a fleeting war. It was not her battle to fight.

7

Buying into the Rhodesian dream

The father of Rhodesian prime minister Ian Smith had been part of the original pioneer stock. Jock Smith had arrived in 1898 with aspirations to mine the country's wealth, lured by the promise of gold. He settled in Selukwe and got involved in trade, mining and later farming. He married Agnes Hodgson, the daughter of a local miner, and their union resulted in three children: Phyllis, Joan and Ian, the latter going on to be the first Rhodesian-born prime minister. While they had not been pioneers, the idea of Rhodesia had been presented to Belle in a newspaper cutting shown to her by her husband. Gregory had come home from work harping on about Rhodesia like it was a new swing record. He read out how Rhodesia was a country with 'vast tracts of unbridled sunshine'. Sitting by their window, with a view of the rolling grey skies, a combination of pollution and impending rain, compounded by the recession of the 1930s, Rhodesia had sounded like paradise on earth to her.

'Taxation is light and land is cheap!' read Gregory.

'Really?!' questioned Isabel, as she exhaled the smoke from her cigarette.

It all sounded too good to be true. She snatched the paper from him, wanting to read for herself.

Like him, her fourteen years of education enabled her to read and write, which is something her own mother had not been afforded.

'The Southern Rhodesia Government in conjunction with the

Imperial Government affords assistance to new approved settlers. They will provide assistance in the form of various cash grants towards steamship fare and a nineteen-year loan on easy terms for payment on improvement on farms.'

It was the farm that had been the bait for Gregory. He had been raised on a farm, and came from a lineage of farmers. Tilling and ploughing the land was in his blood. In a series of unfortunate events, his father had lost their leasehold of 100 acres in Kent, leaving them both disenfranchised. Gregory had been forced to look for work in the city in one of the mushrooming factories that started to dominate the landscape after the First World War. He was now employed on an assembly line at the Ford automotive plant in Dagenham. He loathed his job and each year his contempt for it grew stronger while his wages remained stagnant.

'I really want to give this a try,' he said earnestly.

'It sounds too good to be true,' replied Isabel.

'We have nothing to lose,' he replied, 'and more to gain.'

He was right. They had absolutely nothing to lose by leaving London, and certainly nothing to gain by staying. Born into a working-class family, Isabel was the youngest of six children and the only girl in the family. Her father, a policeman, had been able to earn a living that afforded him the means to educate all of them. However, even with a modicum of education, they had no chance of ever surpassing their working-class origins. She was certain that she would never migrate from their cramped housing flat in Peckham, musty with damp and the lingering smell of gas fumes.

They occupied the top floor of a three-storey walk-up. The difference between living on the top floor and the bottom floor was ten pence. For someone who earned only three pounds a week, every penny counted. But Gregory earned six pounds a week so they were able to set aside some savings. They shared the two-bedroom abode with Gregory's parents who had been homeless and hopeless. Gregory's dad coughed incessantly and some nights she feared his chest would cave in and his lungs collapse. However, the old man's resilience surprised her. He coughed his way into a new day. Both her parents were late. Her father, a bobby on the beat, had met his premature demise while patrolling the East End when he was stabbed to death by vagrants. Her mother had succumbed to the deadly Spanish flu, sneezing her last breath in 1919. Gregory's parents were keen to embrace grandchildren, but Isabel was not ready to birth children into their high-rise of poverty. While Gregory assured her of the treasures of Rhodesia, she still harboured reservations about the unknown. He suggested they visit the High Commission for Southern Rhodesia to make further enquiries. The Commission was welcoming and went on to sell the attractive proposition of life in Rhodesia, offering vast possibilities to the settler with modest capital. They further explained that the land was most suitable for cattle ranching or crops such as maize, tobacco and oranges. Gregory liked the idea of being able to return to his farming roots. They were told that the Steamship and Railway companies were also facilitating the move at reduced fares and carriage. The couple left the office feeling more assured, plodding through a thin veil of mist at dusk, the grey clouds hovering ominously over the skyline. Over the next few days they pored over the illustrated pamphlets of the Rhodesian dream. Isabel became convinced that this was their future. She bought into the life in those photographs. So the rest of the year was spent preparing for their move and they finally emigrated in January 1939 – just nine months before the break out of the Second World War. The timing was apt in that, by the time the huge wave of emigration, post-war in 1945, they were firmly installed on a freehold in Somabhula. They prided themselves on being part of Rhodie settler stock.

When they first arrived, Belle knew instinctively she was home. Her heart sang as the sun kissed her face in a warm reception. Gregory had christened their farmholding 'Belle Acres' because he affectionately called her Belle. She adored the name as it didn't allude to their rather humble upbringing. In Rhodesia, Isabel was given a chance to reinvent herself. In the years that followed she went on to birth three children in quick succession: Estelle, Graham and Paul. Gregory's parents had passed on during the war so they never got the opportunity to meet their longed-for grandchildren.

It was during this time that Mabusi came to be in Isabel's employ. Mabusi was a young, unmarried mother who was unemployed and had a two-year-old daughter, Khiwa, to support. The child took a shine to Isabel's daughter, Estelle, and they became firm friends. Belle liked Mabusi on sight and figured she would fit well into their equation. She wasn't wrong on that score. Mabusi fitted in too well and soon attracted Greg's attention. Often times Belle would catch him staring at her in a licentious way. While she found it inappropriate, she had not felt able to address it. Belle had always been one to sleep through the night, often exhausted by the rigours of the day with three small and demanding children. Then, uncharacteristically, she began waking up at midnight, her hand searching furtively for her husband's body, not finding it and then drifting back to sleep again. This happened for many consecutive nights until one night she woke up and decided to go and look for Gregory. She walked down the long corridors of their single-storey home and heard him before she saw him. Grunting like a wild pig.

Belle had retreated back to their bedroom, taking furtive steps, certain they had not seen her. How could they? She tried to work out how long it had been going on. The revulsion came in waves as she imagined him sticking his pink penis into Mabusi and then hers. She knew in that moment she would never let him touch her again.

She lay awake with her eyes closed, waiting for Gregory to return to their bed. He eventually did when the early morning light peered through their curtains. He started to get ready to begin his day on the farm. After he left, she cried herself into a fitful sleep and woke with a rage that she could not describe. She marched into the nursery and snatched baby Paul from *her* arms.

'Get me some coffee!' she hissed.

Obediently, Mabusi returned with the cup. Belle grabbed the steaming hot cup from her and it splashed onto the rug on the floor.

'Look what you have done, you stupid cunt!' screamed Belle, slapping her across the face.

Mabusi stood stoically, which further infuriated Belle. That night Belle informed Gregory that she was dismissing Mabusi. Gregory did not question her decision or try to convince her otherwise, which she found unsettling. As she turned over to sleep she recalled a conversation she had overheard at the Farmers' Club about how some white men kept black women as mistresses and visited them on the down-low. This had led to the birth of a spate of mixed-race bastards who were taken from their mothers and raised in orphanages. Belle thus decided it would be better to have Mabusi under her nose where she could monitor her and any offspring that might arise from her and Gregory's coupling. So she did what most women of her ilk did at that time: she turned the other way and pretended to not have seen anything or heard anything. It wasn't like she could just get on a ship and return to Peckham. She did not want to, nor did she have the means. They had a good life in Rhodesia, much better than the one she could ever have achieved in London. They had a roaring social life that centred around bridge and bowling at the local country club. Gregory played golf and tennis too. She drove around in a Ford Crestline, which she later upgraded to a sporty Chevrolet.

So she managed the situation the best way she could, rejecting the amorous advances of her husband by continuously pleading exhaustion. Then, when he could no longer tolerate her rebuffs, he stopped making overtures. With time, her bitter resentment towards Mabusi dissolved into relief and gratitude as she realised that Mabusi relieved her from satisfying Gregory's demands. She had been seventeen, sweet and naïve when she married Gregory, who was four years older than her. He had been good friends with her brothers and had met her when she was in nappies and had watched her grow up.

Gregory had always been a doting husband, never flirting with other women or giving them so much as a glance. Now she wondered whether something might well have been going on and she had just not been exposed to it. She surmised that the heat of Rhodesia had stoked his ardour. Gregory had really taken to farm life like a bee to nectar. He loved conversing with the natives, speaking Chilapalapa or what was termed 'Rhodesian speak', a smorgasbord of languages like Afrikaans, isiNdebele and Shona, with other dialects thrown in for spice. He would bellow with pride, *'Mina shala lapa eBelle Acres,'* and Belle would cringe at his efforts to try to communicate with the locals. She never forgot how he had been slapping Mabusi's bountiful buttocks, growling *'Mnandi lapa! Faka. Faka.'*

He had also taken to wearing safari suits and owned a range of them in brown, blue and beige. They exposed his bronzed arms and legs. He wore them with socks and suede Clarks Desert Boots, which famously became known as 'Farmer shoes' and were made by Bata. While every other farmer's wife found Gregory handsome and incredibly charming, Belle now found him repulsive. His amorous pursuits did not stop at Mabusi and rumours began to abound about Gregory's adulterous adventures beyond Belle Acres. So, while Gregory was sowing his seeds and cultivating a handsome future for them, Belle focused on her children. They started their schooling at Chaplin High in Gweru, a school that was older than both her and Gregory, having been established in 1902. It had a solid English curriculum with principles (and a principal) that espoused English ideals. During the school holidays they would holiday in Umtali or Victoria Falls. When Gregory started to make more money, they would fly Air Rhodesia to South Africa, where they could frolic on the whites-only beaches. On many occasions, Gregory would not accompany them, wanting to fully exploit the freedom of being without his wife and three children.

When the boys were older, they became avid rugby players and Belle accompanied them on sporting tours with other schools like

Plumtree and Milton High. Estelle wasn't sporty at all, preferring to read and do ballet. When the boys were at high school, their father was shot in the arm by Farmer Wittstock because he had been cavorting with his wife. Gregory had shouldered the wounds and walked around with his hand in a cast, boasting proudly that 'you couldn't keep a good man down'. It was such a scandal in the Somabhula farming community that Belle stopped going to the Farmers' Club for the Friday-night socials. Gregory was unmoved and continued like nothing was amiss. Wittstock and his wife divorced shortly afterwards. In the 1960s, divorce was considered scandalous and Belle flirted with the idea, considering that the children had grown up. Graham had left high school and enlisted in the Rhodesian army. Estelle was heading out to university and Paul was still grappling with adolescence and high school. Belle decided she would wait till the last child had left home before making her move. By this time the boys were very aware of their father's shenanigans. While Graham lauded his father as a hero, Paul was embarrassed. Estelle was indifferent, as she did not have much of a relationship with her father, whom she rarely saw. Estelle went on to study art history and music at the University of the Witwatersrand in Johannesburg. There she met her future husband, an Afrikaner, Danie le Roux. While the Anglo-Boer War had been fought more than 60 years earlier, Anglo-Boer enmity had not thawed sufficiently. So, rather than a big wedding to celebrate the occasion, Estelle and Danie had a quiet, nondescript court wedding.

That year, Gregory had turned 55 and was full of bravado, bolstered by his new-found wealth and status as a successful Rhodesian farmer. Outwardly, Gregory and Isabel looked like a couple with a pristine marriage. Inwardly, they both knew that love had long since vacated the building. They had even stopped pretending and maintained separate bedrooms, Gregory occupying Graham's room after he left home to join the army. Estelle, who had witnessed the deterioration in her parents' marriage, had encouraged her mother to get a divorce and relocate to South Africa, where she would have asylum of sorts. Belle carefully considered her daughter's suggestion and decided that would be the year of her exit, but then Gregory fell ill. By the time they got him to a specialist, the doctors proclaimed that he had lung cancer and had no more than about six months to live. Belle resolved to hang on – better a widow than a divorcée. The former attracted sympathy while the latter was stigmatised.

She bided her time, waiting for Gregory to breathe his last. She called on Khiwa to take care of him as she felt the task too onerous for her. From her bedroom, Belle could hear him coughing his lungs out, imagining the specks of blood and phlegm landing on Khiwa. Without flinching, Khiwa wiped him down, from his mouth to his orifices. Khiwa fed him, bathed him and held him when he was too frail to move. She often imagined Gregory would have killed himself if he had the strength to save himself from this humiliating end. The illness had rendered him helpless and robbed him of his last vestige of dignity. When Belle knew that his demise was near, she searched his study for his last will and testament. She knew he had one, but was not privy to the contents. When she found it, she was horrified. He had bequeathed to his sons an equal share of the farm. To his daughter, ten thousand pounds and to Mabusi, the farmhouse. To her there had been nothing. Zero. In anger, Belle tore up the will and burnt it for good measure, watching the paper curl up at the edges blackened by the flames.

Gregory passed on shortly after, expiring in Khiwa's arms. Belle was relieved to finally see him go. She planned the funeral with precision and invited the entire Somabhula farming community. While others cried, she remained dry-eyed and apathetic. She was unmoved by the accolades. The sombre affair was followed by tea, accompanied by pretty canapés, creamy cakes and scrumptious scones baked by Khiwa. In the absence of a will, the estate was bequeathed in its entirety to her as the surviving spouse.

8

A life of servitude

Mabusi made her debut into the world in 1928, five years after the colonial settlers became independent of the British South Africa Company and Rhodesia became a self-governing settlement. Mabusi was the first living child after her mother had miscarried nine times. Her mother, maFuyane, had tried to have children for years but was unsuccessful. They had tried everything. Prayer, potions and prophesy and still no pregnancy of hers yielded a child. So maFuyane resigned herself to fate as her husband took on another wife who could bear him children. MaNyoni bore him five strapping sons in quick succession. With each birth, maFuyane nosedived into depression. Her husband only paid attention to her when his other wife was nursing. So when she fell pregnant, it was like an afterthought, unplanned. She waited tensely for the pregnancy to disintegrate into blood and clots but it never did. One month morphed into two and then three. MaFuyane was afraid to even acknowledge her pregnancy lest it dissipate before her eyes. Then, in her fourth month, her belly started to protrude and in her fifth she was able to feel the baby's strong kicks. It was only then that maFuyane began to embrace her pregnancy as it seemed firmly rooted, determined not to be shaken. At nine months, she finally gave birth and it was a painless process as her uterus opened to expel Mabusi, the only girl in the Zwide homestead. The child was christened Busisiwe, meaning Blessed. Mabusi was the nickname she adopted from a very young age and never discarded. She was an extraordinarily beautiful child, with dark, satiny skin and piercing black eyes. She was the apple of her father's eye, who boasted he would receive a handsome dowry for her. This would make her beam with pride because at that age she did not understand the enormity of the statement. She adored her father and followed him around the homestead. He hobbled about from one spot to another, chasing after the shade to shield him from the merciless heat.

Her father had been maimed during the Red Axe rebellion of 1896, popularly known as *impi yehlok' elibomvu*, led by the spirit medium Queen Regent Lozikey, in what was the last attempt of resistance against the colonial settlers. He leaned into his knobkerrie, supporting his weight. As much as it served as a walking tool, this also doubled as an instrument for enforcing discipline in the homestead. Ubab' Zwide loved to regale Mabusi with stories of the good old days before *abelungu* arrived. Her father's eyes always lit up when he narrated the war escapades because he too was an important general.

'The earth we are sitting on is barren, *mntanami*,' he said, prodding the earth with his knobkerrie. 'They deliberately moved us here to these reserves to punish us. In the end, we had no choice but to work for them. How else would we survive?'

He was referring to the Land Apportionment Act of 1931, which divided the land into black and white areas. Her father and his people were allocated unproductive 'reserves', while the whites held onto the lucrative, lush farming land. In the 1930s, the average African man had three main avenues of employment: the mines, the farms and domestic labour. The men who did not wish to surrender to this fate sought work in the gold mines of the Witwatersrand. Mabusi's brothers had gone that route. One by one, she watched them leave their homestead as they were recruited by Wenela, the Witwatersrand Native Labour Association, which was the agency set up by the gold mines to recruit migrant workers. The men who opted to stay earned very low wages of two pounds a month. This they repatriated to their wives, who lived in the villages, cultivating the barrenness of the soil and raising children.

Not only was Mabusi beautiful, but she was blessed with the gift of prophecy. This manifested on a day her father was set to travel to Bulawayo to get supplies for the homestead. Mabusi begged him not to go, insisting he would get hurt. When quizzed on how she had arrived at this revelation, she responded that she had seen his accident in a dream. Of course, no one took her seriously as they felt she was just a young child with an overactive imagination. Zwide left for the trip, but did not make it because his Scotch cart overturned and landed on his chest. For a month he was sequestered in a hospital. Still no one took Mabusi's prophecy seriously, attributing the incident to coincidence. On his return from hospital, a neighbour came to visit her father. When Mabusi saw them sitting outside under a tree drinking a traditional brew, she went to greet them, as was the custom. Then she flippantly told her father's friend that he was going to die. The two old men vibrated with mirth. When the laughter subsided, Zwide sternly chastised his daughter and dismissed her while pressing upon his visitor that his daughter was full of frivolous ideas. Then his friend died. That was when her father started to take his daughter's predictions seriously. From a young age, she would dream and all her dreams would come true. She predicted births, deaths, illnesses and impending doom. By the time she was ten, she was able to tell people's fortunes and foibles. Her father, having seen an opportunity to make money from her gift, had installed her in an empty hut where she could consult. Being educated was not a privilege Mabusi had been afforded. For many girls, education was believed to be a waste of resources because girls were only valuable for marriage, for which no education was required. So Mabusi had not gone further than Standard 4 at a mission primary school. Even on the mornings she had to go to school, her day was prefaced with household chores around the homestead before joining her brothers to trek to school, a distance of 3 kilometres from the homestead. On their return, after discarding their uniforms, Mabusi would continue with household chores, which involved fetching water from the river and then cooking for her brothers. While other children played with wild abandon outside, Mabusi would be attending to a snaking queue of people who sought her services. Her father charged them a goat or chicken, or a few shillings for those who had money. This exhausted Mabusi to the point of shutting down. The dreams ceased. Then the people stopped coming and she was no longer useful to her father.

That was until Sindani Nleya arrived. He was a travelling salesman of sorts, bartering goods in exchange for sorghum, maize and other staples that were in season. When he saw Mabusi stepping out of the granary, he offered her his hand in marriage. She had just turned fourteen when she was betrothed. Romantic love in those days was very much an alien concept. You did not marry for love; it was purely an economic transaction in which a woman's labour and childbearing capabilities were traded in exchange for a bride price. Sindani paid her father five cows as dowry and she became his wife. On arrival at his homestead, she discovered he had two other wives, who looked at her with glaring suspicion, making her very uncomfortable. Mabusi went into marriage revering her husband. He was much older than her. Having completed elementary schooling, she worked out that he was 40 years old, born just before the turn of the century. Their first night had been awkward. She lay prostrate, spreadeagled on the bed as he penetrated her. Mabusi recalled the discomfort and the blood-stained blanket that she had to wash down at the river. This was the part of marriage that took her quite a while to get used to. After many nights of clumsy posturing on her part, her husband commanded his other two wives to teach her the ways of pleasuring him sexually. They had ridiculed her before demonstrating how to handle their husband. For Mabusi, this was the most humiliating element of marriage and she hung her head in shame. On the cow-dung floor she watched the older wife mount the pelvis of the younger one who gyrated her hips in response. Their heads met and their lips locked in a kiss, their tongues teasing and taunting. The older one pretended to thrust into the younger one, imitating their husband's grunts in animation. Then they both collapsed onto the floor with laughter. Mabusi could not help but join in the camaraderie, but as soon as she laughed they drew their faces into stern alignment.

She knew then that being a wife was not what she was meant to do as she preferred to play with the children in the homestead. Her husband had children as old as her and they would play hopscotch together. In the end, the other wives stopped trying to co-opt her into doing any hard labour and let her play with the children. Their enmity towards her was replaced with pity. They started to treat her like one of the children, the only exception being that when all the other children gathered into one hut to sleep, Mabusi would have to serve her husband. She served him dutifully as she had been taught and he, in turn, showered her with love and admiration. She understood, even at that young age, that she would be reliant on her husband for sustenance and that her rights were conferred through him. Mabusi thrived on his love and affection, blossoming into womanhood, her breasts and hips filling out. It was not long before she fell pregnant. As her belly sprouted with life, she knew instinctively she would no longer be able to play with the other children in the homestead and she slowly began to adopt her role as a mother. She gave birth to a creamy white child with wispy white hair and blue eyes and the whispers abounded. Her husband named her Khanyisile for she was the light, just like her complexion. As she grew so did the gossip surrounding this aberration called *inkawu*. The whispers became a scathing indictment on Mabusi, whose husband sent her and her daughter packing because he believed she would bring bad luck to their marital home. Mabusi had contemplated returning to the family home, but realised the shame she would be forced to live with for the rest of her life. She would be called a 'return soldier', *umajika emendweni*. With her status diminished, she would be forced to live under the auspices of her brothers and their wives. Mabusi was clear that she was not going to suffer that fate. Growing up, she had witnessed first-hand how women become pariahs because of their marital status. She was thus forced to find a job on the commercial farms and raise her controversial child on her own.

When Mabusi arrived at Belle Acres, Madam Belle had just given birth to baby Estelle, who she was tasked to attend to. The girl was followed by Graham and Paul. She nursed and raised all three children. The layout of the three-bedroom bungalow was such that her room – or the servants' quarters, as it was called – was adjacent to the kitchen in the east wing of the house. Her room had two entrances, one opening to the kitchen and one to the nursery. Next to her room was the laundry room, where the houseboy did all the ironing after he completed all his other household chores. They were called 'boys', but these were men in their late twenties and early thirties. They also had a garden boy who tended to the garden. All five of them ate their meals on the porch outside the kitchen. That was their space. The kitchen opened to the dining room where the cookboy served breakfast, lunch and supper. After dinner, the Williamses would filter into the lounge, which was across the passageway. The lounge opened out to the veranda where the Williamses would spend many summer nights drinking wine when they had guests. The east wing of the house contained the other three bedrooms. A long passage connected the east and west wings of the house. The Williamses had built the house from scratch and the nursery had been deliberately placed there because Master Gregory said he did not want noise at night. Mabusi was happy with her working conditions and Khanyisile, who was two at the time, grew up in the Williams household. By the time she was five, she was able to speak English fluently, even better than her own mother. The Williams children were enamoured with the plump little girl who had skin like them but features that were not of them. She was co-opted into the family as Estelle's playmate. The children even shared a room, leaving Mabusi to have her room to herself. Initially, she welcomed the reprieve – that is, until Master Gregory started paying her nightly visits. It was a few months after the arrival of baby Paul, the youngest, when he had first appeared. Her first thought had been: is there something wrong with baby Paul? Had she overslept and not heard the baby crying in his crib?

When he was still a newborn baby, Mabusi would sleep with Paul in her own bed. He loved to suckle on her breasts just as his siblings had. It was only when he was much bigger that she relegated him to the nursery. So she was pretty flustered when she woke up and Master Gregory was hovering in her room like a ghost.

'Sshh,' he said, clambering onto her bed.

He told her to look the other way and to face the wall. His hands had lifted her nightdress, cupping her warm buttocks. Without any further preamble, she had felt him prod her legs apart with his erect member. While her body stiffened in resistance, she could not vocalise or react to it. She was powerless in her position; her only response was to submit to the assault. He thrust into her like an ungreased piston. He climaxed quickly, sowing his seed in her crevice.

In the beginning, his visits were infrequent and sporadic like a freak storm. They were unsettling because she never knew when he would appear, which made for many episodes of fitful sleep. She was often filled with dread, thinking of the backlash should Madam Belle ever find out. She would be certain to lose her job and their livelihood. While Madam had never walked in on them, Mabusi knew she knew that morning when Madam slapped her across her face. While Belle had always been abrasive, lashing out at her had not been her style. Mabusi resented the insinuation that she had solicited the violation. That she had asked for it. In that minute something in their relationship shifted like two tectonic plates colliding. An invisible line had been crossed. After that incident, Gregory's visits became more frequent. Her body even started to anticipate them, lubricating in expectation of him. Then one night he asked her to turn around, to face him. They looked at each other squarely in the eyes and he kissed her. Instead of being repulsed by this, Mabusi welcomed it. Soon the perfunctory one session progressed to two. No longer did he rush to vacate her bed, sometimes holding onto her till the breaking dawn, when he woke for his farming duties and she to attend to baby Paul.

When baby Paul was two, Mabusi was fired. Madam Belle had come sweeping into her room like a tornado, searching through her drawers like a deranged person. She had unearthed sweet-smelling bottles of perfume, jewellery and beautiful dresses hanging in her closet. Holding a pair scissors, Belle had torn at them in a violent rage.

'I want you to go!' she screamed. 'I don't care where you go, but just go!'

Mabusi had packed the very few belongings she had in a suitcase and prepared to leave. Khanyisile kicked and screamed, refusing to leave the Williams children, who reciprocated the distress. They had all grown up together, played together, oblivious of their differences and stations in life. The Williams children had wailed uncontrollably when she departed. Paul had thrown the most vicious tantrum, flinging himself to the ground. That had been her saving grace, with Belle, unable to quiet him, conceding defeat and letting her stay.

'You can no longer stay in the house. You will live in the compound with the rest of the farm workers.'

Mabusi accepted her fate as she was relegated to the makeshift farm accommodation, which consisted largely of mud huts.

'What have you done for us to deserve this?' screamed Khanyisile, ashen at their new living conditions.

Mabusi bit her tongue, unable to respond to her feisty five-year-old daughter.

When Gregory came to visit her a few days later, he was ashamed that she had been relegated to a hovel. That prompted him to upgrade all the staff housing because he could not renovate his mistress's home without fixing the others in the compound. Gregory had modelled them on council housing, with open rooms and shared communal facilities like toilets and bathrooms. However, when the construction was complete, he ensured Mabusi's dwelling unit was larger than the others, boasting two bedrooms instead of the standard one-bedroom studio unit. This appeased Khanyisile somewhat, but she still longed to be in the spacious Belle Acres home. She was aware that something in their circumstances had changed and, like everyone else, she knew that Master Gregory only visited their home. He was often spotted leaving the place in the early hours of the morning. Then the rumours began to abound about their affair, which reached Father Silonda's ears. At church one Sunday he delivered a long sermon about adultery, his eyes resting on Mabusi. She left the church and never returned.

9

The odd one out

Khanyisile spent her formative years in the Williams household. By virtue of the fact that she grew up playing with Estelle, she was co-opted into their household. When Estelle was four and was given her own room, Khanyisile shared it with her. Of course, the madam was strict about them sharing a bed. As soon as the lights were turned off, Estelle would invite Khanyi to join her. She would make space for the plump little girl by moving all her dolls to the side. Then they would fall asleep side by side. The first time Belle discovered Khanyisile sleeping in Estelle's bed she was livid.

'How dare you!' she screamed, outraged at the child's audacity to elevate herself from her position on the floor to her daughter's bed.

'I said she could,' said Estelle with staunch indignation. 'She is *my* friend – not yours. Mine!'

'She can't sleep on the bed with you!'

'Why not? You sleep with Dad?'

Unable to proffer an explanation that would satisfy her daughter, Belle had begrudgingly let it go. Gregory had assured her that no harm would come from it, that they were merely friends.

'But she's black!' spat Belle.

'But she is a human being too,' responded Gregory.

From then on, Khanyisile graduated to sitting with the Williamses at the dinner table, her place beside Estelle. Everything Estelle loathed on her plate she passed onto Khanyisile, who wolfed it down with gusto. Khanyisile intuitively knew that her place in the house would be secured by being useful not only to Estelle, but also to every other member of the family. She ingratiated herself into the Williams family. For a while, her position was secure until their unceremonious expulsion from the Williams farmhouse. Khanyi was confused; she searched through her little mind, wondering what she and her mother could have done to deserve this. When she couldn't fathom a reason, she asked her mother, who had no satisfactory response either, save to say that the madam no longer wanted them. The thought of being separated from Estelle gave her the greatest anxiety. The two little girls cried as they clung to each other. As she prised them apart, her mother had tried to reassure them that they would still be able to play together.

When her mother was reinstated into her job, they did play together but not with the same frequency. Khanyi was also no longer permitted to sleep in the house as they were now relegated to the dirty compound. When Khanyi started school, the play dates with Estelle became as sparse and sporadic as the winter rains. While her friendship with Estelle appeared to disintegrate, her mother's and Gregory's solidified. What Khanyi found disturbing was that Estelle's father visited them in the compound all the time. He didn't care about the dirt and disrepair of their home. He looked past that as he sought her mother's company. While she was too young to understand what was going on, she heard things being said. People around her said her mother had bewitched the old man. That he literally ate out of her hands. Intuitively, Khanyi knew there was something not quite right about him being there. Then she rationalised that maybe her mother was lonely and needed a friend. She was lonely too, but making friends in the compound proved to be rather difficult. It was during this time that Khanyi discovered there was something peculiar about her. In the Williams household, she had almost blended in, but in the compound she was noticeable. From observing the other children around her, Khanyi realised that, although their facial features were the same, none of them had blue eyes or skin as light as hers. Whenever she asked her mother why she was different, Mabusi would promptly reply that she was a special child and special children had special qualities. Apart from her appearance, Khanyisile had never felt different, but it was the people around her who went all out to point out her differences. They nicknamed her 'Khiwa' and, initially, she thought it was because she spoke English so fluently. Then, at school, *inkawu* was co-opted into the vocabulary used to address her. While Khiwa sounded affectionate, *inkawu* was downright offensive. She later learnt that it meant white baboon and she had cried, wondering why some children were cruel enough to call her that. Her Grade 1 teacher, Miss Moyo, took her under wing, and told her to not pay any attention to childish banter and that she was a brilliant student. Khiwa sat in front of the class and always raised her hand to answer questions. She was even tasked with helping other children learn English, which instead of making her popular, made the other children despise her even more. Khiwa was often absent from school in summer when the heat scorched her, causing her skin to blister and her lips to rupture. Khiwa desperately wanted to fit in, to be a part of something, but she was often ostracised in one way or the other. Very quickly she became a loner, learning to be her own companion and burying herself in the books Gregory bought for her. Khiwa was a bright child and, because of Gregory's financial support, she was able to progress to high school. All the teachers testified that she was a brilliant student and would go far. There was one particular teacher, Obey Sithole, who paid an inordinate amount of attention to her. If she was struggling with a concept, he took extra time to explain it to her. Often he asked her to stay after school and invited her back to his staff quarters. Khiwa was so fixated on his affection and approval that she didn't think to report him when he started to undress her, play with her breasts and do unspeakable things to her. Those things were eventually spoken about when his horny explorations manifested in her pregnancy, which could not be concealed. An outraged Mabusi had whipped Khiwa mercilessly, leaving red welts on her skin. After her anger abated, she demanded to know who had done this to her. Khiwa had led her to the culprit. Teacher Sithole was vehement in his denial, accusing Khiwa of lying.

'No one does this to my child and gets away with it,' swore Mabusi. 'No one.'

Teacher Sithole had laughed her off, chasing both of them out of his home. While Khiwa never returned to school after the incident, Teacher Sithole never quite returned to himself either. It was said he started losing his faculties. It started with him speaking incomprehensibly to himself and ended with him roaming around naked, masturbating. The school authorities relieved him of his duties, insisting he was a danger to students. He was often spotted roaming around the nearby villages, naked and muttering unintelligible phrases and begging for food.

With the passing months, Khiwa metamorphosed as she accommodated the new life inside her. Her teenage years were obliterated as she evolved into becoming a mother. Simphiwe was born and they made space for her, continuing to survive on the benevolence of Gregory. Khiwa always flirted with the idea of returning to school when Simphiwe was a bit older, but her plans were derailed when her mother went blind. Mabusi had been foraging in the bush looking for herbs when a cobra spat into her eyes. Initially, Mabusi had shrugged it off, treating the inflammation with some muti she kept in a jar. But her eyes remained red, swollen and itchy, emitting a crusty discharge on her eyelashes. It was Gregory who finally insisted she see a doctor, but it was too late as she had developed a corneal ulceration that progressed to blindness. Mabusi was never the same after that and refused to see Gregory. He continued to come to the house, but he began to pay an unusual amount of attention to Khiwa. She was unsure of what to make of his advances because she had not solicited them. She was perplexed. On one hand, she felt powerless to resist, and on the other she was flattered. Not since Teacher Sithole had any man paid her any attention. So she yielded to Gregory's probing hands. While Mabusi slept with her granddaughter, Khiwa serviced him in the other room. Although she was certain her mother knew what was going on, this was something that was not addressed. Yet it became a wedge that caused great animosity between mother and daughter.

When Gregory fell ill, Belle recruited Khiwa to nurse him and she was invited back to live in the Williams home. She was older then, no longer the child with a burning desire to be in the auspices of their tutelage. The Williamses no longer related to her with the warmth of her childhood. That had dissipated and had been replaced with aloofness and coldness. Now that she was older, Khiwa understood why and expected nothing less. Her friendship with Estelle felt like a mere figment of her imagination. Estelle had an air of authority like her mother and bossed Khiwa around. She no longer desired her company as she had friends from university who spent holidays on the farm. They would send Khiwa on errands, get her to run around for them, to serve them. They never missed an opportunity to remind Khiwa of her place in life. It was because of this that Khiwa was determined to do better for her daughter. She made sacrifices to ensure that Simphiwe would get further with her schooling and get further in life.

Before his death, Gregory had presented Khiwa with an envelope. He gave her instructions to give it to Mabusi upon his death. Knowing her mother's reading was elementary, Khiwa opened the envelope.

1 July 1965

Mabusi, my love

In the event that for some reason my will is destroyed, I want this letter to be a testament to the fact that I loved you deeply and cherished what we had. When I die I want you to have the farmhouse. It is the least I can do after everything you have done for me and my family.

Gregory Williams

Khiwa was seething when she finished reading the letter. There was no mention of her. Of what she had done for him. When she returned to work the next day, she smothered Gregory in his bed with a pillow. Like a chicken, he had kicked unconvincingly at first, weak with illness. He had coughed and spluttered before silently succumbing to death. After Gregory was buried, Khiwa waited patiently for the will to be enacted, but nothing of the sort transpired. This was when she confronted her mother and urged her into action.

'We can have the house – it's ours!' declared Khiwa.

'I want nothing to do with that farmhouse,' replied Mabusi. 'Gregory can rot in hell.'

Khiwa was furious.

'How can you just give up like that, Mama? You earned that house. I earned it.'

'I don't want it,' screamed Mabusi. 'Not like this. Never!'

Khiwa eyed her mother quizzically. Did she know what Khiwa had done? She always insisted she could see things. She quickly dismissed her mother's superstitious nature as she stormed off into her room and sat on the bed, rocked with palpitations of anger. Unlike her mother, she was not going to give up that easily. She would bide her time; she had plenty of it.

10

Going up in smoke

The heat of the day was beginning to subside with the setting sun, which painted the sky with hues of burnt orange. Khiwa trudged home after a trip to Gwelo to purchase supplies. As she walked, her fleshy thighs chafed against each other. She could feel the sweat pooling around her armpits and streaming down her back. She breathed raggedly, the walk physically taxing. It didn't matter how many times she walked the path, it never got easier. Walking towards the compound, she was greeted by plumes of smoke furling into the air. Another fire left untamed and left to burn astray, she figured. It was not uncommon this time of the year. Veld fires took root and would run amok. However, as she ventured closer to the compound, she realised that the billows of smoke were coming from her own home. The shopping bags dropped from her hands. Her heart constricted painfully. Her mother. They had left her in the house. She quickly offloaded Velile from her back and lay her down on the patchy grass. On being placed on the ground, the child broke into a loud wail.

'I am coming back now,' said Khiwa, reassuringly, running towards their home, unrestrained by the weight of the baby, but still labouring under her own.

As she neared the house she could see a large crowd had gathered, torching the house.

'Bulal'umthakathi!' they chanted. 'Kill the witch! Kill the bitch!'

Khiwa was engulfed with dread and trepidation, trying to make sense of the scene before her.

'*Kwenzakalani?*' growled Khiwa. 'Where is my mother?'

Nobody responded. Nobody offered any information. She watched in horror as the flames surreptitiously licked the face-brick home. The corrugated asbestos roof was on fire. The fire leapt through the windows. She could feel the intensity of the flames as she drew closer.

'Mama! Mama!' she screamed. 'I need to save my mother.'

Her voice was drowned out by the angry bellowing of the crowd.

'I can't let my mother die in there! I can't.'

'*Uzofa lonyoko. Unyoko ngumthakathi!*' cautioned John, the house-boy, who was at the forefront of the commotion.

The rest of the crowd joined in, reinforcing and elevating his message. Two men tried to restrain her, but Khiwa would not be deterred. Like a wild horse, she bolted towards the house. She could see the smoke escaping from under the door. She touched the doorknob – it was searing hot. She removed the doek on her head and covered the door handle. Opening it, the door gave way easily and she was immediately enveloped by smoke and a burst of heat as the flames escaped the house. She coughed incessantly as she inhaled a great waft of smoke.

'Mama! Mama!' she screamed.

She heard a strangled cough. Her mother. That signal served to fuel Khiwa's hope. Her mother was still alive.

'*Yingozi! Suka. Khiwa. Hamba!*'

Undeterred, Khiwa pushed through the fire.

'I am coming, Mama,' replied Khiwa, thinking of running to the bedroom to get a blanket. That way she could wrap them both in it to at least shield them from the fury of the fire that was spluttering noisily.

She fell to the floor, deciding it might be better to crawl where the flames would not reach her. The home was now engulfed with fire and thick smoke. She was soaking wet, sweating profusely from the combination of the heat, exertion and fear. The fire was fierce and threatened to obliterate everything in its path. The letter. It was in the wardrobe. That was the only proof they had to claim the farmhouse. There was no way she could let the letter go up in smoke. With fierce determination, Khiwa crawled towards the bedroom, oblivious to the screams or the raging fire around her. She had to get to the letter before the fire did. There was a loud crashing sound. It flattened her. She tasted the dust and ash beneath her. She tried to move. She couldn't. The weight forced her down. The heat engulfed her. She felt her hair singe as it caught alight.

That afternoon, as on most weekends, Melanie took Bradley out riding on her horse. It had a buddy saddle, but she could sense his apprehension as he clung to her T-shirt as she picked up the pace. She galloped gently through the bushes and came to a bundle that turned out to be Velile splayed on the ground in her flannel blanket. That was when they were confronted by her anguished cries. She recognised the blanket; Adrienne had one just like it. After she slid off the horse, Melanie scooped Velile into her arms. She felt light. She stopped crying and her eyes twitched in recognition.

'Bradley, I'm going to leave you here with the baby. Don't move. I need to check what is happening at the compound.'

When Bradley was settled on the ground, Melanie placed the child in his lap. She was sceptical about leaving them there unattended, but she had no choice. There was no way she could carry them both on the saddle.

Bradley touched the baby's face and ran his fingers through her soft, downy hair.

Melanie galloped towards the compound and saw that a ferocious fire had taken hold and was spreading to other houses in the settlement. With urgency, she galloped back to the house to call the fire brigade, but by the time they arrived a row of houses had already been razed to the ground. They had not been able to contain its wrath and it had consumed everything in its path.

PART 2: THE ROAD TO LIBERATION

The first step towards getting somewhere is to decide you're not
going to stay where you are.
JP MORGAN

Part 2: The Road to Liberation

The first step toward getting somewhere is to decide you're not going to stay where you are.

— J.P. Morgan

11

Limbo

Goodbyes were never proffered when one was embarking on such a journey. Simphiwe and Douglas simply left for their honeymoon – what was supposed to be a weekend affair in the city of Bulawayo sponsored by Melanie. They caught a train from Somabhula to Bulawayo to Plumtree. By virtue of being black, this afforded them only an economy-class ticket. It was the first time for Simphiwe to alight the brown- and beige-painted steam locomotive with the words 'Rhodesian Railways' printed in yellow and, as someone who had never travelled beyond her home from the farm to school, this was an exciting experience. Economy meant they had to endure the hard benches, which did not convert into sleeping berths, replete with linen and bedding as was the case in the other classes. While they were unsuitably uncomfortable for sleeping, for the first leg of the journey Simphiwe was unable to sleep. When she finally succumbed, it was on Douglas's lap while he sat upright, enduring the discomfort. The train chugged along with whistles and stops until they reached their final destination in the small town of Plumtree, fondly called kuTitji by the locals, which meant 'railway station' in Kalanga.

On arrival in Plumtree, Simphiwe hung back as Douglas approached strangers for directions to the war effort. A gentleman advised them to walk through the bush until they crossed a river and then they would be in Botswana. Another man repeated the same instructions, as if he was being deliberately cryptic. It appeared that the road to freedom was cloaked in parables.

'*Liyadabuka etshonolanga, libeselikhomba eMpumalanga. Ngokwesifitshana lizaphambana lesifula. Ngokuchapa lizafika eBotswana. Bakhona abanye labo abay' empini.*'

The directions were so vague, and even as Douglas probed further, the man merely responded that they should proceed northwards before turning in an easterly direction, which left them confused. Frustrated and hungry, they decided to deal with their hunger first. They were able to locate a kiosk and drank Cokes and enjoyed a steaming hot meal of chicken curry and rice. They did not know it then but it would be the last gratifying meal they would have in years.

While eating, they overheard a group of young men talking about the war effort. Douglas craned his neck to hear more, but then decided to get up and confront them. The young men said they were part of the ZAPU youth league and were preparing to cross over. They were an amiable group so Simphiwe and Douglas joined them. Simphiwe was keenly aware that she was the only female, but the men seemed unbothered. And that was how the six of them began to trek on foot.

The Ramokgwebana border crossing was 10 kilometres from the town, and so they began their trek through the bushes to Botswana. The sun was merciless, beating down on their backs, but they were unperturbed, fuelled by the excitement that liberation awaited them on the other side of the border. At the border post, Douglas made furtive enquiries as to where the Joshua Nkomo training camp was located. An official instructed them to wait for a truck to transport them to the Tsetsebe police station in Francistown and pointed them to a tree where they congregated with the swarm of other recruits. They conversed noisily among themselves about freedom and liberating the country. The group was a mix of Ndebele, Kalanga and Shona people, all united with a common goal. There was an abundance of youthful exuberance that had not yet been curtailed by cautious maturity. There were many other women too, which piqued Simphiwe's spirits. The mood was infectious and everyone was high on hope. They didn't even realise how long they had been waiting before they were piled into a truck like cabbages and transported to a crowded dormitory, where they would reside for the next three weeks. There were no bathing facilities and they all had to relieve themselves in makeshift buckets outside the building. The following morning they were roused from their deep slumber by a whistle. Like her counterparts, Simphiwe jumped to her feet, got dressed and quickly made her way to the assembly area. Here they were separated into platoons and then sections. The morning began with a toyi-toyi session.

'*Dolo phezulu! Simudza gumbo!* Knees up!'

People were jumping with knees high and, in her enthusiasm, Simphiwe jumped up until her knees reached her chin. Every day began with this military drill. However, as the days passed with no sign of food, the energy for this activity started to wane. The liveliness had been dashed and replaced by anger and desolation. One by one, they saw their comrades drop like flies because of hunger. Those who weren't dying of hunger were being killed. Rumours spread that there were infiltrators among them who working for the enemy. This made things tense as people were unsure who to trust or who to avoid. Simphiwe couldn't even lift her head because she was weak. Douglas sat stoically beside her, cradling her head in his lap, trying to put on a brave front. There was no organised feeding programme and everything was haphazard and nobody seemed to know anything. The police officers marshalling the area eventually organised that a beast be slaughtered and cooked. That night people ate till their stomachs were taut, not knowing when the next meal would arrive.

The following day a list of names was called and both of them were on it. Once they had formed a sizeable group, they were moved once again and shepherded into a waiting chartered military aircraft. Like most recruits, it would be their first time on an aeroplane, which was both an exhilarating and frightening feeling. Simphiwe held onto Douglas in fear. He assured her they were going to be fine, concealing his own apprehension. However, when the plane took off into the air she felt a heady feeling, like the one she experienced when Douglas filled her and propelled her on an orgasmic flight. She held his hand tighter and he squeezed hers in acknowledgement. They had not coupled in what seemed like ages and she wondered if there would be room for them to reconnect when they arrived at their new destination. She didn't know where they were heading until they were informed that they were disembarking in Lusaka, Zambia.

On arrival they were met by uniformed ZIPRA military high command, among them Alfred Nikita Mangena and Lookout Masuku. Up until that point, Simphiwe had no idea of the military organisation of ZAPU. She was not politically conscious and had just risen to the challenge to join the armed struggle. In her naïveté, she had not borne the full weight of signing up.

It was at this juncture that Simphiwe felt the importance of what they were doing and that somehow her contribution would count for something. From the airport they were ferried to the Nampundwe transit camp where they were sorted like bottles on a factory conveyor belt. They were segregated according to age, sex and physical fitness. Anyone younger than sixteen was assigned to finish off their schooling. When asked why she was there, Simphiwe promptly stated that she was there for military training. The commanding officer eyed her warily before assigning her to the group earmarked for that. Then they were sorted according to gender because men and women had to live in separate camps. Simphiwe waved weakly to Douglas as she was ferried away with the other women to VC Camp, the acronym translating to 'Victory is Certain', which housed all the female recruits. Her heart constricted with the pain of being separated from him. She hadn't anticipated that they wouldn't be living in close quarters, but the war did not respect marriage – nor life, for that matter. This she would discover under the most brutal circumstances.

12

Victory is certain

The female recruits arrived at the camp and the gates were manned by female soldiers, but you couldn't make that out when they were kitted in their military attire. Simphiwe was alarmed that there was no one to receive them when they got to the camp. The place appeared to be deserted. Victory Camp was a farm stationed 35 kilometres outside Lusaka and it was here that Simphiwe's transition from a civilian to a soldier would begin. Victory Camp was previously used as a base by the MPLA (People's Movement for the Liberation of Angola) during Angola's own fierce civil war against the Portuguese.

Such was the benevolent nature of liberation struggle movements of bequeathing assets they no longer needed that the Victory Camp was donated to ZAPU when the MPLA was returning home after the Angolans won the war. It was sparsely built and included a structure nicknamed 'the Palace'. There was another dwelling that housed the commander and commissar, and Simphiwe and the other recruits were accommodated in cone-shaped tents. Simphiwe discovered how porous these tents were during the rainy season when the water would seep through, soaking their blankets. It was no surprise that the camp became a breeding ground for lice. While rain could be an unnecessary inconvenience, the rainy season also gave comrades an advantage, as it meant there was an ample supply of water in the camps. The rain also stimulated the growth of lush vegetation, which provided thick foliage and acted as a natural camouflage. It felt like the rainy season had conspired to give the liberation struggle stalwarts a natural advantage. In some camps, cadres grew their own food and the maize sprouted with the rainfall. Simphiwe realised that food was a scarce commodity in the camps and highly sought after. They subsisted on a diet of *isitshwala* and beans or sour milk. On days when there wasn't much, preference was given to the younger recruits. There was no kitchen or dining facility and all cooking was done outside in large barrels. Food was consumed while squatting or sitting outside. Beyond the clearing of the camp were miles of bush, where they were often relegated if it was felt the camp was not safe.

It was only after a whistle was blown that female recruits emerged from the ground where they were hiding and began to populate the space. They moved in an orderly fashion until they converged on what Simphiwe soon came to know as the assembly point. A woman decked in military fatigues and wearing a black beret marched to the front. A whistle was nestled around her neck. She introduced herself as Commander Jane Ndlovu and her deputy as Commander Audrey Ndlovu. Simphiwe would soon learn that these were not their real names but noms de guerre that they assumed during warfare. Commander Jane addressed them with such authority and, while she was of a small build, there was something powerful about her. She didn't have a microphone, but her voice carried to the last row. 'We welcome you to Victory Camp. This is your first lesson. Whenever a vehicle arrives at the base, we take cover, comrades. This is because we do not know whether these cars come carrying friends or foes. We must always be on our guard. We don't trust you either. We don't know if you are here to help us or infiltrate us.'

Simphiwe felt a chill run down her spine at those words. Were they not all fighting for the same side for the same change?

'We are not here to promote tribalism. We are here to win a war. We are one people here. Forget that you are Kalanga, Ndebele, Ndau or Zezuru. We are all here for one cause. We all speak one language with one voice. If you have any tribalism, spit it out right now.'

Comrade Jane Ndlovu further explained to the recruits that she had arrived in Zambia a few years before, in 1974, and at that time there were very few female recruits. Her speech was followed by the registration process, and it was during this process that they were all quizzed harshly about their age and origins.

'Why are you here?' asked the commissar.

'I am here to fight for my country,' replied Simphiwe.

The commissar laughed in her face, 'What do you know about fighting?'

'Not much,' replied Simphiwe, 'but I am here to learn.'

The commissar eyed her guardedly, 'Are you sure you want to join the military effort? You finished Form 2 so you can proceed with schooling. We will need educated people once the war is over.'

'I want to fight,' reiterated Simphiwe, determined to lend to the cause. She hadn't come this far to pull out now.

The commissar scribbled something on the paper she was holding and told Simphiwe that from henceforth she would be known as Victory Silwane. From that moment, Simphiwe Nzima ceased to exist.

The day began at 4am with Jane's whistleblowing. Simphiwe had slept fitfully the night before due to excruciating period pains. After giving birth to Velile she'd forgotten about the inconvenience of menstruation. Her periods had ceased, but since she was no longer breastfeeding her cycle had resumed with the associated cramps. She felt them in her back and in her abdomen. She had tried to use some torn and discarded cloths to absorb the menstrual blood because they had no access to cotton wool in the camp.

'I'm not sure if I should go today,' explained Simphiwe to her camp mate, Rugare Hondo.

'Are you sure you want to miss training? Remember what happened to that recruit who skipped training?'

Simphiwe remembered very well how Comrade Joyce Huni had

been made to run 5 kilometres with a backpack of bricks as punishment. On completion, she had fainted and the commanders had been unsympathetic and had poured cold water over her. Not wanting to suffer the same fate, especially in the dead of winter, Simphiwe dragged herself to the training session, which began with a 5-kilometre military toyi-toyi and running with a backpack of stones strapped to your back or sometimes holding a rifle. This was to prepare them for the eventuality of being in the bush and carrying weapons. That morning Simphiwe couldn't keep up with the rest of the pack, falling behind as the uneven terrain seemed to further frustrate her efforts. She was feeling dizzy and faint because they had not eaten in days and didn't even feel herself collapse in a heap on the ground like a pack of cards. As she lay on the ground trying to collect herself, she felt the military boot of the commander in her side.

'Get up!' she commanded, with no mercy in her eyes. 'Do you think this is a field trip?'

The pain in her side was excruciating but Simphiwe forced herself to stand up. She held back her tears because crying would be a sign of defeat.

'You must be tough!' intoned the male commander. 'We are in a war!'

'I have my period,' cried Simphiwe. 'It's making me weak!'

The commander laughed. 'You think the enemy will spare you in the bush because of your periods? The Rhodesians aren't moved by menstrual blood.'

He prodded her in her side with the rifle, forcing her to her feet. She used all her remaining reserves to run back to the camp. Later that day Commander Jane came to visit her and she was sympathetic to Simphiwe.

'You will get used to it. We all did, eventually,' she said.

Simphiwe nodded mutely.

'As for the blood, you will eventually stop menstruating too. We all did at some point.'

After she left, Simphiwe succumbed to her tears. Since her arrival at the camp, that had been the first act of kindness she had received. She yearned for home and her grandmother in the cosy comfort of Belle Acres. She cried and the tears flowed liberally, as did her blood. There was no water to wash and the blood dried on her thighs, as did her tears.

Joshua Nkomo visited the camp frequently, dressed in his signature general's uniform replete with epaulettes and brass buttons. He was a colossal man with a staggering presence and the leader of the ZAPU party and supreme commander of its military wing, ZIPRA. Affectionately known as 'Father Zimbabwe', he had started the nationalist movement in the sixties. ZANU was a splinter group that broke away from ZAPU. His visits boosted the recruits' flagging morale, especially on cold rainy days when they had not eaten much. As they stood in lines as he made his patrol and inspected them, Simphiwe felt he genuinely cared about them. He'd ask if they were okay and they would respond that they were indeed, even if they were far from it. Then he would break into song: 'Ze Zeee ... Zimbabwe.'

He would tell them that victory was close, but they had no way of knowing and could only take his word for it. In the camps, they were cut off from news flow, from everything really. Simphiwe knew of girls in the camp who had snuck out to go to Lusaka. Some had lovers there or relatives who had gone to Zambia in the 1940s and 1950s to seek employment and further their education. These brave girls would often return to the camp with stories about the bustling city life. Sometimes they brought food back with them and many of them returned pregnant. As much as Simphiwe wanted to escape the treachery of camp life, she was scared of being caught. The punishments meted out by the commanders were always harsh and meant to humiliate, and Simphiwe wanted to stay out of trouble as much as possible. She never did learn the fate of those women who eventually gave birth in the camps because she was deployed to Mkushi at the beginning of the next year.

13

Stranger in Moscow

Douglas and many of the other male recruits were sent to the JZ Moyo Camp II in Solwezi in the northwest of Zambia. The camp had been christened after Jason Ziyaphapha Moyo, the vice president of ZAPU who had perished in January 1977 when a parcel bomb exploded in his hands. The camp was run by senior cadres, most of whom had been trained in the Soviet Union. The recruits embarked on a ten-week training course that comprised Physical Training, Political Education, Armed and Unarmed Combat Tactics, First Aid, Military Intelligence, Topography and Military Engineering, and it was during this time that the commanders scouted for recruits who showed great potential. These were earmarked to complete their training programme overseas. Douglas was selected for the task. He only found out on the day they were to depart that they were actually leaving Lusaka. As Douglas had quickly come to learn, everything in the military was shrouded in secrecy. Even their final destination was a secret. Douglas felt apprehensive because, while Lusaka was not home, it was familiar and he was surrounded by what was recognisable. It was the reassuring presence of other cadres that emboldened him to take the next step in his journey.

They departed from Lusaka International Airport in the middle of the night and he was given a passport with his new combat name: Jones Sibindi. Unlike his maiden flight from Botswana to Lusaka, this one was longer and lasted four hours. He was unable to sleep, his eyes were wide open throughout the entire journey. They disembarked at Addis Ababa International Airport, which was teeming with black people, but the languages being spoken were unfamiliar to Douglas. This made him feel even more alienated and he figured it would only get worse the further they flew from Lusaka. After a two-hour stop-over, they caught a nine-hour flight to Budapest. Douglas's anxiety heightened with every hour spent on board and he envied the other passengers who were able to sleep effortlessly through the voyage. When they eventually landed, Douglas thought the expedition was over – only to be told they had to board another flight, which took them to Moscow. The changeover was thankfully quick because it was bitterly cold and they had arrived in Russia at the beginning of the winter season. Like the rest of the new recruits, he was dressed in-appropriately for the chilling weather in a khaki shirt and shorts and he felt the biting cold in his bones. Moscow temperatures of minus 3 degrees Celsius were a shock to the system, having emerged from summer temperatures in Lusaka of 31 degrees Celsius.

The Russians were fully prepared to receive them at the airport where each recruit was given a coat and a balaclava to insulate them from the cold. Just when he thought the trip was finally over, Douglas found himself strapped into the seat of another flight. He was emo-tionally and physically exhausted, tired of putting on a brave front. Even though he was in the company of other comrades, he felt fright-ened and very alone. At times like this he wished he had a friend, a confidante that he could pour his feelings out to, but living in the camp had taught him to be wary of people. You never knew who you could really trust. A friend could easily turn into a foe.

As he wrestled with his feelings, he eventually drifted off to sleep, but it was short-lived and fitful. Three hours later, they were deposited at the military training centre on the outskirts of the city of Simferopol. Douglas later learnt that Simferopol meant the 'city of usefulness' – as it was christened by Catherine the Great – and this, here on the Crimean peninsula, would be their home for the next eleven months. From the aeroplane they were quickly shepherded onto insulated trucks to be shielded from the biting cold. On arrival at the centre, they were met with piping-hot bowls of soup called schi that he could taste was a combination of cabbage, carrots and potatoes. The accompanying bread was black in colour, which Douglas initially eyed with suspicion, but his hunger was less discriminate. Later they would joke that once they attained independence, black bread had to be the staple to demonstrate their dominion. No more white bread, only brown and black. Used to sparse meals, Douglas was pleasantly surprised when the soup was followed by a plate of beef stroganoff. As ravenous as he was – and he did shovel his way through the meal – he just couldn't find the taste for the beef strips, cream and mushroom dish. Later he would expel every little morsel. Dessert followed with a slice of the Russian cake, smetannik, made with sour cream and accompanied by Russian tea. While he had not entirely enjoyed it, the three-course meal felt like a celebratory feast. He was not accustomed to such generous helpings of food because it was so scarce in the camps and they had often gone hunting to subsidise their paltry diets.

Following the meal, the recruits were to undergo rigorous examinations to reveal any hidden illnesses or physical irregularities. They were quarantined for three weeks while undergoing the tests. They were relieved of their old clothing, which was burnt, and allocated clothing better suited to their new surroundings. Once Douglas had passed the medical scrutiny he was allocated a room in the training college. He was given a new wardrobe of military boots, combat uniforms and warm, heavy winter coats. While he was warmed by the Russian reception he remained very wary of white people. Would they be mistreated under the tutelage of these Russians? He hadn't known what to expect being in a foreign land and alone in his room that night he let out all the pent-up tension bottled inside him. The appearance of being brave and fearless had taken its toll on him. For the first time in months, he slept well, a combination of exhaustion and relief.

Their day began with a run when it wasn't snowed under, which it often was and even sunny days seemed like they were buried under six feet of snow. Grey skies and the Siberian winds left the recruits mind-numbingly cold. It took Douglas a while to warm up to the wintry climate and even longer to the food. His palate could not get accustomed to the borscht soup made with thick red beetroot, and he found solyanka soup too spicy and would try to fish out the chunks of meat while setting aside the walnuts that swam in it. He grew to love shashlik, Russian kebabs, though they were not served often. He soon discovered vodka, which became the only thing to warm his soul when he was feeling lost and desolate.

They lived in isolation as their movements were confined to the academy. They were not permitted to interact with the local population in the surrounding villages, not that they had the time. However, there was limited interaction with other trainees in the academy from uMkhonto weSizwe (MK) and other liberation parties. Then a band of female recruits arrived and he was immediately taken with Nonkululeko Sizwe, an MK cadre. She was a tall, big-boned young woman with a fierceness he found attractive. She was bald, with a round face and big eyes that looked at him with longing. He often avoided her intense gaze because he felt he was betraying Simphiwe by being attentive to another woman. Nonku was determined to win his affection. One night it rained heavily in the camp. The type of storm where the thunder rumbles like a bomb explosion. The lightning struck like a flashlight being turned on and off. All Douglas could see were Nonku's pert breasts and long sinewy legs as she strode into the room.

'I'm scared,' she whimpered, climbing into his bed.

'Nonku!' he gasped. 'Should you be here?'

'Do you want me to leave?' she asked, searching for his penis underneath the coverlet.

She felt him spring to life in her hands. She knew he had not been with a woman in ages as he rarely entertained them. She had often wondered if he was incapable, uninterested or asexual, but as his erection pulsed in her hand she knew for certain he was none of those things. They made love that night as the rain pelted against the windows like the force of his ardour as he penetrated her.

'Don't stop,' she said, wrapping her legs around him like a python. He knew then he was trapped.

She never left his bed after that.

The training programme was structured and rigid, leaving no time for anything else. After a brisk wash in the mornings, they would settle down to breakfast. They ate kasha, a buckwheat porridge, followed by blini, pancakes that they ate with fruit or mincemeat. They would be presented with political news, which they had to read and critically analyse. This was followed by intense classwork. The academic component of the programme was built on the foundation established at the holding camp in Lusaka, with the addition of the Russian language. The political training encompassed political ideologies with a strong emphasis on Marxist philosophies, and the military training covered both mechanical and chemical warfare. They would then break for lunch, which always included a hearty soup and generous serving of meat or chicken. Afternoons and some nights were filled with practicals, namely artillery training. After supper, their evenings were filled with more political analysis and ideologies. They watched old footage of the Russian army waging war against Germany.

Douglas's fighting spirit was further ignited, as was his nationalism and a strong desire to win the war. Up until then, Douglas's knowledge of European history had been limited, but the months in training gave him a crash course.

He learnt that most African countries had once been autonomous and enjoyed self-government. There had been no borders, no restriction of movement, but the powers that be deliberated and decimated the continent, cutting and carving borders. It shocked Douglas to learn that old white men sat in a room with complete disregard for culture and linguistic considerations, quibbling over the destiny of Africans. And here they were all these years later trying to dismantle those decisions of nineteenth-century Europe and the yoke of colonialism.

Douglas also learnt about the Bolsheviks and the abdication of the tsar from his throne and his subsequent exile, where his entire family was slaughtered before they could be rescued. Douglas was intrigued that while the oppression back home was white on black, this was white on white. He learnt that it was driven by class, with the royal family oppressing the general masses as a result of their birth and privilege.

His third and most painful lesson came when he learnt about the Second World War. He came to know of Adolf Hitler and his programme to 'cleanse' German society of individuals viewed as racially inferior to his perceived idea of the Aryan race. Douglas was most astounded by the hate exhibited by this man and further learnt, with horror and much consternation, about the Nazi concentration camps that were initially meant to accommodate 'communists' and 'enemies of the state', but were later expanded to include Jehovah's Witnesses, Jews, Romas and anyone else considered 'asocial', like homosexuals. He learnt of the brutal termination of millions of lives at the six extermination camps and it was during this time that Douglas began to question the veracity and existence of God. If God were truly there, why would he allow the slaughter of millions of innocent people? Who did God represent if not the weak and subjugated? His faith began to flounder while his anger gained a foothold.

There were other lessons beyond the classroom that no military instructor could impart. They visited agricultural co-operatives on state-owned farms when spring sprung in April. The idea of co-operative farming held a lot of appeal to Douglas because it meant there was equitable access to land and farming opportunities. No one person, like Paul Williams, had a monopoly over the land and the means of production. Beyond the farms, it was the first time Douglas was exposed to living in what appeared to be an integrated society. They took excursions into Moscow and, while there were few blacks living in Moscow at the time, it gave him a taste of what it would be like to live in a society where there was no curtailment of freedom and no segregation. So, although they were living in a snow-white country, they were not ostracised. The stares were borne largely of curiosity rather than outright racism. Before they left, they spent the last two weeks of summer in the port city of Odessa. He went with Nonku. They were bathed in sunshine and the Black Sea rolled before them. Douglas felt that he had come to the end of his odyssey. This was his first foray into the sea and he dipped his legs into the saline waters. For the first time he felt relaxed and, as his feet caressed the sandy beach, he wanted to imprint the memory in his mind. He promised himself that one day he would return here with his wife and daughter. He did not say that to Nonku because he felt depressed at the thought of leaving her behind.

'Will we ever see each other again?' he asked.

'Let's live for the moment,' she said, kissing him surreptitiously. 'We are at war. Who knows if we will live or die.'

That was Nonku: feisty and fearless, bold and brazen. It made him feel less guilty about leaving her behind. That night, as they lay in bed, his arms draped around her, he had a dream about Simphiwe and his daughter. In the dream it was the middle of winter and they were playing in the snow. Simphiwe was marvelling at how cold it was as she helped Velile to build a snowman. Then from nowhere an army truck traversing the snow came hurtling towards them, staining the snow with its dirty tracks. He dived forward to try to save them, but the truck bulldozed them, leaving a slathering trail of blood. He woke up, drenched in sweat.

14

Casualties of war

It was a well-known secret that Paul's brother, Graham, was part of the Selous Scouts, a paramilitary unit that operated independently and was responsible for intelligence gathering and other missions.

Graham had secretly recruited a few black boys to join them on spying missions. They were posted to ZANLA camps in Mozambique and were paid handsomely for supplying the secret service with intelligence. One such boy was Temba, whose father had grown up at Belle Acres and who Graham trusted implicitly. But he could use the threat of killing his family if the boy decided to turn on him. Temba did no such thing. He delivered critical information and, with his photographic memory, Temba was able to sketch camp layout plans, which was useful in corroborating aerial photographs.

Unfortunately, Temba was caught and had his ears cut off and his tongue cut out. The terrorists had not killed him because they wanted to send a message. They dumped him, barely conscious, at the Rhodesian army base outside Umtali. He had been murmuring Graham's name over and over again and died just before Graham could get to him. Out of respect for his family, Graham decided not to throw Temba's body down a mineshaft, as was often the case with many casualties of war. Instead, he had transported his body to Belle Acres and dumped it in the bush where he knew there was a strong likelihood that it would be found. That way, Temba would be given a decent burial without being compromised in any way or being labelled a sell-out. However, Graham's good intentions went awry. Innocent children playing in the bush stumbled upon the foetid body. His mother could not understand why her son was without a tongue and ears and her husband couldn't provide any explanation without giving away the role he had played in getting their only son enlisted in a war he had no business fighting.

Once they had buried Temba, his mother went to consult a sangoma. After throwing bones in the air, the sangoma insisted that it had been a ritual killing for muti purposes. She didn't explicitly enunciate a name, but simply said: 'The person who did this lives at Belle Acres and has lived there for a long time.'

The bereft mother reached her own conclusions and, with a group of angry residents, had stormed Mabusi's home. She had denied the accusations levelled at her and pleaded her innocence, but her pleas fell on deaf ears. Vigilante justice prevailed and they torched the house.

It was the middle of winter when Graham returned from what he deemed a successful mission in Mozambique. He wouldn't divulge many details other than to say they had been behind the annihilation of the Chimoio camp. On this visit, he didn't come alone; he was in the company of a young and feisty blonde-haired woman who introduced herself as Jane Mordon. In all the time Melanie had known Graham, he had never been serious about a woman. Over the years, Paul and her had speculated that he might be gay, but arriving at the house that day, arm in arm with Jane, dispelled that idea.

Jane was a BBC journalist and she and Graham had met in a pub in Chimoio where she had been covering a story while he was on an intelligence mission. Melanie was secretly envious of Jane, who reminded her of herself and what she could have become. Over dinner, Jane told them she had covered the war in Angola and later Mozambique.

'I became the African correspondent for BBC two years ago,' she stated. 'I used to be in the Middle East.'

'She's a daredevil like me,' boasted Graham proudly.

Melanie had not been able to understand the attraction between the two. Jane was a worldly and well-travelled woman with a global outlook on life, while her brother-in-law had an insular view and was bigoted and racist. Perhaps Jane would provide him with some much-needed enlightenment. But Melanie still wasn't sure what she saw in Graham apart from rip-roaring passionate sex that they were all made very aware of every night.

Melanie hadn't revealed to Jane that she had studied journalism. She felt inferior for having studied, only to then become a housewife. She hadn't even made it to the newsroom, something she always regretted. She was doubtful that Jane would have judged her, but she judged herself.

From their lengthy interactions, Melanie discovered that Jane was covering a lot of the Rhodesian politics and offered insights beyond the propaganda being published in the papers and punted on the airwaves. Casualties were being under-reported on both sides and victories over-reported.

'Ian Smith is under pressure to settle. He can't afford to wage a war on both fronts,' stated Jane.

The growth in the sizes of the ZANLA and ZIPRA camps was a constant headache for the Rhodesian army. This put a lot of pressure on the country, with her smaller army, less manpower and a low conscription base. Emigration was high because many joined the so-called 'chicken run', fleeing the conflict. Rhodesia was being forced into negotiating an internal settlement, which was rejected by both Joshua Nkomo and Robert Mugabe.

Undeterred, the Rhodesian prime minister had gone on to broker a deal with a rather unlikely alliance of political stalwarts that included a reverend, a bishop, a chief and a businessman.

'It's not going to stick,' said Jane authoritatively. 'The OAU won't hear of it.'

'Tell me more,' said Melanie, pulling up a chair, keen to hear more about the workings of the upper echelons of power.

She offered to pour more tea, but Jane opted for a whiskey instead, even though it was only 11am.

This is how Melanie came to learn about the war, through intimate conversations that made the issue personal rather than something impersonal and generic that she only read about in the newspapers. It felt like Jane was preparing her for the worst.

Even in the midst of war, the stream of visitors to Belle Acres didn't slow down. A few weeks after Graham and Jane left, Melanie welcomed her parents. While she visited them often, they hadn't ever been to Rhodesia, until that summer at the height of the war.

Bernard and Elsie le Roux arrived with a trail of coordinated leather Samsonite luggage. Bernard looked relaxed in a fedora, striped golf shirt and coffee chinos, and a light-blue sweater draped around his shoulders that matched his blue eyes. Elsie wore a striped coffee-and-yellow sundress. She was already fanning herself with her huge straw hat that had flattened her perfectly coiffed hair. From the time she was a young girl, Melanie couldn't remember her mother ever not being done up. She always looked perfectly put together, not a strand of hair out of place.

'It's hot as hell here,' she remarked as they drove from the airport.

'The weather here is no different to Johannesburg,' remarked Paul.

'It always feels like a sleepy hollow here,' commented Elsie.

'Rhodesia is in the sticks,' added Bernard, unimpressed by the little he had already seen.

He did, however, remark that it was clean and the wide streets were welcoming when they drove through the city. But he hated the buildings and the Victorian architecture; the English had really left their imprint on the city. They had lunch at the Cape to Cairo Restaurant on the corner of Grey Street, a building based on the concept of Cecil John Rhodes's dream of constructing a railway from Cape Town to Cairo.

After lunch, they proceeded on to the farm where they were going to spend the rest of the week getting to know their grandchildren. They spoiled them with clothes from department stores in South Africa like Stuttafords and John Orr's.

'We even bought stuff for the piccanin,' chirruped Elsie.

'Mom, please,' chided Melanie. 'Her name is Velile.'

Elsie distributed the gifts, which were received with unrestrained delight. The girls both received dolls, a Barbie for Adrienne and an assortment of Fisher Price dolls for Angel. Brad received a fleet of Dinky toy cars and some Lego.

'I was actually surprised they sold black dolls,' giggled Elsie.

Angel threw her doll aside and screamed that she also wanted a Barbie doll.

'What an ungrateful piccanin!' sniggered Elsie.

'Mom!' scolded Melanie. 'You should know better than to not give them the same!'

Adrienne reacted quickly and gave Angel the blonde-haired, blue-eyed Barbie and Angel was quickly mollified. The grandparents played with the children until they pleaded exhaustion and went to take a nap.

When they woke, the sun was going down and the heat was not as unbearable so Paul took them on a guided tour of Belle Acres, ending at the compound. Bernard was unimpressed with the dilapidated workforce housing.

'You need to do better, Paul – workers are your assets,' admonished Bernard.

'The housing was fine. We had a fire two years ago that destroyed most of the buildings.'

'A veld fire? How unfortunate,' piped up Elsie.

'It wasn't a veld fire … It was actually more unfortunate than that,' said Paul.

Paul then narrated how the fire had started. When Paul had finished, Elsie held her hand to her chest, as if to still her rapidly beating heart.

'Did she die?' she asked, her voice almost a faint whisper.

'She died and her daughter Khiwa died trying to save her. Khiwa was our maid,' responded Melanie.

'Khiwa was also Velile's grandmother,' explained Paul. 'That's how we ended up taking in Velile. She was orphaned after both her grannies died in that fire.'

'Oh my, that's tragic,' said Elsie, having new-found empathy for the child.

'But, Paul, that was two years ago. Why haven't you fixed the compound?' asked Bernard. 'Imagine these people waking up to that memory every day!'

Paul was taken aback. 'How the hell is this my fault? It was their stupid superstitions that caused this.'

'Your brother started this. You need to fix this. You can't afford to have unhappy workers, Paul. It is a labour-intensive operation on this farm and you need these people more than they need you. I averted many strikes simply because I paid people a bigger wage. I recovered my money elsewhere. If you and my daughter want to live a long life on this farm, you better fix this mess.'

Melanie stood quietly beside her father, silently rooting for him. While she knew her father's impetus was not philanthropically motivated, she still supported it. The end result would be beneficial to the workers. They returned to the farmhouse in silence, where the strained mood was broken by the happy chatter of the children monopolising their grandparents once more. After dinner Bernard pulled out his chequebook and scribbled across the paper.

'You are obviously cash-strapped and clearly things are tight with the sanctions on the country, but I have money that I can give you to sort out that mess at the back.'

Paul was hesitant about accepting money from his father-in-law.

'I would never be able to pay you back,' replied Paul.

'I am not asking you to pay me back. Just do it for the workers. Social investment they call it.'

Paul accepted the money and Melanie could no longer suppress the smile on her face.

15

The final destination

Her parents departed after a fortnight, leaving what felt like a vacuum to Melanie. Their departure coincided with Paul's birthday. Melanie was miserable to see them go and had tried to convince them to stay for the party, but they had already made plans, which included a three-day weekend sojourn in Caribbea Bay. Melanie had really enjoyed having her parents around and being able to show them their way of life. In quiet moments together, her mother could not help suggesting that they could give Paul and Melanie more money. As her laatlammetjie, born fifteen years after her two sons, Elsie was fiercely protective of her daughter.

'Mom, we're fine,' said Melanie reassuringly.

Elsie didn't understand how Melanie could have traded in her former life for this.

'I do love him, Ma,' she assured her, seeing the concern in her mother's eyes.

Elsie was mollified and burst into laughter. 'It can only be love, my darling. Even Belle left this shit for greener pastures.'

They had both laughed and hugged lovingly.

Paul had been particularly anxious when they told him of their plans to holiday in Kariba because of its close proximity to Zambia. The Zambezi River bordered Zambia and ZIPRA and, with speedboats donated by East Germany, they could make incursions across the river into Rhodesia.

'There's a lot of dissident activity that end,' said Paul.

The Elephant Hills Country Club opened in 1974 with its signature Gary Player golf course, and had been bombed into closure in 1977. The Victoria Falls Hotel was not spared either. ZIPRA insurgent activity was targeting the tourist assets to further cripple the economy. Paul had recently read that tourist arrivals had plummeted from 340 000 per annum in the early seventies to the current levels of 79 000.

Melanie's dad mocked him. 'Come now, old boy, don't tell me you are afraid of a few terrs? Smithy has everything under control … He's guarding the front.'

He had gone on to pat Paul on the back and he stiffened, finding his father-in-law rather patronising.

Paul had heard enough horror stories from Graham about the terrorists and he didn't take the threat of them lightly.

'And besides,' added Melanie's father, 'we're flying. Everybody says the terrs are on the ground.'

Bernard and Elsie left a few days later and Paul and Melanie stood on the balcony at Bulawayo Airport and watched the plane take off.

Sun-kissed and relaxed, Elsie and Bernard boarded the flight on the Viscount Hunyani and were two of the 58 passengers on board. The flight was full and some passengers had to be waylaid to the next flight. Even against the background of a struggle, people were still holidaying. While lives were being lost, others were born. People got married. They went on honeymoon. Life carried on as if nothing was amiss.

The flight from Kariba was lively, its passengers a mixture of old and young. It was a relatively short flight and they expected to be landing in Salisbury within the hour. Minutes into the flight, the air hostesses wheeled out their trollies and began serving drinks. High in the clouds, the passengers were oblivious to the squad of ZIPRA lieutenants on the ground eyeing the flight suspiciously.

Using a Strela surface-to-air missile, they shot at the aircraft and watched as it began to lose power and hurtle downwards towards the canopy of trees below. The plane crashed and burst into flames. Eighteen passengers survived the crash-landing and escaped the wreckage, but before they could make sense of what had happened, armed cadres appeared. Douglas was part of the operation. For the first time since completing his training, he was physically confronted with the enemy. He had been anxious to get onto the ground and become part of the action. He was eager to apply his new-found knowledge of warfare and tactics in real combat with the authors of his oppression.

It had been his first time in open ambush and he had experienced a feeling of fear and exhilaration. Until that day, he had never killed another human being and he recalled the face of the man who begged him and pleaded for mercy. The man was wearing a fedora with a blue handkerchief in his white shirt and, without a second thought, Douglas had pulled the trigger and the bullet had torn the man's scalp apart. The blood splattered onto his military fatigues and, after that first shot, Douglas fired several more. On leaving the site, he was satisfied that there were no survivors. However, the rescue team that followed a day later found eight who had lived to tell the gruesome story of how they had narrowly escaped death. Unable to identify their assailants, they described them as machine-gun-toting men baying for blood. It was all over the news, eliciting responses of shock and horror. In a BBC interview flighted on television, Joshua Nkomo took credit for the disaster. Until then he had been regarded as a timid man, but that display of aggression showed that he was far from it. His justification for bringing the plane down was that it was believed to have been carrying the commander of the Rhodesian security forces, Lieutenant General Walls. While Rhodesians expected international condemnation, the act was met with profound silence.

Melanie, together with Paul and thousands of others, attended the memorial service at St Mary's Cathedral. It had been years since she had stepped into a church. She was moved by the outpouring of grief that spilled into the courtyard. Thousands had come to pay their respects. Melanie's brothers, Anton and Christiaan, both flew up with their spouses to bid farewell to their parents. They held hands and cried through Reverend John da Costa's impassioned eulogy.

'Belief must bring action. And if you believe in God you must do something about it. And yet churches, even in our own dangerous times, are more than half empty all the time.'

Melanie's parents' death had felt bizarre. Even after the memorial service she was in denial. She couldn't believe that they were really gone. Why should she? It wasn't like they had buried their bodies. Once the disbelief subsided, she started going to church to deal with her anger. She dragged Paul and the children with her, who went because that was the only place she would agree to go. She never left the house and was enraged by the injustice of it all. It angered her that a whole war was being fought because of white dominion and the refusal of a white minority to cede and make concessions to a black majority. The whole thing was unsustainable and the wave of independence was sweeping across Africa. Who would be stupid enough to think they could stem it? Smith had been stubbornly supporting a war that had not only resulted in the loss of lives, but had also cost the economy millions because of UN sanctions. It had become apparent that Rhodesia could no longer afford the war, the treasury coffers running dry. And because there had been mass emigration, they didn't have the manpower to continue fighting.

Melanie's anger finally gave way to a debilitating depression. She had not been able to smile through the haze of sadness that enveloped her. Even the girls giggling as they played together could not stir her to life. The rest of the year rolled by in a blur and when the new year was ushered in, Melanie prayed that it would be better than the last. They marched off to vote in the referendum, shuffling along in the queue at the voting station. Everyone agreed that Smith's proposals were ridiculous and that he was throwing the whites under the bus.

'What choice does he have?' asked Melanie. 'The way I see it, his hands are tied behind his back.'

'He can fight. We're winning battles,' responded Paul.

Melanie rolled her eyes heavenwards. She could see through Rhodesian propaganda. They reported low casualties, yet every day someone they knew lost someone in an ambush or a landmine explosion. Melanie had stopped reading the newspapers and Paul accused her of being out of touch with reality. She wanted to curate her own reality, because that was the only way to preserve her sanity. The results of the referendum came out and 85 per cent of the whites had voted in favour of the new proposals. Paul had dismissed the result.

'It was obviously rigged. You know Smithy and him wanting to control the outcome.'

Melanie eyed her husband pitifully. Like many of their friends, he wanted to carry on living in this utopia of white supremacy.

Then reports came through that another plane had been shot down by another Russian Strela, but this time around there were no survivors. It was a Sunday afternoon and they were at the club in the company of the Watsons. Security at the club was tight, with doors barricaded and a fully stocked rifle rack in case there was an unexpected ambush. This was how they lived. Nobody travelled at night any more and long-distance trips between cities were not advisable because the Rhodesian countryside was teeming with terrorists. Still they enjoyed a Sunday beef roast with potatoes, gravy and peas and had just finished dessert when the news came through about the second plane. Melanie excused herself and went to the bathroom. She vomited the entire three-course meal in a series of spasmic groans and sat on the toilet seat crying. Cheryl found her weeping uncontrollably after her absence at the table became apparent.

'I feel like I'm losing my parents all over again,' she wept.

'Bloody Joshua,' Cheryl responded. 'We thought he was better than Mugabe, but he's a heartless fool. How do you kill a plane full of civilians?'

Melanie sobbed harder, clutching her sides. The pain and outrage echoed by Cheryl reverberated among all white Rhodesians.

Many more atrocities would be committed and there would be no censure from the world, but the victims would remember the silence.

16

Operation Gatling

The sun was rising, casting a light on the stoep of their Belle Acres home. Simphiwe was on her knees, scrubbing the floor. It needed to shine before she went to school and, even though she was anxious about being late, her mother was very uncompromising when it came to her shiny stoep.

There were bloodstains on the stoep that morning and Simphiwe was confused because she couldn't ascertain where the blood came from. Was it Velile? Where was her daughter? She looked up and saw her mother and grandmother approaching in the distance, both wearing black dresses with puffy sleeves. The hems swept the ground, gathering dust and the bristly needles of blackjacks. They were chatting amicably and when her granny saw Simphiwe, her eyes were wide open, which startled Simphiwe. Immediately, she jumped to her feet and raced towards her grandmother. She wanted to hold her face and look into her eyes, but when she tried to hug her, the older woman stepped back, avoiding her embrace. Simphiwe was perplexed. Her grandmother was never aloof; it was her mother who was cold.

'*Yini, Gogo?* Why *usenza* so?'

Her grandmother did not respond. Simphiwe looked to her mother, trying to seek reassurance from her, but her mother's face was unyielding, her lips drawn into a tight line. Simphiwe was confused. What had brought about the change of mood so suddenly?

'Go back,' they said. 'Go get your child. You can't come with us.'

'Where are you going? I want to come!' argued Simphiwe.

'*Buyel 'ekhaya, Simphiwe,*' chastened her grandmother.

And then, in unison, they turned their backs on her and marched off. They held hands and started running, their bodies getting smaller and smaller until she could no longer see them. Simphiwe felt excluded. Why did they not want her to go with them?

Simphiwe woke up bereft. Tears were running down her face and she wiped them away, relieved that it had just been a dream. But she was sad that she was waking up at Mkushi Camp and not in the solace of their cosy abode at Belle Acres. It had been over eight months since they had arrived at Mkushi, the training camp for female recruits located 125 kilometres north of Lusaka.

The camps were all close to the capital as Nkomo thought that would insulate them from possible attacks from the Rhodesian army. He had a long-term strategy to build ZIPRA into a formidable army. With the help of the Soviet Union and Libyan air force, they would enter the country through three entry points: Kariba, Victoria Falls and Wankie. ZIPRA would eventually storm the capital of Salisbury in a climatic end to the war.

Simphiwe emerged from her foxhole that morning. Mkushi was well established and had over 50 marquees, but the women rarely slept in them, choosing instead to sleep in the trenches for safety. It was hard to get sleep in the camps, mostly because they were on edge all the time as the Rhodesian army had been militant in their foray into Zambia.

It was 8.05am. Simphiwe knew the exact time because Douglas had gifted her a beautiful gold-plated Casio watch on his return from Moscow. He had managed to get it smuggled to her in the camp with the people who brought in food supplies. Normally, it was hidden in her foxhole, and she only wore it at night when she went to sleep. But that morning she didn't feel like taking it off as it made her feel closer to her husband. She hadn't heard from him in months and communicating via letters was in any case difficult as the camp commanders read all the correspondence.

There was always talk of infiltrators, that the Selous Scouts had planted spies among them. She fingered the watch gently. It showed the hours, the minutes and the seconds, and time seemed to drag or maybe it was because they were all so hungry. It had been two weeks since they had last received food rations so there was hardly anything to eat. The women made their way to the assembly area for the morning parade and the camp commanders stood upfront. There were 914 trainees who filed out for the parade that day and over 1 800 people in the camp. They were kitted out in khaki trousers and shirts, their Afros hidden under their berets.

During the course of the morning, Commander Jane Ndlovu intercepted Rhodesian military communication on her radio and learnt that Freedom Camp was under attack. Freedom Camp was located on Westlands Farm, 15 kilometres north of Lusaka. It housed the high command of ZIPRA, and it was where operations were planned before execution. She convened an urgent meeting in her underground bunker to alert her commanders that the enemy had attacked the camp and that they had to be vigilant. Following the meeting, the commanders then alerted the women to assume a defensive position in the trenches. They were advised that they could emerge in small groups to get what little food there was from the kitchen because lining up would make them vulnerable.

Commander Jane's intelligence was indeed correct. A few hours earlier, fuelled by copious amounts of aggression and gumption, the Rhodesian SAS had invaded Zambian airspace. Squadron Leader Chris Dixon, commander of the Canberra bomber, had called the Lusaka International Airport from his cockpit.

'Lusaka Tower, this is Green Leader,' he began by way of introduction. 'This is a message for the station commander at Mumbwa from the Rhodesian air force. We are attacking the terrorist base at Westlands Farm. This attack is against Rhodesian dissidents and not against Zambia. Rhodesia has no quarrel, repeat, no quarrel, with

Zambia or her security forces. We therefore ask you not to intervene or oppose our attack. However, we are orbiting your airfield at this time and are under orders to shoot down any Zambian aircraft that does not comply with this request and attempts to take off. Do you copy?'

'Copy that.'

'Roger, thanks. Cheers!'

While this might have sounded like dialogue from an action movie, it was real life and the horror of the onslaught soon unfolded. The SAS had instituted the first air strikes on the Freedom Camp, targeting their 8.30am parade. The strike force comprised Canberras, Hawker Hunter jets and K-Car helicopter gunships. Four Canberra aircraft dropped Rhodesian-made alpha bombs and, hitting the ground below, the bombs rebounded into the air and exploded with ferocity. Four K-Car helicopter gunships followed. K-Car is an acronym for Kill/Command and that is exactly what they did that morning.

Each K-Car had a crew of three: a pilot, a gunner technician and fire-force commander. Their faces and hands were smeared with 'Black is Beautiful', the camouflage cream created by Rhodesians to disguise themselves and make them less conspicuous so they could easily infiltrate black spaces.

The assault from above was synchronised and well choreographed, and the unsuspecting victims below fled in terror, dispersing in different directions, taken by surprise. It was a bloodbath and very few escaped the claws of death that day. Some dodged the bombs only to be burnt alive or shafted by the bullets. In the aftermath of the Rhodesian orgy of killing, the bodies of the dead lay strewn on the ground, covered with a film of congealing blood. Millions of dollars' worth of ammunition had been destroyed, buildings decimated and reduced to rubble, but the Rhodesians were not done. One camp down; they were on a mission to destroy two more. And Mkushi was next.

Simphiwe was part of the last group to go to the kitchen that morning. The hot food was finished and there was only milk left, served out of huge barrels. It reminded her of Belle Acres, except this wasn't farm-fresh milk straight from the cow. It was powdered milk that had been mixed with gallons of water. It was so watered down, but Simphiwe was past caring or complaining. She knew that when the war effort was over they would milk their freedom for all it was worth.

While drinking their glass of milk, Simphiwe and her friend, Rutendo Garwe, chatted. They had both been transferred to Mkushi and had become good friends over the months. Simphiwe was draining her cup of milk when she noticed low-flying helicopters whirring above them. She checked her watch. It was 11.45am. Rutendo was confused because they had not been alerted that the Zambians would be doing an air patrol that day. Then they heard Commander Jane's whistle, a sign for them to gather at the assembly point. The girls looked at each other in confusion. The commands were conflicting; they had first been told to hide in the trenches and were now being called to parade. Nonetheless, they made their way there and discovered that Commander Jane had been captured and it was a Rhodesian army official blowing her whistle.

'Run!' she commanded. 'Run!'

But it was too late. Napalm bombs dropped and exploded with fury. Simphiwe was catapulted into the air and landed on her back with a resounding thud. She lay motionless and when she opened her eyes, she saw pillars of smoke forming black tunnels in the sky. It was as if she was floating, looking down at her prostrate body. One hand lay next to her body. Blown off.

Like frightened rabbits, some girls had remained hidden in the tunnels. They had met their explosive end when bunker bombs were hurled into the trenches. The camp was enveloped in chaos, with girls running in different directions, colliding into each other. The orderly drills they had practised were forgotten in the mad desperation to flee. Some girls were on fire, flames engulfing them. The smell of singeing hair, burning flesh and toxic fumes thronged the air. It was in that commotion that Mabusi and Khiwa appeared to Simphiwe in their long black dresses. This time they didn't run away from her and her mother had tears streaming down her face. She was clutching her head, pained by the slaughter around her.

'Asambe mntanami. Asamb'ekhaya,' she beseeched.

'Hayi, Simphiwe, sala, asikafik 'isikhathi sakho,' replied Mabusi. 'Your time hasn't come yet.'

'Hayi, Mama!' rebutted Khiwa angrily. 'Ngeke ngimtshiy 'umntanami. I can't leave her to die here! Asambe Simphiwe! Asambe!'

Then they started to bicker. Mabusi was telling her to stay and Khiwa was telling her to go. Who was she supposed to listen to? She chose to adhere to her granny's instructions as Mabusi had always been the voice of reason, the voice she listened to. That was when she came to. She started coughing as she inhaled smoke and struggled to get up as she tried to propel herself up, but realised that one hand was no longer there. She felt blood trickle down her face and touched her head. The shrapnel had hit her. She had just managed to sit up when she saw Rhodesian paratroopers landing, wielding menacing rifles.

Simphiwe knew instinctively that if she remained where she was she was going to meet her death sooner rather than later. Trigger-happy Rhodesians fired a volley of bullets in every direction. With an incredible amount of effort, Simphiwe managed to stand. She felt light-headed and slowly hobbled along, swept up in the stampede. She decided to run towards the bush. Many other women were heading in that direction, towards the river. They threw their burning bodies into the water, not knowing that napalm burned in water, and their screams pierced through the air. Simphiwe's small steps were curtailed when she felt a searing pain tear through her leg. She fell to the ground, face down, and felt the feet of frightened women run over her. She buried her face in the grass and bit on her tongue to try to stave off the pain. She didn't have the willpower to stand up.

Douglas was part of the team of men who volunteered to clear the camp. The river was bloodied with the decimated corpses it carried. They pulled bodies from under piles of rubble while others were buried in the trenches. Very few torsos were intact, limbs broken and bowels split open. A few girls were still alive beneath the rubble, severely wounded, but life still pulsed weakly through them. There were no screams, only stunned silence. As the rescuers worked through the carnage, Douglas was hoping to find Simphiwe. And then he saw it. Her hand with the gold-plated Casio watch, blackened by the blast.

17

The peace brokers

A few days before Christmas, they woke to the news that the war was over. It was almost as if the British wanted to conclude the Rhodesian mess expeditiously and celebrate Christmas lunch without a war hanging over their heads like a noose. Douglas was rather perplexed about the ceasefire agreement that had been signed at Lancaster.

Following the ceasefire, ZANLA and ZIPRA had to surrender their arms and the soldiers had one week to report to the sixteen designated assembly points around the country manned by the Red Cross. The location of these assembly points was suspicious to Douglas. Only four of them were located in the urban centres and the rest were on the periphery of the rural areas. Wouldn't that make them easy targets? Douglas, like many of his counterparts, didn't trust the disarmament process. He didn't trust the Rhodesian forces and knew first-hand how brutal they were. What if this was all a ruse?

Douglas recalled his encounter with the enemy when they had been ambushed in Hwange. It had been his first experience of one-on-one combat. Unlike taking the aeroplane down, his fight had been with an armed soldier whose skills matched his own. He decided he wasn't going to give up his weapons. His gun was like his penis and he felt vulnerable without it.

But soon thereafter, they had to surrender their weapons and accept that the war was over, with no decisive victor. He felt betrayed by the brokered settlement. To think they had survived rapid falls and steep gorges crossing the Zambezi just for them to concede by signing a piece of paper. He thought of the ones who had not survived the treacherous crossing, who had been defeated by the river when their dinghies tipped over, or simply extinguished by the Rhodesian forces under a barrage of bullets. When he reflected on the brutality of it all, he felt that this was a cop-out. He thought of Simphiwe and became angry. They had come all this way – and for what? Talks started to abound that their leaders had betrayed them in signing the Lancaster Agreement. While they were being slaughtered in the trenches, their leaders were selling them out while in oak-panelled boardrooms in London.

Douglas, like many of his comrades, had no understanding of the negotiations that had occurred behind the scenes and which had culminated in the Lancaster Agreement. After Ian Smith had forged ahead with his internal settlement of 3 March 1978, he had ushered in a Zimbabwe-Rhodesia headed by Bishop Abel Muzorewa. However, it had not received international endorsement because it excluded ZAPU and ZANU. The OAU's objection had been the loudest. The elite group of African states had been established in 1963 as the Organisation of African Unity to share ideas on political ideologies and Pan-Africanism.

Ethiopia had hosted the inaugural event in Addis Ababa. Ethiopia always walked with an air of superiority. 'We are gathered here today to promote African unity and solidarity in the face of white imperialism,' preened Ethiopia at the ceremony.

Ethiopia was a sight to behold and commanded attention when she walked into the room. Her features, with her sharp pointed nose and high cheekbones, were striking. Her mop of curly hair was piled on top of her head, with a few tendrils hanging on her face. Tall and svelte, she looked sensual dressed in a traditional habesha kemis made of fine handwoven cotton. Elaborate Tibeb patterns were embroidered on the material, with multicoloured threads on the cuffs, the hem and the collar. She was soft-spoken, but firm. It was a grace that came from never having been colonised by oppressive imperialists. Apart from a five-year stint when Italy had forced himself on her, occupying her against her will, she had lived independently. Ethiopia had an air of autonomy.

The OAU was a small, intimate group of sixteen states that used their collective power to not legitimise the new Mickey Mouse government constituted by Smith and his motley crew.

It was at the first Commonwealth Heads of Government meeting held in August 1979 that the frontline states made their position very clear. Margaret Thatcher had just come to power in Britain and it was her ascension that was to have the greatest impact on changing the fortunes of Rhodesia. She had zero empathy for the Patriotic Front and referred to them as 'terrorists like the IRA'.

'The Patriotic Front is the only legitimate party that represents the interests of all Zimbabweans,' said Zambia, draped in a red kitenge with blue geometric squares.

Tanzania nodded in agreement, her kofia almost toppling over. She wore a loose-fitting, white kanzu that swept the floor. Zambia was hosting the delegates in Lusaka, despite the fact that a war continued to rage in her backyard.

Up until then, Nigeria had not spoken, but she blustered into the conversation with authority. She was a buxom beauty, big-breasted, with big buttocks. When she walked, the corridors of power shook. Her head was draped in a headdress that matched her orange Asoke-print dress, with a pleated umbrella Gele forming a halo around her head.

'We can't have this nunsense!' she declared, waving a large manicured hand in the air. The gold chains on her wrists clanked noisily together. She had gold chains draped around her neck, some disappearing into her bosom. Her ears were pulled down by the weight of her gold earrings.

Britain side-eyed her, thinking her to be rather gaudy. She, in contrast, looked rather prim and proper in a white pussybow blouse teamed with a tailored blue jacket and matching pencil skirt. She wore a strand of pearls that she played with as the discussions unfolded. She spoke in a low and measured voice, carefully pronouncing each syllable.

'It is for the benefit of everyone here to support the settlement and put an end to this Rhodesian debacle.'

Britain was tired; her last colonial outpost was behaving like a typical last-born, causing trouble and prone to throwing tantrums. She wanted to shake the African dust off and never have to set foot on African soil again.

'Listen oho, mebbe you didn't hear us the furst time. We will not support any settlement that doesn't include Nkomo or Mugabe. I make no joke, oho. If you support this stupidity, Nigeria will stop buying all British goods and services. And I mean all, oho.'

Britain winced and the other OAU states watched as she twitched nervously in her seat. Everyone in that room was aware that Nigeria was the biggest consumer of British exports. Nigeria knew her strength. She had black gold in the form of the oil fields of the Niger Delta and Abuja nestled between her thighs. With the click of her gold-adorned fingers, Nigeria went on to nationalise the assets of British Petroleum in protest so as to curb the supply of oil to Rhodesia and South Africa. She didn't stop there and went on to flood the markets with millions of pound sterling, which sent the stalwart currency into jitters of nervousness.

'I don't joke, oho,' repeated Nigeria, making a hissing sound with her lips. 'Support Smith and see what we will do, oho.'

Britain needed no further prompting. She knew where her toasted bread was buttered. She addressed her counterparts and reiterated that the Crown had every intention to grant Rhodesia independence, but it would not happen under the current circumstances. She pointed out the flaws in the proposed constitution, which, she said, were not representative of the country's demographics. With pursed lips, she would not legitimise the new state. Her inaugural address was met with wild applause. Afterwards, Australia, Jamaica and Zambia rallied around her. They egged her on to convene another conference to outline the modalities for a new Rhodesia. Basking in the adoration and wanting to ride on the momentum, she agreed. That was how the Lancaster Agreement came into being, with Britain as the venerable host.

Robert Mugabe, leader of the ZANU party, was a reluctant participant and felt these meetings were diverting his attention from the war on the ground. He was quite happy directing the war effort from his villa in Maputo. Had things gone his way, he would have continued the war till the last man standing. The way he saw it, Rhodesia would eventually capitulate. Nevertheless, it was the combined pressure of Samora Machel of Mozambique and Kenneth Kaunda of Zambia who made him relent. The effects of a protracted war were taking their toll on their individual economies. They threatened to close the ZIPRA bases in Zambia and the ZANLA bases in Mozambique if the two did not present a united front and show up at the talks. It was no secret that Mugabe and Nkomo loathed each other. Forty-seven plenary sessions later, over a period of three months of haggling and heckling, the Lancaster Agreement came into effect and brought the war to a decisive end. There were no victors; it was a brokered peace settlement.

18

Homecoming

Following the ceasefire, the high command of both parties flew into the Salisbury airport amid wild cheers and a hearty welcome. They were like film stars on the red carpet. Unlike the A-listers of the liberation struggle, Douglas was among those who arrived by train. Others in the lower command had bussed in. Instead of converging at the assembly points as they had been directed, Douglas had headed straight to his rural home.

He boarded a bus at Renkini Bus Terminal, which was a hustle and bustle of activity and teeming with commuters, transport touts and vendors selling everything from a biscuit to a bucket of sorghum. Douglas bought himself a Fanta orange and a packet of spongy buns. Animated and boisterous conversations were taking place all around him. Some were screaming at the top of their voices.

'Thief! Thief!' screamed a woman as a man sprinted through the crowd, darting between vendor stalls. Two burly men took it upon themselves to chase the so-called thief. He was caught and a crowd gathered as he was thrashed mercilessly. Douglas decided not to be distracted by the vigilante efforts lest he missed his bus home.

He made enquiries from the transport touts and they directed him to the bus he needed to board. The bus was lined with rows of seats and it reminded him of boarding a flight, except that had been less chaotic. There were no assigned seat numbers like on the aeroplane and it was a haphazard and clumsy process. People's luggage lined the passageway and he had to climb over a 10-kilogram sack of maize that was obstructing the way. It was a painfully hot day and the windows were closed, the odours of food, sweat and impatience converging to create a stuffy atmosphere. He found a seat near the front because he wanted to be close to the door in case there was a need to escape. A hen clucked noisily under his seat. Douglas opened his window to let in some fresh air and a stream of discordant sounds flowed in from outside.

Living in the camps, Douglas had been separated from society for a long time and seeing so many people in one place made him nervous. Suddenly there was a loud crackling sound in the bus and instinctively Douglas dived to the floor.

'It's just a bus with a bad exhaust,' said the driver, who had seen Douglas in the rear-view mirror.

Dusting himself off and feeling embarrassed, Douglas rose to reclaim his seat. He could hear the giggles of the passengers behind him, who obviously thought he was being paranoid. He hated that the bus had to be full before they could depart, because sitting around and waiting made him edgy. He was not used to being idle. Finally, when the last passengers boarded, a mother with a troop of noisy young children, the bus rolled into motion. One of the children, a little girl, caught his attention. She must have been three or four and his Velile immediately came to mind. He was looking forward to being reunited with his daughter. But first he had to go home.

As the bus hummed its way through the Bulawayo CBD, Douglas marvelled at the tall buildings and wide streets – such a change from being cosseted in nature. The vibrancy of city life was soon, however, replaced by the mundane scenery of long brown grass and tall thorny trees with brown leaves that dotted the landscape. He was eventually lulled into a deep sleep but woke with a start when the bus came to a halt at a roadblock manned by armed officials like him. One climbed aboard the bus and took a cursory look around before instructing the driver to proceed. The bus continued to meander through the rural landscape. Fields were empty with the relics of dried-out maize stalks and Douglas figured that the harvesting for the season must be complete. He finally disembarked near a lone tree signalling the turn-off to his outpost. He walked a few kilometres, passing a motley collection of mud huts clustered around nothingness. There was no development, just sprawling unproductive reserves of bushveld. On occasion he would meet the odd person and they would greet each other and ask after each other's health as though they knew each other. It was just the way of the world in these parts. No introductions required, just acknowledgment.

As he was nearing his home, he saw two young girls walking towards him. They were walking hand in hand and laughing gaily together. He was immediately drawn to the taller of the two, who was walking with a measured gait, as she reminded him a lot of Nonku. He had never forgotten Nonku and often wondered what had happened to her. The girl's friend was shorter and more voluptuous, with breasts that caught his eye as they jiggled as she walked. He suddenly felt a stirring in his loins; it had been years since he had been with a woman. He felt like his libido died with Simphiwe, but now it felt like it was being resurrected. He called out to the girls in greeting.

'Linjani mantombazana?'

They giggled in response. He wasn't sure what was funny and even adjusted his beret. Maybe they felt intimidated by him in his army fatigues.

'Hawu, girls,' he chastened gently, 'don't you want to greet a war-weary soldier like me?'

'We do,' said the taller one, talking for both of them.

She reached out her hand and Douglas held it.

'I am Jones Sibindi,' he said, introducing himself by his war name. Even though he was no longer in combat, he was no longer Douglas.

'I'm Theresa,' she replied, 'and this is my cousin Tabitha.'

'Holy Moses,' he replied. 'I am surrounded by angels.'

They both chuckled again and his face lit up with a smile. He felt his pulse quicken with excitement, flushed with the potency of his awakening libido.

'So, Theresa, how do I get to see you again?'

She explained that she stayed koNkala, the homestead across the river. He promised he would visit later that evening. Tabitha then insisted that her uncle would not allow it. Theresa added that he fiercely guarded his kraal and not even wild animals could get through the fence.

'I am a soldier,' he said confidently. 'I can get through anything. I have been to places you could never imagine.'

They girls both laughed, the sexual innuendo not lost on them.

'I'll see you later … Don't fall asleep too early.'

They parted with the promise of a rendezvous cloaked in darkness. His pace quickened as he walked towards his own homestead. While he didn't turn to look back, he could feel the girls' eyes boring into the back of his head. Their pockets of laughter floated in the air like light, soapy bubbles bursting with anticipation.

As he finally reached his home, an enclosure with six huts, it was his mother who saw him first. She rose from her place on her grass mat and ran towards him. Douglas dropped his rucksack and raced towards her.

'Duggie! Duglus! *Mntanami*,' she screamed, '*umntanami bakithi!*'

He was ensconced in a crushing embrace and choked with love. Not since childhood had his mother held him like that and in that moment he welcomed it. He found solace in her arms and imagined himself as a little boy of five, shrouded in the innocence of childhood and not tainted by manhood and the ugliness that came with the war. The tears escaped from his eyes and he didn't fight them, allowing them to flow, unrestrained. He didn't have to pretend with her and, as he cried, he felt all the tension and anxiety start to leave his body.

'I thought you were dead, *mntanami* – so many people have died. I didn't want to be that mother who has to bury her child.'

Her face too was wet with tears. They held onto each other, afraid to let go. Very soon their hug was expanded to include his siblings and other members of the family. He could feel little children tugging at his feet, trying to get a piece of him. In their eyes he was a champion.

This was a hero's welcome home.

The day unfolded with ceremony and grand gestures and a goat was slaughtered in his honour. His mother apologised that there were no cows left in the kraal and blamed it on the hardships of the war. She didn't have to narrate it; her face was lined with suffering. Douglas wanted to smooth the creases of worry.

'Everything is going to be all right now, Mama,' he assured her. 'We have won the war.'

'*Shuwa mntanami? Shuwa sibili?*'

Her voice was questioning, disbelieving.

'I assure you, Mama, life will be better for all of us. Otherwise it will have all been a waste. People would have died for nothing. So many deaths, Mama, so many.'

He allowed his voice to trail off. He did not want to burden her with the heaviness of the war. Instead, he regaled them all with stories of life in the camps and the antics of his comrades. Even in the midst of the turmoil, they had allowed themselves to laugh, to poke fun at each other.

At his mother's homestead, they ate together and appraised each other on what had been happening over the three years since they had seen each other. Douglas couldn't bring himself to tell them about Simphiwe. The wife he had lost to the war. The time passed quickly and soon the sun was setting. He excused himself, wanting to take a bath. His sister had heated the water for him over an open fire. He had told her it was unnecessary because he had been bathing in cold water for so long that he was used to it. He splashed the soothing warm water over his body. As he was getting dressed, his uncle peered around the door.

'*Mtshana*, there are things you need to do now that you are back.'

As Douglas dabbed himself dry with a frayed towel, he wondered what these things were. His uncle's tone was sombre and his face reflected the gravity of the matter.

'You need to cleanse yourself spiritually. Of all those people you killed in the war.'

Douglas trembled slightly. He often had nightmares. Of dead faces flashing in his dreams. Sometimes he could even smell the fear, the blood.

'I will do it, *malume*,' he replied, without hesitation.

'There's a woman not far from here ... I will take you to her tomorrow. She will cleanse you. You need to remove that aura of death, otherwise it will taint you and those around you forever.'

Douglas nodded and borrowed some clothes from his uncle. They were ill-fitting, but that didn't matter – he was certain Theresa had been impressed by his uniform earlier that day and wouldn't mind what he was wearing.

He made his way to the Nkala homestead in the dark. He felt like he was back in the war, doing field reconnaissance. He surveyed the homestead from a distance and saw people seated in the kitchen, around a dying fire. He observed as, one by one, the elderly family members went to sleep. The girls were the last to leave and he felt safe in the knowledge that they slept alone and decided to approach them stealthily.

'*Yimi*,' he announced, as he pushed the door of the hut. There was no resistance. They had deliberately left it open for him.

Tabitha was already in bed, while Theresa sat on top of it, her feet dangling over the side. She rose to meet him in the middle of the room. He kissed her soft lips and, without any preamble, undressed her. She helped him remove his clothes, her hands running all over his hardened body. The glimmer of light from the moon exposed the desire that shone on their faces. They fell to the floor onto the cowhide mat and it tickled his back as Theresa ignited his already inflamed libido. He mounted her with urgency, unable to restrain his passion. He came fast, spurting all his pent-up yearning into her. His release was accompanied by a guttural groan that emanated from deep within. This made Tabitha giggle as she turned to her side.

'I'm sorry,' he said to Theresa, collapsing on her. 'It's been so long.'

'It's okay,' she replied, stroking him. 'You have the whole night to please me.'

He kissed her, cupping the firm breasts that beckoned to him. His lips followed and he sucked on them while his hands danced between her legs. His fingers got caught in the bushy hair as he searched for the nub of her clitoris. He stroked her until she was gasping and groaning with pleasure. On the bed, Tabitha reached between her own legs, her own longing stoked.

Douglas mounted Theresa, taking his time with slow, measured strokes. She writhed beneath him, her pelvis grinding against his groin. He felt her body tense as she was gripped in the throes of an orgasm. Her hands tightened around him but he didn't stop. He kept thrusting into her with purposeful intent and she came again. Tabitha came too, a strangled scream escaping from her lips. Douglas was spurred on and turned Theresa around. He had her on all fours as he pummelled his way to another orgasm. He was pulling her towards him, wanting to go again, but Theresa pleaded exhaustion. Tabitha volunteered herself to the task. '*Hawu*,' said Douglas, '*lawe futhi?*'

Tabitha nodded, straddling Douglas, impaling herself on his throbbing penis. She was hot and wet and he kissed her hungrily, cupping her full ripe breasts that were like melons in season. Tabitha gyrated her way to a climax and they came together in a fusion of frenzy. Afterwards, he lay between them, flanked by their adoration.

'So what must happen here? Now I must marry you both?'

'Yes,' replied Theresa, rolling onto her side, feeling satiated and satisfied, stroking his firm body.

'Yes,' concurred Tabitha, 'you have to take us both.'

Douglas kissed one and then the other. They were right – he was going to wife them both.

The harried knock on the door alerted them and Douglas swiftly rolled beneath the bed.

'Who is it?' asked Theresa, climbing to her feet and quickly covering herself with a sarong that was lying on the floor.

'Are you okay?' came a gruff voice. 'I thought I heard strangled voices.'

'*Si* right, baba,' replied Tabitha authoritatively.

Douglas listened to the footfall of feet getting farther and farther away before rolling out from under the bed. He kissed the girls goodbye and got ready to leave. They were upset that he was not going to stay the night.

'I will see you both tomorrow,' he said.

He ran into the night, feeling euphoric. The girls had given him an enthusiastic reception befitting a war-weary soldier. He truly felt like he had conquered.

19

The aftermath

As they counted down to the new year, there was an air of uncertainty. The Williams family converged at the Somabhula Country Club, but their community had thinned. The new year began with the country preparing for elections. There was fierce campaigning all over the country as candidates tried to woo voters to the ballot box. In some quarters it was felt that there was more coercion and less wooing. The general election was held on Valentine's Day and, as promised in the Lancaster House Agreement, there were two voting rolls: the common one and the white one, which guaranteed the white minority twenty seats. Ten parties contested the inaugural elections, but the results showed that only four had been taken seriously by the electorate.

From the comfort of their living room, Melanie and Paul watched the live broadcast of the election results on television. ZANU-PF had won in a landslide victory of 57 seats.

'I can't believe he's that popular!' remarked Paul.

'Do you think they rigged it?' asked Melanie.

'You bet my fucking arse they did!'

ZAPU had won a meagre twenty seats, a huge blow to Joshua Nkomo. Smith's Rhodesian Front won twenty seats and Muzorewa's United African National Council just three seats. This meant that Robert Mugabe would become the prime minister of Zimbabwe. The news was received differently in various quarters. For the black populace, it was met with profound jubilation and crowds of black people thronged the streets of Salisbury, waving the flag in the air. Hundreds of young black men were carted in flatbed trucks, chanting ZANU slogans and waving their fists in the air. It was a terrifying sight for many white business owners, who quickly locked their businesses and fled the city. Those cocooned in office buildings watched from their windows, frightened by the number of Mugabe supporters who were bussed in to cheer their new leader. Those in government buildings began the tedious job of shredding evidence. Anxious white mothers fetched their children from school early. The morale among the white Rhodesian troops plummeted and many cried in despair. There was a fear in the air that hung like a thick fog of pollution over the city. Fear of retribution, fear of nationalisation, fear of uncertainty, fear of the unknown.

A news reporter on the ground was stopping people for random interviews, asking what their expectations were of the new government. Employment was a common response. People wanted jobs and better pay and equal opportunities in the workplace. Others articulated the need for good schools, hospitals and better housing. The reporter approached a few whites to get their views on the result. Many professed they were devastated by the outcome and betrayed by the role the British government had played in the Lancaster Agreement. An elderly woman with perfectly coiffed hair articulated her disgust: 'I'm frightened because we lost the war. Mugabe's victory stinks and the British stink with it.'

Some remembered what had occurred when Mozambique gained its independence and a law was enacted that those of Portuguese nationality could either renounce their citizenship or become Mozambicans. Those who did not want to do so had to leave the country within 24 hours with no more than 20 kilograms of luggage. Repatriation planes were arranged to charter people back to Portugal. While the Portuguese government made provision to accommodate the returnees, they were met with open hostility and failed to integrate fully into Portuguese society and were always treated as second-class citizens.

But Mugabe was quick to provide assurances that he would pursue a policy of peace and reconciliation between whites and blacks. In a national broadcast he stated, 'We would want to see them live in this country, free from any restrictions, free from any victimisation. To us, we cannot practise racialism in reverse; we just cannot do it in principle. As far as we are concerned, they are entitled to serve the nation as the blacks are entitled to do so. And hence we would want to see them develop a greater sense of security, a greater sense of confidence, a sense of belonging. This is our message to them.'

'I don't believe him,' said Paul, switching off the television. 'He's a communist. He'll murder the fucking lot of us.'

'Paul, don't be so dramatic,' snapped Melanie. 'The whole world is watching. Let's see what happens. Only time will tell.'

She picked up her car keys, feeling stifled by being in the house, surrounded by the air of negativity.

'Where are you going?' asked a concerned Paul.

'I need to get some groceries,' she quickly replied.

It was a lie; she just wanted to drive around. Over the last few months, she had been caged in the house like a frightened bird. Following the death of her parents, she had been engulfed in a cloud of depression.

'I'm coming with you,' Paul said. 'It might not be safe.'

Leaving the farm, they were met with chanting, dancing and ululation from the farm workers. Paul figured there would be no point in insisting that any work get done for the rest of the day. Where there were celebrations, people were peaceful. They were all tired of the war, tired of the hardships that came with it.

At the supermarket, Melanie bumped into Cheryl, who could not stave off her tears.

'Oh my God, Melanie, what is going to become of us?'

Melanie stifled her annoyance as she hugged her friend, trying to offer some comfort. She had been trying to run away from negativity only to walk right into it.

'We're leaving,' said another lady who was throwing things into her trolley. 'We're not going to stick around for this shit.'

'We can't leave,' sobbed Cheryl. 'We don't have the money. Everything's tied up in the farm. We have loans up to our necks. We never thought it would come to this.'

'We're not leaving either,' replied Melanie. 'It's okay; we'll sit it out together.'

The lead-up to the election had been fraught with tension and fear. Graham had explained to Melanie and Paul that Mugabe was not supposed to have won the election and there had been several failed attempts to assassinate him.

'We've been trying to eliminate the bastard since Maputo,' said Graham, taking a long drag of his cigarette.

They were seated on the patio, having drinks. For the most part, they were not celebratory; it was just easier to drink in Mugabe's victory. The more they drank, the looser Graham's tongue became and he started divulging secret state operations. Curled on a chaise lounge, Melanie listened intently because Graham's stories were always filled with drama and intrigue.

'You know,' slurred Graham, 'after the ceasefire, we were briefed that under no uncertain terms should Moogarby win the elections. He was a marked man after that.'

Operation Hectic was what it had been code-named and involved the elimination of certain political stalwarts, including Robert Mugabe.

Graham went on tell them about the foiled attempts on Mugabe's life after he had addressed an election rally in Fort Victoria. A radio-activated explosive device was used to carry out the ambush, but there were miscalculations and Mugabe's vehicle narrowly missed the explosion and he escaped. After that foiled attempt, a plan was made to kill him on a trip to Bulawayo to address another rally at the city stadium. That operation had been planned down to a T, with Selous Scouts planted everywhere.

'We were confident we were going to nail the bastard, but you know what? He got off the plane, and when he reached the bottom of the steps he announced that he was cancelling the rally.'

Paul was aghast. 'Are you serious? Just like that?'

Graham nodded. 'Just like that. We don't know who tipped him off, or maybe he just had a hunch. Wily man that, but he got back on the plane.'

And just like that Mugabe had escaped death yet again.

Graham stomped out his Kingsgate cigarette and lit another. Melanie was concerned that after Gregory succumbed to lung cancer, Graham might meet a similar demise. She tried to gently caution him about his excessive smoking but he only laughed and joked good-naturedly that if he could survive the war then he could survive lung cancer.

'I can only imagine that these attempts on his life made Mugabe paranoid,' continued Melanie, weighing in on the conversation between the two brothers.

'He's always been paranoid,' replied Paul, stroking her leg. 'You just need to listen to his speeches.'

'But how did *all* the assassination attempts fail?' asked Melanie.

Graham shook his head. 'Even with all that careful planning, the manpower and the ammunition, the powers that be decided it wasn't going to happen. And it didn't – and now here we are.'

He wore a defeated look on his face. 'We tried everything to stop this. There was even a plan to rig the elections, but it was set aside because nobody actually thought Moogarby would win.'

Graham laughed, but there were tears streaming down his face. Melanie reached out and patted his shoulder gently. She'd been reticent at first, fearing a rebuttal, but Graham was receptive to her consoling touch.

'So what's the plan now, Graham?' asked Paul. 'You going south to Pretoria?'

Graham surprised them with his response when he told them he'd decided to stay put. Melanie decided she was going to truly welcome the new government, while Paul continued to express deep reservations as he mourned the downfall of Rhodesia. Yet even in his grief he could not bring himself to join the exodus of Rhodesians fleeing across the border into South Africa in droves. A few opted for Australia and the United Kingdom. Overnight, people packed up their disillusionment and parts of their lives into suitcases and boxes and left. 'For Sale' signs sprouted up all over the suburbs. Estate agents were kept tremendously busy as well-resourced blacks purchased homes in the previously white suburbs. Thus began the slow process of racially integrated neighbourhoods. The greatest source of dread for everyone was that standards would start to fall. Not just neighbourhoods, but schools and hospitals. Melanie was unperturbed and, while many of her cohorts left, she was clear that she was not returning to the mess of apartheid. It was estimated that over 300 000 left Rhodesia and the 150 000 that stayed became a tight clique that observed the changes with keen interest.

20

The house of stone

Independence Day celebrations were slated for a month after the election. The Prince of Wales flew in to represent the Crown. Not since 1960 had any member of the royal family set foot on Rhodesian soil. At 32, the dashing prince, who was still very much an eligible bachelor, was dressed in a white naval uniform decorated with gold epaulettes. He had been received at the Salisbury airport a few days earlier by Mugabe and introduced to the inaugural government. More than a hundred delegates arrived to attend the independence celebrations. Salisbury airport was a hive of activity as the dignitaries flocked in.

The fanfare began with a state banquet hosted at the Meikles Hotel on the eve of Independence Day. Distinguished dignitaries and guests all filed into the hotel, accompanied by their spouses decked out in splendid gowns. It was truly an eclectic and cosmopolitan mix of people and colours swirling around the room, a moment filled with promise of the new dawn of democracy. Melanie had been glad to be a part of the buzz.

The air was thick with optimism. Mugabe appeared to be making a concerted effort to accommodate the white minority population. When he constituted his new government, he elected Denis Norman, a white farmer with no prior political experience, as the Minister of Agriculture. When called to the ministry, he was head of the Commercial Farmers' Union, and while Denis had initially expressed reservations at taking up the post, he had risen to the responsibility. Paul knew

Denis from his farming circles and from the CFU, the 'old boys' club' of farming. This gave Paul and his ilk some much-needed reassurance that at least their interests would be protected, if not represented. Land had been a contentious issue and the final outcome in the Lancaster House Agreement was that existing property rights would be respected. The incumbent government could only acquire land for resettlement on a willing-buyer/willing-seller principle. The British government pledged to support the process, but this was the clause that would come back to bite them in their arses.

While people were merrymaking and networking, there was another behind-the-scenes attempt to sabotage Britain's relinquishment of power. This time the threat was not internally engineered; it was external. It was not in the best interests of South Africa to have a stable and functioning Zimbabwe on their doorstep, because State President BJ Vorster feared that if that happened, Zimbabwe would become the hub for insurgents fighting the apartheid regime. Operation Barnacle was being coordinated from the high offices of Pretoria in South Africa. Their strategy was simple: assassinate Mugabe and plunge the newly formed republic into chaos. Remote-controlled explosives concealed in traffic-light boxes were to be installed on the route that Mugabe was to take to the Rufaro Stadium for the Independence Day celebrations. But Mugabe's security detail was ahead of the game, and although it allowed Mugabe's motorcade to proceed along the designated route, Mugabe himself was in a car in a smaller convoy on an entirely different route. He arrived at the stadium unharmed and the independence celebrations continued without a hitch.

Paul and Melanie sat in the VIP section, adding to the smattering of white faces among the sea of black that filled the stadium that night. While most whites stayed at home to watch the festivities or cry over them, Paul and Melanie were privileged to be a part of the live proceedings. Paul felt an air of superiority to be in such close proximity to power. He couldn't wait to narrate the events to the boys when they met at the next braai and was almost annoyed that everything progressed so smoothly. He'd been hoping for fireworks of sorts, perhaps even a hiccup or two.

Melanie had thought it was odd that Nkomo, a tall man of some stature, was essentially tucked away behind the sound system in an obscure corner of the stadium. She wondered why he was being so obviously sidelined. The combined choral force of the three armies sang 'Nkosi Sikelel'iAfrika' and the ceremony was presided over by His Royal Highness, the Prince of Wales. Reverend Canaan Banana was to be president of the new republic – a constitutional role, ceremonial at best, with little real power. Nkomo had been offered the post, but had declined it, preferring a more active role in government. The joke in Rhodie circles was that the country was now, without a doubt, a banana republic. As Banana was sworn in, Melanie observed that he lacked the confidence and quiet assurance Mugabe exhibited. Even as he recited his oath, Banana's voice sounded shaky, like someone desperately in need of God's help. Mugabe, by contrast, was bold and assertive. On that podium that night, the church and the judiciary were both represented and they would become critical players in the new dispensation. The newborn country would adopt Christianity as its official religion; African spirituality would underpin it.

There is something auspicious about the midnight hour. It represents a crossover, the beginning of a new day, a victory over the darkness of the night that precedes it. In the Bible, it was midnight when Boaz discovered Ruth lying at his feet. It was at midnight when the Israelites began their exodus from Egypt. It was at midnight when Paul and Silas were praying to God and singing hymns and suddenly a violent earthquake shook the foundations of the prisons and everyone's chains became loose. And so it was at midnight that Zimbabwe was birthed. The name Zimbabwe was derived from the words *dzimba dza mabwe*, 'the House of Stone'.

The Union Jack was lowered and Paul's heart sank. He felt like a newborn baby whose umbilical cord had been severed, but he had none of the security of being in his mother's arms. As the Zimbabwean flag was raised, Melanie felt a surge of hope. She reached for Paul's hand and squeezed it.

'Darling, we have crossed over.'

'God help us,' he replied. Paul had never been a believer, but at that moment he felt they needed divine intervention.

The seven-coloured flag, with its horizontal stripes of green, gold, red and black, was hoisted into the air. A white triangle contained the Zimbabwean 'golden' bird, fashioned on the iconic soapstone birds that stood proudly atop the walls of the ancient city of Great Zimbabwe. Paul explained to Melanie that they had been moulded on that of a bateleur eagle.

'The bird is of great spiritual significance in the Shona culture. It's supposed to represent protective spirits and messengers of the gods. The Greeks have nothing on African mythology.'

Even as he said it, Melanie could tell he was being facetious.

With the political protocol complete, the way was paved for the real attraction: Bob Marley and the Wailers. While Melanie was not a fan of reggae, she had yet to come across anyone who didn't know who Bob Marley was. It was also her first time seeing him in person, his swinging dreadlocks in tow. He had flown to Salisbury with his band and PA system. She'd been impressed that he had chartered a Boeing 707 from London at his own expense, and his entourage had overnighted in the run-down Skyline Hotel on the outskirts of the city. This was because all the fancy hotels were booked out as Salisbury was heaving with dignitaries and foreign journalists. Apparently, Bob Marley spent a great part of the day in Mutoko, sampling the local weed. When he took to the stage that night he was higher than the Zimbabwean flag. There was a stampede as the crowd surged forward to get a glimpse of the Rastafarian icon who had supposedly kept the comrades company in the camps singing 'Buffalo Soldier'. Tear gas was sprayed into the stadium to disperse the crowd. Bob didn't even get a whiff of it he was so high on the moment. When the furore had died down, Bob Marley took the microphone and declared: 'Viva Zimbabwe', to which the crowd roared in elation.

PART 3: THE DEMOCRATIC DREAM

For to be free is not merely to cast off one's chains, but to live in a
way that respects and enhances the freedom of others.

NELSON MANDELA

PART 3: THE DEMOCRATIC DREAM

For to be free is not merely to cast off one's chains, but to live in a way that respects and enhances the freedom of others.

NELSON MANDELA

21

A marriage of convenience

It was early in the New Year when Douglas reported to the Filabusi assembly point. Like many ZIPRA comrades, he had been reluctant to converge there. In contrast, the Rhodesian security forces had been the first to retreat to their bases at the end of 1979. The powers that be had agreed that while demilitarisation took place, the two guerrilla armies could remain armed. This proclamation was reassuring to most guerrillas.

Douglas entered the assembly point armed to the hilt, his rifle slung over his shoulder and his pistol nestled in his pants. In his backpack he carried a few grenades so, while it wasn't heavy artillery, the light ammunition gave him the much-needed assurance that he could retaliate if he was attacked.

The elections took place in February that year while they were still at the assembly points. They collectively shouldered the defeat of ZAPU in solidarity. The soldiers felt they had been cheated. While the news of ZAPU's defeat was staggering, it had also been anticipated. The Soviet Union had issued many stern warnings of this eventuality, constantly reiterating that winning an outright battle was better than succumbing to their fate at the ballot box. Any room for challenging the result was removed when a chartered British flight landed at Salisbury airport and the ballot boxes were loaded onto it and flown overseas. This ensured that there would never be an electoral challenge.

After the conclusion of the elections, the demilitarisation process was declared to be over. Douglas was apprehensive about what would happen after the Commonwealth Monitoring Forces left en masse. They were now at the mercy of their victors. Under the new dispensation, everyone was born again as a new person, forgiven for the sins of their past. Nobody could be lawfully tried or persecuted for any human rights abuses they may have committed. And there had been many on both sides. However, while much of it was forgiven, the victims had not forgotten and their wounds continued to fester.

From Douglas's understanding, they were being held at the assembly points while awaiting integration into the Zimbabwe National Army, which would be formed by merging the Rhodesian National Army with the guerrilla armies of ZANLA and ZIPRA.

The former managed to retain some of its key personnel, but many of the disillusioned Rhodesians from infantry, intelligence and security forces resigned en masse. They were reconstituted into the South African Special Forces Brigade known as the Reece Commandos.

The offers were good as soldiers wouldn't lose rank on transfer and their pensions would still be honoured. Others, like Graham, stayed on as saboteurs and secret agents. While they worked inside Zimbabwe, their orders were issued from Pretoria.

South African president PW Botha had a simple strategy at that point: to destabilise Zimbabwe in order to prevent her from being an ally to any liberation struggle party, namely the African National Congress. The apartheid regime went further and assisted in the creation of dissidents who were unleashed on Zimbabwean soil under the banner of Super ZAPU. Their mandate was to cause terror and instability in the newly formed country. In so doing, she would be too distracted to pay attention to the apartheid state next door. This was in spite of Mugabe's repeated assurances in which he reiterated that he had no desire to get involved in South African political affairs. He was more preoccupied with trying to consolidate his position at home.

Mugabe tried to woo Joshua Nkomo with the post of presidency, while Mugabe himself would be prime minister. Nkomo declined this overture and Mugabe was affronted. In his mind, the rejection of this political proposition was misconstrued to mean that Nkomo and ZAPU were not committed to rebuilding and national cohesion. Yet Nkomo had refused the role solely on the grounds that the presidential tag was ceremonial and he wanted to be actively involved in government. So, while he was awarded the Ministry of Home Affairs, it was clear from that point onwards that any attempt to bridge the enmity between them was lost. And so began the battle of the giants. Douglas recalled the African proverb that says when elephants fight, it is the grass that suffers. The grass was about to get flattened with the weight of these two men.

By virtue of being armed, guerrillas were not permitted to leave their assembly points. Douglas felt the Rhodesian Security Forces were receiving preferential treatment because they were allowed to move in and out of their military bases. Douglas hated that they were being held like caged birds. When were they going to enjoy the freedom they had fought so hard for? Like many others, Douglas breached the ceasefire and went to see his mother. Leaving the assembly points while armed was considered an act of rebellion.

While some guerrillas were peaceful, some did terrorise the civilian population and many violent skirmishes were reported. Oftentimes persuasive methods were used to get guerrillas to return to the assembly points. Many of Douglas's friends were still at large, languishing in the rural countryside. Initially, Douglas flirted with the idea of defection, but his convictions led him to remain at the base, although he remained disturbed by the guerrilla arrests taking place.

In May and June 1980, 400 guerrillas were rounded up and thrown into Khami Prison. What provoked Douglas's ire was that it appeared that ZANLA ex-combatants who defected were dealt with leniently, yet ZIPRA ex-combatants received harsh reprobation. The term 'dissidents' started to be thrown around loosely and applied liberally like lotion to ZIPRA ex-combatants. He couldn't shake the feeling of apprehension and deep suspicion of the new murky waters they were now wading in.

22

A tale of two cities

When Bradley started Grade 1 the Williams family decided to set up
a temporary abode in Bulawayo to be close to the children's school,
Whitestone Primary. Paul had been resolute that he couldn't have
his wife driving over 200 kilometres every day on the school run. He
lamented his family's safety because while there was an illusion of
peace in the country, the looming threat of dissidents had not been
eliminated. *The Chronicle* would report of farmers being ambushed by
dissidents and people driving on major highways were not spared.

They decided to acquire a second home, a four-bedroomed bungalow in the affluent suburb of Burnside. The house was built on a
rocky outcrop with sweeping views of sprawling acres of land. After the mass exodus of many people in the white community, houses
were fairly cheap. They had purchased the house from a family who
had immigrated to South Africa and, although it was in pristine condition, Melanie added her personal touch, customising the bedrooms to
suit each of the children's personalities. Cars for Bradley, pink ponies
for Adrienne, and Disney cartoons for Angel.

They each had their own bedroom, but the girls often slept in
hers. Melanie didn't mind; she was not accustomed to sleeping alone.
For the first time in their married life, she and Paul were living apart
for at least four days a week as he was stationed back in Somabhula, managing things at Belle Acres. She welcomed the girls' presence
in her expansive bed and when Paul had business in Bulawayo and

stayed overnight, the girls would scamper off to their bedrooms like little mice.

On Friday afternoons, they all climbed into Melanie's Land Rover and headed back to Belle Acres. So Melanie and the kids lived in the city during the week and enjoyed the beauty of the countryside and being back at Belle Acres over the weekends.

Esther loved the new set-up. While she had grown up at Belle Acres, *emaplazini*, being in the city was a welcome change. Although domestic work generally confined her to the precincts of the Williams' home, her weekends saw her venturing out. Initially she would go back to Belle Acres with Melanie and the children and spend the weekend with her parents, but that was before she discovered her mother's relatives in Matshobane. Her mother's sister, *umam'dala*, lived in a two-bedroomed house with her two daughters. They also shared the home with another family who lodged in the spare room. All ten of them were crammed together in close quarters. It was in stark contrast to Esther's spacious servants' quarters where her cottage had a kitchenette, a bedroom and an adjacent bathroom. But it was quiet and lonely there, so she suffered the cramped quarters for the company.

'See you on Tuesday,' said Melanie as she backed out of the driveway, her eyes shielded by a pair of Ray-Ban sunglasses.

'Not Monday?' replied Esther.

'Exeat weekend,' replied Melanie. 'We'll be in Vumba.'

'Enjoy, Mum!' exclaimed Esther.

Melanie didn't want to be called 'madam' so Esther deferred to 'Mum' instead. At 30 years old, Melanie was only five years older than her but Esther still deemed it inappropriate to call Melanie by her first name, even though Melanie insisted she didn't mind. Esther adored Melanie and enjoyed working for her and the children. Adrienne and Angel waved frantically at her from their car seats and she blew them both a kiss. They were like her own daughters and had grown up in her arms.

After the electric gate closed behind her, Esther retreated to her servants' quarters. She took off her starched pink uniform and stepped into a pair of bell-bottom jeans and a tight-fitting viscose shirt. It was only since moving to the city that she had started wearing trousers. At the farm she would never dream of it lest she be accused of being forward, but in the city the girls were open-minded. Initially, her cousins had laughed at her, calling her a VK (*vele'khaya*), but she soon learnt to dress like them and eventually, when she inherited Melanie's old clothes, started outdressing them. Melanie had trendy pedal pushers, bell-bottoms and other beautiful clothes she bought in South Africa. Esther also inherited a vast collection of corked heels and platform shoes. She combed out her Afro until it glistened in the sun and smeared Ambi Fade Cream on her face to lighten it. While the 'Black is beautiful' epithet was being bandied about, nobody really bought into it. She learnt this from her cousins, who had laughed at her dark complexion, calling her 'midnight magic'.

No longer wearing her uniform, nobody could tell Esther was a domestic worker and walking to the bus stop she got a lot of catcalls. They were mostly from the garden boys in the area and she ignored them. They were not in her league.

Most women her age were married, but Esther was thankful she had waited because she would have just married some nobody from the farm. Instead, she had a boyfriend by the name of Munyaradzi Chiota, who everyone called Munya. He had grown up in Bulawayo and, while he was Shona, he spoke isiNdebele fluently. He had been lodging across the street from her aunt's house when they met in Entumbane. The two suburbs were separated by Luveve Road, but their growing love bridged the distance and he had been her main motivation for going to Matshobane every other weekend. They would walk through the streets of the township together and he would buy her a Coke and some sweets. Sometimes he took her into town and they would have hot chips and chicken and then go and watch a movie at the Kine 600 Cinema. She'd never been to a movie house so seeing the people on the big screen was exciting. The first time they watched *Blue Lagoon* she had sat on the edge of her seat, thinking the actors were going to jump out. Munya had laughed at her, mocking her gently.

'It's no different from television,' he teased her. 'It's called the big screen.'

Munya liked to watch action films with a lot of fight scenes and gun-toting men like Clint Eastwood in *Bronco Billy*, Jackie Chan in *The Big Brawl* and Robert Carradine in the epic war movie, *The Big Red One*. While Esther hadn't yet figured out what she liked, she knew she hated the violent films. She had thoroughly enjoyed *Fame* and made a song and dance about it and realised where Melanie got her current dress sense from. She dressed like the ladies in *Fame* with black tights and luminous green, pink and yellow crop tops. Esther always thought she was brave to walk around with her bum uncovered but Munya thought that such dressing was indecent.

After watching *Blue Lagoon* a few times and seeing Brooke Shields and Christopher Atkins's sexual awakening, she and Munya embarked on a sexual adventure of their own in the confines of his bedroom. He had to cover her mouth with his hand because she was groaning in gratification as he penetrated past her inhibitions. Because he lodged in a house with three other people, they rarely had privacy. Urban migration from the rural areas had been rampant during the war. Although the Rhodesian government tried to protect villagers in some tribal trust lands, it became near impossible in the end and many started to flee their homes, seeking refuge in the cities, which were failing to accommodate them all. Because of the limited space available, people ended up living on top of each other. Munya had applied for his own house, but his name was still on the waiting list. Esther couldn't wait till they had a place of their own.

Early Monday morning, Munya departed for work. He left Esther sleeping as she wanted to make the most of her day off with the family away until the next day. She eventually got up at 9am and cleaned his room. She scrubbed the floors and polished them till they were gleaming. She hand-washed the laundry in a silver tub while gossiping with the wife of the couple who owned the house. Unlike the suburbs, everyone in the township spoke to each other over the fences between their homes. Everyone knew everyone and they would invariably get to know your business.

'It's good that you are here,' said Mavis to Esther. 'There are girls who come here trying to campaign for Munya's affections.'

'You can't shepherd a man,' replied Esther, 'but a good sheep will always find its way home.'

Mavis laughed good-naturedly, 'I will keep watch for you, my sister. I will ward off the flies.'

Later that afternoon, Esther ironed Munya's shirts, flattening out the creases. He didn't have an electric iron like Melanie's that glided across the clothes so it took her longer than usual. Melanie also had a washing machine that made her load much lighter. When she was done with the ironing she started making preparations for supper. Munya didn't have a fridge so she walked across to the butcher to buy some meat. The streets were not empty like the suburbs; they were teeming with people and alive with conversation. Children played in the road, dodging the odd car. On her return, Esther passed some children from Helemu Primary School in their signature blue uniforms playing hopscotch in the streets, kicking up the dust. A man came past and chased the children off.

'*Hambani emakhaya bokhijani. Namhlanje kulempi!* Go home, children. There's a war today.'

Esther did not take much notice and thought it was his way of chasing the children off the streets because otherwise they'd play outside till dusk. She got back to the house and started frying onions. Every so often she looked at the gate, waiting for Munya to arrive home. He finally did and was carrying two paper bags from Greens supermarket. She ran to meet him, throwing her arms around him.

'I could get used to this,' he said kissing her gently.

'Same here,' she replied, leaning back into him.

They had an early supper and retired to bed. Without a television to entertain them, they created their own drama in the bedroom and after a marathon lovemaking session, they fell asleep in each other's arms. They were woken hours later by what sounded like a hailstorm on the asbestos roof. Munya got out of bed and was going to go ask Mavis's husband what was happening, but he was stopped in his tracks by the staccato of gunfire reverberating around the house. He immediately dived to the floor and instructed Esther to do the same. They found refuge under the bed and held each other, trembling with fear. The rolling explosions followed and came in varying degrees of intensity. And with each explosion, Esther kept thinking that it was her time. That the next explosion would be the final one. Yet the commotion went on all night and she and Munya remained under the bed, afraid to move, lying in a pool of their own urine, enveloped in the stench of fear. They lay wordlessly, comforted by the other's presence and reassured by the sound of the other person breathing. Esther was relieved when dawn broke, but the gunshots had still not subsided.

'I think we are at war,' said Munya.

Esther's face was wet with tears. The closest she had ever come to witnessing war was in the movies they watched on the big screen. She had never envisaged she would wake up to it.

'We need to get out of here,' he said, 'otherwise we won't make it alive.'

After a short lull, they finally emerged from under the bed, got dressed and went outside. Mavis and her husband followed suit and the four of them ran out into the street and joined a large convoy of people apparently making their way to the railway station. In droves, civilians fled the township and Luveve Road was a scene of utter carnage, littered with dead bodies. Esther tried not to stare. A battalion of men in army fatigues was camped at a stream between Entumbane and Emakhandeni. Aside from the movies, Esther had never seen armed men and they scared her. As she and Munya continued walking, they heard helicopters skirting the air above them, and from a loudspeaker the voice of Lookout Masuku began addressing the crowds.

'*Bafana? Kwenzakalani? Asibekeni phansi izikhali!* Boys? What is happening? Put down your arms.'

They finally made it to the railway station where many families had found refuge and spent the night there. The following morning, they were told to return to their homes as calm had been restored.

While life supposedly returned to normal, Esther felt far from being her usual self. In a strange way, she felt soiled by the events that had taken place. Like a veil had been lifted and she had been indecently exposed to an ugly reality that she couldn't make sense of. When she arrived at work on Wednesday morning, it was to a hostile reception. She stood awkwardly while Melanie ranted and raved at her about professionalism and how her unexplained absence had been an inconvenience to her and the children.

'Paul said I should fire you for this, but I defended you, Esther. I told him it wasn't like you to not show up for work. You could have at least tried to call me to let me know you weren't coming!'

'I'm sorry, Mum. I almost got shot.'

Esther handed her the newspaper that Munya had bought. Melanie never read the news and so her eyes scanned the article, widening in disbelief. She was hit by the realisation that while they both occupied the same country, they were living in disparate worlds. It was a tale of two cities. Melanie was immediately filled with guilt and started making Esther a cup of tea. She apologised profusely and offered to give her the rest of the day off, but Esther refused, insisting she wanted to keep busy. She didn't want to sit alone with her thoughts, with the sounds of gunshots, explosions and hapless screams lodged in her subconscious.

'I thought I was going to die,' said Esther, collapsing into a chair. 'I honestly thought it was my time.' She started to cry, the fear and anxiety of the past few days pouring out. She had been too stunned to cry about it up until this point.

On their return home, she and Munya had commiserated, trying to piece their experiences together with the neighbours, collectively addressing their anguish. One man explained how they had been chased from the beer hall and jumped fences to get to their homes. Some families lost members in the crossfire. When she left the township, people were hanging black cloths and removing curtains to let the community know they were in mourning. That some among them had not survived. Men, women, children. The violence had been indiscriminate.

'Maybe you should stop going to the township on the weekends until things stabilise, Esther.'

'My boyfriend lives in the township, Mum,' explained Esther. 'How will I see him?'

'Maybe he can stay here with you until things settle,' suggested Melanie.

'I'll suggest it to him,' replied Esther.

Munya was agreeable and Esther welcomed the move because after that night she was certain she would no longer be able to sleep alone. Every time she closed her eyes she saw dead bodies. Things exploded in her head, and even the sound of popcorn on the stove unnerved her.

One afternoon Bradley had come charging into the kitchen with his toy gun and she had yelped in panic and jumped back in fright.

'I'm just playing with you!' he laughed, rushing off to terrorise the girls. It had taken a while for Esther to regain her composure.

She was relieved when Munya arrived that weekend. Of course, Paul thought it was a bad idea, but Melanie argued that having a man on the premises would be a deterrent to thieves and that Munya was a decent bloke who had a decent job in town. Melanie eventually grew quite fond of Munya and often invited him inside for a cup of tea and to quiz him about the politics of the country. Munya professed not to understand much about the whole ZANLA/ZIPRA thing and said that for the most part they had all been living together peaceably with no tribal dissension. From then on, Melanie made sure to buy the daily newspaper to stay abreast of what was happening in the country.

23

The battle of Entumbane

Douglas's term at the assembly point came to an end when ZIPRA ceded its crack regiment to the Rhodesian forces. They were a group of men who had been trained in the Soviet Union but with little experience in active combat. Douglas was part of the unit and this accelerated his absorption into the army. He was given orders that he would join Brady Barracks on 11 November. He was looking forward to leaving; the atmosphere at the assembly point had become highly charged with a potent mix of tension and testosterone.

With the isolation and living conditions, soldiers were becoming restless. However, a month before they were relegated to be integrated, they received orders that they were going to be resettled temporarily at housing schemes in either Chitungwiza or Entumbane. This was meant to be a temporary reprieve while the barracks were under construction. Since tribal integration was one of the aims of reconciliation, they assigned equal numbers of ZANLA and ZIPRA ex-combatants to both housing schemes.

In October, Douglas was one of the 12 000 who moved into their new abode in Entumbane, the suburb deriving its name from the hillock where King Mzilikazi was buried. The guerrillas who weren't accommodated continued to languish at the assembly points.

Douglas moved into a four-roomed house that he shared with other cadres. The police had been wary of moving armed ex-combatants in such close proximity to the civilian population, separated only by a high security fence, but Douglas loved that they were living in the vicinity of ordinary people. The assembly points had been so isolated and cut off from human habitation.

On his sporadic forays into the township, Douglas tried his luck with the local girls. It had been a while since he had been with a woman and he missed their warmth. The city girls were not as easy as the rural ones. They were demanding and at that time soldiers were receiving a paltry allowance of Z$100 – money they spent recklessly because they didn't have to buy their own food.

Buying cigarettes at the supermarket one day, he bumped into Esther. He recognised her doe eyes. Although she was a few years younger than him, they had grown up together at Belle Acres. He was overwhelmed with excitement at seeing a familiar face. He gleaned from their conversation that she was a domestic worker and earned Z$30 a month. He spoilt her and bought her sweets, a cream doughnut and a Coke as he knew she couldn't afford such luxuries. He liked that Esther wasn't wearing any make-up; she hadn't been tainted by the city. A lot of women had powdery white faces and wore bright red lipstick and tight pants. He still preferred his women demure-looking and wearing dresses. Esther was wearing a floral sundress with yellow platform heels, but he could tell she wasn't comfortable in the heels as she swayed unsteadily as he walked her home.

'So will you be my girlfriend?' he asked hopefully.

'I already have a boyfriend,' she replied.

'But *udli mali yami? Udlelan' imali yami wen'ungafuni?*'

Esther was taken aback by his reaction.

'I said,' he repeated, 'why are you eating my money when you clearly don't want me?'

'*Hayi suka, Douglas,*' she replied, 'is it by force or fire?'

He slapped her hard across the face. She folded over like a pack of cards and fell to the ground. He hit her repeatedly, undeterred by the crowd gathering around them. Esther managed to crawl away and stood up, took off her shoes and ran home.

'*Futsek! Sifebe sothuvi!*' hissed Douglas.

Those who had witnessed the backlash hadn't dare intervene. The township was charged with nervousness since the arrival of the uniformed men in their army-print fatigues.

Douglas sat and chilled with the guards for a while, exchanging small talk, when a group of ZANLA cadres arrived. They were talking volubly among themselves. They greeted each other and then the cadres defaulted to Shona. Douglas had learnt Shona while in a battalion with some men from Mashonaland and could understand what the men were saying.

'These *dumbumkuru* guys are arrogant,' remarked one flippantly.

Douglas was affronted that they had made a jibe about Joshua Nkomo, who was the butt of many fat jokes.

'Humble yourselves,' said another. 'You lost the war.'

'We lost the elections, not the war,' the man replied.

'Sore losers! We won fair and square,' said another.

Douglas clenched his fists tightly. He would have taken the men on, but he was unarmed. On entering the camp, they had to leave their weapons in the armoury for safekeeping.

Clashes like this were common in the camps. ZANLA men were prone to throwing insults at them. If they weren't saying it, they were singing derogatory songs meant to provoke anger and humiliate them. Things really came to a head when Enos Nkala, the then Minister of Finance, addressed a rally at the White City Stadium. His speech was the ember that sparked the violence that broke out between ZIPRA and ZANLA.

'From today the PF ZAPU has declared itself the enemy of ZANU (PF). The time has come for ZANU (PF) to flex its muscles. Our supporters must now form vigilante committees in readiness for those who want to challenge us. There must be a general mobilisation of our supporters. Organise yourselves into small groups in readiness to challenge the Patriotic Front ZAPU on its home ground. If it means a few blows, we shall deliver them. If the police do not want to act according to the specific instructions I have given, then we shall proceed with those to whom the instructions have been given.'

Douglas was among the many ZIPRA combatants who listened in consternation. Apprehension rose like a dark cloud, spreading an aura of gloom across the entire camp.

Douglas wasn't sure what sparked the fighting, but the Monday following the rally, he was woken up by frantic knocking on the door.

'*Ndoda ziyatsha lapha!*'

Douglas leapt to his feet and dressed quickly. He joined the stampede to the armoury to secure a weapon. He was fast on his feet and managed to outrun some comrades to the entrance, which was being choked by the soldiers fighting to get past each other. The ZANLA men had already mounted their mortars and bombs were flying in the air, exploding with pent-up aggravation.

Douglas grabbed a rifle and other small armaments and joined the insurgency. The ZIPRA battalion called for further reinforcements from their other battalions. A full-on battle ensued, spilling out from the camp and into the surrounding settlements. Many innocent civilians were caught up in the crossfire. For two days a battle raged, guns blazing with heavy artillery brandished by soldiers.

The fighting was quelled with the deployment of Hunter jets, the commanders appealing to their armies to reach a ceasefire. Fifty-five perished in the ambush and over 500 were injured. The residents of Bulawayo were slapped with a curfew. This became known as the first battle of Entumbane.

24

The battle of the giants

Following the first battle of Entumbane, Douglas read with growing angst and concern of the nine ZAPU comrades who had been arrested. Earlier that year, in June 1980, parliament had voted to extend the state of emergency. This gave the state authority to detain anybody for 30 days if they were believed to be a threat to peace and stability. No reasons needed to be furnished. You could just be picked up in the middle of the night and thrown into prison. Douglas started to realise just how precarious the situation was and that members of their party were under attack.

Douglas was incorporated into the army as a private and, while the Rhodesian Security Forces were co-opted into the Zimbabwe National Army without change in rank, no attention was paid to the experience or training he had received in the Soviet Union. The Rhodesians were generally sceptical about incorporating guerrillas into the ranks because they felt they were highly undisciplined and would create problems in the regiment. It was against this background that Douglas tried to assimilate into a system that was determined to spit him out. He took his grievances to his battalion commander, Colonel Ngozi, who had merely laughed in his face.

'Your ilk is full of shit. I don't care if you were a colonel in the bush – here you will earn your rank, boy!'

'This is not fair. We should all be treated fairly!'

'Life is not fair. Get the fuck out of my face.'

What further pissed off Douglas was that Colonel Ngozi wasn't that much older than him and, from what he had gleaned, had a modicum of education. However, it seemed the Colonel did not want to be challenged and, from that day onwards, Colonel Ngozi made his life a living hell. Douglas tried to get himself moved to another battalion, but the Colonel blocked his move and had him thrown into Khami Prison for a few days to teach him a lesson. In solitude, Douglas had time to reflect on his future in the army. He felt like he was embarking on another armed struggle. Even in the army, the conditions of service were not fair: he was earning a salary of Z$105, while a white private started on Z$285 and received an allowance of Z$24.36 if he was single. He wondered if this was the price they were paying to convince the white population that they were secure, with nothing to fear. Where was the change they had been promised? The Lancaster Agreement had pledged that the Africanisation of state institutions would take place. Yet here he was, in an army riddled with white men. His friend, Private Mutero, reminded him that they had been fighting a system and not the white man.

'The system stinks,' replied Douglas vociferously. 'They're still monopolising all the positions. And the blacks who are getting them, well, you know ... they are connected.'

'Change will come,' assured Mutero. 'It's still early days.'

Douglas balked at the suggestion. 'Early days my arse.'

The year ended and 1981 eased in, but Douglas felt his optimism wane – despite even the wild New Year's Eve parties that had gone on into the early hours of the morning. If anything, he had drunk a quarter of his pay that day and another quarter he had spent on a prostitute he had picked up at a beer garden. The rest he had sent to his mother to cover her over the festive season.

January was a particularly long month. Not only was Douglas broke, but he was angry too. He had learnt with dismay that Joshua Nkomo had been demoted to Minister without Portfolio, and he and many of his ZIPRA cadres were disgruntled by this new development.

When month-end came around with their long-awaited pay, they converged at a beer hall in Ntabazinduna. Among them were disabled ZIPRA ex-combatants who had been wheeled in. They vocalised their grievances over cold bottles of Black Label, which failed to cool their rising resentment.

'Nkomo needs to resign from that government,' lambasted Douglas.

He echoed the sentiments of many who felt that Nkomo was making too many concessions.

'I didn't lose my limbs for this shit!' spoke another ex-combatant.

'This is not serving us,' countered another ex-combatant.

It is not really clear what happened, but a war of words transpired with some ZANLA cadres who were also drinking there. Fuelled by alcohol, the underlying tension exploded into fights and soldiers broke rank and opened fire. The fighting was picked up at the Entumbane settlement and hence this became known as the second battle of Entumbane. Since Douglas had been co-opted into the ZNA, he was supposed to stay out of the fighting, but his sense of duty would not allow him to sit back while his comrades were massacred. Other battalions, such as Essexvale, Glenville and Connemara, joined in.

The battle raged on and the city of Bulawayo was brought to a standstill. Furtive calls were made on radio urging people to remain in the safety of their homes. The town centre was deserted and businesses closed their doors, not wanting to get caught in the crossfire. The railway service was suspended. Melanie kept the children home, but Bradley didn't care about missing out on school; it was fun being at home. They played Scrabble, Monopoly and other board games, and Melanie tried to distract herself while the children played in the garden, oblivious to the turmoil unfolding around them. They remained cocooned in the house that entire week and her only communication was with Paul on the telephone. He kept insisting he wanted to be with them, but she urged him not to travel.

The battle had spread all the way to Connemara Barracks in Gwelo, the presence of armoured tanks rolling through the streets of Bulawayo bringing the battle to their doorsteps. For six days the battle raged and on the seventh day the white-commanded RAR battalion, with its jet fighters and helicopter gunships, was called in to subdue the unrest. They were heavily armed with clay mortars and tanks, and it took them a day to restore law and order. The death toll stood at 800, with bodies laid out at the city morgue for kith and kin to identify. Douglas's friends were among those death statistics and it broke his heart that the war had now disintegrated to blacks killing each other. He heard that his friends residing at Entumbane were evacuated and moved to Woolendale Rifle Range, while the ZANLA okes were taken to Godlwayo. He was suspicious of the separation – now that they were perfectly segregated, they would be lynched. This time there was no press coverage of what transpired, the events unfolding almost in obscurity, but forever etched in the minds of those who were involved. Douglas felt the anxiety in the pit of the stomach when the Minister of State Security called for the disarming of all soldiers. This created panic and many soldiers started hiding their firearms and concealing weapons.

Douglas got into a lot of trouble for his participation in Entumbane. He had been 'arrested' and was stripped naked and held by one of the battalions of the Rhodesian forces. He felt betrayed by the Rhodesian army that had openly attacked ZIPRA who were now seen as instigators of the battle. A commission of inquiry was established to look into the disturbances but, as Douglas suspected, nothing came out of it. The vindication they were hoping for never came. Instead, they were heavily punished for participating in Entumbane, his pay docked for six months. Questionnaires were being circulated and they were asked to detail exactly what they had done in the camps. Douglas was highly suspicious of this enquiry and threw it away. He became a rebel and refused to show up for drill or take part in the weapons training, which he felt was repetitious. Colonel Ngozi once again threw him into Khami Prison for insubordination. It was during this time that Douglas seriously contemplated his future. The demobilisation programme had come into effect because the army was just too bloated to absorb everyone. Those already in the ZNA could leave and many of his comrades had started to do so. Douglas felt the Z$185 that would be offered monthly for a period of two years was certainly better than the current victimisation he was experiencing. Other veterans had gone on to join the SEED programme, where they worked on state-owned farms, trading their guns for gardening tools. The whole thing held very little appeal for Douglas. It just evoked bad memories of his time at Belle Acres. By the time he was released from prison, Douglas had made up his mind: he would demobilise. However, that night as he slept in the dormitory, he was woken up by Mutero, who urged him to leave immediately.

'You need to go now, Douglas; there are orders to kill you.'

Douglas did not stay to ask questions. He simply got up, grabbed his firearm and furtively made his way out of the camp, disappearing into the dark night.

25

The fugitive

That Friday, Melanie returned to the farm with a boot laden with shopping from Haddon and Sly and Meikles. The children escaped from the car, leaving her and Esther to lug the bags into the house. Esther had gone with her, claiming she wanted to spend some time with her family on the farm. Melanie was offloading the car when a man in army fatigues came around from the back. The bags fell from her hands and hit the ground. She had heard about dissidents running amok, attacking people in their homes. Esther started screaming when she saw who it was, which only served to amplify Melanie's trepidation. Douglas held his hands up to show them that he was unarmed and that he meant no harm.

'I am so sorry,' apologised Douglas. 'I didn't mean to scare you. It's me, Douglas.'

Esther slunk away in dread. Her first thought was that Douglas was there to finish her off. She had not forgotten that beating. He had left her with black eyes and a split lip. Munya had nursed her back to health and she told him that she had been assaulted by a soldier for rebutting his advances. She hadn't divulged that they knew each other because that would only have served to complicate the issue.

Melanie didn't recognise Douglas straight away as she had only met him once at his and Simphiwe's wedding. He had changed dramatically since then. His face was firmer, more angular. His body had hardened, his physique brawny. His sleeves were rolled up and she could see his muscled arms.

'Doug … Douglas … ?'

'Yes, Madam, it's me.'

'Where is Simmy?' asked Melanie, expecting her to pop into view.

'She's dead. She didn't survive the war.'

Melanie's face fell in shock. She held her hand to her chest.

'Oh no, Douglas. I am so sorry.'

'It's awful and I don't know if I will ever make peace with it, but she's gone.'

'Well, let's go into the house and I'll make you a cup of tea.'

Melanie hollered to Esther to fetch the groceries. Douglas didn't feel it was his place, but for some reason he found himself bending to pick up the items. He didn't know why he deferred to that. It was no longer necessary. They had won the war, so why was he still behaving like he was subservient to Melanie?

They were having tea in the lounge when Paul walked in with the girls, having just come from their riding lesson. Douglas immediately jumped to his feet when he saw Velile. She had big almond eyes, like her mother, which sparkled in her sweet round face. She was a short, tubby girl with stumpy legs. Her hair was sectioned into four pigtails.

'Vee, this is your daddy,' said Melanie, by way of introduction.

Without hesitation, Velile bounded into his arms. He scooped her up and lifted her into the air. Velile grabbed a clump of his hair.

'Your hair's like mine,' she said matter-of-factly.

Douglas was overcome with emotion. She was so grown-up. He held her for a long time and couldn't hold back the tears. After a while he sat on the couch, balancing Velile on his knee.

'That's my sister Adrienne,' declared Velile, 'and my brother Bradley.'

Adrienne and Bradley came forward and greeted him. He smiled. He realised that the children had achieved what the adults had failed to do. To bond beyond the racial divide. His eyes were brimming with tears.

'Why are you sad, Daddy?' asked Angel, her tiny finger trying to obliterate his tears.

'I'm not sad, my girl. I'm just happy to see you.'

Melanie shepherded her children out of the room, giving Douglas and his daughter time to get to know each other. Paul followed her out. When they got to the kitchen, the children bombarded her with questions. Is he coming to stay with us? Has he come to take Velile? Don't let him take Velile, please, Mommy! Velile belongs with us. She's our family.

Melanie had no answers and quickly parcelled them off to Esther, giving her and Paul some privacy.

'So this is it – he's come to get her,' said Paul.

'I think so,' croaked Melanie.

Paul could sense her tears bubbling beneath the surface and pulled her into his arms.

'I told you not to get attached to her, Mel.'

'I couldn't help it,' she sobbed.

Paul rubbed her back soothingly. 'This is for the best, Mel.'

'But I can't bear the thought of losing her, Paul!'

After dinner, Melanie took the children to bed, leaving Douglas alone with Paul. They had barely spoken at dinner, their eyes hardly meeting. Douglas had been uncomfortable sitting at the table, but his daughter occupied the space with ease. He marvelled at how at home she seemed. It felt surreal when, only a few years ago, Douglas wasn't even permitted over the threshold of the house.

'What really brings you here, Douglas?' Paul asked.

Paul didn't trust his motives one bit. It had taken a lot for the black brigade to come down to earth after the euphoria of the celebrations. Some workers began harbouring grand ambitions of usurping their positions. Esther, like many domestic workers, thought she would become the madam of the manor. Many male labourers thought they would wake up and own a share of Belle Acres. None of this happened. If anything, life post-independence was a honeymoon for the white people. While they might have lost political power, they still retained economic control and all their privileges.

With the lifting of sanctions, everything was in plentiful supply. No more fuel rationing or long winding queues. Shop shelves were well stocked and they could shop to their heart's content. For many whites who had chosen to stay, it was business as usual and business was brisk. The Somabhula Country Club reopened and Friday night drinks resumed. They continued to play badminton, tennis and squash, and on Saturdays they congregated on their sprawling farms for braais. On Sundays they had lunch at the club. The changes were few and immaterial, mostly cosmetic and superficial.

Rhodes and Founders Weekend, which used to commemorate Rhodes's birthday, became Heroes Weekend, with a memorial park, Heroes' Acre, established outside Salisbury. It was built and designed with the assistance of North Korea, key architects in the training of the 5th Brigade, which would slaughter many civilians in the years to follow. The joke among Rhodies was that it was the 'Gooks and Spooks' weekend. They all took their boats out to Binga or Kariba for the celebratory weekend.

'So? Why are you here, Douglas?'

Douglas shrugged his shoulders. 'I came to get my daughter.'

'Ah,' said Paul, 'I thought as much. Where will you take her?'

'What does it matter to you? She's my daughter, after all.'

'We've looked after her all these years, Douglas. I care what happens to her.'

Douglas looked down. He didn't want to appear ungrateful, but he wanted his daughter back.

Paul shook his head. 'Do you fancy your old job back?'

'No, Paul. I would never work for you again.'

Paul laughed. 'You think you're better than that?'

Douglas shook his head. 'I don't think I'm better, I know I am,' he replied with a confidence that unnerved Paul.

Paul eyed him warily. A few years in the war had turned him into a condescending bastard.

'I'm truly thankful for everything you and Melanie have done raising Velile, but let me take my child. It's my turn now.'

Paul accepted the proposition. He had no alternative, but it pained him – Velile had become part of their family.

'I have one more favour to ask, Paul. Can I spend the night here? We'll be gone tomorrow.'

Paul was aghast. 'You're leaving so soon? You aren't even going to give the kids a chance to say goodbye?'

'It's for the best,' replied Douglas. 'I hate goodbyes anyway.'

Melanie had been listening quietly, fighting back her tears. She was too heartsore to join them, knowing that Douglas really was going to take his daughter back. While she was happy that he had come to assume his responsibility, she was devastated at the thought of being relieved of hers.

'You can sleep in the guest room,' Paul answered.

'That's not necessary,' replied Douglas. 'I'll sleep in the compound. I'll be more comfortable there.'

'Don't be silly, Douglas – you're better than that now,' responded Paul.

Douglas wasn't sure if Paul was being ironic or sincere, but when he laughed, Douglas felt compelled to laugh too. The tension between them was slowly dissipating.

'Can I offer you a whiskey?' asked Paul, pouring himself one.

'I prefer vodka,' remarked Douglas.

'Russian vodka?' asked Paul, pleasantly surprised at Douglas's choice of drink.

Douglas nodded. 'Pour me one and I'll tell you all about it.'

They spoke well into the night, chatting about Douglas's Russian excursion. Glasses were emptied and refilled and Melanie could hear them laughing together. It was midnight when Paul finally slid into bed beside her, snuggling close.

'He's really not a bad guy.'

'He never was,' replied Melanie. 'You just never took the time to get to know him.'

The following morning the girls came tottering into their room just as they did every morning. Paul had risen at dawn so the girls lay on either side of Melanie, hugging her on both sides.

'Where is my daddy?' asked Velile. 'I want to hug him too.'

'He's in the guest room,' replied Melanie.

Velile, without any prompting, went to seek out her dad. She wanted to curl up beside him the same way Adrienne did with her father. She returned a few minutes later looking downcast.

'Daddy's not there,' she said.

'Maybe he's in the lounge,' said Melanie, clambering out of bed.

'Daddy!' shouted Velile. 'Daddy, where are you?'

Melanie went into the guest room and saw that the bed had been made with military precision. Almost as though it had not been slept in. She made her way downstairs to the living room, but there was no sign of Douglas there either. Esther reported that she had come in at 7am and there had been no one in the dining room or kitchen.

'Maybe he decided to go to the compound to see his old friends,' said Melanie.

Velile looked panicked and Melanie scooped her into her arms and reassured her that her daddy had taken a walk and would be right back.

An hour later, a ZNA Land Rover pulled up outside and three uniformed men climbed out and knocked on the door.

'We are looking for a Comrade Jones Sibindi,' they declared.

'I don't know who that is,' said Melanie.

They handed her a picture. It was Douglas and he was in his army uniform. Melanie swallowed hard. Should she retract her statement and say she didn't know him by that name?

'We have reason to believe he spent the night on these premises, Ma'am.'

'No one by that name slept here,' replied Melanie, deciding to stick to her original story.

'Ma'am,' said the one man earnestly, 'harbouring dissidents is a crime.'

'I have done nothing of the sort! You can search the house.'

They walked in and the men rifled through the house, searching high and low. Melanie was tense, wringing her hands nervously. Within fifteen minutes they were satisfied that there was nowhere he could possibly be hiding in the house. Then they asked Melanie to get into the car and accompany them to the compound. Melanie almost wet herself with anxiety, but steeled herself to go with them. Her knees were shaking uncontrollably and she was fighting hard not to break down. The girls were screaming for their mommy, but Esther quieted them. She knew Paul was out in the fields and she quickly radioed him. In the compound, the men went from door to door, quizzing every household and showing them a picture of Private Jones Sibindi. Nobody had seen him. Nobody had heard of him.

'What has this Jones Sibindi done?' asked Melanie as they were heading back to the farmhouse.

'Like we said before, he is a dissident. He is wanted for murder.'

Melanie felt a shiver down her spine. They handed her a poster. It had an image of Douglas on it and a reward of $1 000. They wanted him dead or alive. Paul arrived just as the army truck was reversing out. He looked concerned and when Melanie handed him the poster he exploded with rage.

'Fucking hell, we had a dissident in our house!'

'Ssshh,' said Melanie putting her hand over his mouth.

Douglas had woken up in the early hours of the morning and helped himself to a pair of trousers and a shirt that had been hanging in the guest bedroom. They fitted him perfectly. He bathed and shaved his head and his beard and then headed into the bush where he made a fire and burnt his uniform. At the sliver of the first sign of morning, he headed out, his firearm tucked safely into the crotch of his trousers. He was a man on the run; he was a fugitive.

26

The burning house

After the second independence celebrations, Zimbabwe decided to rename her capital Harare. Angel grew up in the 'new' Zimbabwe and so Paul and Melanie, Angel's guardians, thought it an auspicious time to adopt Angel and make things official. After her father's disappearance, they knew it would be prudent for them to change her last name so that no connection could be made to the dissident Douglas Nzima/ Jones Sibindi. And so she became Angel Velile Williams. A mistake was made on her birth certificate when the 'a' was dropped from the name Angela, but they decided to leave it, not wanting to go through the administrative headache of getting the birth certificate amended and reissued. No one called her Angela anyway. For the most part, she was called Gel or Ange, and Melanie affectionately called her 'Angel'.

Angel was five years old when she started primary school, with Adrienne and Bradley a few classes ahead of her. In her striped red dress and white socks, just like Adrienne, Angel was used to uniformity as Melanie always dressed the girls in a homogeneous style. Bradley often complained that he felt left out, so if the girls were wearing blue dresses, he would be kitted out in a blue shirt and trousers.

On her first day of school, Angel held her mother's hand tightly. This was the first time they would be separated because Angel had grown up attending the nursery school on the farm and there her class had been predominantly black and very familiar. She had cried and clung to her mother and Mrs Robertson gently prised mother and daughter apart, coaxing Angel with reassurances that she would be fine. Mrs Robertson was a delightful rotund woman who wore flowing pinafores and who everyone found endearing. She spoke in a gentle voice and soon became Angel's second favourite person after Melanie. Angel started looking forward to going school and while there was partial racial integration at the time, she was one of only five black children in a class of 25. She was a shy and coquettish child, but soon made a handful of friends. She didn't feel alienated as the children pretty much all played together at break time. Angel loved school and never felt a sense of being black as she had at the farm. At school nobody really noticed colour and they played and played until the tintinnabulation of the bell signalled home time.

Birthdays were a big thing in the Williams household and were celebrated with much spectacle and splendour. With her birthday in February, Angel was always the first to celebrate every year. Adrienne's birthday was in April, Bradley's in June, Paul's in August and Melanie's in September. Angel was particularly excited to be celebrating her sixth birthday because she was going to invite her new friends from school and not just have her siblings and farm friends there like she had back at Belle Acres. They had a Mickey Mouse-themed party after a trip to Disney World the previous year had started a Disney obsession. Her parents gifted her a pink bicycle with training wheels and a basket on the front. Her initials AVW were imprinted on the side bar.

Adrienne's eighth birthday then swung around just before the first term holidays and she decided on a My Little Pony party. She had a big collection of the little ponies and even coloured her hair purple. Adrienne was gifted a life-size doll's house by her parents. It was made with wooden panelling and Melanie had painted it white with a pink door. She pimped it up with pink trellised windows and decorated the outside with images of Adrienne's ponies. The doll's house sat at the bottom of the beautifully terraced garden, surrounded by its own white picket fence. The interior was fully furnished and kit-ted out with a miniature green four-plate stove and an oven. Next to it was a gold fridge covered in glitter and studded with star stickers. They were toy versions, modelled on the real thing. There was a blue wash-basin stand especially for Adrienne's dolls. In the centre of the room was a tiny table with the cutest tea set and a small purple clock on the wall. Angel thought the house was the most beautiful thing she had ever seen and, as she ran her fingers over the glossy yellow kitchen counters, she could not help being consumed with envy. Adrienne's gift eclipsed hers by miles.

'I hope I also get this for my next birthday,' said Angel, staring dreamily. 'We could be neighbours,' she said to Adrienne.

Adrienne draped her arm around her and matter-of-factly said, 'I'll give it to you when I get tired of it, Angel. You and I share every-thing, remember?'

Angel had been upset. She wanted her *own* doll's house. She didn't want to share everything with Adrienne. Once Adrienne cut the ceremonial ribbon, the children all promptly migrated there from Brad's treehouse and the doll's house became the centre of their out-door play.

One afternoon they had congregated there with a tall jug of fresh-ly squeezed orange juice and chocolate cake Melanie had made for them. Adrienne had set up tiny teacups and teapots on the lawn. They all gathered to play house.

'I'm going to be the mom,' announced Adrienne authoritatively.

'I'll be the dad if you are going to be the mom,' said the next-door neighbour's son Steve, who was also Bradley's best friend and spent a lot of time at the house. Standing next to Adrienne, he kissed her playfully on the cheek.

'Sies, man!' shrieked Brad. 'That's yucky!'

'Grown-ups kiss all the time,' replied Adrienne defiantly. 'Steve will make a good dad.'

'I'll be the driver!' declared Brad. 'I'll chauffeur everyone around.'

His obsession with cars was immense and Herbie was all the rage at the time.

'We need a maid,' insisted Adrienne. 'Every house has a maid.'

All five pairs of eyes landed on Angel.

'I don't want to be a maid!' said Angel emphatically. She pointed to Carla, who was also part of their friendship circle.

'Let *her* be the maid.'

'Maids are black. And you're the only black person here – you *have* to be the maid,' said Adrienne casually.

'It's okay, I'll be the maid!' volunteered Brad. 'Carla, will you be the driver?'

Bradley then raced back to the house and ran back as fast as his sturdy, growing legs could carry him. He had smeared his face and hands with the black shoe polish that Esther used to keep his Bata school shoes shiny.

'Am I black enough?' he asked on his return. 'I can be the house-boy.'

They had laughed at him before agreeing that he made a great houseboy.

'So what are *you* going to be then, Angel?' asked Carla curiously.

'I'll run the supermarket,' Angel quickly replied. 'You're going to need a place to buy your tea and biscuits.'

Angel set up shop using Brad's Lego pieces. Later, when Brad's friends from the compound came to join them, Adrienne assigned them to be garden boys. They didn't complain and enthusiastically picked up the toy shovels and forks from the shed. The memory of that day stayed with Angel and it would always anger her. She hated it that they were never given a choice and that there was never any role reversal in their play. Subconsciously, she started to develop an inferiority complex.

One Saturday afternoon Adrienne and Bradley rode off on their bikes, but Angel couldn't keep up with them so she kicked her bike to the side of the road and walked back to the farmhouse in a huff. Once she had calmed down, she ventured down to the doll's house with a box of matches she had found in the kitchen. She had no idea what over-came her, but she lit a match and set the pony-print curtains alight. The silky viscose fabric burnt quickly and the fire soon spread. Luck-ily, Esther saw the blaze and managed to put it out before the doll's house was razed to the ground.

Esther smacked Angel's small hands.

'You don't ever play with matches again, do you hear me, An-gel?' she admonished.

'It must have been an accident,' said Melanie, coming to Angel's defence.

'I didn't mean to,' cried Angel, sobbing in Melanie's arms.

The incident was brushed aside, but Paul still hung onto it. He didn't believe Angel was innocent and wasn't ready to absolve her. The following Sunday, when Melanie was at a party with Brad and Adrienne, a party that Angel hadn't been invited to, he decided to have a word with her.

'Let's take a walk, Angel,' suggested Paul, leading her down to the doll's house. One side was blackened from the flames of the fire, but the structure remained intact and would just need to be fixed up to regain its glory.

'Why did you burn Addie's doll's house, Angel?'

'I said I was sorry,' replied Angel, her face crumpling up like tis-sue paper. 'I didn't mean to.'

'That's a lie, Angel! You wanted to burn it down!'

'I promise I didn't,' replied Angel.

'I'm not your mother – I can see right through you, Angel. Why did you burn it?'

Paul pinched Angel on her arm until tears were streaming down her face.

'Okay! I did!' said Angel, owning up to the crime. 'I don't know why … I'm sorry.'

Paul then grabbed her and pulled her over his knees and spanked her with an open hand until she was howling like a hyena. He stopped and let her cry until her tears were dry and she was no longer hic-cupping and then he unexpectedly hugged her. Angel was confused because she hated being hit, but she welcomed Paul's hug. It was the first time he had ever held her.

'Don't ever do that again,' he warned, pointing a threatening fin-ger at her.

'I won't,' she whimpered, a combination of fear and reverence in her voice.

Angel never made mention of the incident to Melanie because she didn't want her mom to perceive her any differently after the inci-dent. She was grateful that Paul didn't say anything either, and from that day on Angel vowed never to get on his bad side ever again.

27

The turbulent teens

The nineties ushered in the high school years and the Williams children were all carted off to boarding school. Angel had already spent her last year of primary school in boarding school because her older siblings had gone on to high school. And, by then, Melanie declared that she was exhausted from doing the school run, homework and living apart from her husband.

Bradley was a boarder at the prestigious Falcon College in Esigodini and Adrienne and Angel were at the sister school, Girls' College. Esther and Munya got married and moved up to Harare. Paul and Melanie sold the Burnside house and bought a luxury penthouse that Melanie fitted out with resplendent furniture in Ascot's Kenilworth Towers. The lock-up-and-go arrangement worked perfectly if they needed to come into town for sporting weekends.

While Adrienne loved boarding school, Angel felt unhinged. Puberty came with innumerable challenges and unlike her sister, who was tall and slender, Angel was short and curvy. It was the era of Christy Turlington, Linda Evangelista and Claudia Schiffer, the poster girls of what it meant to be beautiful. Even when Naomi Campbell broke onto the scene, Angel knew she couldn't remotely compare herself to her. She dieted relentlessly, but that only succeeded in cinching in her waist while her hips and buttocks remained resolutely in place. She started to starve herself, and by the time she turned fifteen she had developed a serious eating disorder. Melanie picked it up and Angel was frogmarched to a psychologist. In her office, Angel attempted to explain her anxiety and her feelings of not belonging.

'You need to fall in love with yourself,' the psychologist impressed upon her.

Looking at herself in the mirror Angel hated everything that was reflected back at her. How was she supposed to love this? How?

She hated her hair. It was stiff and tightly coiled like a spring and she resented that she didn't have flowing long hair like Melanie and Adrienne. Even the hair salon Melanie patronised had 'no idea what to do with it'. When she was much younger, Esther had offered the suggestion of straightening it with a hot comb. But even when it was secured in a ponytail it didn't have the swishy swing like Adrienne's and that frustrated Angel no end. Her pigtails were stiff and rigid and, after swimming, her hair would shrivel, leaving her to go through the painful process of straightening it again.

Angel recalled that when she was little, Esther would grab her to sit between her thighs to make her keep still and then plait her hair and roll them into buns, coiling them with black thread. Melanie would tie red ribbons around the buns. Melanie thought Angel looked so cute, but Angel secretly wished she could have hair like Melanie's.

She was sixteen when she discovered Dark and Lovely No-Lye Relaxer. It felt like liberation in a box and finally gave her the long and silky straight hair she wanted. But she couldn't swim once her hair had been relaxed because it would become frizzy and lose its sheen.

She hated that she had big brown eyes and that they were not blue like her siblings. And while it had never bothered her before, she started to resent her brown skin. She hated that she was the only brown person at the table when everyone around her had peachy-coloured skin. She wanted to fit in, not stand out. It didn't matter at primary school, but in high school the colour divide was more obvious. The black girls tended to group together at break time and the white girls sat in their own little cliques. By default, she had always congregated with the white girls and, by virtue of being Adrienne's little sister, got roped into her clique of friends. In Form 1 she had tried to make friends with some of the black girls, but they eyed her with suspicion. First they didn't understand why she had a surname like Williams when she was neither coloured nor white. That was when the lying began.

'I'm American,' lied Angel. 'I was orphaned and then the Williams family adopted me.'

She was too ashamed to tell them that her lineage could be traced to domestic workers who had serviced the Williamses for years. Her low class filled her with a deep sense of shame. More so because the parents of the black girls she went to school with were all professionals. They were accountants and actuaries, CEOs and CIOs, dentists and doctors, economists and engineers, lawyers and leaders, pharmacists and physicians, politicians and paralegals.

'Where in America do you come from?' asked one of the girls.

'Orlando, Florida,' she said confidently.

By the time she was twelve, Angel had holidayed in cities all over America, Europe and Asia, plus they had travelled extensively in Africa. She was a world citizen, so convincing the girls that she was American wasn't difficult. But instead of this bringing her closer to the girls, it alienated her further because they couldn't relate to her. Culturally, they were miles apart and she couldn't speak any of the local languages. She didn't listen to the same music and, while the black girls were all about nineties' R&B, she listened to groups like The Cranberries, Roxette and Take That. She didn't behave like the other girls either. Her mannerisms were white. She spoke white. They soon started calling her a coconut: black on the outside, but white on the inside. When Angel failed to crack those circles, she retreated.

The girls were at the age when they were starting to take notice of the opposite sex or, more importantly, being noticed by the opposite sex. But nobody paid attention to Angel. The white boys didn't look at her, not in *that* way. The black boys might have been interested, but because she wasn't moving in their circles she never stood a chance. Valentine's Day was always a torturous day for her and while Adrienne would be inundated with flowers and gifts from her flock of secret admirers, Angel didn't receive a single card.

'You can have my chocolates,' offered Adrienne that afternoon as they lay curled up on her bed, rifling through her gifts.

'So I can be fat? No thanks!'

'Ange, you're not fat,' said Adrienne. 'I'm just offering you the chocolates so that you don't feel left out.'

'I don't want your handouts, okay, Addie! I don't!'

Angel had stormed off in a huff and Adrienne had rolled over and carried on eating the chocolates. Back in her own room, Angel stood in front of the mirror scrutinising herself. Trying to understand why no one loved her, she cried herself to sleep that night. The following morning, in a contrite tone, she approached Adrienne and asked her to set her up with someone for the Valentine's Day dance that weekend.

Adrienne sashayed down the stairs in a tight, red-leather ruched dress with a plunging neckline and dangerously low back that showed off her bronzed tan. She did a little twirl and threw a dazzling smile, tossed her head back, her sleek blonde hair bouncing as she did so. Melanie couldn't help staring at her from the bottom of the stairs. She and Adrienne had argued about the dress because she had insisted it was too sexy for a girl her age, but Adrienne had argued that it was exactly the look she was trying to achieve. She was tall and slim, and when she walked into a room her presence was felt. She had always been a bit older than her years and had a sophistication and coolness about her that belied her tender age of seventeen. If her mother had her way, Adrienne would have been immortalised as a seven-year-old. Melanie couldn't believe how time had transformed their lives. If felt like yesterday that Adrienne was an adorable little girl running around in nappies, or a pimply tween walking around in bright pink tights and baggy sweatshirts. It also seemed like yesterday that Bradley was brooding around the house, a gangly teenager sporting short, spiky, blond hair. Now he was heading to university to study Law; a decision that father and son were still fighting about. Paul had wanted him to study towards a BSc in Agricultural Economics or a business degree, but Bradley had no inclination for either, insisting he had no interest in running the farm or taking it over one day. Naturally, this upset Paul terribly.

'Honey, you look beautiful,' enthused Melanie, crouching to take a picture of her.

'I know,' replied Adrienne, pouting for the camera.

She twirled and struck a few poses.

'You know you look wonderful, my baby,' said Paul.

Adrienne smiled triumphantly, her eyes lighting up, basking in her father's adoration. Melanie stood with her hands crossed over her chest, watching from the sidelines. She had always been envious of their relationship and had felt excluded, remaining on the fringes.

'Ange, please bring my jacket!' called Adrienne.

'Why don't you get it?' chastised Melanie.

Looking up, she saw Angel standing at the top of the stairs, looking hesitant and shy. It seemed that with every year she grew shyer and withdrew into herself. Such an introvert, whereas Adrienne was such an extrovert. Sometimes she wished Adrienne could pour out half of that confidence to Angel.

'I'm right here,' replied Angel, racing down the stairs holding Adrienne's jacket.

'Ange, you look gorgeous!' proclaimed Melanie.

'Thanks, Mom,' replied Angel, even though she didn't feel it.

She was wearing a strapless dress with a tight-fitting bodice that flared into a puffed skirt with a polka-dot tulle underskirt cut mid-thigh, leaving her shapely stocking-clad legs on view. Her braided hair was piled on top of her head. The dress had been Melanie's choice and Angel had complied in her good-natured way. Their relationship was not marked with dissension, but rather quiet accord.

Melanie told the girls to stand together for a picture.

'My lovely girls.'

'For a moment, I didn't recognise you!' chirped Paul. Adrienne went bounding into his arms. She had always been his favourite child and, although Melanie had always tried to show no favour to any of the children, Paul went out of his way to make sure everyone knew that Adrienne was the apple of his eye. Adrienne loved the attention and received it everywhere she went. At school, the teachers adored her. She was beautiful, intelligent and athletic and played hockey and tennis and swam for the national team. She had been the obvious choice for head girl and wore a blazer full of colourful scrolls award-ed for academic achievement. It also helped that her parents donated generous amounts of money to the school governing body. Outside of school, Adrienne was the reigning horse-riding champion.

Unlike her sister, Angel wasn't sporty, so she played the piano and did ballet. She knew she wasn't the best and had come close to quit-ting when Paul admonished her for not getting the lead role in *Swan Lake*. But, like Adrienne, she *was* studious. She had to achieve the same grades, because anything less would have been unacceptable. When she surpassed her sister, Paul didn't comment, but if Angel under-performed she would be severely reprimanded.

'I am not sending you to a private school to fuck around! I'm forking out thousands for your education.'

Whereas Melanie had gone out of her way to make Angel feel like she was part of the family, Paul went out of his way to remind her she wasn't.

They were later joined on the patio for drinks and canapés by their longstanding neighbours, the Watsons. Carla was also attending the Christian Brothers' College Dance for the first time. They were waiting for Adrienne's date to pick them up, as he had volunteered to drive even though Paul had tried to insist they be chauffeured there. Adrienne loathed the idea; if they went with Bab'Fuyane, the driver, they wouldn't have the freedom to party after the dance. Paul always made sure he met the young men his daughters were cavorting with and so, while they waited, Melanie took more photographs. Adrienne was relieved when her boyfriend, Luke Wittstock, finally arrived, her face sore from all the fake smiling. Initially, when they had started dating, Paul had been against it because the family had never fraternised with the Wittstocks. Adrienne had dismissed him, insisting that it had been years since Grandpa Doug's scandalous affair with Luke's grandmother. Adrienne was resolute in her love for Luke and didn't see why she should be made to suffer. For Paul, the time lapse hadn't been long enough, the memory still fresh in his mind. He would have preferred if she dated one of the Watson boys, but Adrienne had never fancied Steve or Stuart. They were like her big brothers and they'd all grown up together. Farming stock tended to stick together.

While Adrienne sat upfront with Luke, Carla and Angel sat together in the back. Carla was Angel's only friend – at least the only one she never had to explain herself to. While they had been forced upon each other because of proximity and familial relations, they had genuine affection for each other. During the journey they were able to unpack their individual excitement about the dance. Carla was going with Craig, a sixth-former she had nursed a crush on for the longest time. Angel had been set up with Anthony, who was part of Luke's clique of friends. It wasn't that Angel disliked Ant, as he was affectionately called; they just had nothing in common. He was a jock who played first-team rugby. He was athletic and participated in all team sports, while Angel avoided the sports ground altogether. He was part of the cool kids, while she hadn't made the cut. Even their music tastes were vastly different. He was a Bon Jovi and Van Halen fan, while Angel abhorred rock.

Ant arrived at the dance half drunk and nearly stuck the corsage down her dress. Angel had only agreed to go with him because

Adrienne had insisted, and she did want to be part of the fanfare and ceremony. The function had been well organised and was hosted by a local hotel. Tables encircled the dance floor, streamers and0 balloons hung from the ceiling of the banquet hall and lights dazzled in a brilliant kaleidoscope when the disco lights came on. They reflected off the girls' dresses, creating a spectrum of vibrant colour. Two of Adrienne's friends, Ellen and Linda, and their boyfriends, were at their table. Angel figured that the only reason she was tolerated by everyone was by virtue of the fact that she was Adrienne's sister. They were nice-enough girls, but Angel always felt like she never quite made the grade.

'Why are you *so* serious?' remarked Ant.

His words were slurring into each other. She'd almost forgotten he was there.

She smiled weakly, 'Sorry.'

'Come on, let's dance.'

Angel obliged and Ant stumbled his way onto the dance floor. They joined the others who were all dancing to Roxette's 'The Look', swinging and swaying and singing along. Angel spotted Luke twirling her sister in his arms. Adrienne was really enjoying herself and seemed very taken with her boyfriend. They had been dating for over a year and Adrienne said she was going to marry Luke – she was very definitive and decisive about that. Angel had never had a boyfriend. There just didn't seem to be any boy who interested her. Most of them were childish and all they wanted to do was to get to third base so they could remove your top and fondle your breasts. Maybe she'd give it a try one day. They all danced till the song ended, and then 'I Can't Help Falling in Love' by UB40 came on and Ant pulled her roughly into his arms. She felt awkward and was relieved when a fast song came on. Then they were dancing again, arms flailing in the air, hips thrown from side to side. After entreaties of exhaustion, Ant led Angel back to the table for a drink. He tried to force his brandy and Coke onto her, but Angel resisted, preferring her non-alcoholic punch.

Alcohol wasn't permitted, but they'd managed to smuggle it in some-how.

'It's so hot in here,' said Angel, fanning herself with the menu.

'Let's go outside and take a walk – I could do with some air!' suggested Ant.

Angel knew instinctively that she should have refused, but she decided to go along anyway. It was a beautiful night and the streets were almost deserted. Ant took her by the hand and they walked with their fingers intertwined. Angel almost forgave him for being less than sober. He leaned in for a kiss and she willed herself to savour the feel of Ant's warm lips on hers. She parted her lips, allowing his tongue to probe and tease. She ran her fingers through his dark, wavy chestnut hair. It wasn't as soft and curly as Bradley's. Nobody could ever know that they had crossed that line as they were siblings and a shared kiss between them was nothing short of incestuous.

Ant's tongue was forceful, not gentle like Brad's. She quickly re-gretted her decision and gently nudged him away. She didn't want to lead him on.

'Stop it!' she said.

Ant stared at her in alarm, 'Why? What's wrong? You're being a tease. Farm girls don't give it up?'

'Let's just go back inside,' she said, in a voice much harsher than she had intended.

They walked back in silence. The magic had been broken. Angel knew that she couldn't run away or hide from the images in her mind.

28

It started with a kiss

While the other girls were sharing the details of their first kiss and giggling about it, Angel cowered in shame about hers. She couldn't tell them her first kiss had been with her brother. One night they were watching A Nightmare on Elm Street *together. Everyone was asleep and they were on the couch, sharing a blanket. When there was a scary scene, Angel buried her face in Bradley's chest. At some point, they bumped heads and their mouths found each other. She felt his lips on hers and for a fleeting moment they pressed into hers. They stayed like that, their bodies quivering. Bradley's tongue caressed her lips, exploring and tantalising. The kiss was as sweet as chocolate truffles with a syrupy middle. Angel had enjoyed being in his arms, feeling desired and wanted.*

'Brad, stop!' she said pushing him away. 'We can't do this.'

'Angel, uh … I'm sorry,' he apologised, running his fingers through his hair. 'I don't know where that came from.'

He swallowed hard. Angel stood up, almost trying to create a healthy distance between them.

'Brad, we must forget this ever happened. You're my brother.'

She rushed off to her bedroom, slammed the door and locked it. She had contemplated discussing the incident with her psychologist, but she didn't trust her enough so she decided it would be her secret.

When they arrived at the farmhouse on Sunday she was surprised to see Bradley's red Mercedes AMG roadster parked between their parents' Range Rovers. The sound of rock music that filled the air was further evidence that he was there because their parents listened to ABBA and Neil Diamond. Angel's heart stalled. She hadn't seen Brad since that night and she wasn't sure how she would react when she saw him again. Adrienne and Carla jumped out of the car like calves released from a stall to greet Brad. Angel sat in the car, trying to gather herself. Her emotions were all over the place. It had been months since the kiss, but as she ran her tongue over her lips it could've been yesterday.

A knock on the window snapped her back to reality. It was Bradley.

'Hi, hi,' he said. 'Are you avoiding me?'

'Not at all,' replied Angel getting out of the car. They hugged, rather awkwardly at first, but then relaxed in one another's arms. When Bradley released her, then held at her arm's-length, studying her with his intense gaze.

'My, my ... look at you!'

She averted her gaze, not wanting to meet his.

'And what's this?' asked Bradley, pointing at her braids.

He wanted to run his fingers through her silky hair, which always smelled of jojoba and coconut oil. He held her, squeezing her fingers, not wanting to let go. He looked good; suntanned and bronzed. He had let his hair grow, his floppy chestnut curls covering his coral-blue eyes. He was wearing a blue T-shirt, which clung to his lithe muscled body, and an equally tight pair of jeans. He didn't have any shoes on, he rarely ever did. They had played like that as kids, the soles of their feet connecting to the earth below.

'How was Italy?' she asked.

Bradley had opted to take a gap year before starting university and spend some of it travelling through Europe. He and Steve went to Italy, landing in Rome before moving on to Venice and then partying their way along the Amalfi coast. But then Bradley's euros ran out, and he had cabled home to ask for more money, but Paul had refused so they came home.

'Well, I'm back!'

'Welcome back,' she replied

'I'm happy to be back,' he replied.

'Are you guys all right out there?' asked Steve, standing in the doorway. 'Lunch is ready.'

'Coming,' replied Bradley hurriedly and they walked into the house to join the others. He had been wary about his reunion with Angel; she hadn't left his mind for a minute.

Melanie's heart was full as they sat down for Sunday lunch. She was happy to be surrounded by her family and their friends. The conversation was boisterous as the boys told everyone about their shenanigans on their Italian tour and made everyone laugh. Melanie cooked a spread on Sundays, just how Paul always wanted her to, as she'd eventually got round to taking those culinary lessons. She was delighted to see everyone slice through their roast lamb and enjoy the roast potatoes and vegetables. A huge bowl of roasted beet and rocket salad with butternut and feta cheese and sprinkled with walnuts stood in the centre of the table. Now that the dairy operations had been expanded to include a processing plant, they had a line of products under the Crème de Mel-k range that included cheeses, yoghurt and ice cream, predominantly for the EU export market. After her parents' demise, Melanie had inherited a huge sum that she had injected into the farm. They had mechanised the milking operation and built a factory and office space. This was even more of a reason why Paul was upset by Bradley's decision not to join the family farming operation.

'So where's next on your bucket list of travels?' asked Cheryl, Steve's mom.

'I'm not funding any more of this mischief,' stated Paul. 'If Bradley wants money to travel he's going to have to do some work here on the farm.'

'Dad, you know how I feel about the farm,' Bradley responded. 'I just don't feel comfortable that you own all of this and the workers who actually do the labour don't have equity in it. Like, how is that even fair?'

'How can *you* talk about fairness, Brad? You're spending the money we make on this farm like its water. Whose money do you think paid for that car you're driving? That penthouse you live in? Drop the sanctimonious horseshit with me, Brad. Until you can actually earn a living, don't bullshit me about equity.'

There was an awkward silence around the table that Melanie tried to fill by asking if anyone wanted dessert. She offered them a choice between blueberry cheesecake and strawberry popsicles. The jovial mood was further spoiled by a call from Estelle, Paul's sister, informing him that Granny Belle had suffered a heart attack. Paul's mom was the only surviving grandparent – her husband, Uncle Scotty, had died in the early nineties after suffering a debilitating stroke.

Melanie spent the rest of the afternoon getting ready for her and Paul to leave to go see her mother-in-law. An hour later, they were flying out on a chartered Cessna. Paul was visibly upset, both about his mother and his son.

'Maybe we should have had that third child, Mel. I might've had a son who actually wants to inherit all this,' mumbled Paul as they boarded their private jet.

Melanie laughed. 'I'm only 42 – we could always try.'

'Let's,' suggested Paul, kissing her playfully.

Melanie kissed him passionately until the pilot coughed and they pulled apart. They settled down in the spacious interior of the jet, which could seat twelve people and a cabin crew of two.

'He'll come around,' she said, placing her hand over Paul's.

She would sit Bradley down when they returned, Melanie decided. They were building a generational legacy, after all.

29

Dangerous liaisons

Bradley had been up all night, sleep eluding him, so he decided to go for a jog around the farmhouse. He was hoping to outrun his thoughts, and was mad at himself for what had transpired the previous night. They had gone to the Farmers' Club, which had been upgraded to the Somabhula Country Club. Replete with an 18-hole golf course, gym and tennis courts, Angel was used to being the only black person there other than the staff. They ordered steak and chips and the guys ordered beers. Angel decided she was going to have a drink and, even though she was underage, Brad let her. The boys were adamant that if she were going to drink, it would be best if she did it with them. They were all doggedly determined to get inebriated and introduced Angel to vodka cocktails and gold sambuca shots. Stuart and Adrienne egged everyone on and Adrienne took Steven on in a shot-for-shot contest and promptly proceeded to outdrink him. They were the noisiest table in the establishment, their talk animated and the laughter loud and raucous. They were eventually asked to leave because they were disturbing the other diners. Angel was glad they were leaving because she felt giddy and light-headed. She took tentative steps out of the club and nearly missed a step and was relieved when Brad caught her.

'I got you,' he said, putting a protective arm around her.

She nestled into him, feeling safe and secure in his arms.

It was a little after 1am when they got back to the farm. The drinking carried on in the newly installed bar, but by this time Angel's

world was spinning so she made her way to the kitchen to make herself a strong cup of coffee. She was leaning against the counter, waiting for the water to boil, when Bradley waltzed in, making her jump.

'God, you gave me a fright!' she laughed nervously.

'Why are you so jumpy?'

'Blame it on the sum-boo-car,' she replied, her speech slurred.

'Make one for me too,' he replied. 'I feel like kak!'

He pulled her into his arms.

'Dance with me.'

Angel laughed, 'There's no music, silly.'

'We'll make our own,' said Bradley, pulling her into his arms.

'*This* is silly!' she said, laughing and gently chastising herself.
'Silly me. Silly Angel.'

'Sshh,' he replied, 'you're missing the tempo.'

So she allowed herself to be led by Brad.

'We used to dance all the time as kids, Gel. I miss that,' he said,
burying his head in the nape of her neck, drinking in her flowery
scent. He wanted to hold onto the moment, pause it so that she would
never leave his embrace. How he longed to run his hands all over her
beautifully svelte body and remove the clothes that were a barrier between them. Then he felt her pull away from him. Startled, he looked
up; he had been enjoying rocking gently on her shoulder.

'The water,' she said with a smile.

The kettle had been boiling for several minutes. The steam had
condensed into little droplets on the wall. She switched off the electric
kettle. She felt the warmth of Bradley's closeness. The familiar smell
of him. She felt his hot breath on her neck. Angel gasped when she
felt his hands go around her slim waist. She let go of the kettle and
found herself turning in his arms until she faced him. He pulled away
and stared at her with his dreamy coral-blue eyes. They kissed, more
decisively than the first and oblivious to the fact that someone could
walk in on them.

He kissed her slowly and Angel felt her knees give way. She felt weak and slipped against the counter. They both reached the floor and all she wanted was to kiss him over and over and over again. He kissed her deeply, more assured by her responses. The kiss was like fire building, soft flames gently licking at her desire. When she finally extricated herself from him, she was engulfed with a heady combination of guilt and desire.

She stood up, balancing against the counter. It was like she was regaining her senses and the craziness that had overtaken her a few minutes ago was clearing like a fog.

He wanted to protest, but she put a finger over his mouth.

'Brad, you promised,' she said.

'I'm sorry,' he replied. 'Actually, dammit, I'm not sorry. I want you, Gel.'

She ran out of the kitchen, unable to deal with his confession. He slammed his fist into the counter, frustrated by his inability to rein in his feelings or even process them.

Ten kilometres later, sweating profusely, Brad collapsed with exhaustion on the landing. He'd been hoping he would sweat out his all-consuming thoughts of Angel. Steve had joked that he needed an exorcism except Bradley hadn't found that funny. He had turned to Steve in confidence, looking to unburden himself, rather than open himself to ridicule.

He hated himself for having thoughts that baffled him. He wasn't supposed to feel this way about Angel. She was like a sister. It was crazy for him to be in love with her. It felt incestuous. Angel wasn't his blood sister, though – that ought to count for something, right? He was desperate, clutching at any glimmer of hope. But deep down he knew it wasn't possible. He'd have to accept that Angel could never be anything more to him, and whatever other feelings he had for her he had to banish forever. But he had tried in vain; God knows he'd tried. He'd tried to forget, ignore and toss aside his feelings for her for so long. There had been other girls in his life, but he had never felt anything for them. Nothing stirred inside him when he was with them. He only felt alive when he was with Angel. Seeing her was torture, like a worm being dangled in front of a fish. He cradled his head in his hands and wanted to cry; it was a hopeless situation.

The ringing of the phone propelled him to his feet. It was his mother, calling from the hospital to give them an update. She also was keen to know if everything was all right at home.

'Yes,' replied Brad, smiling at the irony of his response.

'Granny Belle is stable. She's going to make it.'

At 73 years old, Granny Belle was as tough as nails. They had lost Grandpa Scotty two years earlier and, although Brad had never actually said it, he wished the Lord had taken Granny Belle instead.

He tried to avoid his grandmother as much as possible because she was both narrow-minded and prudish. Their dislike of each other was mutual and Granny Belle had threatened on countless occasions that she would write Brad out of her will.

'We're probably going to stay here for a few more days until Granny Belle is discharged. Please stick around and drop the girls at school and keep an eye on things.'

Bradley had been contemplating leaving, wanting to avoid the awkwardness between him and Angel.

'Don't worry, Mom. I'll take care of everything,' replied Bradley.

'And feed the dogs. And water my plants.'

'Mom, don't worry,' said Brad. 'You just worry about Grannny right now.'

'Thanks, darling. I won't worry – and your granny's going to be just fine. Hang on, your dad wants a word with you.'

Paul came on the line. His father didn't have much to say besides asking after everyone and summarising what Melanie had said. He was brusque in his delivery and then said goodbye. His mother came back on the phone.

'Love you, darling, and give my love to the girls.'

'I love you too, Mom. Bye.'

Bradley hung up thinking how sweet his mother was, albeit a little overbearing at times, but he figured it made up for his father's apathy.

The rest of the house stirred at midday, hungover and lethargic. Bradley prepared brunch for everyone and then carted the girls back to school as it was the end of their exeat weekend. Angel hoped that by the end of the week he would have returned to Harare, but she was pleasantly surprised when he arrived to pick them up on Friday afternoon. Angel was conflicted – she didn't want him to go, but she didn't want him to stay either. Adrienne had already made plans to drive back with Luke, which meant Angel would be alone with Brad.

She was surprised that he had survived at the farm that long, but Bradley insisted he was merely holding the fort and that their parents were set to return on the weekend. He offered to buy her lunch and suggested Pizzaghetti or La Gondola. Both were tempting, but she settled on the former. Walking into the establishment, they were immediately accosted by the fragrant aromas of Italian food. She ordered a pepperoni pizza while he settled for pasta Alfredo. The Cranberries were crooning softly in the background and Angel joined in the chorus, proclaiming she was 'in too deep and such a fool'. She felt the words keenly. It felt like Brad had her wrapped around his little finger. She started to flirt with the idea that they were on a date and that he wasn't her brother, but a man she adored whom she had met on the streets of Bulawayo.

'How's school?' he asked.

'Same old boring stuff,' replied Angel.

'Tell me about the boring stuff – I want to hear it.'

Angel told him all about the goings-on at school and he listened attentively, laughing every now and then at the funny antics of high-school girls. When Angel had exhausted the topic, she asked him about his wanderings and plans for the future.

'I was hoping to continue touring Europe, but you heard Dad. He won't give me another cent. Maybe I can get Mom to speak to him for me.'

'Working isn't such a bad idea either,' teased Angel.

Bradley ran his hand through his hair in obvious frustration.

'Gel, I can't do this farm shit. You know me – this life isn't for me.'

'I *know*,' she replied, 'and I know Paul too.'

She'd never been able to bring herself to call him Dad. It just had never seemed right.

'I'm going to have to start uni in September. Mom has the money. She would have given it to me, but you know Dad ...'

The whole situation with his dad was getting him down, so he changed the subject. He started to quiz Angel about her date. Steve had mentioned something to him in passing that he had heard from Carla.

'Who's that punk I heard you went with to the dance?'

'Ant? He's just a friend.'

'He'd better be. I don't want anyone corrupting my little sister.'

As he said that he ran his fingers through her hair, ruffling it a little. He could no longer resist the urge.

'You're so protective over me!'

'That's what big brothers are for. *Right*?'

'Wrong!' laughed Angel. 'One day you are going to have to watch me getting married!'

'I don't ever want that day to come,' he replied, looking at her straight in the eye. He was serious; there was nothing frivolous about the statement. Angel turned away and stared down at her half-eaten pizza. One day she would have to deal with Bradley bringing home his bride. Hopefully, that would happen when she was much older and could afford to move far away from the farm.

She wanted to laugh the moment away, but her throat was dry. She took a bite of her pizza instead.

'We should go,' he said. 'We can get the rest of your pizza as a takeaway.'

'Brad?' she said. 'Thank you. For everything.'

They slipped into silence on the drive home. Bradley turned up the music and Roxette filled the interior of the car. They sang along to every song, which didn't allow for any further conversation anyway. Bradley dropped her off at home and said he was meeting Steve at the club. Angel felt slightly miffed that he didn't invite her, but took it in her stride and decided to take her horse for a ride.

The sun was going down and Angel knew she had to saddle up and return to the house before it got dark. That was when she heard the hooves of a horse galumphing towards the river. It was Bradley. Her heart started galloping in her chest. The river was a secluded place, running along the eastern boundary of the farm. Angel loved going there and walking along the riverbank that was full of bulrushes dancing in the wind, combing her feet through the sand. It was her peaceful place to connect with nature.

'I knew I'd find you here,' said Brad.

'I didn't want to be found,' replied Angel.

'You can't keep avoiding me forever, Gel.'

'Look, Brad,' said Angel, 'I'm at a loss how to act towards you. Since we kissed, it's been strange between us.'

She stared down at the ground, at her feet. She'd never been articulate and didn't know how to express the confusion she felt. She looked up at him, bewildered and confused. In her youthful naïveté, she was unable to process the intensity of her feelings.

'We had a lot to drink that night and I was tipsy and I don't really know what came over me, Brad. It was a mistake—'

'Angel, it wasn't a mistake. I wanted to kiss you. I've wanted to kiss you for a long time. The alcohol just gave me the courage to do what I've been dreaming about for so long.'

Angel was quiet, astounded by his confession. She was even more surprised when he took her hands in his.

'I'm not going to say I'm sorry for what I did, Angel, because given another chance I will kiss you again.'

Angel smiled at him, feeling a heavy burden evaporate from her chest.

'Now that we are both sober, can I kiss you again?'

'And what happens after the kiss?'

'I don't know, Gel. All I know that is I love you and I want to be with you.'

He pulled her into his arms and kissed her. Angel stretched her toes, leaning into him. He had always been taller than her. She felt a wave of heady sensations spread through her body and her heart was beating fast, pounding in her ears. As she surrendered to his kiss, to her emotions, she knew they had crossed that invisible line and there would be no turning back. He started to undress her, her clothes falling to her feet.

> Like autumn
> Her leaves were shed
> Breath taken, he admired
> The scene that she conjured
>
> He stripped himself
> Of all the bark he had
> Muscles flexed, body taut
> Hardened yearning, his to flaunt
>
> He kissed her
> He caressed her
> The tips of his fingers
> Tracing the desire that lingers
>
> He lifted her
> Holding her with care

Like a vase of porcelain
For his touch is certain

Upon a bed of grass
He placed her
He lowered himself
While she opened herself

His kissed between her thighs
It gave him such a high
Her soul released a fluttering sigh
Her orgasm was nigh

They coupled
Their arms tangled, like vines
Their legs entwined
Their mind and hearts aligned

They moved in unison
The sun dappling over their bodies
They reached the highest peak
Language only lovers speak

She cried out his name
As she came, again and again
Tears of joy spilled from her eyes
He was moved as he heard her cries

The earth moved beneath them
The heavens shook above them
How intense was his love
For this woman called Angel, his dove.

30

A change of heart

Paul and Melanie returned to Bradley having had a change of heart. He declared boldly over dinner that he was committed to farming and wanted to learn the ropes. Paul was delighted and didn't care what had prompted it – he just welcomed it. Paul was quick to introduce Bradley to Tyrone, the farm manager, who was to guide him through his internship. He didn't want to leave anything to chance in case Bradley changed his mind.

Bradley was up at the crack of dawn with the rest of the staff. Tyrone showed Bradley around, but there would be no preferential treatment just because he was the boss's son. His day began in the yard with the milking operations. From the yard, the milk was channelled to the factory. The Williamses were no longer running a fledgling operation; theirs was now a thriving and highly profitable business. While he'd always appreciated that they had money, he'd never realised how it was earned. It was physically gruelling work, mentally taxing and he wasn't sure whether he was cut out for it. Apart from the hard work, Brad was happy to encounter his childhood friends Spencer, Honest and Thabo who were part of the staff. Spencer was the production manager and Honest worked in the accounts department while Thabo was in quality control.

'Are you happy here?' he asked them one afternoon when they were having lunch in the staff canteen.

'Very happy,' replied Spencer. 'We're paid well and we have free accommodation here on the farm.'

'We have a good life here,' reiterated Thabo. 'Your father is a tough nut, but he means well.'

They laughed uneasily.

'So are you going to take over this ship?' asked Honest.

'Possibly,' replied Bradley.

Before his internship, he hadn't been fully aware of the size of the operation or the export markets they serviced. The nineties were characterised by the liberalisation of the Zimbabwe economy, while the politics was becoming more protectionist as the country eased into a one-party state.

The only party Bradley had was when the week ended and Angel returned from school. It took a lot of restraint on both their parts not to tear at each other with raging passion. They had to play platonic when they accidentally brushed against each other in the kitchen. Or when their eyes met across the dinner table, their feet entangled under the table, a prelude to their lovemaking. Bradley would wait until the house was quiet before sneaking into Angel's room. They would lock the door to make sure they wouldn't be rudely interrupted. They played music in the background to drown out their avid lovemaking. Take That's 'Pray' became the soundtrack to their blossoming love affair. When Paul and Melanie got hooked on Rod Stewart's 'Have I Told You Lately That I Love You', they hijacked that track too.

Schools closed for the term and Angel was home for the duration of the April holidays. They all went on a family holiday to Mauritius and while Angel shared a room with Adrienne, she snuck into Brad's room every night. They were inseparable. They took long walks on the beach and secretly kissed under the moonlight.

On their return, their secret nightly rendezvous continued unabated. Summer gave way to winter and the cold made it even tougher for them to extricate themselves from each other when a new day dawned. One morning, at 4am, Brad had overslept and collided with his father in the hallway as he was making his way back to his room.

The look of sheer guilt on his face was in contrast to the utter astonishment on his father's.

. 'What the hell is going on?' asked Paul.

'Dad … I can explain,' stammered Bradley.

'You've got a lot of bloody explaining to do!' said Paul angrily. 'Go to bed – we'll talk in the morning. Oh fuck, it's already morning. Just go to bed!'

After breakfast Paul decided to resume the conversation. Bradley was on edge and wasn't been able to eat much of anything. Finally, he resolved to tell his father the truth and insist that he had not done anything wrong.

'What exactly is going on, Brad?' was the first question Paul threw at him.

'Angel and I are in love,' came the answer.

'What? She's your sister, Bradley! We fucking adopted her.'

'Technically, she's not my sister, Dad – not in the biological sense of the word – and I love her. Honest to God, I do.'

'We all love her, dammit! Did you even think this through, or is it that you just couldn't contain your lust? You took advantage of her, Brad! Imagine if people got wind of this? You'd be charged with statutory rape!'

'Dad, that won't happen – we love each other. I'm nineteen years old, old enough to know what I want from life. And I want to marry Angel one day.'

Paul ran his fingers through his hair, expelling a mouthful of air like a dragon breathing fire.

'Brad, I don't want to hear another word about this. Whatever is going on between you two, I want it to end. Do you hear me?'

'Dad, I'm not a kid. You can't order me around.'

'Bradley, as long as you are living in this house you'll—'

'Dad, I'll move out of your house if that's what this is going to come to. I love Angel and there is nothing you can do to change my mind.'

'You move out and I will cut you off financially, Brad. Let's see how you'll finance this little flirtation of yours. End this bloody affair! End it, Brad. Today. Then you can make plans to go to uni in Europe.'

'Europe?'

'Yes. Isn't that what you wanted all along? You can go to Oxford and do your law degree. Start with summer school. It'll keep you out of trouble before the semester begins.'

Although his father had finally conceded, this is not the way Bradley had wanted it to happen. However, he figured it could buy him and Angel some time. If he studied, he would be in a position to pursue a career and his burgeoning love for Angel. He knew deep down that this wasn't a fleeting love affair. He loved her and he wanted to be with her for the rest of his life.

Angel, however, was inconsolable when Brad told her about his imminent departure. Her sobs tugged at his heartstrings, stretching them taut until his head ached. He reassured her that everything was going to be okay, but as he boarded a commercial flight a few days later he was no longer so certain.

Paul called ahead to inform his mother, 'He'll be there for a few days before connecting to London.'

'Why the sudden change of heart?' asked Granny Belle.

'He's been fucking Angel. Can you believe it, Mom?'

'Of course I can,' replied Belle flippantly. 'She seduced him. Just like her grandmother seduced your father.'

'This is what scares me, Mom. It is like history is repeating itself right under my bloody nose.'

'She's eyeing the money, Paul. What better way to get her claws into it than through Bradley?'

Paul felt sick to his gut. He'd been wrong about Angel. She was just like her grandmother and great-grandmother before her.

The mood at dinner that evening was strained, Angel and Brad's absence glaring. Her parents were both quietly angry for different reasons. Adrienne, tired of stewing in a pot of tension, dished a plate of food to take to her sister.

'No eating in the bedrooms,' said Melanie. 'You know that.'

'Mom, Angel's upset,' replied Adrienne. 'I don't think she's ready to face either of you.'

'Addie, I think we handled the situation pretty well, all things considered,' replied Paul.

'No you didn't,' retorted Adrienne. 'I don't actually see what the problem is.'

'How long has this been going on?' asked Melanie, realising Adrienne knew more than she was letting on.

'All his life, Mom. Am I the only one who noticed that Brad has always been smitten with Angel? He has been puppy-eyed over her for her for years.'

'Stop it, Adrienne,' shouted Paul, slamming his fork down. 'That's absurd! Are you out of your *mind*?'

'Dad, what is really so absurd about this? Is it because Angel's *black*?'

Paul stood up and stormed off without finishing his supper. Melanie gave her daughter a look of remonstration.

'Addie, did you have to take it there?'

'Well, somebody had to, Mom. I just don't see what the big deal is about Brad and Angel.'

'Ange is your sister, Addie. It's incestuous! Frankly, I'm so disappointed in both of them.'

'Mom, we're not related!' Adrienne rolled her eyes. She wasn't really interested in what her mother had to say. She stood up and took a plate of food to Angel, which she pushed aside and refused to eat. Her face was wet with tears as she mourned Brad's abrupt departure from her life. Adrienne put a consoling arm around her and they cried together.

The following morning Angel woke to a reassuring call from Bradley to tell her that he had arrived safely in Johannesburg. He went on to assure her that he loved and cared for her deeply and that the distance would not diminish his love. After telling him how much she loved him, Angel hung up – only to see Melanie standing in the doorway. Her insides flipped as she wondered how much of their conversation Melanie had overheard. Gingerly, Melanie entered the room and perched on the end of the bed next to Angel.

'Ange, we didn't send Brad away to punish you. We love you and what you and Brad are doing is wrong. Paul had to send Brad away.'

'Mom, you don't understand; I'm in love with Brad.'

'Angel, honey, you're underage. You shouldn't even be having sex! You're too young to appreciate what love is. Besides, people in love do no act as irresponsibly as you and Brad have. Did you and Brad ever talk about STDs, pregnancy or the consequences of sleeping around?'

Angel lifted her head and stared at her mother.

'Sleeping around? Is that what you think we're doing, Mom?'

'Angel, you have to forget about Brad in romantic terms – he's your brother. Please focus on your schoolwork; you're too young to have this kind of relationship. You'll meet lots of men when you're older.'

'I don't want other men. I want Brad!'

Paul was standing at the door; he had been eavesdropping on their conversation.

'I don't care how old you are, Angel, it's never going to happen. Over my dead body will you and Brad be together.'

Angel stared back at him, a deep loathing in her eyes. It would have to be over his dead body then. He wasn't going to stand between her and the love of her life.

Bradley started his first year at Oxford in September 1993 while Zimbabwe was still reeling from the impact of the 1992 drought that had precipitated a recession. Angel, trying to stave off her own depression, was grappling with her Cambridge O-levels. While Zimbabwe had decolonised, the curriculum had not. In 1994 she embarked on her A-levels, the two-year course in preparation for university. While she had hoped to study in London, where she would be closer to Bradley, her dream was dashed when Adrienne started applying to South African universities. She knew she would have to follow the same route of going down south.

The year 1994 had heralded the first democratic elections and the political landscape was changing. Nelson Mandela became president, while Robert Mugabe was knighted by the Queen. None of these events moved Angel. They paled in comparison to a call from Bradley or a letter sealed with a 'Kiss from a Rose', which was now their new song. They spoke all the time, their conversations primed towards the day in the future when they'd be reconciled. They had a concrete plan in place, premised on her eventual move to South Africa. There, they would be able to meet up, unfettered by Paul's authority. Similarly, Angel would be free to travel to see Bradley in London. They just had to get through the next two years.

When Angel embarked on her final year in 1995, the country was plunged into another drought, while the economy continued to suffer in the throes of the World Bank-sponsored Economic Structural Adjustment Programme. Rising inflation, declining wages and growing unemployment were the least of Angel's worries as she buried herself in Geography, Physical Science and Maths and studied conscientiously to ensure she got the grades that would secure her university entrance. Alanis Morissette kept her company through the late nights. Adrienne left for the University of Cape Town, but it was in her absence that Angel started to flourish, finishing school without Adrienne to shepherd her through it. This also afforded her the opportunity to grow into herself and out of Adrienne's shadow. While she missed her sister, Adrienne was bad at communicating and would send an email once a quarter and call every now and then. Through their sporadic communication, Angel learnt that she had settled well into her veterinary science programme. Luke was there too, studying viticulture and oenology, so they had moved in together into an apartment off-campus. While their love life was flourishing, Angel felt like hers was floundering. She physically missed Bradley and that was not something their lengthy long-distance trunk calls could diminish.

Their monthly telephone bills were evidence of the long-standing communication that disheartened Melanie. She knew she couldn't expect them to never talk again – they'd always have the sibling connection – but she was wary that they were fuelling their romantic one. While she had not read them, she saw the letters postmarked from London. Paul had too. He opened every one and sealed them again.

'I'm going to put a stop to this shit once and for all,' declared Paul one morning.

'Paul, they're not having sex, that much we know, and we can't ban them from talking to each other.'

'Melanie, your naïveté scares me sometimes,' replied Paul. 'I'm enough of this nonsense.'

For his twenty-first birthday, Paul and Melanie handed Bradley the deed to his trust fund, thus allowing him to access the millions set aside for him since birth. The lawyers had drafted the papers, but Paul had instructed them to insert an addendum: a caveat that stated that if Brad pursued any romantic relationship with Angel Velile Williams, he would forfeit all funds. The financial umbilical cord would be cut off and severed for life and he would have to forge ahead in life without the millions bequeathed to him.

Angel had written her last exam the day she got the call from Bradley. She was preparing to go out and celebrate with Carla.

'Hey, lover!' she crooned into the phone.

'Hello, Angel,' he replied, his voice subdued.

'Everything all right?'

He usually sounded so happy when they spoke, but now he sounded brusque and offish. She was taken aback.

'You know, Gel, I've been thinking things over these last few days. Dad's right.' On hearing 'Dad's right', Angel instinctively knew the conversation was about to take a turn for the worse. Anxiety forced her to settle on the chair and she began to coil the telephone cord around her wrist, listening to Bradley's stilted delivery.

'I was wrong to pursue you, to use you for my own selfish gratification. I crossed a line that I should never have. I violated you, and for this I am truly sorry.'

His words deflated her buoyant mood. Gone were the tender words that evoked warm and fuzzy feelings inside of her.

'Ange? Are you still there?' he asked.

She cleared her throat.

'Yes, Brad, I'm here.'

'Say something,' he prompted. 'Anything.'

'I don't know what to say,' she replied. She was shocked and taciturn.

'You will always be my sister, Gel. That's something we will always have. We can't ever be anything else, you and I. I'm going to go for therapy to deal with this and I suggest you do the same.'

'Okay, Brad. Bye, Brad.'

She hung up . The phone rang again, much louder than the ringing in her head. She ignored it. Instead, she sat and replayed their conversation over and over in her head. Pause. Rewind. Replay. When Carla arrived to pick her up for the party, she still hadn't moved. They were supposed to be meeting up with other girls for the end-of-exams celebration.

'You okay, Angel? You're not even dressed!' bemoaned Carla.

'I'm too tired to go out,' replied Angel. 'I think it's the exhaustion.'

'You just need a shot of Bioplus,' replied Carla dismissively. 'We're going to party!'

Her effervescent mood still failed to rub onto Angel, who was slowly fetching her scattered emotions from all over the floor and plastering on a brave face.

That night Angel drank without prompting, hoping to numb herself of any emotion. Uncharacteristically, she danced on the table and promptly toppled off. She went home with Ant who she had bumped into. The plan was to have sex, but as they were getting undressed, she started throwing up. Every cocktail, every tot of vodka, every shot of tequila was spewed onto his bedroom floor. He wasn't impressed, but he helped her out of her clothes, showered her and wrapped her in a towel and then put her to bed. Angel cried in his arms. He thought she was dying of embarrassment, not suspecting it was anything more than that. When Ant dropped her at home the next morning, in his blue Nissan Pulsar that spluttered noisily, Paul was standing on the porch with Melanie. They both looked at their watches as Angel made her way to the stairs. A raging monologue was taking place in Angel's head as to whether to greet them or ignore them. Paul quashed the idea when he greeted her.

'This the time to come home?' he asked.

'I'm sorry,' replied Angel. 'We stayed out too late last night.'

'You couldn't have had the courtesy to call?' asked Melanie.

'I'm sorry, Mom,' apologised Angel, looking down at her feet. 'It won't happen again.'

'Damn right it won't' shouted Paul. 'You're grounded and don't you dare come home with some coloured oke again!'

'What?'

'You heard me,' replied Paul. 'Don't be cheeky with me, Angel. This is my home and I set the rules.'

Angel swallowed hard, fighting back the tears that threatened to surge forth. She apologised again and retreated to her room where she closed the door on her pain. She threw herself on the bed and convulsed with tears. In the background Roxette was crooning plaintively. It must have been love.

Part 4: The Occupation

The people who occupy a territory determine the
nature of the society in that region.

Arthur Kemp

31

Mating Mariska

From the time Bradley started university in London, he lived off-campus in a charming two-bedroom apartment in the affluent suburb of Clapham. The flat was owned by his parents, one of their many assets scattered around the globe. He resented that he still lived under his father's roof, even if it wasn't on the same continent. He hated that his parents still pulled the purse strings of his future. And he hated himself even more that he hadn't had the courage to walk away from his inheritance but had walked away from love.

He hated coming home to an empty apartment every day. While his mother had done a fantastic job of furnishing it with stylish quintessentially English furniture, he still felt alone and desolate. The emptiness was a reflection of his life. He wondered whether he shouldn't have stayed in residence instead; at least that would have staved off his loneliness a bit. But Paul had reminded him that the flat didn't cost anything, so it wouldn't be financially prudent to pay to stay somewhere else. He switched on his stereo so at least he could hear voices other than those in his head. Sinéad O'Connor's euphonious voice strained over 'Nothing Compares to You'. He exhaled noisily; some songs were triggering.

He made his way into the kitchen and looked in the fridge. There was nothing there aside from a wedge of cheese and a carton of fruit juice; he'd forgotten to go shopping. He slapped his forehead – he had actually passed a Marks & Spencer every day on his way home. He closed the fridge and decided that he wasn't hungry after all. But the stirring in his belly would not abate so he ordered Chinese food to be delivered. While he waited, he got into the shower and let the water rain down over him. He started to think about Angel and the fun they once had when he snuck into the bathroom when she was in there and they had made love in the shower. The thrill was always heightened by the fact that they could get caught – until they were. They would make love over and over again, as if tempting fate. Insatiable, their desire had no beginning or end. It was like playing a CD with one song flowing into the next.

As the water ran down his face, he felt the tears emerge. He cried as the pain of letting Angel go filled him to the brim with nothingness. They were supposed to be together, making plans for a future. He questioned his life choices. When he felt like this he wanted to call his father and tell him to screw his trust fund, but he knew that he needed to get his degree and not get emotional about it.

It tore him apart that he and Angel were no longer in each other's lives, tangled like grapevines. Sometimes the only thing he wanted after a long day was to pick up the phone and call her, just to hear the sweet timbre of her voice, but he couldn't even do that any more. He loved her so much and his need and desire for her were so deep it was painful. He scrubbed his body hard as though he was trying to remove all memory of her touch. Of her soft hands gently caressing his torso. Of her lips forming small wet kisses across his body. He could smell her as though she was in the shower with him. Sometimes she came to him in his dreams and they would make love. Bradley would wake up sweating and would be filled with frustration when he realised she wasn't there. That she was no longer a part of his life. He turned off the shower and reached for a towel. He was still drying himself when the doorbell rang. Must be his food order, he thought.

He never had many visitors – nor did he have that many friends. His mates from school never stopped by and the only socialising they did was when they went pub-crawling. He liked to drink and it had become a 'passion' of sorts. The doorbell rang again.

'Coming!' he shouted, wrapping the towel around his waist.

As he opened the door, it he realised it wasn't his Chinese food, but a girl by the name of Mariska from his Italian class. He had to take a language as one of his courses and she was studying Linguistics so that is how they had met.

'Hi, Brad,' she said. 'I hope I'm not too early.'

Bradley stared at her blankly, trying to register why she was there.

'You said you needed help with your assignment and I offered to help, remember?'

'Oh yeah,' replied Bradley, wanting to slap himself for being so forgetful. 'Thank you for coming,' he said, opening the door wider and inviting her in. Mariska had great legs and was showing them off in a flared mini skirt with a grey sweater. Her tousled dark brown hair was secured in a ponytail and her emerald-green eyes sparkled when she spoke. She had a well-defined face with a sharp jawline and a long, pointed nose. Bradley quickly excused himself and retreated to the bedroom to dress.

Mariska's gaze shifted from his muscled torso to the well-appointed surroundings of the flat. She was impressed; his wasn't typical student digs. She settled on the couch, fluffing the yellow damask cushions behind her. When Brad returned, the Chinese food arrived and he apologised for ordering only one carton and suggested they share. She declined the offer.

'I actually have food in the car. Greek moms, you know! When I told her we would be studying together she insisted that I bring some food in case you were starving!'

Brad laughed. 'Your mom sounds like mine – a feeder!'

They went down to Mariska's car and took out a picnic basket laden with food: a Greek salad, moussaka, dolmades and warm shish kebabs. Mrs Georgio was clearly a great cook and Bradley tucked into the feast.

'Home-cooked food always tastes better,' marvelled Bradley, wolfing down a kebab. He could taste the love and dedication in every mouthful.

'I should do this more often,' teased Mariska.

'Can you even cook?'

'Yes, I can!' replied Mariska. 'I make a killer instant pudding!'

They both laughed and when the food was finished Mariska reached for a bottle of wine from Brad's well-stocked wine rack. They sipped on the wine as they worked through the assignment. Mariska was a natural at languages and told Bradley that she wanted to be a translator. The wine flowed, glasses refilled until the bottle lay empty on the floor.

'I really shouldn't,' Mariska said when Brad offered to open another bottle. 'I still need to drive home.'

'Then sleep over,' suggested Bradley. He was really enjoying her company. 'Take my bed. I'll sleep on the couch.'

'Hmmm … okay,' agreed Mariska, after considering Brad's suggestion for a moment.

They had gone to bed together, the wine loosening any inhibitions either may have had. Darkness receded and gave way to the dawn of a new day and Bradley woke up hungover and got up right away, immediately regretful of what had happened. Mariska rolled over and stretched her arms out … An empty space beside her. Where was Bradley? How had she not felt him move? When had she fallen asleep?

Bradley was out on the balcony, drinking a mug of coffee. He couldn't help feeling guilty about what had happened the previous night, that he had taken advantage of Mariska. The fact that he had been feeling alone, both emotionally and physically, didn't justify the way he felt he had used her. A physical release – that's all it had been for him. He didn't feel anything for her. He was about to go inside and apologise to her when he felt her snake her arms around him. He exhaled deeply. This wasn't going to be easy; he had made an impression on her, it seemed.

'Hey,' she said in a dreamy voice.

'Hey, Mariska,' he said, disengaging himself and turning to face her.

He put his mug down on the table and gently cupped her face in his hands.

'Mariska ...' he began. 'Last night—'

She could read the solemn expression on his face and his grave tone told her that he wasn't about to say what she wanted him to.

'I don't know how to tell you this without hurting your feelings, but ...' continued Bradley.

'You don't have to say anything, Brad. I know what happened shouldn't have happened.'

Bradley felt relieved; at least they were on the same page.

'I'm really sorry, Mariska.'

Mariska was dismissive. 'Don't overthink it, Brad. You and I are cool.'

With the awkwardness behind them, the two went on to become friends. She would spend many such nights at Brad's flat, but nothing physical ever happened between them. Sometimes they would go to the West End and catch a show together, or they'd go clubbing, eat out or stroll through the city together. Mariska introduced him to her friends and slowly his life began to be populated with new characters and colourful conversations that often went on until the early hours of the morning. Mariska was always there. Dependable and reliable Mariska with the laughing eyes.

32

Sounds of blackness

University offered Angel the liberation to explore her identity beyond the confines of Belle Acres. She deliberately chose to study at the University of Pretoria, far from the influence of Adrienne at the University of Cape Town. Melanie and Paul accompanied her to orientation week. She'd been hoping to go alone with Melanie, but Paul tagged along too, steering her through the enrolment process at the Faculty of Natural and Agricultural Sciences. There had been no negotiation about the courses she would take; Paul was quite clear that she was to come home every holiday and start working on the farm.

'There are no free rides here,' he stated.

Angel was allocated a room in the student residence. But when Pauline, her startled roommate, found out she was black, she quietly arranged to move out. While Angel had always been aware of racism, she had never experienced it quite so blatantly. She had grown up sharing a room with Adrienne, so that had never been an issue. Hell, they'd even shared a crib. When Pauline moved out, Angel wasn't sure how to deal with the rejection. When she mentioned it to her parents, Paul had been dismissive – just a matter of personal preference, he said – but Melanie was adamant that it was indeed racism. While they had never had deliberate conversations about racism and discrimination, this would be one of many more first-hand encounters Angel would have.

So it was that Angel got a new roommate, a black girl by the name

of Anele Ngcobo, and they became firm and fast friends. Anele introduced her to two of her own friends, Tshepo Mabuyane and Seipati
Molefe. They were initially curious about Angel's background; it was
odd that a black girl carried a white surname and was unable to speak
any of the vernacular languages. Angel was about to fish out her Florida story, but decided to be honest about how she came to be adopted
by the Williams family. She had expected condescension, but instead
Tshepo had revealed that her grandmother had also been a domestic
worker and had gone on to educate her mother who had become an
accomplished lawyer. Angel felt a liberating sense of relief.

Once they got past that initial hurdle, Angel soon became part
of their circle. She even started referring to herself as Velile, dropping
the name Angel completely. She began to resent that she was not able
to converse in Sesotho, Xhosa and Zulu and envied her friends who
switched seamlessly between the various languages, which they often did when they claimed to have exhausted their 'English bundles'.
They called her *mlungu* and even though it was used with affection, it
secretly riled Angel. She felt excluded from the cultural loop.

Anele was studying African history and started to school Angel
on her origins.

'Do you realise we are related?' she asked Angel one afternoon
over lunch.

'What do you mean?' replied Angel, pushing her hamburger
aside.

'Your King Mzilikazi fled here during the Mfecane.'

'Okay, you need to tell me this juice,' replied Angel, perking up
with interest.

Anele began to narrate to her how, when Mzilikazi came of age,
he joined the military and became a lieutenant under Shaka Zulu.
Anele herself was a proud Zulu girl from Vryheid, so she enumerated
the strength of the Zulu Kingdom under the indomitable Shaka Zulu.

'King Shaka adored Mzilikazi and made him the commander of
amabutho of the Khumalo clan. He was like his right-hand man!'

As a favoured general, Mzilikazi held court in close proximity to Shaka Zulu and became an acute observer of his methods. On his return from a successful military campaign, Mzilikazi did not surrender the captured cattle, as was the modus operandi. While Shaka Zulu did not assume any impertinence behind this act, it certainly was intentional on the part of Mzilikazi. And so, when Shaka sent a group of envoys to Mzilikazi to enquire about the missing loot, Mzilikazi – in a display of wilful insolence – returned the envoys empty-handed and held onto the plunder. Mzilikazi was not stupid and knew that this move was likely to earn him the enmity of King Shaka, so he quickly evacuated his people. As a fugitive, fleeing the wrath of Shaka, he and his renegade nation travelled up north in search of a new home, clashing en route with laagers of migrating Boers. This forced Mzilikazi even further north, until he and his followers finally crossed the Limpopo River. They were rolling stones, gathering tribes that they assimilated into the Ndebele way of life. Mzilikazi eventually settled in around 1838 in what is known as Matabeleland South Province, where they established the Ndebele kingdom.

'The Basotho called them *maTebele* and this is how it came to be known as Matabeleland.'

Anele went on to expound about the territory in the east. *Etshonalanga* was inhabited by *amatshona* – or the tribes that came to be collectively known as Shona. Having never studied African history, this was an 'aha' moment for Angel. She could write essays on Napoleon Bonaparte, but nothing on Mzilikazi, who established his Ndebele kingdom bounded by the Zambezi River in the north, the Limpopo River in the south and Mashonaland in the east.

Mzilikazi initially established his nation at Intabazinduna, with Inyathi as his capital, but the settlement was later abandoned when his senior wife, Queen Loziba, died and the nation migrated to Mhlahlandlela in the Matopo district. Mzilikazi often initiated random cattle raids into Mashonaland. Having adopted the militancy of Shaka Zulu, the Matabele were aggressive. Once they had massacred the men, they would incorporate the women and children into their own kingdom. Until his death, Mzilikazi would successfully defend the Ndebele kingdom from encroachment by the whites.

'We need to accord you honorary Zulu status,' declared Anele. 'You are one of us!'

'Bayete!' piped up Seipati, making them all erupt with laughter.

After their conversation, Anele took Angel shopping in downtown Pretoria. They purchased a white T-shirt, which she teamed with a black skirt, and Anele brought her a beaded belt to wear around her waist and elaborate neckpieces for around her neck. She wore sandals made of leather and cowhide. Kitted out in Zulu regalia, they held a brief ceremony in her room and Anele made Angel recite her clan names:

'Nzima, Phakathi waboNkosi, Mabhud'akaMthiyane, Nkuni kazothiw' amakhosikaz. Gavu elimnyama ngentamo, Juba lapha kuyababa kuthi hheeee, wena owagogoda umuntu ngenduku yakhe, abanye bemgogoda ngezabo!'

Anele, Tshepo and Seipati ululated and danced around her. Angel felt a strong sense of belonging, of kith and kinship. Even after her initiation ceremony – and after Anele taught her how to wrap them – Angel continued to wear Zulu headscarves and accessorised with Zulu beads around her neck, arms and ankles. Melanie was intrigued when she saw Angel and also started wearing Zulu beads, prompting Paul to sing Odyssey's 'Going Back To My Roots' off-key, and Angel couldn't help but laugh.

From that point on, Angel was intentional about embracing her Africanness. She started to make a concerted effort to blacken herself. When she was growing up, there had been no markers for blackness and her life had been devoid of black music, black art and even black food. But now, in this new, as yet unchartered area of her life, she discovered Kwaito music and fell hopelessly in love with the group TKZee. Posters of Tokollo were plastered all over her wall as she thought he was the hottest man she had ever seen. While R&B pop culture started to infuse her life and she was dressed like Da Brat in crop tops and baggy jeans that hung off her bum, she still wore a Zulu headwrap. The girls introduced her to Boom Shaka and suddenly Angel saw in Thembi Seete someone who looked like her. She started to embrace her curves, her hips and her bum. She started falling in love with herself and who she was.

Sometimes her hair was braided and adorned with Zulu beads. Paul often joked that she was going through her 'black phase'.

'Sounds of blackness is home,' he would say when she was home for the holidays, which only served to piss Angel off even more. She deliberately ate in the canteen with the workers and was intentional about making friends there. She made a concerted effort to start learning isiNdebele and started hanging out at the compound on weekends. It was during this time that she sought out her grannies' graves. They lay side by side: Busisiwe Mabusi Nleya 1928–1977 and Khanyisile Khiwa Nleya 1945–1977. Slowly she was starting to gather up the jigsaw puzzle pieces of her life and piece together the identity of Angel Velile Williams. Who was she? What was she? Where did she belong? For the longest time, she had felt like she was floating around with no real roots. She had no markers for her identity so she now clung to whatever she thought they were.

33

University of life

In her quest to fit in, Angel started dating Andile Thwala, who was studying Engineering. They had met in the library when he was poring over textbooks piled high with titles like *Fluid Mechanics* and *System Engineering*.

The attraction was immediate and she spent a great deal of her first year combusting energy in Andile's bed. He was a scholarship student, straight out of the hood of Soweto. He, however, was always cash-strapped, whereas she was always flush with cash, so her girl-friends were wary of his intentions. They cautioned her to be careful of not 'being used', but Angel dismissed their concerns. She felt validated by the attention she got from Andile and would do anything for him. Melanie and Paul were generous when they wanted to be, but on occasion, when she was too embarrassed to ask them for more money, Adrienne was only a phone call away. Her first year passed by in a blur of binge drinking and riotous parties – many of which she funded, so she rapidly became popular. Deep down, however, she knew it was all superficial, but still she craved acceptance and desperately wanted to belong.

The result was that she failed four core modules in Economics and Financial Accounting that first year. She didn't just fail – she failed spectacularly. She sat staring at her exam slip with 30%, 35%, 39% and 24%. Andile was nonchalant about it and said it wasn't the end of the world and she could simply repeat the exams.

'You don't know Paul Williams,' Angel replied.

That night, while the girls were celebrating getting through their first year, Angel had far too much to drink. At the club, Andile started kissing Seipati in full view of Angel and, devastated, she fled. Andile ran after her, claiming it was a mistake.

'I know what I saw!' she screamed, unsteady on her feet.

'*Uyabhora*, man!' he replied. 'Let me take you home.'

'We're both going home. I won't let you come back for her!'

'There you go with your insecurities,' replied Andile. 'Always a killjoy.'

They climbed into Angel's VW Golf. Despite not having a driver's licence, Andile always drove. When Angel started crying, he turned on the radio to drown out her cries, Arthur's 'Kaffir' blaring from the stereo. Andile stepped on the accelerator and Angel stopped crying when she saw the dial go from 100 kilometres an hour to 160.

'Andile! Slow down – you're going too fast.'

'Fuck off,' he shouted, pushing his foot down even harder on the accelerator.

He turned up the volume on the stereo, with Arthur now screaming in Angel's ears. She held her hands up ... and that was the last thing she remembered.

A head-on collision with a long-haulage truck on the N3.

The car crumpled like a shell and all Angel could remember was her feeling squashed up in the passenger seat. Her head was badly hurt and blood oozed down her face. Then, suddenly, she was aware of the car door being opened by two portly women in long, flowing black dresses. Her vision fuzzy, she couldn't see them clearly. They unstrapped her from her seat and carefully extricated her from the car, going to great lengths to ensure they didn't hurt her further. She could feel the larger buxom woman breathing raggedly, exhausted by the effort. The other worked quietly, but tirelessly. They eventually managed to pull her from the car and deposit her body on the side of the road. She was unconscious when she was found.

It remained unclear as to how Angel had managed to survive the wreck. Andile died on the spot. Although she mourned the debilitating loss, she also quietly thanked the good Samaritans who had saved her life; this, it seemed, was a pivotal moment in her life, finally realising that she was not alone, that there were guardian angels looking out for her. But now she had been left to pick up the pieces of her life, and had to come to terms with her dismal performance at university. Naturally, Paul was livid, but Melanie remained calm and collected.

'You can always rewrite the exams, Angel. Maybe Agriculture just isn't for you. Don't stress too much – just focus on getting better.'

'She's just wasting her life with all the drinking and partying. They're all the same; these kids will never amount to anything. It doesn't matter how much we do for them,' said Paul, acidly.

His words stung.

'Paul! Be kind ... She's just come out of a really bad accident,' admonished Melanie. She then turned to Angel and suggested she might want to start going to therapy again.

'She doesn't need therapy!' shouted Paul. 'This is the result of bad company and bad choices. Is this it, Angel? Is this the path you've chosen for yourself?'

'I'm sorry,' replied Angel softly, folding and unfolding her hands in her lap.

She was reminded of the day when Paul smacked her for setting fire to Adrienne's doll's house. She felt that small.

Having to spend December's summer holidays with her leg in a cast, she was in a sour mood; sullen-faced, she hardly left her room. Bradley sent a postcard from Brighton, 'Get well soon' scribbled on the back in his untidy scrawl. Postcard from hell, she thought as she shredded it. Instead of making her feel better, the card made her feel worse. In cruel irony, the radio began to play The Cardigans' 'Lovefool' and she couldn't reach her ghetto blaster to turn it off. She started weeping with the chorus, finally crying herself to sleep. When she woke, two women in black toga dresses were standing at the foot of the bed. Her heart raced erratically when she recognised them from the scene of the accident. They were the women who had rescued her, but now a deeper realisation struck her: she knew them. She wanted to acknowledge them, to thank them, but while her mouth was wide open, no words came out. The radio was still on, No Doubt singing 'Don't Speak' almost as if to reinforce her silence and she stuttered in frustration.

'You're better than this, Velile,' said the younger albino granny. 'We didn't save you so that you could drown in self-pity.'

Angel continued to mutter a mouthful of nothingness, desperate to respond but unable to. In her sobriety, she now knew where she had seen them before. Melanie had shown her pictures of her grandmothers at her parents' wedding when she was much younger. It was her albino grandmother who really stood out for her.

'You need to pull yourself together,' said the old woman. 'We're counting on you.' She scribbled on Angel's plaster cast and the two then turned their backs and left. Angel woke up screaming – she had suddenly found her voice. She felt awkward when Melanie came rushing through the door and turned on the lights.

'Sorry, Mom, I didn't mean to wake you up. It was just a bad dream.'

'It's okay, Angel,' Melanie replied, hugging her. 'I'm here for you. *We* are here for you.'

Angel would have dismissed the dream as a nightmare, but then she saw the words 'We love you' engraved on her cast.

Later that day, Angel decided to pull herself out of her mood and limped her way to visit her grannies' graves, picking fresh peonies from the garden and laying them on the graves.

As it turned out, the vision was instrumental in Angel pulling herself up by her bootstraps. While she still hung out with Anele, she stopped drinking and partying and began to focus all her efforts on getting through her degree. After Paul blatantly refused, Melanie had graciously agreed to pay the tuition for her to repeat and Angel made sure she passed every module with distinction. That, in turn, set the tone for the rest of her varsity years. She finally completed her degree in 1999 and was awarded the Vice Chancellor's prize for the best results. With Paul and Melanie seated in the front row at her graduation, she was glad to have proved Paul wrong. He clapped the loudest and stood up when she was capped. Adrienne and her long-term boyfriend, Luke, were there to share in the moment, just as Angel had done for them the previous year.

Angel's euphoria was, however, short-lived when she spotted Bradley in the audience with his girlfriend, Mariska, who up until then had only ever been mentioned in passing. Angel felt her stomach churn with anxiety. Bradley had not been home in more than six years and the only reason he would be back was if he had met someone and it was really serious. Mariska was everything Angel wasn't: slim and green-eyed, with tousled dark brown hair that cascaded down her back. She put on a brave face as they posed for family photographs, but Angel was feeling overwhelmed by her insecurities. She couldn't help think she was the black sheep of the family. She hadn't touched a drink since the car accident, but that night at the dinner celebrations she reached for the bottle of champagne.

'Angel, are you sure that's a good idea?' said Melanie.

'It's just one glass, for crying out loud!' countered Paul and egged her on as they toasted to her success.

What was supposed to have been a beautiful night was blighted by Mariska's presence. For years, Angel had secretly entertained thoughts of being reconciled with Bradley. That somehow they would find their way back to each other. Mariska's presence was a rude reminder that none of that would ever happen. Her supposed happy ending was now tainted and bittersweet.

34

The belle of Belle Acres

As the turn of the century loomed, the entire Williams family converged on Belle Acres for the hustle and bustle of the Christmas holidays. Melanie was thrilled; it had been years since they had all been together under one roof. Even Granny Belle flew in. They tried to get her to use a wheelchair but she stubbornly refused. She was a whole eighty years, balancing on her walking stick, which she raised and poked at people at will. Her grey hair framed her face and shone in the sunlight. Her face was lined with deep wrinkles that looked like furrows in a cornfield that had just been ploughed. Even at her advanced age, her eyes were alert, despite being weighed down by heavy bags under them.

'Hello, Mabusi,' she said to Angel, much to Angel's annoyance.

'It's Angel,' she replied pointedly.

'Oh sorry, Angel, it must be my dementia.'

Granny Belle had been diagnosed with early-onset dementia in her sixties and her memory and focus had become progressively worse over the years.

And then, a few minutes later, 'Mabusi, please make me a cup of tea with a slice of lemon. Only you know how to make it the way I like it.'

Angel rolled her eyes, but marched to the kitchen and made the tea. Compliance was easier than trying to correct Granny Belle, who stubbornly clung to her old ways. Standing on the sidelines, watching the heartfelt exchanges and reunions, Angel was probably the only one annoyed by the onslaught of guests and all the hugging and kissing.

Granny Belle had travelled with Graham and Jane. The couple had no children, Graham always quite categorical that he did not want any. Jane was a tall, slender woman with dark hair and dark eyes and, more receptive towards Angel, and reached out to hug her.

Paul's sister, Estelle, who looked like a younger and better-preserved version of her mother, was with her husband, Danie. Danie was in his sixties, with a balding head and piercing green eyes encircled by a silver-grey beard. They had two grown children, both of whom had declined the invitation. This was a relief as it spared them all the onslaught of four noisy children running amok in the house. So it was a Christmas reunion for the Williams siblings and their mother. Had Gregory been alive, he would have completed the family portrait.

Bradley and Mariska flew in from London and, while Mariska was bubbly, with a sunny disposition, it wasn't enough to thaw the iciness Angel felt. After everyone had settled in, they all went on a hike led by Graham, who was determined to show off the bush-tracking skills he had gathered during his time in the Selous Scouts. He now worked on a game farm in Namibia and Jane was a freelance writer.

They had a picnic on the grassy riverbank. Melanie had prepared a platter of cold meats and cheese and the Chardonnay flowed freely. After lunch, Brad went canoeing with Mariska. Imagining them navigating the river, choked in places by tall, slender reeds and papyrus that swayed gently in the breeze, Angel felt like he was rowing over their shared memories. Had he forgotten how they had swum naked in the river after he had made love to her for the first time on the bank? Angel was immediately assailed by the memory.

Needing an escape, she set off to visit her grannies buried side by side in the cemetery, little wooden plaques identifying their graves. Angel made a silent pledge that one day she would build them proper tombstones so that they would not seem so obscure and irrelevant.

Angel greeted her grannies with reverence and apologised for being away for so long. She busied herself clearing the overgrown weeds around the graves and plucked dwarf red poppies that were growing wild and laid them on the graves. Then she sat on the twin mounds that had flattened with time and spoke to her grannies earnestly, articulating her constant sense of desolation, of feeling out of place.

'*Linjani boGogo?* I feel so lost. Unloved. I'm so lonely here.'

She started to weep, crying softly, her tears falling on their graves, wetting the ochre-red soil.

'Can you even hear me!' she sobbed, overwhelmed by frustration and feeling ignored.

It was like she was speaking into a void of nothingness. She got up and walked back to the house. When she arrived back, Melanie was in the kitchen preparing salads and Graham had started the fire for the braai. She could see the smoke coiling into the air accompanied by raucous laughter.

'Are you joining us?' Melanie asked Angel hopefully.

'Yes,' replied Angel, throwing her arms around her.

Melanie hugged her back with equal fervour and Angel sobbed into her chest until her tears subsided.

'I know this is hard for you,' said Melanie. 'I know what you are going through. I loved someone once before Paul. We couldn't be together, so I know how you feel, but you will get through this,' said Melanie in a reassuring voice.

Angel was surprised. 'I always thought Paul was your first love.'

'He wasn't my first, no, but he's certainly my last.'

Angel hugged her back and felt that she was being heard. Melanie wasn't addressing her just as a parent but rather as a woman. She knew she needed to move on with her life, so she resolved to put on a sunny facade and join in the camaraderie.

The merrymaking continued long after the last steak had been polished off and, one by one, the guests began to plead exhaustion and went to bed. When Angel was left with Graham, she knew this was her cue to leave. She was tired of hearing about how Mugabe had fucked up the country and how it had gone to the dogs. She headed off to the Jacuzzi, martini cocktail in hand. She'd lost track of how many she had consumed. As she sat in the water, she felt randy and decided that, since she was alone, she would play with herself, the jets of the water spraying between her legs.

'Can I join you?' asked Bradley, who didn't wait for her to respond and climbed into the water and sat opposite her. Angel felt embarrassed and wondered how long he had been standing there, observing her. She held her hand to her chest, a startled expression on her face.

'I thought you were asleep.'

'That was just an excuse to get away. When Uncle Graham started his Rhodie stories, I said I was tired.'

They both laughed, the water rippling with their energy.

'I don't know how Jane puts up with it,' responded Angel.

'She doesn't. She was the first to head off to bed, if you recall.'

They laughed again as they recalled how fed-up Jane had looked.

'He gets like that when he's had too much to drink. Starts talking about the Bush War.'

'God help us. He must just write a book and get over it,' joked Angel.

There was a pause and Bradley stretched his legs until his foot touched the apex between Angel's legs. A voice in her head was telling her to get out of the water, but another was telling her to stay. She was conflicted. When Brad's foot slowly started rubbing her she knew it was game over for her. She expelled a deep breath, her breasts beckoning seductively to him beneath the water.

'It feels good to be back,' he smiled, his eyes not leaving hers.

Angel couldn't conceal the effect his proximity had on her. Beneath the water, her thighs were shaking and so was the glass she was still holding in her hand.

'How long are you here for?' she asked, trying to pretend nothing was happening in the warm current of water.

'Just until the 27th of December, and then we'll spend two days in Kariba and another two at Victoria Falls. And then it's New Year's Eve in Cape Town. Are you joining us?'

'No, I'm not,' replied Angel indignantly. 'And, besides, we need to start preparing the farm for the new season.'

Bradley manoeuvred himself in the water, brushing against her. The small talk was boring him, a mindless distraction from the real undercurrent of passion between them.

'Come here,' said Bradley, pulling her closer. She could feel his warm breath on her shoulder. Angel still shivered at his touch and couldn't understand why after all this time she still responded to him in that way. What was it about him that made her heart beat so fast?

'I want to plough you,' he added seductively.

She felt a jolt of electricity run through her when he placed his hand on her back and she started stroking his bulging erection through his wet shorts.

She straddled him, easing herself onto him. His hands cupped her buttocks as if moulding them. It was a starless night and the area around the Jacuzzi was only dimly lit. Their mouths locked in a tumultuous kiss and they both came with the same turbulence of the water foaming around them. Angel finally pulled away as the waves of rationality and regret washed over her.

'Brad, what the fuck are we doing?' she said.

'Please don't do this, Gel. You wanted this as much as I did.'

He was incorrigible. How dare he blame her when his girlfriend was sleeping upstairs?

'Why did you kiss me?' he asked, almost shouting. 'You can't tell me you don't feel the same way about me.'

'Brad, *you* ended this, remember?'

'I can start it again, Gel. Just say the word and I will end it with Mariska tonight. Say it, Gel, and I'll do it. Tell her it's over.'

Angel could feel droplets of sweat condensing on her forehead and her exposed back.

'No, Brad! No!'

He angrily slapped his hand onto the water, causing a splash. She climbed out of the Jacuzzi and rushed back into the house. A trail of water following her footsteps.

The next day was Christmas and everyone was slow to rise, but Angel had risen with the sun. Waking up early was a force of habit for her. She swam a few laps in the shimmering sapphire Olympic-sized pool while Bradley stood on the balcony of his bedroom watching her intently. He looked at her admiringly.

She wasn't tall, but neither was she short, fitting perfectly under the crook of his shoulder. She wasn't skinny, but had undulating curves and a flat stomach dimpled by a belly button. Her hips were wide and inviting and she had long, strong, firm legs. She had dark, smooth skin that almost shone with a glowing lustre. Her hair was flattened in cornrows. Her big black eyes had an unusual power that lured people to her. She was the kind of person people always looked at even though they might dismiss her without a second thought. Her nose was pert and her mouth full and ripe. To him, she was perfection. When Angel emerged from the water, he was mesmerised by the sight of her in a white swimsuit with a plunging neckline. It was a remarkable contrast against the chocolate-coloured richness of her skin. Everything about her seemed deliberately sensual, so sensual that he was forced to suck in his breath when she walked by. He stood and watched her until Mariska saw him on the balcony and walked up behind him.

'Darling,' she crooned, snaking her arms around him.

He turned in the circle of her arms and kissed her. She could feel the bulge in his shorts.

'Let me take care of this,' she said, leading him back to the bed.

She kissed him slowly on the lips. He responded to her and that was all she needed to spur her on. She kissed him more passionately and he kissed her back with equal fervour, his hands running through her hair. They soon fell onto the carpet, his mouth roaming down her chin and her slender neck. He sat up and hurriedly pulled off her pyjama top, exposing her pert breasts, which he licked, sucked, squeezed and kneaded. It felt so good, and Mariska moaned and groaned appreciatively, encouraging him to continue. He did, licking her stomach, her thighs. He licked her all over until she was writhing helplessly with pleasure. Then he took her with swift fast strokes and they both climaxed in a frenzy.

'Aah, Gel!' he cried out.

It was a passion killer for Mariska and she felt her whole body slacken. Bradley slumped on top of her like a sack of potatoes.

'I'm sorry, Mariska,' he said, trying to smother her with kisses.

She pushed him off brusquely and made her way to the bathroom, slamming the door so hard that he felt the floor reverberate. He knocked on the door, apologising profusely for what he called a 'slip of the tongue'. It wasn't the first time that had happened; sometimes he even called out her name in his sleep.

'Will you *ever* get over her?' screamed Mariska.

'I *am* over her,' he replied. 'I swear to God, I am. I don't know where that came from. Maybe it's seeing her after all these years.'

'I knew I shouldn't have come here,' shouted Mariska. 'This was a mistake. You and I are a mistake'

He could hear her crying softly behind the door and Bradley felt wretched. When she finally emerged an hour later, they were late for Christmas lunch, which was served promptly at midday. They missed the starters of mussels in a creamy white sauce, but joined in time for the second course of a tender turkey stuffed with celery and sage served with spears of asparagus. By the time dessert was served, everyone complained that they were more stuffed than the turkey, but couldn't resist the Christmas pudding with custard. Granny Belle licked her fingers with relish before asking Angel to make her a cup of coffee.

'It's fine, I'll get it,' volunteered Adrienne.

'Why? That's why we have hired help. What do you think we pay Mabusi for?'

'Granny, that's Angel,' said Adrienne, correcting her for what must have been the hundredth time.

When Adrienne returned, Luke was down on one knee and she dropped the cup of coffee. Considering how enamoured the couple still were with each other, the proposal came as no surprise to anyone. They were enveloped in a cloud of congratulations and hugs. And then, not to be outdone, Bradley announced that he and Mariska were also getting engaged. Now *that* was a surprise to everyone, including Mariska. She and Bradley had talked about settling down one day, but it was always in passing and non-committal.

Once everyone had settled down after the surprise turn of events and once the toasts had been made, Melanie clapped her hands excitedly at the prospect of two weddings in the Williams family.

'So, any idea when you all want to get married?' asked Paul.

'We're thinking August,' replied Adrienne. 'Somewhere in the winelands.'

'April for us,' said Bradley. 'I can't wait a minute longer,' he said, gazing at Mariska, who seemed equally surprised by the urgency.

'Seal the deal, Mariska,' cheered on Granny Belle.

'This calls for another toast!' announced Paul.

With their glasses filled with Dom Pérignon, the family toasted Brad and Mariska. While they all laughed, the irony was not lost on Angel. She had been observing the couple keenly. Bradley was trying too hard and although she didn't want to say it, he was making the biggest mistake of his life.

35

For whom the wedding bell tolls

Angel was glad to leave the nineties behind and embrace the noughties and the challenges that came with it. She was a fully fledged employee at Belle Acres and proudly wore her badge as farm manager. To make room for her, Tyrone had been moved to operations. Her day now began at 6am, but by the time she had woken and had her first cup of coffee, Paul was already up. While he no longer needed to marshal operations, he was still an early riser, up at the crack of dawn, as a force of habit. He had become Angel's mentor, guiding her and training her to take over the farm one day. This was not something many 22-year-olds could boast about, but she had stepped into the role and risen to the challenge. Standing in front of the mirror, kitted out in her safari pants and shirt and brown leather Doc Martens, she felt a lot better about herself than she had in years. Her hair was braided in cornrows, a practical and easy-to-manage style for her active lifestyle on the farm. She had discarded the doek and now only wore it on weekends.

They were laying a new irrigation system and she was overseeing the process. As she drove around the farm, it continued to amaze her to see the vast tracts of bush cleared to make way for the crops. As a child, there had always seemed to be an endless stretch of bush, but most of it now accommodated the extensive crop cultivation of wheat, soya and maize, all used for the animal feed to support the growing herd of cattle. The fields were green with the sprouting maize crop that had been planted in October and had now started to ripen. The soya crop had been planted mid-November and they were rotating the cultivation of soya with winter wheat. The fields were filled with labourers pulling out weeds that competed with the soya for space. The farm's operations were still very labour intensive, but Angel was happy that they could provide jobs and therefore sustenance for thousands in the area.

After parking the bakkie at the side of the road, Angel headed through the fields on foot and, as always, was greeted with admiration. She made time to engage in small talk and crack jokes with the workers and, while her isiNdebele and Shona were not flawless, she still tried to converse with the workers as much as she could in their own languages. She was acutely aware that there were very few women in her position and it made her feel that much prouder of her accomplishments – even more so when she attended Farmers' Union meetings with Paul, confirming for her that farming was a male-dominated occupation. She was the only female farm manager and often the butt of sexist jokes.

When she was done with the field inspection, Angel passed through the dairy section to check how things were faring. This took up most of her morning and at midday she returned to the office to work on the budgets for the year ahead. She was expected to present the budget and progress to the board every quarter. The rest of her day was spent behind her computer, working out how to minimise operational costs in order to maximise profitability. She also oversaw the marketing for a product line that included cream cheese, yoghurt and dairy shakes. These were the products they exported and it was a part of the job she enjoyed immensely. She liked working with the tangible, nurturing the process from the ground until it became a unit on a spreadsheet.

Her workday typically ended at 6pm when she returned to the farmhouse for dinner with Paul and Melanie. Despite them always making her feel welcome, sometimes she couldn't help but feel like a third wheel when she was around them. She admired how enamoured they were with each other even after so many years. How they cuddled when they watched television together. Theirs was the kind of relationship she wanted for herself one day. Sometimes she felt like she was intruding on their time together and would slip off to her bedroom, using the time to flip through old family albums and listen to music. She yearned for the day that she had a family of her own.

They still trekked to the club every Friday evening, but the good thing was that more black people now fraternised there and Angel made some friends among the black farmers and managers. On weekends, she hung out at the compound with her workmates.

Apart from that, her life remained lonely, revolving almost entirely around work. It felt like too much of an effort to try to revive old high-school friendships, especially as many had now left the country anyway. And, while she missed the companionship of a man, she had no idea where to even begin on the dating scene.

January finally rolled into February and the Valentine's Day weekend of 2000 when the referendum was to be held. Angel lamented somewhat about her lack of a date, the absence of romantic love, as she shuffled along in the winding queue with Paul and Melanie as they prepared to cast their votes. Paul had given all the labourers the weekend off to vote.

It wasn't long after the resounding 'No' vote that Angel flew to Victoria Falls for Brad's wedding late one Saturday afternoon in April. It had been a deliberate decision to arrive only a day before the wedding so as not to get caught up in all the fanfare and festivities leading up to the day. Things had been awkward between them since the Christmas Eve incident in the Jacuzzi and Angel was running low on her 'keeping up appearances' reserves. From the airport, she took the waiting shuttle to the Victoria Falls Safari Lodge into which the entire wedding party had been booked. After checking in, she sat at the bar on the balcony overlooking the waterhole where elephants had converged for their own sundowners. She was soon joined by Luke and Adrienne, who had only just surfaced from an afternoon nap, and they regaled her with stories from the rehearsal dinner the night before.

'Looks like I really missed out. What's the plan for tonight?'

'Hopefully, some sleep!' replied Adrienne. 'I want to be fresh and rested for the wedding tomorrow.'

'We have Brad's bachelor party!' said Luke with a naughty grin.

'Please just make sure my brother makes it to his wedding in one piece and not too hungover,' warned Adrienne. 'Otherwise Mariska will have your head on a stake.'

'That's Steve's responsibility,' said Luke, who looked like he was raring to go.

'Well, you and I will have a chilled night together,' said Angel, looking at Adrienne.

'Absolutely,' agreed Adrienne, who was looking forward to catching up with her sister. It had been four months since Christmas and the communication between them had been erratic.

'I thought you were bringing someone to the wedding?' said Adrienne.

'I decided to swing solo,' replied Angel.

'Ahh, so you still haven't met anyone?'

The answer was no. Not since AD (Andile's Death). The accident was something she rarely spoke about, but it had been that long since she had been with someone. One or two guys had propositioned her at work, but Angel didn't want to complicate things, especially considering her position as farm manager. Adrienne immediately started scrolling through her Nokia 3310. Angel knew that look; she was looking for someone she could hook her up with.

'Don't you dare!' shrieked Angel.

They both laughed.

'Maybe I'll meet someone at the wedding,' said Angel.

'Yes, that's a real possibility actually – so I promise to stop meddling like the big sister that I am!'

The sisters bonded over vodka cocktails and Adrienne updated Angel on preparations for her August wedding. Much later, they headed to the boma for dinner and were joined by their parents and other guests from the wedding party. The mood was convivial and Angel couldn't help misting up with tears. It was after midnight when she finally got to bed, utterly exhausted. She missed breakfast, but quickly ordered room service because, with the hangover she had, there was no way she would get through the ceremony. She showered and changed into a pink satin cowl-neck dress that clung seductively to her curves. When she got downstairs to the lobby she almost collided with Granny Belle.

'You look ravishing, Mabusi. That colour really suits you.'

'Thank you,' replied Angel, without saying anything further. All she wanted was to escape Granny Belle, and so they made their way onto the shuttle that was ferrying guests to the venue. Once Granny Belle was settled in the front, Angel made her way to the back of the bus. Everyone was excited and the mood was effervescent.

'Who are you with? The bride or the groom?' asked a middle-aged white man seated next to her.

'The groom,' she replied.

The man went on to espouse how in awe he was of the beauty of Africa. He drew the words out in a lazy drawl; she'd already worked out from his accent that he was from America. He spoke animatedly about how he and his wife had toured the Victoria Falls and gone on a 'suffari' in 'Wankie' National Park. He told Angel they would be going to South 'Afreecar' after the wedding to spend a few days in Cape Town.

'You really should add Chimanimani, Nyanga and Vumba to your list before you leave Zimbabwe. That is the holy trinity of the Eastern Highlands,' suggested Angel.

'Maybe the next time we're here,' he replied. 'We're friends of the Georgios, Mariska's parents. We've known Nicoli and Chris for years. Mariska grew up right in front of our eyes – such a lovely girl. Bradley is a lucky man.'

Angel wasn't sure who was luckier, Brad or Mariska. The man

continued to rattle on about Mariska and how marvellous she was, and all the while Angel simply smiled politely. By the time the shuttle finally came to a stop at the venue near the banks of the Zambezi River, she'd had her fill of Mariska and her virtues. Angel remained in her seat, determined to lose the man, but that meant she would be forced to escort Granny Belle who was the last to disembark. Angel felt obliged to help her and so they tottered off together, hand in hand. Angel had to slow down so that Granny Belle could keep up. She was leaning on her walking stick, cursing repeatedly under her breath.

'Why couldn't they get married in a hotel like normal people? Now we have to go bundu-bashing!'

'Apparently, Mariska fell in love with the falls when they holidayed here last year,' said Angel, hoping to mollify Granny Belle.

'So many white people,' observed Granny Belle. 'I had no idea there were any left in this country.'

Granny Belle paused to catch her breath and rested one hand on her hip. After a few seconds, they resumed their slow walk.

'Should you even be walking this far?' asked Angel concerned.

'Of course,' replied Granny Belle. 'I need the exercise. I've really overdone things with all the eating and drinking since we've been here. I'll be glad when this circus is over and we can go home.'

When they finally arrived at the seating area for the ceremony, a white woman approached them and asked who they were with. The groom or the bride?

'I will sit where I want,' retorted Granny Belle. 'At my age, I've earned the right to sit wherever I want.'

The woman recoiled, slightly affronted, and then turned to Angel.

'And you, ma'am? Your name?' she asked Angel, not quite sure where to direct her while scanning the guest list.

'She's with us,' snapped Granny Belle. 'She's a Williams.'

Granny Belle was having a rare lucid moment. Angel suppressed a smile. She was filled with a strange sense of pride to be identified as a Williams, especially coming from Granny Belle's lips.

'Don't you want to sit near the front?' asked Angel.

'No. Don't you know it's always more fun at the back?' Granny Belle chuckled animatedly. 'And, besides, it will be easier for me to get up and go to the loo if we need to,' she added. 'You'll help me won't you, Mabusi? Estelle finds it annoying when I ask her. Don't ever get old, Mabusi. I've lived long past my sell-by date.'

Angel chuckled, dismissing any annoyance she should have felt at being referred to as Mabusi. She decided that for the duration of the wedding, she would make peace with being referred to as her great-grandmother. Granny Belle exhaled deeply before settling her weight on a slatted chair capped with garlands of roses. The chairs had been arranged in rows overlooking the Zambezi River and a make-shift chapel set up on the riverbank, draped with lace and wreaths of flowers.

The antelope and springbok grazing on the other side of the river formed the perfect backdrop to the nuptials. It was clearly a fascinat-ing sight for many of the international guests who were enthusiasti-cally capturing the scene on the disposable Kodak cameras that had been placed on the chairs for everyone to make use of. It was a beau-tiful day to get married and the guests were basking in the glorious heat of the afternoon sun. They had been given a choice of a parasol or hand-held fan and Angel opted for a parasol, which she held over Granny Belle, fanning herself furiously with her other hand.

Slowly the chairs filled up with guests. Granny Belle shifted slightly, not quite trusting the chair to carry her weight.

'Mabusi was a good woman,' said Granny Belle, in yet another of her rare lucid moments.

Angel perked up; it wasn't every day that she heard things said about her great-grandmother beyond her servitude.

'You know, I blamed her for sleeping with Gregory, but it wasn't her fault. It was his. He was the problem. For years, I didn't want to accept that he raped them both.'

Angel was astounded by the old woman's revelation. Her throat felt dry; she wanted to probe Granny Belle further, but knew that this was not the appropriate setting. She knew, too, however, that Granny Belle might not remember the conversation a few minutes later.

'We were worried when you and Bradley started your affair. I thought to myself, is history repeating itself? Maybe we did all get it wrong … Maybe he does love you. I saw you that night in the Jacuzzi, you know. I was sitting by the window because I couldn't sleep. I struggle to sleep nowadays. Mabusi and Khiwa don't stop harassing me. When you get to my age you're bound to have made a lot of mistakes. I know I made so many and I'm really ashamed of them.'

Granny Belle picked up her handkerchief and dabbed her eyes. Angel was tongue-tied. As unsettling as this information was, she didn't know how to react. She lay a reassuring hand on Granny Belle's. An uneasy truth made her shift uncomfortably in her seat. They say Granny Belle had dementia, that she was losing her mind, but Angel considered that she might not have lost it after all. Estelle then appeared and tried to shepherd Granny Belle to the front. Granny Belle obstinately refused.

'I'm fine here with Mabusi. You'll take care of me, won't you?'

Angel nodded. Rolling her eyes, Estelle thanked her and then flitted off to the front-row seat next to her husband, relieved at not having to be burdened by the aged matriarch.

'My firstborn, Estelle – she's married to that white capitalist over there,' said Granny Belle as Estelle scuttled off.

Angel expelled a noisy breath. She didn't want to hear about Danie; she wanted to steer the conversation back to Mabusi. Or had Granny Belle already lost that train of thought?

'Marry well, Angel. That's the best thing you can do for yourself. And put aside a stash of cash for those rainy days that will inevitably arrive.'

'Did you have rainy days in your marriage?'

Granny Belle threw her hands in the air, and then leaned in closer to Angel and whispered, 'I had storms, Angel. Life with Gregory was one big storm. He's probably still whoring down there in hell!'

Angel's curiosity had been sparked. She wanted to learn more about this man.

'I found peace with Uncle Scotty, God bless his soul. There's peace that comes with marrying a man who loves you,' said Granny Belle.

Angel allowed the words to percolate.

'Melanie is loved, but I don't know about Jane. I don't think Graham has it quite together. It's the war … It messed with his head,' continued Granny Belle.

Angel was certain that, had it not been for the violin quartet that started playing, Granny Belle would have continued her unrestrained chatter.

At that moment Bradley, accompanied by his best man, Steve, strode in, joined by two other groomsmen all wearing cream chinos that matched perfectly with the African savanna and the long, sunburnt grass, with white shirts and bow ties. Angel's heart constricted when her eyes came to rest on Bradley. A knee-jerk rejection. The bridesmaids followed in swathes of burnt-orange silk, and finally the bride glided down the makeshift aisle in a dazzling strapless, figure-hugging mermaid dress. On her head she wore a beautiful crown of white roses interlaced with baby's breath.

'She's a beauty,' whispered Granny Belle.

Angel nodded numbly. Why was she even here? What the hell was she thinking? She couldn't hold back the tears that escaped from her eyes.

Thankfully, she was not the only one weeping as Bradley as Mariska exchanged vows. The difference, however, was that theirs were tears of pure joy while hers were of sheer sadness. Granny Belle put a consoling arm around her and said softly, 'You're in love with my grandson, aren't you? I can see it in your eyes.'

Angel fought back the tears and found herself leaning into Granny Belle. In that moment, she realised she no longer existed for Bradley.

He hadn't even noticed her among the guests; he only had eyes for Mariska. Her heart broke even more at the way he looked at her when reciting his vows. He used to look at her like that.

'I, Bradley Simon Williams, take you, my darling Mariska, to be my lawfully wedded wife. I promise to love you faithfully. To protect and to provide for you. To honour and cherish you. Through the highs and lows. Through our triumphs and failures. Through sickness and health. For richer and richer.'

There was no 'poverty' in their vows and the guests chuckled at the modification.

'I, Mariska Helena Georgios, take you, Bradley, to be my lawfully wedded husband. I thank you for choosing me. The same way I I choose you, forsaking all others. And I will continue to choose you every day of my life. I take you, flaws and all,' she chuckled, 'the same way I offer myself to you with all my faults and foibles. I promise to challenge and encourage you; to honour and respect you. To love you completely and consistently all the days of our lives.'

The rest of the ceremony passed in a blur of rites and rituals. Rings were swapped. Kisses exchanged and the registry signed. With the service concluded, the finality of the moment settled in Angel's mind and she knew without a doubt that she had lost Bradley. Forever.

36

Cultivating fear

Barely a week after their nuptials, Bradley woke to the horrendous news that a farmer, David Stevens, had been murdered. The BBC carried rolling coverage on how Zimbabwe had declined into lawlessness following the farm invasions in February of the same year.

His wife, Mariska, stirred beside him.

'Are your folks all right?'

'I hope so,' replied Bradley, crawling out of bed.

They were back in the two-bedroom apartment in Clapham, but Mariska was scouting around for a bigger place in Kensington. He picked up his cellphone and 'Mom' flashed across the screen. It rang interminably, with no answer. Then he called Angel and she picked up on the second ring. He walked through to the living room, feeling like he needed some privacy.

'Hi, Angel. Is everything all right down there?'

'On our side it is,' she replied, tersely.

'I'm watching the news and saw the awful bulletin about Stevens.'

'We've been following the story here too,' replied Angel. 'It's breaking news.'

The unprecedented farm invasions had occupied the news since February, with militant war veterans crying for land redistribution. However, up until then, the invasions had not resulted in any casualties. Details were still sketchy, but it had been reported that Farmer

Stevens had been abducted from his farm in Murewa, 75 kilometres outside the capital in a farming area of Mashonaland East. The violence of his death sent shockwaves throughout the entire country. Farmer Stevens was apparently driven into the bush where he was tortured and killed. Stevens' friends from the farming fraternity, Gary Luke, Steve Krynauw, Stuart Gemmil and Ian Hardy were also abducted when they tried to come to his aid. They were beaten black and blue, concussed and comatose, presumed dead. But they'd lived to tell the story, bruised and bandaged, talking to the press from their hospital beds. Bradley paused to watch the coverage on television.

'I can't believe I'm alive,' said Krynauw in a shaky voice. He was on the verge of tears.

'It's fucking unreal what is happening,' reported eyewitness John Osborne from his hospital bed. He'd been lucky to escape, 'These guys are not playing; they mean business.'

Bradley turned the volume down and directed his attention back to his conversation with Angel.

'Gel, are you guys safe?' he asked.

'I think we are. No one has invaded Belle Acres. Yet.'

'Please ask the folks to call me and keep me posted on any new developments, okay?'

'Will do,' replied Angel, hanging up.

He hated that she had been so abrupt with him, that their conversations were so clipped and polite. When he cut the call, Mariska was standing behind him expectantly.

'It seems everything's fine there, for now.'

'What's the long-term plan? Evacuation?'

'I really don't know ... Angel didn't say much,' replied Bradley, running his fingers through his hair.

The situation back home was making him anxious and he hated that he was so far removed from everything.

'Couldn't you at least speak to your dad? He probably has a better handle on the situation,' remarked Mariska.

Mariska was annoyed that Bradley was conferring with Angel; his parents were right there on the ground and he should be talking to them directly.

'I did try to call, but they didn't pick up.'

'You ever think of going back?' she asked.

'No, not with this kak going on,' replied Bradley.

'And if things were okay, would you go back?'

Bradley had thought long and hard about it, but he'd acclimatised to life in London. He'd been living there for more than five years and had started his first year of articles with a firm on the Canary Wharf. He'd forged some formidable friendships during his university days and they were a tight-knit group, young and upcoming professionals making a fairly good living. It was a different life, yes, but one that he had fully embraced. He and Mariska had a bustling life. He'd adopted the football culture and on Sundays they camped at the Royal Bell to watch a game. This would be followed by a jaunt at Jazzmins. They clubbed at the Fridge in Brixton, Caesars in Streatham at Circus in the West End. Mariska enjoyed going to the theatre to watch musicals and the ballet and he even accompanied her occasionally, even though it wasn't his thing. His life was full and he couldn't imagine living anywhere else.

His response placated Mariska considerably; as long as he harboured no intentions of returning to Zimbabwe, their marriage was safe. Even though she was married to him, Angel remained a very real threat to Mariska's happiness.

The death of David Stevens sent reverberations of fear through the farming community. Not long after, another farmer, Martin Olds, was shot on his farm after it was invaded by a legion of war veterans and youth militia. Melanie couldn't understand Paul's dogged determination to remain in Zimbabwe in the face of such danger and her uneasiness grew. When another farmer, Willem Botha, was killed, Melanie was adamant that she was leaving. These were not strangers; they knew some of these people and, while they might not have fraternised with them socially, they'd often met at the Commercial Farmers' Union or at cattle auctions and agricultural shows. Their children had gone to the same schools.

'I'm not going to wait to have a bullet put in my head,' proclaimed Melanie.

'You're being rash,' replied Paul. 'Playing right into their hands. This is exactly what they want us to do, scare us into leaving.'

'Angel, are you coming with me?' asked Melanie, ignoring Paul.

Angel didn't know that she had a choice in the matter and felt conflicted. She understood why the squatters were so militant, agitating for land. It was their birthright. She understood the need for land redistribution and equity, but while she could empathise with them, she also felt that this might not be the best way to do it. If she stayed at Belle Acres, she would be alone with Paul without the buffer of Melanie.

'I'll go,' declared Angel.

That night she packed a few things into a suitcase. Undecided as to what to take and what to leave, the photographs of her parents were the first thing that went in, followed by a few items of clothing. Exhausted, she collapsed into bed and decided to continue packing in the morning. Sometime in the middle of the night, her grannies arrived in flowing black gowns with puffy sleeves. She was woken by them tussling over her suitcase. Khiwa eventually overpowered Mabusi and wrestled the suitcase away, emptying the contents onto the floor. Angel woke with a start. She would have dismissed it as just another dream, but the items she had packed were strewn all over the floor.

'I'm staying,' announced Angel the following morning at breakfast. 'I still have a job to do here.'

While Melanie was staggered by the decision, she didn't try to persuade Angel otherwise. Paul patted her gently, proud of her stance.

'This is our land,' he said to her later. 'Melanie wouldn't understand – she wasn't born here. We were.'

37

Invasion

Angel had to profess her ignorance on the land question in Zimbabwe. While she was aware of the history of the inequality of land owner-ship in the country, she hadn't understood the depth of it. She was horrified to learn that over 90 per cent of the arable land in the country belonged to six thousand white farmers. When she shared the statistic with Paul, he quickly debunked it.

'That's bullshit,' rebutted Paul. 'Where did you read that? Since independence, there are over a thousand black farmers.'

Paul went on to explain that the land resettlement programme had begun prior to the year 2000, but at a snail's pace. It was reported that half a million people were on the waiting list for land and only 52 000 families had been resettled.

'But that's still a tiny number compared to the number of disen-franchised people in this country!' insisted Angel.

'Listen here, Mugabe was never committed to land reform in this country. He is gassed up because he is now under pressure with the war veterans.'

'Politics aside, do you agree there is a need for land redistribu-tion, Paul?'

'Whose side are you on, Angel?'

'Your side,' she replied quickly. 'Of course I don't support the land invasions and am sure the land could have been distributed a better way, but I understand people's desperation.'

'Angel, this has nothing to do with the land. It's got to do with how we all voted in the 2000 elections. You've got lots to learn. Let's go have some coffee and I'll tell you all about it.'

They sat down and Paul started to school Angel on the politics of the country. Up until then she'd never taken much of an interest or any political stance and hadn't voted, even though she had been eligible. Paul explained that after the annihilation of ZAPU in the eighties, Zimbabwe had effectively become a one-party state. Edgar Tekere had tried to form ZUM in opposition to Mugabe in the nineties, but his attempt had failed to gain traction and was violently squashed. It appeared that a new political opposition had emerged in Zimbabwe called the Movement for Democratic Change. MDC. In what had not happened since Independence, the party had won 57 of the 120 electoral seats.

'Mugabe lost in all the urban constituencies. I reckon that if the elections were free and fair, he would have lost in some of the rural constituencies too, but that's a story for another day.'

Angel vaguely remembered reading about Mugabe's resounding loss, but she didn't understand the implications.

'I reckon Morgan Tsvangirai stands a good chance of winning the presidential elections,' continued Paul. 'Mugabe is feeling threatened, which is why he's acting out. This thing with the war veterans is just a side show to intimidate us whites.'

'Are you going to vote for Morgan?' asked Angel.

Paul edged in closer, as though there were others listening in on their conversation, even though it was just the two of them.

'Of course I will,' replied Paul. 'Not only am I voting for MDC, I'm backing him too. A lot of us are funding Tsvangirai's campaign. The country is ready for change, Angel. Mugabe is out of ideas.'

Angel nodded, hating that she could contribute very little to the conversation, but this was at least the start of her political education. She started to read the newspapers, all four of them – *The Daily News, The Chronicle, The Herald* and *The Standard* – as well as the pink paper,

The Financial Gazette. Paul cautioned her to be aware of the propaganda, especially in state-owned papers. She started listening to the news and became more aware of the biased reporting and coverage. The ruling party ZANU-PF dominated when it came to media coverage and very little airtime was given to the opposition.

At first, Angel had been reticent about staying behind on the farm with Paul, but as the days unfolded, they found an easy routine around each other. They ate dinner together every night and had vociferous conversations about politics. Paul even took her to MDC meetings. While it sometimes felt clandestine, Angel was happy to be included and it made her feel like a real stakeholder. Even her circle of friends expanded as they high-fived each other with the open palm, the greeting of the MDC.

In August of that same year Paul received his Section 5 notice declaring that the government wished to acquire Belle Acres. This was promptly followed by a Section 8 informing him that they had 90 days in which to vacate the property. His first reaction was to try to get into telephonic contact with the Minister of Lands, Agriculture and Rural Settlement. Paul prided himself on the fact that he had Minister Joseph Made on speed dial. While he wasn't a member of the ruling party, he made regular donations, so the Section 5 notice was a source of great concern since he had been given several assurances that his farm was not on the hit list.

'This is a mistake,' said Paul confidently. 'Our farm is not supposed to be on the list. We're running a productive operation here. We provide employment to hundreds.'

He didn't have to enumerate the benefits to Angel – she was well aware of them. But she knew that the farm invasions were a very real threat.

'This is absurd!' agreed Angel.

'I'm not leaving here, Angel' replied Paul. 'This is my home. I was born in this country and I've done so much for it. I'll die here if I have to.'

Paul spent the next couple of days trying to get hold of the minister, but was diverted to his deputy, who merely took his messages and promised that the minister would get back to him. By the time a group of war veterans showed up at Belle Acres, the minister still hadn't got back to him. The crowd arrived in a flatbed lorry and when the security guards tried to bar them from entering, they were threatened by the machete-wielding crowd. In the end, they conceded defeat and allowed the armed group to head up to the farmhouse. At the front was a man by the name of Cain Mao Nzou, who marched up the long, winding driveway flanked by sunburnt winter grass. The group settled at the bottom of the garden and erected a makeshift camp. Ottilia, the domestic worker, watched them from the kitchen window and counted more than 40 individuals – a mixed group of women and men, young and old, which made her question the validity of these 'veterans' all having ever actually participated in the war.

They hacked down Bradley's old tree house and used the planks to light a bonfire that they congregated around. They called it a *pungwe* and it burnt through the night. Every night there was singing and dancing, accompanied by the thumping of a drum. The day the group arrived marked the last day Paul enjoyed a restful night. Just as he drifted off to sleep, the drums would start up again, beating incessantly, and the voices would rise to an annoying crescendo.

Every morning Paul stood on the balcony of his bedroom, observing the occupants below. His nerves were frayed and the lack of sleep was becoming evident in his eyes, his brow permanently furrowed in anxiety. Angel could tell that the ordeal was wearing him down. Even his hair had seemed to whiten considerably since the arrival of the group. Angel urged him to try to get some sleep during the day when relative calm prevailed because the contingent spent the day sleeping, exhausted from their activities during the night. Angel, in the meantime, continued with their farming operations, but the mood was tense and fraught with anxiety. When Mao heard they were still operating, he was livid. They ambushed the workers at the compound and warned them of harsh retribution if they continued working for Paul. Harsh beatings were meted out.

'We fought for you!' barked Mao. 'But you want to continue to be oppressed by the white man. Stop this stupidity!'

At that point, some of the workers were recruited into the struggle and were co-opted to set up camp in the garden. For many, it was the first time they had ventured beyond the compound. Angel was not spared any of their callous retribution.

'Sistren,' Mao warned, 'we are watching you. Black people like you are sell-outs and we know how to deal with you.'

'I'm no sell-out,' replied Angel. 'If we don't continue ploughing and planting, we won't be able to pay any of these people.'

'*Nyarara mhani! Voetsek,*' he roared. 'What you even pay them? We see you running around here in your fancy cars because you fucking the baas! Every other black person lives in the compound, but you sucking your *murungu's* cock.'

He slapped her hard across the face. A clap of thunder and Angel felt her ears ringing.

'You are a stupet beech. What can you tell me? What do you know? I fought for this country. I lived in the bush so you can stand here and tell me nonsense!'

'*Murove!*' came the voices of the contingent. '*Mutengesi!*'

They began to beat her. Some used wooden sticks and others their balled and angry fists. When she folded and fell to the ground, they kicked her mercilessly. It was only when she was lying on the ground, barely conscious, that they left her. Some spat in her face in disgust. Ottilia and Paul came to her rescue and she was ferried to hospital, her face and body pulpy and bruised. She spent a week in hospital, drifting in and out of consciousness. Every time she opened her eyes, Paul was at her bedside and, when she closed them, her grannies were there on the fringes of her subconscious.

38

Shots fired

After Angel's bloody confrontation with Mao, the occupation became a fully fledged rebellion or *jambanja*. The contingent took over the Jacuzzi and bathed in it every morning until the motor packed up from overuse. Then they turned their attention to the pool, diving into the sapphire-blue waters as a reprieve from the blazing heat. It became a common sight to see Mao lounging by the pool, outstretched on a sun lounger smoking Paul's Cuban cigars.

For sustenance, the occupiers slaughtered a cow, the blood spilling onto the green grass, flattened by the constant stomping of feet. The carcass was hung from the remnants of Bradley's tree house, attracting a swarm of flies. It took the occupiers a week to get through the carcass and not one part of the animal went to waste. They braaied the cuts of meat and made stew with the offal. Those who arrived at the farm looking lean and mean fattened up considerably with each passing day. A contingent of dedicated women cooked in three-legged pots to ensure that all the comrades were fed. They helped themselves to cutlery, crockery and glasses from the kitchen and combed through the pantry for whatever they needed. Ottilia posed no resistance, simply because she didn't want to antagonise them. They helped themselves to the bountiful supply of alcohol in the bar. This helped energise their nightly *pungwe* sessions, which were accompanied by weed smoking, making them even more boisterous. When that finally ran out, they forced Ottilia down to the cellar where they raided the wine racks.

After they had depleted the groceries in the kitchen and pantry, Paul resolved to eat at the club because he wasn't going to feed the thugs on his property. But the looting didn't end in the kitchen; the women ran riot in the house, trying on Melanie's clothes. They shared her dresses, shoes and handbags, much like the Roman soldiers after they crucified Jesus. Thankfully, Melanie had left with her prized jewellery. Once they started stripping the walls of the paintings and other decorative ornaments, Paul knew there would be no stopping them. It would be pointless, but he nevertheless filed a police report of theft and vandalism of property. The police promised they would follow up but never did. Locking doors was futile because the contingent had already broken all the locks and stolen the gold-plated doorknobs. Paul knew it was over when they tore out one of the sandalwood doors and used it to fuel the fire that burnt through the night. For forty days and forty nights this went on.

'*Hondo ye minda!* The war for the land,' they chanted. '*Nyika ndeyedu.* The land is ours. *Pasi nevarungu!* Down with the white man.'

Paul had stopped making calls to the minister and deferred to the police, who refused to get involved, claiming that the matter was beyond their jurisdiction.

'You're supposed to maintain law and order! My farm manager was badly beaten by these hoodlums.'

'Well, what did she do to provoke them?' came the station commander's reply.

'What the fuck is that supposed to mean?'

'*Iwe murungu! Nyarara!*' cautioned the police officer. 'This is not Rhodesia. Check your tongue.'

They threatened to arrest Paul for unruly behaviour.

'I have illegal squatters on my farm,' Paul exhaled noisily. 'All I want is that you ask them to leave.'

'We've told you before. This is for the courts. Take your grievances there.'

Defeated, Paul left the station. They were on their own.

Paul tapped into their radio network, communicating with other farmers. Their conversations were a roll call of survivors offering support and sometimes condolences to the families of farmers who had been lynched. The group was getting smaller and smaller, with most farmers eventually capitulating to the invaders and leaving.

When news of the assault on Angel reached Melanie, she was irate. Paul had tried to keep it from her, but Ottilia kept her up to date with everything that was happening on the farm.

'What will it take, Paul? Do you want them to kill my daughter before you see how much danger you're in?'

For the first time since the whole fiasco had begun, Paul broke down on the telephone, floored by his tears.

'You should see her, Mel. Those savages almost butchered her to death.'

Melanie couldn't hold back her own tears.

'Mel, they've trashed the place,' he sobbed. 'They're destroying everything we ever worked for.'

'Paul, listen to me,' said Melanie sternly, knowing that she had to be the voice of reason. 'You've done your bit. It's time to move on.'

'Mel, Belle Acres is my life. I've given everything to this place. I was born here, for crying out loud. I have every right to be here.'

'And I understand that, darling, but for the safety of you and Angel, you need to leave. We can start over. Since Adrienne and Luke bought that farm in Paarl, they're doing well.'

Adrienne and Luke had their entire lives ahead of them. Paul couldn't envisage starting over at his age and living in exile like a refugee in a foreign land. He sobbed into the mouthpiece. His whole life was going up in smoke.

'Paul? Are you there?'

Melanie was infuriated by her husband's stubbornness. She couldn't understand the hold Belle Acres had over him. They had all left. Granny Belle. Graham. Bradley. Adrienne. He and Angel were the only ones left.

'Darling,' she cooed into the mouthpiece, 'we're going to be grandparents soon. Don't you want to watch the sunset while playing with your grandchildren? I still want to travel the world with you. We never finished our bucket list of countries to visit. You promised that we would go on an ocean cruise around the world, remember? Just you and me. We can do that now.'

Paul continued to sob into the mouthpiece, his convulsions rocking his body.

'I love you, Paul,' said Melanie. 'We've got so much to live for. Please ... leave Belle Acres. I don't want to have to spend the rest of my life without you.'

'You're right, Mel. I'll leave ... I love you too.'

'I don't believe it! You've always loved that farm more than me.'

They laughed and Paul felt some of his anguish dissipate. Melanie had a way of smoothing his rough edges. He knew he wasn't an easy person to live with.

'I love you, Mel. You're the love of my life and I am doing this for you. Only you.'

Paul hung up, a lingering smile on his face.

As night set in, the chanting from the squatters grew in its intensity. He grabbed his revolver and stormed outside, firing three shots into the air. Angel woke with a start. Woozy from the medication, she shuffled fearfully downstairs, wondering what had happened. She'd been discharged from hospital a day earlier, her shorn head wrapped in a muslin bandage.

'*Mese budai pano apa!*' All of you get out of here! shouted Paul in Shona, making sure he could be heard loud and clear.

'Paul, don't do this,' shrieked Angel, coming up behind him, hands flailing in the air.

'We're not leaving here,' replied Mao. 'If anyone's leaving, it's you. And if you keep this shit up, you'll leave in a coffin.'

'Paul,' begged Angel, 'let's get back in the house.'

'Yes,' agreed Mao, 'listen to your beech.'

'*Handibvi pano!*' hollered Paul belligerently, waving his firearm in the air. 'This is *my* land. My father paid for it. I have every right to be here. None of you fucking minions will ever own this land.'

His words incensed the crowd, who had been hankering for the slightest provocation.

'*Batai murungu!*' commanded Mao.

His lieutenants pounced on Paul, undeterred by his threats to shoot them. The men easily overpowered him, wrestling the gun from his hands. Angel pleaded with Mao to let him go, apologising profusely on his behalf.

'You're next,' warned Mao, looking at Angel. 'Don't think we're going to spare you. You're a traitor.'

They were now beating Paul with sticks, pounding his flesh, machetes slicing through it. Angel flinched, their assault triggering memories of her own attack, still fresh in her mind. Her wounds were raw. She knew what they were capable of. With everyone embroiled in the orgy of violence, she retreated into the house unnoticed. She radioed to the other farmers in their circle to alert them of the attack; they warned her to leave immediately.

'Please send reinforcements – they're going to kill him!'

Angel knew there was no way she could drive away from the farm unseen. They would tip the car over if they had to. The only place she could think of fleeing to was the compound. She ran into the night as fast as her legs could carry her. Her grannies ran with her, steering her down the well-worn path. She'd hide out with Ottilia until the madness subsided.

The sun soon rose, but Paul did not rise with it. His spirit had departed from the earth he so loved, only his limp, bloodied body remaining, hanging from the windmill like the carcass of a quartered beast.

The contingent that had beaten him to death had then returned to the farmhouse like hungry hyenas baying for Angel's blood. The dawn of the new day hadn't dissolved their feral nature. They called on her to come out of the house and were infuriated by the lack of response.

'Sistren!' screamed one of the lieutenants. *'Budai mumba. Ticha pisa imba yacho, newe futi!'* Get out of the house! We will burn you and the house!

Still there was no response, so they marched inside in search of Angel.

'Let's burn the house down!' declared one of the lieutenants.

'No,' replied Mao, 'we were given strict orders not to.'

'Nani?' screamed another lieutenant. 'I say we burn the house down. I say burn it!'

There were collective screams of 'Burn it down!' and Mao couldn't stem the rising tide of fury. It was agreed – the house needed to fall just like the owner.

'Pisa imba!' they shouted, drowning out Mao's protestations. Burn the house!

They baptised Belle Acres with a splash of diesel they found in the barn, and another lieutenant set a match to it. The house lit up as red flames sparked to life, fanned by the growing inferno of anger.

Belle Acres combusted in a blaze. For the invaders, this was their Jericho moment.

39

Out of the ashes

A police contingent finally arrived at the scene of the carnage at around 7am, an hour after the fire brigade. The entrance, which had previously been barricaded, now allowed easy entry and exit. Paul's bloodied body was lowered from the windmill near the barnyard. Bludgeoned to death, his lifeless body was encrusted with blood, his skin mottled with blue and purple patches. Angel was required to accompany the corpse to identify it at the police station. She cried through the entire process, but received little sympathy from the sergeant on duty.

As they completed the paperwork, Angel wondered how she was going to tell the family.

The Carters, who lived 20 kilometres from Belle Acres, were there to give her moral support.

'We phoned the police soon after you called,' reported Cain Carter. 'It seems they eventually sent someone after the fire started.'

'We drove out, but the entrance was barricaded,' said his wife, looking at her feet.

'And then we left, Angel. We were too scared,' said Cain, shame-faced.

Angel understood their fear, but she was silently angry that Paul had died alone. That no one had attempted to rescue him. How often had he gone out on a limb for neighbours when they sounded the call for help? She recalled the number of times he had gone out on searches when a farmer in their area had been abducted.

News of Paul's death was reported in the newspapers the following day. They recounted that he had been killed in a skirmish after he opened fire on the legion of war veterans and militia squatting peacefully on his land. They deliberately omitted the part about him being battered to death. This made Angel's head crackle. As she sat hugging a mug of coffee in her hands, she wondered whether she would ever be able to erase the image of Paul's lifeless body from her mind.

Taken in by the Carters, she eventually called Melanie. She had already been informed and the two spent close to ten minutes crying on the phone. There were no words, just tears.

'After the funeral you can relocate to South Africa to be with the rest of the family, Angel,' said Melanie.

'Yes,' replied Angel numbly; she had no more fight left in her.

Then she remembered that her passport had been in the house and had been lost in the fire.

'I'll have to apply for a new one and you know how long that takes. Running for my life, it never occurred to me to get my handbag.'

When Angel finally hung up, her eyes were puffy and swollen, her body still bruised from the beating.

'I'm so sorry, Angel,' said Marge Carter, rubbing her shoulders soothingly.

'And I lost my family pictures. All of them.'

She knew the headache it was going to be to replace her passport but how would she ever replace the only memories she had of her parents? How could she ever recreate that?

'I can't do anything. I'm stuck!' cried Angel.

'You can stay here as long as you need to. We will try to help in any way we can.'

'I just want to lie down,' said Angel, her head throbbing.

Marge gave her a mild tranquiliser, which knocked her out and she woke only the next day. At first she felt disorientated, not sure where she was, but then it all came rushing back to her. The shocking realisation that Paul was dead.

Panicked, she went in search of Marge.

'I need to go back. I need to go back to Belle Acres.'

'Angel,' said Marge placating her, 'I don't think that's a good idea.'

'I need to go back,' she replied with a burning urgency in her voice. 'Take me back.'

Begrudgingly, Cain and Marge drove her back.

To their surprise, the war veterans had vacated Belle Acres. If it wasn't for the smouldering remains of the farmhouse, Angel might think she had dreamed up the whole nightmare. Cain and Marge were equally surprised that the intruders had left.

'Maybe to escape persecution,' surmised Marge.

'What persecution? How many farmers have been killed since this whole fiasco and no arrests have been made? We're just sitting ducks.'

They surveyed the ruins, devastated by the carnage and the tremendous loss. That was how each member of the family felt when they finally arrived, one by one.

When Melanie arrived on a commercial flight a day later, the Carters accompanied Angel to the airport because she was still too frail to drive. On seeing Melanie, Angel dissolved into tears. They cried together, shouldering each other's pain.

'Maybe if I had stayed ...' Melanie blamed herself for leaving. 'I could've knocked some sense into him.'

'Don't say that, Mom – you would've probably been killed too.'

'Maybe dying with him would have been better,' cried Melanie. 'I can't deal with this pain.'

Melanie mourned Paul in so many ways. She had lost an adoring, albeit stern father to her children. The tenderness of a lover. A safe space to be herself. A friend she could confide in. She knew Paul had his faults, but right now she chose to focus on the good and to water down the bad. Angel didn't know how to console her and was relieved when Adrienne arrived the next day.

Her sister, however, was a walking mess.

'Dad!' she sobbed. 'Daddy! How can Daddy be dead? How, Angel? How?'

Adrienne's face was red, painted with anguish. She sat quietly, her body wracked by sobs. Of all the children, she had been the closest to Paul and she felt his loss ardently. To her, he had been the perfect, doting father. Kind and considerate, he'd been her loudest cheerleader. Her hero.

Graham and Jane arrived later the same day. If Graham felt any grief, he hid it well at first, downing one whiskey after another until Jane said it was too much. It was then that he finally caved in, collapsing under the heaviness of trying to keep it together.

'What's too much, Jane? Mourning my brother?'

Estelle wore her sorrow stoically. She dabbed her eyes with a handkerchief and took over as the caretaker of everyone else's emotions. Danie was the same, comforting others but keeping his own emotions in check.

For the duration of her stay, Melanie stayed at the Kenilworth penthouse with Adrienne and Luke. Compared to the farmhouse, it felt small and crowded. Paul's siblings happily checked themselves into the Holiday Inn. Granny Belle had been too frail to make the trip and Estelle reported that they had been forced to admit her to a nursing home, her dementia progressing rapidly. Her two dedicated nurses constantly complained that Granny Belle suffered from severe hallucinations at night. She would often wake up screaming, claiming she was being tormented by Mabusi and Khiwa. No one took the assertions seriously. If anything, they had simply increased her medication, sedating her so that she slept most of the time.

Angel had been tasked with picking Bradley up at the airport – a task she had tried to worm her way out of, but Adrienne was just too over-whelmed with grief to drive. Melanie was paralysed with sorrow and had barely left her chair since her arrival. Luke insisted that it was best that he stayed with the women and that Brad would need Angel's support. And so, begrudgingly, she had agreed. As she drove, her hands were unsteady on the steering wheel. She kept telling herself to calm down. When she laid eyes on Bradley, she felt a little faint, as if the last vestige of strength was leaving her. He stared at her blankly for a long time. When he removed his sunglasses, his eyes were bloodshot. He spoke first.

'Is it really true? Is Dad gone, Gel?'

'He is. Gone-*gone*.'

Bradley closed his eyes. 'God, why are you doing this to me?' he murmured. 'Why?'

Slowly the tears fell like the beginning of a light shower of rain.

Angel was crying too, her lips trembling.

'Bradley,' she croaked. 'I'm so sorry, Brad!'

They moved towards each other, slowly and awkwardly. They clung to each other, seeking comfort. They'd both had a difficult relationship with Paul and mourning him was complicated. For a significant period in her life, Angel had resented him and, even in his death, she was filled with ambivalence. He had been a mixed-up and complicated man. A part of Angel hated him, yet the other part loved him and deeply admired him. It was only in the last few years on the farm that she had come to appreciate him and they'd formed a bond of sorts. She'd come to understand him better, realising that underneath that brusqueness he meant well. Bradley understood that because he too had borne the brunt of that side of his father.

In between the crying, their lips found each other and they started kissing. They kissed with wild abandon and with a fierce passion that seared through them. Nothing was said as they let their mouths communicate where words would no longer suffice. Grief had made Angel vulnerable and only Bradley's consuming love could soothe her pain.

The drive from the airport to the flat was achingly long.

'Is everyone staying at the penthouse?' asked Bradley.

'No, just us. Estelle and Graham are at the Holiday Inn.'

'I think I should stay there too,' replied Bradley. 'I need to be alone.'

He insisted they head to the hotel first so he could check in and freshen up.

The receptionist immediately assumed they were Mr and Mrs Bradley Williams and handed him the keys. Angel swallowed hard, a stark reminder that he was very much married. As soon as they were inside the room, Bradley scooped her into his arms and kicked the door shut behind them. He threw her on the bed and found his way on top of her. They kissed again and again, tearing at each other, frantically removing the clothing that separated their bodies. They made love with a burning urgency, her whimpers of pleasure intermingling with his groans of ecstasy. Brad rode her like a stud, following the sensual rhythm of her body. They rode past the frontiers of morality, past the sobering reality of their situation. They arrived together in a realm of delight and pure sexual gratification, lost in the spontaneity of orgasmic pleasure. They made love again and again until they were both spent, their lovemaking helping to assuage their pent-up pain and grief. As they professed their love for each other, Angel felt as though she were hallucinating.

'Brad, this isn't a dream, is it? I really am here.'

He touched her face again and kissed her swollen lips.

'You are, Gel, and I love you with all I have,' said Brad for what seemed to be the hundredth time that day.

'Brad, I *really* love you. I feel like I haven't been living these past few years.'

He understood what she meant. She didn't have to explain – he knew precisely what it felt like.

'Gel, I was scared you would hate me forever.'

'I could never hate you.'

'I don't want to lose you ever again.'

'You won't, Brad,' she told him, holding him tight. 'But ... Mariska ...'

He silenced her with a kiss. He didn't want to ruin the moment with the grating reality of their discordant situation.

Instead, he held her and didn't say anything. He wanted to hold onto the moment. It was the finality of death that made everything else seem pressing and urgent. They both felt the need to express feelings that had been contained and suppressed for years. It was the realisation that the only thing they had was time and it was passing quickly. It could not be arrested or stored. There was so much Brad wanted to say, so much he wanted to tell her. He wished he could make up the time they had lost, the time he knew they could never recover. They talked about neither the present nor the past; in that moment, being in each other's embrace was all that mattered. Reality set in, however, when the evening fell upon them and knew that parting was inevitable.

'We have to go,' Angel said.

'Yes, I know,' Brad replied.

He was ready to face the rest of the family.

'Gel,' he said taking her hand in his, 'I need you.'

'I got you, Brad,' she replied.

Every night, Angel lay in Bradley's arms, him professing he couldn't stand to be alone. They comforted each other and found solace in each other. Mariska arrived a day before the funeral and fetching her at the airport was a huge reality check for Bradley. His father had been a good husband and that was a trait he wanted to emulate, but his father would never have approved of him and Angel, he knew that. Dare he defy him in death? When he laid eyes on Mariska as she made her way out of Arrivals, he vowed to be a better husband. Bradley regretted that he and his father had not been closer, that their relation-ship had been fraught with tension and fallouts, and he was remorseful that they had not managed to iron out the creases when he was alive. He hoped to rectify the mistakes he'd made with his father by doing better with the son Mariska was carrying.

Mariska looked exquisite in a thin-strapped, long, white voile dress teamed with white espadrilles. Her chintzy bangles clanked together as she embraced everyone, offering her condolences as everyone congratulated her on her visible pregnancy. Angel realised then that she had to abort any ideas she had entertained about her and Bradley being together. She felt rotten, sick to the core. How could she even contemplate taking him from Mariska and their unborn child? When they finally laid Paul to rest, Angel vowed to lay her feelings for Brad to rest too. She would bury them six feet under.

As they shared their collective memories of and stories about Paul over the next few days, no one focused on his faults. Nobody made mention of his flaws or foibles. No one spoke of the raging arguments they'd had with him; instead, they remembered only the warm and insightful conversations he sparked. Angel knew that talking about that other side of him would be like betraying his memory. They had grown close in those last few months before he passed on. Looking around at the people who attended the funeral, she knew everyone had experienced Paul differently. He was different things to the many different people in his life. In that moment, Angel quietly accepted that she was too. That it was possible to be many things and that they could all be true. She looked at her own life and wondered what people would say about her at her own funeral. Who was she? What was she, Angel, really about?

40

The inheritance

After the funeral, the family converged at the firm of attorneys Coghlan and Welsh for the reading of the last will and testament of Paul Williams. Angel walked in with no expectations of receiving anything from him and walked out a millionaire.

Paul had bequeathed Belle Acres to her. While it had come as a shocking revelation, no one else around the table was fazed by the announcement.

'He wanted you to have it,' said Melanie with authority. 'He said you were the only one who loved it enough to run it well. The farm-house actually belonged to Granny Belle, but she insisted that you have it,' added Melanie.

'I don't know what this even means,' declared Graham. 'Since the fucking government has taken it over and those munts burnt the fucking house down.'

For Angel, it felt bittersweet. Inheriting the farm was supposed to be a big thing, but circumstances had reduced it to nothing. Or rather, she inherited what they termed a 'contested asset'. In addition to the farm, Paul had left her a lump sum of £100 000, which was being held in a nominee account at Lloyds Bank in the United Kingdom. At the current exchange rate, that made her a millionaire.

'Take your money and start over in another country, Angel. Leave this godforsaken place,' advised Estelle, as she packed their bags to leave.

Paul had been generous to his siblings and gifted them £10 000 each. Bradley and Adrienne, of course, had their trust funds, which they had been drawing on since they were 21. Bradley also received the Clapham apartment, while Adrienne was bequeathed the Bulawayo penthouse. Melanie would inherit the remainder of his million-dollar estate, which the lawyers advised they would start working on getting wrapped up. Melanie was going to be a wealthy widow, especially considering all that her parents had left her.

'We'll be together soon,' Melanie assured Angel as they hugged each other at the airport. She had been last to leave after everyone else had said their goodbyes.

Since Paul's death, Angel had been staying at the Kenilworth apartment, but now that everyone had gone, she felt bereft and decided to return to the farm. It was hers now, even if it was just on paper.

Preparing for the funeral had kept Angel busy, occupying her time and energy. There had been the service arrangements, the catering and flowers, calling everyone and constantly being with people. Now that it was over and the busyness had stopped, she had no idea what to do with herself in the hours, days and weeks that stretched ahead. The workers were delighted to see her when she arrived at the farm, but there was an insidious feeling of collective helplessness. They too had witnessed Paul's bloody murder and now their fate remained suspended in mid-air. Angel didn't know what was going to happen next. The farm wasn't occupied and there was no one she knew she could contact. She called a meeting with all the workers huddled in the courtyard.

'Thank you all for coming. As you all know this has been a terrible time for my family … For all of us. We've laid Paul to rest. Some of you were there and I thank you for the support. I know you are probably wondering what comes next and I wish I knew what to tell you.'

'What happens to our jobs?' asked one worker. 'The only reason

I stopped working is because Mao threatened us, but I want my job back.'

Many more confessed that they had joined Mao's occupation out of fear of harassment and even death.

Angel did not doubt the veracity of their assertions; she'd been there – she'd seen it. As the workers continued to voice their concerns, Angel realised that they had also faced the collective trauma of Mao's invasion.

'I was raped and beaten by one of those militia men,' confessed the nurse who ran the clinic on the farm. 'They wanted cash and I said that our facility is free ...'

Her voice broke and Angel reached out to her. Many more workers confessed to being beaten for not joining in the *pungwes*. Standing among the workers, Angel realised that there was a much bigger problem at hand – and that was continuity. She would fly out in a few weeks to begin a new life in South Africa, but what would become of these people and their families? These thoughts tormented her. This was her farm – it was her responsibility. Was she just going to pack up and turn her back on everything?

'So you're just abandoning us here?' asked Ottilia, as Angel made her way to the car.

'No,' replied Angel. 'I'm coming back to the compound.'

Ottilia threw her arms around Angel, weeping in ragged gasps. Angel slowly began to soften in her arms and hugged her back.

Angel didn't want to be alone; she doubted she'd ever be able to sleep alone again. Before Melanie had left, they shared a bed and she wasn't able to fall asleep without a sleeping pill. Every time she tried, she'd have vicious nightmares. If it wasn't Mao thrashing her, it was Paul crying out to her. Melanie had suggested Angel return to therapy and while she promised she would, she dreaded making the appointment.

Angel headed to the stables. She hadn't been there in a while and her horse, Queenie, whinnied excitedly when she saw her. Angel kissed and stroked her tenderly before mounting her. They picked up an easy gait and Angel galloped across the farm, admiring her land. Every inch of it was hers. It was an exhilarating feeling being a landowner. She didn't care how long it would last, but she was going to relish the feeling for the moment. She visited her grannies' graves and went through her usual ritual of clearing the graves and laying flowers.

Being at the farm filled her with an indescribable sense of peace. As she walked through the fields, it was as though he was more alive than dead. Even as the wind whistled in her ears, she felt like he was speaking to her. Riding past the ruins of Belle Acres filled her with anguish, tempering the exuberance she had felt earlier. She couldn't hold the tears back. It was too soon to be here, she decided, and continued to the office block beyond the paddocks, which had not been destroyed by the fire. The offices were deserted, but to avoid the sense of idleness that threatened to overwhelm her, she immersed herself in admin work. She sent emails to the staff advising them to return to work. Slowly they returned and started populating their desks, and by the end of the week the office was up and running again.

'What happens to the farm?' they all asked at the inaugural staff meeting.

'We'll start farming again,' she replied. 'Until they occupy us again.'

And so the workers picked up their tools and went back to ploughing, sowing and milking. Two weeks passed. Then three. Then four. There was no word from the government about the farm occupation and so Angel continued as though the Section 8 notice had never been served. Her new passport eventually came through, but she decided she wasn't going to leave just yet. The workers needed her and so she picked up the reins and assumed leadership. It was what Paul would have wanted. He had groomed her for this.

Weeks rolled into months and the year ended in relative calm. Every day Angel made it a ritual to comb through the papers, reading about another farmer who had become yet another murder statistic, but eventually there were no more. There was still considerable uncertainty about the future and so, on the advice of her lawyers, Angel repatriated a lot of the family's funds, smuggling it out when she travelled to London for the Christmas holidays. She gave all the workers generous bonuses and by the time she left on holiday everyone was happy.

While a white Christmas in London was a novel experience, she didn't want to be there, but as this was their first Christmas without Paul, her absence would have been conspicuous. She arrived on Christmas Eve and every minute in the presence of Brad and Mariska in their new Kensington home was excruciating. Her feelings for him had not died; if anything, seeing him had simply resurrected them. He appeared to be happy, playing the role of doting husband and loving father. They deliberately avoided each other and even when they embraced, their eyes did not meet. They were never alone together, always a buffer between them.

Angel vowed that would be the last time she put herself through that kind of torture. After Christmas, she and Melanie left for Paris. They stayed at The Ritz in the heart of the city overlooking the Place Vendôme. Melanie had insisted on paying. A porter carried their bags to the eleventh floor and as Angel walked into the suite she marvelled at the finery and luxury. While they had holidayed in Paris when she was a child, they had never enjoyed such opulence.

'Life's too short,' remarked Melanie. 'Let's enjoy it while we can.'

They drank to that, whether it was coffee at a cosy outdoor cafe or Moët at fancy champagne bars. They shopped at the high-end stores on the Champs-Élysées and Angel purchased her first Dior bag and a gold watch at Swarovski. While she still wore her African doeks, she discarded the beads. She preferred to wear gold bracelets and gold earrings and also decided she liked silk shirts and tailored pants teamed with Chanel pumps. Her personal style was evolving into one of Afro-Euro chic. Melanie totally loved the transformation.

'You need to start looking like the million dollars that you are, Angel.'

Angel was becoming. And she loved this newer version of herself.

Part 5: The Afterlife

Every story has an end, but in life, every ending is a new beginning.
Unknown

PART 5: THE AFTERLIFE

Every story has an end, but in life, every ending is a new beginning.

Unknown

41

Changing faces

Belle Acres continued operations uninterrupted well into 2002, but it felt like they were caught in the eye of a storm as bedlam and anarchy whirled around them. While Angel had made no attempt to rebuild the farmhouse, she built her own two-roomed abode at the compound where she resided among the staff. This was supposed to have been a temporary arrangement, but the longer she stayed on the farm, the more permanent her residence appeared to be.

Everything seemed to be on a downward trajectory. Mugabe won the 2002 presidential elections and, in response, the value of the Zimbabwean dollar plummeted. Before the farm invasions, she needed only Z$24 to purchase one American greenback. Now she needed Z$55. The loss of value was staggering, but bigger loss was to follow. The loss of autonomy.

A few days after the results of the election were announced, a Toyota Land Cruiser rolled into Belle Acres, followed by a MAP75 armoured personnel carrier painted different shades of green. Uniformed soldiers looked out of the open-topped hull, their rifles pointed menacingly. Angel spotted them from the balcony of her office and broke out in a cold sweat.

They parked outside the office and the soldiers disembarked, spreading out like they were going to institute a hostile takeover. There was a pervasive feeling of tension and Angel strode out to meet the army officials in their green-and-brown camouflage uniforms and green berets with the ZNA insignia and the gold bird. The image of her father flashed before her.

'Gentlemen, good morning,' she said, greeting them politely.

'It's General Ngozi,' replied the taller of the two officers leading the men, lowering his steely gaze on her, 'and this is Colonel Pfuti.'

'How can I help you, *General*?'

He laughed. It was a dry, brittle laugh devoid of any mirth. The colonel stood beside him, a deadpan expression on his face. He was clearly used to the General's ways.

'I just want the keys to my farm,' the General replied smoothly. 'This property now belongs to me.'

Angel felt the anxiety pool in the pit of her stomach, spreading down her legs, which suddenly felt like jelly. The much-dreaded proclamation had arrived. This was *her* farm. It was her land. He couldn't take it from her.

'I'm Angel Williams. I inherited this farm from Paul Williams after he died,' she declared boldly.

The General convulsed with laughter. It came deep from in his belly and made him paroxysmal. This time the colonel joined in the laughter, making a mockery of Angel's declaration.

'The owner of this farm was served with the regulatory notices under law. What you two might have agreed upon is none of my business.'

'Pillow talk,' chuckled the colonel making the General laugh unabashedly.

'He was actually my father,' replied Angel, thoroughly annoyed by their insinuation that she had had sexual relations with Paul. 'He adopted me as a child and when he died I inherited Belle Acres.'

'And the first thing I am going to do is change that bloody name,' said the General vociferously.

'And what are you going to call it?'

'Bloody Acres,' he replied cockily.

There was more voluble laughter. Angel twitched in irritation, trying to suppress her rising anger.

'Who is the farm manager?' asked the General.

'I am,' she replied.

They laughed even harder and it made Angel fume that they thought they would belittle her simply because she was a woman.

'Come, I'll show you around,' she volunteered, determined to show them her capabilities.

She began with a tour of the office, introducing him to her small staff complement. She drove them around the farm, showing them the fallow fields that were ready to receive the seeds. She took them through the dairy operation and explained that, while the yields were low, they had been running a profitable business. Angel noted with pride that while the number of milk producers in the country had dropped from 323 to 283, Belle Acres was still in the fold.

She ended the tour with a visit to the compound where she showed him where the workforce was housed. The General was visibly impressed.

'So you're not just a pretty face after all,' he remarked.

'No, I'm not,' snapped Angel, piqued that she was being reduced to the sum of her looks. 'I'm actually in the process of studying towards a master's degree in Land Management.'

'Oh, really?' said the General, seemingly captivated.

One of Angel's New Year's resolutions was to complete her master's. With no social life to speak of, she decided she would use her free time to study. Here she was, caught up in the maelstrom of land reform, and it seemed ingenious that she should write about it. And so she decided to focus on the land redistribution programme.

By the time they had completed the tour of Belle Acres, the General appeared convinced of her competence.

'Well, you've passed the interview. I'll keep you on. You can run the show, but on *my* terms.'

Angel knew there was something sinister in his words and it left her unsettled. This was *her* farm – why was she negotiating terms on her farm?

'Here's what we're going to do. First, I'm firing every single person who works here.'

Angel was taken aback. 'Why? These people have worked here their whole lives!'

'That's why I am firing them. Their loyalties lie with you, not me. So, let me repeat myself … I'm firing everyone and they will have to reapply for their jobs. I will ascertain who stays and who goes.'

Angel realised then that she was going to lose the farm and decided that she wasn't going to stay on – not under the General's conditions. She was relieved that she had taken out the money when she had, that she had not invested in rebuilding the farmhouse because that would certainly have been a sunk cost.

'I don't think I want to stay under these conditions,' replied Angel.

'I don't care if you go,' replied the General. 'I'm not even sure I can trust you. I need people around me I can trust.'

Angel wanted to curse, but held her tongue.

'Call all the workers. I want to address them. They must know there's a new sheriff in town.'

After the General's address, the workers walked away in sombre spirits. They complained bitterly among themselves before expressing their disgruntlement to Angel.

'There's nothing I can do about it,' she said, feeling helpless. 'I'm not going to stay here and work for that man.'

'At least you have a choice to leave … What will happen to us?' asked one worker and then another and another until all their voices were competing to be heard. Angel held her hands up in resignation.

'I don't have the answers. I wish I did, but I'm not in charge here any more!'

She retreated to her own quarters, overwhelmed by the sudden turn of events. They had been compulsorily acquired. Management of Belle Acres had changed face.

42

Angel's abduction

Her family had warned her to not get too invested in the farm, that this day would always come. She started tossing some clothes into a suitcase and began to pack away the things of value she had slowly started to accumulate. Ottilia walked in and quickly offered to help. Angel was appreciative of Ottilia's loyalty and threw herself on her bed.

'I'm coming with you,' said Ottilia. 'Whatever happens, I'm not staying here.'

'I don't blame you ... There's nothing left to stay for.'

Angel started to cry, assaulted by myriad emotions: the sense of displacement, the disgruntlement, the unfairness of the whole situation. This was her home. Her umbilical cord was buried somewhere on this farm. Her grandmothers were buried here. Her entire life had played out on Belle Acres. Ottilia comforted her, trying to assuage her pain.

'The sooner we leave the better. I can't stand being here,' said Angel.

Angel turned on the television, which happened to be on the news broadcast. A group of war veterans were threatening to boycott the funeral of Chenjerai 'Hitler' Hunzvi if he was not awarded hero status. The leader of the Zimbabwe National Liberation War Veterans Association (ZNLWVA) had been lauded as the champion of the land resettlement programme, but had succumbed to cerebral malaria – or at least that was what was being reported in the press. Like Paul, he died at the age of 51. Angel felt little sympathy on hearing of his demise, blaming him for the chaotic land reform. He'd been an instigator of so many of the country's woes and, having spent many years exiled in Poland, it was doubtful whether he had even fought in the war.

'*Mxim*,' smirked Ottilia, walking in with a cup of hot chocolate. 'To think he won't see the results of the mess he created.'

Angel remembered the vociferous remark Chenjerai once made to a white farm manager that had been quoted in several publications. 'Do you know why they call me Hitler? It's because I am the biggest terrorist in Zimbabwe. I am the most dangerous man in this country. And you must do what I tell you.'

Even Mao was not in the league of Hitler Hunzvi. A doctor by profession, Hunzvi had been elected to a position of leadership in 1997. He made headlines when he interrupted Mugabe's annual address at Heroes' Acre but his brazenness had not ended there. Hunzvi had led the war veterans to the party headquarters, where they stormed a politburo meeting demanding compensation for thousands of disgruntled war veterans. Hunzvi felt that the war veterans had not been adequately compensated for liberating the country.

Timing is everything and Hunzvi's timing was perfect. His ascension came after Mugabe won the 1996 presidential elections. However, even with his resounding win, low voter turnout at the polls signalled to Mugabe that his popularity was waning. He knew better than to alienate the war veterans and so he succumbed to their demands of a lump sum payment of Z$50 000 each and a monthly pension of Z$2 000. Then the Zim dollar crashed and it took Z$10.50 to purchase one greenback. While Mugabe thought he had appeased them, the war veterans were back after the money had run out, demanding that the Z$2 000 be increased to Z$4 000. The blackmail didn't stop there; they wanted land too and, eventually, with no more money to placate their growing appetite, Mugabe capitulated to their demands and so the land grab began.

'I'm so tired of this!' said Angel switching off the television.

She would leave early the following day, she decided. She no longer wanted to be weighed down by people's haplessness, especially since she was no longer in a position to help. She felt guilty that she had other options and knew that if she stayed any longer she would be guilt-tripped into staying. She fell into a restless sleep, tossing and turning with anxiety about the future. Her grandmothers appeared to her in a dream. They too appeared agitated, strutting about the room, their long black dresses sweeping the floor. They were carrying her suitcases.

'*Hamba, Angel. Hamba!*' they insisted.

Angel lifted her head, drowsy with sleep.

'I'm going,' she replied.

'Go, Angel. You need to go now,' they said in unison.

Angel, still groggy, half opened her eyes. It was 10.55pm and there was no way she would be driving to Bulawayo at this hour.

'I'll go in the morning,' she replied, turning on her side.

'Go now,' they implored. 'Vuka, Angel. Vuka!'

There was an incessant pounding on the door and Angel sat up, wiping her eyes. The knocking got more frantic, so Angel climbed out of bed and slipped on her gown.

'Open the door or we'll break it down!'

Ottilia hung back in fear as Angel opened the door to two soldiers. They grabbed her, entwining their hands with hers so that she could not get away.

'Hey! Hey, what is this? What's going on?' she shouted, kicking them with her unrestrained legs.

'The General has called for you.'

'Called for me for what?'

'Let's go. You'll get to ask questions when you are in his presence.'

And so, having gagged her to muffle her screams, they bundled her into the night.

Panicked, Ottilia sent an SMS to Melanie. It contained three words.

They kidnapped Angel.

43

The General's angel

When the General later recounted how they met, he would proudly proclaim that he abducted her. That he had sent his men to seize her in the middle of the night and they had travelled over 300 kilometres with her before she was deposited like a prized possession in his presence.

'That's how much I wanted her,' he would brag to his guests, who would be seized with a combination of amusement and shock at his boldness.

'The minute I laid eyes on her I knew she was going to be mine.'

She remembered that night differently, without the tinge of romanticism, but with a great deal of realism. She'd been terrified as she was bundled into a Puma truck. They drove for kilometres on end to what seemed to be nowhere. The General never considered his actions intimidating, that he had physically subdued her into submission.

'She lived in a hovel. At the workers compound, but now she's queen of this castle.'

At this point, people would turn to Angel and marvel at her good fortune – an angle that compounded the overall effect of his version of the story. It made it more laudable that he'd rescued this poor woman from the clutches of poverty. The story always made the hairs on the back of her neck rise.

She reached for her gold-plated fork, wanting to stab him with it. He liked to tell the story over dinner when they had visiting dignitaries or were entertaining esteemed friends. He loved to posit himself as the knight in shining uniform who had liberated her from a life of destitution and paucity. She'd smile and nod good-naturedly because the General would never tolerate being contradicted, even more so in public. This was the narrative he was happy to punt because her real life story didn't quite sit with him.

The night she had been apprehended by his men, she had peed herself in fear. She had cried inside, imagining her death. While tears streamed down her face, her cries were raging internally. She told herself over and over again to be brave, silently repeating that she was strong, hoping the affirmation would bolster her failing strength. After hours of driving, they'd finally arrived at a house with high walls and an armed sentry. They'd driven through an open gate and up a long, winding driveway lit by soft lamps. It was then that the full grandeur and splendour of the house were revealed. The General was indeed the king of this castle. And a noisy one at that, with a raucous party on the go.

The long sloping driveway was clogged with luxurious cars of different makes and sizes. A grand double-storey home sat at the top. The balcony was well lit, giving an illusion of a glittering jewel. Whenever Angel thought back to that night, it felt ludicrous that she arrived at the General's party in her satin pyjamas. Which is why no one would ever understand that, despite being brought to a party teeming with guests, he really had kidnapped her. 'Why didn't you scream for help?' was always the obvious question. Or alert one of the guests that you were being held against your will? Would they have believed her anyway? Or would they simply have thought she was high on something?

She had been shepherded into the house that night and escorted to a bedroom, a plush suite with sumptuous carpets and velvet drapes. She had showered, crying as the water pelted against her body, the sound of the water drowning out her weeping. By that point she had still not seen the General, nor had he laid his eyes or hands on her, but she had a strong sense of foreboding about what was going to happen next. When she emerged from the bathroom, she wrapped herself in a fluffy white towel. She stepped out onto the balcony that overlooked the swimming pool, where the party was in full swing. The partygoers were dancing to Oliver Mtukudzi belting out from the loudspeakers. The entire place was patrolled by armed soldiers. Angel knew she was trapped and even if she had tried to run, she wouldn't get very far. And where would she run to? She had no idea where she was; she was literally hemmed in.

She exhaled noisily as she prepared to get dressed. A uniformed helper had already placed a box on the bed containing three pieces of scant, lacy lingerie replete with garters. She was presented with a choice of two dresses and compared to the racy lingerie, they were demure. She was more comfortable with the choice of dress, but the lingerie was too risqué for her taste.

'Am I supposed to wear this?' she asked.

'Yes,' replied the woman. 'And when you are done, you are to come downstairs and present yourself to the General.'

'And if I don't?' she taunted.

The stern-faced matronly-looking woman looked at her and smirked. 'You don't have a choice, my dear. My advice to you? Play along. You don't want to get hurt.'

Angel felt a chill run down her spine and shivered with unease. She shifted her attention to the gowns that had also been placed on the bed. Both were from the Prada Fall 2002 collection. One was an asymmetrical dress with one shoulder and the other a thin-strapped, black Grecian dress with leather straps. She chose the second for its simplicity – she wasn't going to try to be glamorous while held captive. For her feet, she had a choice between Steve Madden black-sequinned kitten heels or black mules with gold floral motifs. She chose the former as she rarely wore heels and wasn't about to make her debut in them that night. Everything was a perfect fit. She had only met the General for a few minutes on the farm, so how was he able guess her size?

Angel's hair was short, cropped close to her scalp and accentuating her face. Her big, almond-shaped eyes were still puffy from crying, her distress visible even as she tried to wipe away the glaring evidence.

There was a knock on the door before it was immediately opened and standing there was the General. He stared at her with his deep-set eyes. His gaze was dark, hooded with desire. Angel looked away from him.

'Are you ready?' he asked.

'Do I have a choice?' she replied.

He roared with laughter. 'That's what I like about you, your feistiness.'

Angel eyed him circumspectly, her eyes narrowing with disdain. His arrogance was nauseating.

'So, how did you guess my dress size?' she asked.

'I didn't,' he replied. 'My ex-girlfriend is the same size as you.'

'Oh, so it's a one-size-fits-all now, is it?'

'Women forget that they are dispensable,' chuckled the General. 'That they can be easily replaced.'

Angel held onto those words, unsure whether it was a veiled threat or a callous observation. He then took her by the hand, leading her outside for a meet-and-greet. He introduced her as his girlfriend, throwing a possessive arm around her. Angel stiffened at his touch.

'*Bhebhi rangu,*' he declared with pride, '*anonzi, Angel.*'

Her smile was tight and her eyes twitched nervously as she moved beside him. Then she saw him – Mao – standing at the edge of the pool nursing a whiskey. Her chest tightened and her heart started to pound. She was unaware that she was trembling, but the General felt it.

'What's wrong?' he asked.

Her breathing was sharp and shallow, her heart flapping in her chest like a frightened bird.

'I'm not okay,' replied Angel, leaning into the General, her legs shaking, unsteady on her feet.

Mao started to advance towards her and she folded over. She felt herself sink to the floor, but the General caught her before she hit the ground. He seemed genuinely troubled by her reaction. A doctor in the crowd suggested they carry Angel into the house – and that was how she left the party, having passed out from an anxiety attack.

Angel woke the next day flustered and confused, trying to make sense of the events of the night before. The General was lying beside her, his arms draped around her. This sent her into a flutter of panic.

'It's okay,' he said, holding onto her, cocooning her in his embrace. 'Everything is fine. You're safe with me.'

'Where is Mao? He was here. At your party. That man … He terrorised me. You have no idea what he did!'

'Don't worry about him – he's gone. He'll never bother you again.'

'What does that mean?'

'It means exactly that. I have taken care of him; he will never harass you again.'

Angel relaxed, at least sufficiently to turn in the circle of his tight embrace.

'Don't worry, my Angel. I am not going to hurt you.'

She looked the General in the eye, searching them. They gave nothing away. He had dark circles and bags around his eyes that could only have been accumulated from years of inadequate sleep. His face was lined with wrinkles, his angular jaw softening only when he smiled.

'Are you going to take me home?' she asked. 'I want to go home.'

'This is home now,' he replied. 'Your home is here with me.'

He ran his fingers down her tawny brown skin, in perfect contrast to his dark onyx complexion. She quivered at his touch.

'Let me love you,' he said, propositioning her. 'What is the worst thing that could happen?'

Angel felt a lump form in her throat. Yet again, what choice did she have but to succumb to his advances? His hands were large and, as he caressed her, his strokes were gentle and deliberate. His kisses were light, his tongue inquisitive and probing. While she was certain she didn't desire him, her body betrayed her and responded to him.

Bradley had been the last man she had been physical with and she felt ashamed of her body's unabashed receptiveness to the General as he strummed the chords of her innate desire. His long fingers played a symphony between her ebony thighs until she was singing a chorus of pleasure. His eyes never left hers, spurred on by the silky wetness as she climaxed, her pupils dilated with gratification. She shuddered as he raised her legs, placed them on his shoulders and entered her, his movements slow and calculated. Angel was in awe of his size, but his movements were slow and deliberate so that her body became receptive and she gripped him tightly as he thrust his way to his own orgasm.

Even after all these years, Angel still flushes at this memory.

44

Sleeping with the enemy

They were married three months later. Angel had wanted a low-key, private ceremony on a remote island with white sandy beaches and shimmering blue waters. But the General had other grand ideas and his prevailed. They were married at the Wild Geese Lodge, a secluded wildlife sanctuary in Mazowe Hills with at least five hundred guests in attendance. Melanie was one of them and she couldn't help thinking it was like being at a political rally rather than a wedding. She was the only member of the family who attended. Adrienne had made it clear that she would not attend, because doing so would feel as though she was betraying her father's memory. She had been vociferous in her disapproval.

'How can you marry a man who had a hand in Dad's murder?' she hissed.

'The man who killed your dad is dead, Adrienne.'

After leaving the General's party that night, Mao had lost control of his car. Drunk, he had driven off the kerb and his car was found wrecked on the side of the road, his body burnt beyond recognition.

'Angel, why are you doing this? After everything Dad did for you, this is how you repay him? By marrying one of his enemies?'

Angel had hung up on her and that was the last time they'd spoken. Unsurprisingly, Bradley and Mariska had declined the invitation too, so the wedding was attended by people Angel didn't even know. It was the General's wedding. The president was in attendance and, at 78 years of age, he had just won his fourth term at the helm of the republic. It had been another election marred by state-sponsored violence and victimisation of the opposition. But none of that mattered – the highly decorated generals had secured him yet another victory.

Melanie was concerned that the General was almost 30 years older than Angel. There were a lot of other things that concerned her too.

'He's old enough to be your father, Angel,' was the first thing she said when Angel announced her pending nuptials. But Angel insisted that it didn't matter, that she was delighted she was going to be the General's wife.

'He *is* actually older than my father,' said Angel unashamedly. 'But age ain't nothing but a number,' she sang ruefully, alluding to the title of the hit song.

Angel and her friends had been part of that pervasive generation that had grown up on Aaliyah's hit single.

'You need to hook me up with a general!' piped up Anele.

The girls were in awe of the General. He was tall and imposing and his dark olive skin shone like the gold epaulettes on his uniform.

Melanie had not met the General prior to the wedding, despite having made several attempts. He'd refused to meet her, stating emphatically that he loathed white people. The General was relieved that Angel's family was not coming to the wedding. There were some whites from the business and farming community, but the General insisted that these whites were different.

Melanie was with Angel in her bridal suite as she dressed. Her varsity friends, Anele, Seipati and Tshepo, were part of her bridal entourage. Apart from Ottilia, they were the only familiar faces. They drank Veuve Clicquot and made merry, empty bottles littering the dressing table among the tubes of lipstick and pots of make-up. 'I don't even recognise myself,' proclaimed Angel, looking at herself in the mirror as she ran her fingers through the thick Peruvian weave that cascaded down her back.

'The only person who needs to recognise you is Simba,' replied

Melanie, standing behind her and embracing her.

It was odd to hear anyone refer to the General by his first name. Simba Simboti was his birth name and Tongayi Ngozi his nom de guerre. He had illustrious struggle credentials, having joined the war of liberation in 1973 and even after the war hadn't discarded the Ngozi part of his name, choosing to become General Simba Simboti Ngozi.

'How well do you actually know this man, Angel?' asked Melanie.

'Well enough,' replied Angel. 'And we'll continue to get to know each other.'

'Do you love him?' Melanie probed further.

'He loves me. Surely that must count for something?'

'Angel, that's called empathy, not love. Do you love him?'

'Yes. I love him,' replied Angel.

Melanie wasn't convinced. What was the allure of the General? Angel had grown up around money so that certainly couldn't be the reason.

'I hope you're not doing this for the farm,' said Melanie.

'Of course not,' replied Angel dismissively. 'I've made peace with losing the farm.'

Melanie didn't believe her, but now was not the time to pursue it. It was Angel's day; it was supposed to be happy, not filled with recrimination.

'Let's go, girls! We can't keep the General waiting!'

Melanie covered Angel's face with the foot-long veil and they made their way out of her suite. Angel floated down the red carpet looking angelic, her dress covered entirely in lace. Granny Belle would be proud, she thought. She was marrying well and into a position of power. The General wrung his hands nervously as Angel approached. This was his third marriage. The first had been a no-frills, civil ceremony, and while the second one had been a huge celebration, he hadn't had the money that he had now. This wedding was grander, more of a self-actualisation of what he really wanted. Angel was the trophy wife. They were joined in holy matrimony by a priest, but neither of them 'do' church so it was more ceremonial than religious. The General didn't believe in God or the Church, insisting that religion was the biggest tool of colonisation. A hoax played on the black man.

'Bloody Robert Moffat and his cohorts,' he'd said. 'Fuck those missionaries.'

'But you love the missionary position,' teased Angel.

He'd laughed and decided to colonise her in the confines of the bedroom with his missionary masterstroke.

They spent their wedding night in Harare and then drove out to the General's family home in Vumba the following day. Angel discovered that the General suffered from aviophobia – an intense fear of flying that meant that he would travel nowhere that required him to board a plane. And this was also the reason he'd declined all diplomatic postings abroad. In fact, the more Angel got to know the General, the more she realised how frightened he was. He might have instilled fear in others with his commanding presence, but he remained fearful of the unknown and they always moved around with a well-armed security detail. In the beginning, Angel found it disconcerting to always be in the company of the guards, but the General insisted someone was out to kill him. He hadn't even eaten at their wedding because he believed there were people there who would try to poison them.

'Why would anyone want to kill you?' asked Angel.

'I wouldn't have got this far in life without enemies,' he replied candidly, 'and you, by virtue of being my wife, are also a target.'

They passed through his ancestral home nestled in the Vumba mountainside, straddling the Mozambique and Zimbabwe border. The home was made up of a circle of thatched, refurbished rondavels, electrified and fully furnished with modern amenities. The rustic charm of each hut held no trace of the General's impoverished upbringing.

'It's what pushed me to join the struggle in 1973,' explained the General.

'I wasn't even born yet,' responded Angel.

His parents were late, but his siblings were all still alive and treated Angel with reverence. She knew it was only because she was his wife and, had the circumstances been different, she probably would have been running around the homestead like a headless chicken like all the other *murooras*.

His brothers and sisters feared him more than they respected him. The General instructed her not to accept any food or drink from the family while they were there and whispered in her ear that his sister was a witch. He insisted that he could not sleep in the village because he feared being choked in the middle of the night, so they stayed at the spectacular Leopard Rock Hotel. The sweeping vistas of the mountains from their room were in stark contrast to the rustic charm of the homestead. The General was a restless sleeper and hardly ever slept through the night. Sex soothed him, so when he woke up in the middle of the night from an intense nightmare, he would reach for her.

With their visit to the family homestead over, they drove up to Nyanga and stopped at World's View. While it had been a foggy morning when they set out, the mist had lifted, unveiling panoramic views. Angel remembered that sunset as a child and it never grew old. The views were so arresting that the General said he felt as though he saw angels appear in all directions.

'I used to gaze at that sunset for hours,' said the General wistfully. 'It's a sign. You and I were meant to be.'

They checked into the Troutbeck Resort, where they spent three days cavorting in the lap of nature. They fished, went horse riding and hiked through the picturesque mountainside, which the General knew intimately. He told her he felt at peace there and explained how he trekked for days through the pine and wattle forests and hiked the mountains to cross over to Mozambique to join the war effort. He was passionate about being a soldier and went to great lengths to explain to Angel the military strategy of ZANLA during the war and how ZANLA had politically mobilised local communities in the *pungwe* system. They had a network of young civilian men called *mujibhas* who provided the guerrillas with logistical support. *Chimbwidos* were the female equivalent, but their duties differed from their male counterparts.

'They also satisfied us sexually,' chuckled the General.

A *pungwe* began when darkness fell and villagers would have to provide the guerrillas with food. After eating, there would be singing and dancing and the sharing of political ideologies and dogma. *Pungwes* went on all night. Villagers who did not join were viewed with suspicion and were often accused of being sell-outs. Lynchings were commonplace and many villagers met their end by simply failing to cooperate with guerrillas. Angel couldn't help thinking that this was the same strategy Mao and his cohorts had used when they occupied Belle Acres – a cut-and-paste methodology.

They posed for photographs next to the terraced Nyangombe Falls, its waters cascading like a bridal veil. The General told her it was on the banks of this river, the Nyangombe, that the notorious 5th Brigade had been trained. Angel professed her ignorance of the unit and the General explained that the squad had been recruited solely from ZANLA guerrillas stationed at the Tongogara assembly point. They were specifically trained by the North Koreans and were answerable only to Mugabe. Even their uniforms were different and were crowned with red berets.

'They were used to quell the insurgency in Matabeleland,' explained the General. 'We averted civil war in this country. ZAPU was a threat to peace after independence.'

He went on to further explain that the signing of the Unity Accord in 1987 cemented the relationship between ZAPU and ZANU.

'Just like you and me,' he added, snaking a loving arm around her waist.

From Nyanga, they crossed the border into Mozambique and spent the first few nights in Chimoio. The General told her his memories of the area from when he resided there during the struggle. Chimoio, located 17 kilometres north of the city of Chimoio from which it derived its name, was the biggest ZANLA base. It was a heavily populated area and the thirteen camps housed over 700 ZANLA cadres.

This had been the headquarters of Robert Mugabe and his commanders, Josiah Tongogara and Rex Nhongo, chosen because it was so isolated and would have made it less vulnerable to complete annihilation. Being in close proximity to a FRELIMO base meant Rhodesia was reluctant to attack it because they did not want to start a fight with FRELIMO. Distance from the border made both camps inaccessible to the Rhodesian forces. It was too long a distance to travel without being spotted.

'I think we got too comfortable thinking the Rhodesians wouldn't do anything to us as long as we were on Mozambican soil, but on the 23rd of November 1977 they attacked us,' explained the General.

Angel realised that that was the year she had been born; she would've still been in nappies.

The General went on to narrate how they had risen that morning, emerging from the trenches like meerkats, and lined up for the morning parade. The commanders on duty noted a lone aircraft flying high in the sky. They were quick to dismiss it, thinking it was Samora Machel coming to pay them a visit. The Mozambican president would fly in from time to time to consult with the high command. Deciding to err on the side of caution, the parade was nevertheless disbanded. As the comrades were dispersing, more planes swooped in like eagles on the Chimoio base camp. Bombs were dropped and the ground shook with the impact, enveloping the camp in a cloud of dust. A mass stampede ensued as comrades ran for cover. But it was too late. After the hail of air strikes, paratroopers dropped down to the ground. With the ambush over, the attackers scooped up their manpower – some dead, but mostly alive – and finally there was a lull as the helicopters retreated. The smell of burning flesh permeated the camp; dismembered limbs were strewn on the ground. The air filled with the cries of wounded survivors, some gasping for air, grappling with death. There were howls of anger and despair as comrades made their way through the wreckage, stepping over shrapnel.

'I survived that bombing, Angel. It was the worst of its kind ... Thousands died that day. Women and children. I really grew to hate the white man that day, with all my heart.'

As he had narrated the carnage, a lone tear rolled down his cheek. Angel gently wiped it away. It was in those fleeting moments of vulnerability that Angel was drawn to the General.

45

Immaculate conception

From the ashes, they began reconstruction on Belle Acres. The General had the plans drawn up because he wanted a big house, eight bedrooms in total. He told Angel that he had grand expectations of her filling their home with children. He was childless. Angel learnt that his first wife had been killed in a car accident when she was driving home with their three kids and they had all died, while his second wife had been unable to have children. On hearing this, Angel was determined to give the General a brood of children. Falling pregnant was, however, not as easy as she had envisaged.

It wasn't for a lack of trying but even with the amount of copulation taking place, nothing happened. Every month, Angel's period arrived like clockwork. While the General didn't say anything, he was anxious about the lack of conception. Angel's gynaecologist assured her that there was nothing wrong, that there were no discernible obstructions to conception. On hearing this, the General decided to consult one of his spirit mediums. He had a few at his disposal. After throwing a few bones on the mat, the sangoma declared that Angel needed cleansing.

They had gone down to the river at Belle Acres, and Angel had been commanded to strip naked and bathe in the river. She was thankful for the bulrushes that grew along the water's edge because they provided her with a cover of sorts. The bulrushes danced softly in the breeze, which made Angel shiver slightly as she waded into the water. Memories of her and Bradley skinny-dipping and making love resurfaced and her skin prickled with the memory. Angel wondered if the sangoma was a mind reader too. She had no faith in the accuracy of these spiritual healers and only went along with it to placate the General. The sangoma waved her *itshoba* in the air, a wand made from a bushy animal tail. She splashed it in the water and sprayed Angel while muttering inaudible incantations. Angel was given a bottle filled with water and seaweed that she was told to drink every day. When she returned to the farmhouse she emptied the bottle and replaced it with aloe vera juice. She then placed it in the fridge next to a selection of other concoctions the General drank every day.

That night, Angel had a vivid dream in which she was running across a field of roses, a handsome man running after her. He was enveloped in light and laughter and they were both naked. As she ran, she turned back but could not see his face, only his long hair. When he caught up to her, he kissed her passionately and they fell on the ground, drunk with laughter and passion. Even as they fell into the thorny rose bushes, the thorns piercing their skin, they were unperturbed by the discomfort. They continued to kiss passionately, the heady scent of roses filling her nostrils.

'I love you so much,' he whispered to her over and over again.

'I love you too,' she replied.

They continued kissing, he making the sweetest love to her.

But then a strong wind suddenly picked up, gusting in from nowhere, and blew her lover away.

'No, don't go!' she cried. 'Please don't go! Come back to me! Please come back. Don't leave me!' she screamed. 'Don't!'

When she opened her eyes, she was relieved that it was just a dream. The General turned on the light, obliterating the darkness.

'Angel, are you all right?'

'Oh!' she cried out, hugging him tightly. 'I must have been having a bad dream.'

He hugged her back, squeezing her tightly. He continued to hold her in his arms, stroking her damp hair.

'You were crying, Angel.'

'I was just scared,' she muttered.

'Scared of what?' he insisted, probing her. The General didn't take bad dreams lightly.

'I was just scared … in the dream,' replied Angel, turning away from him.

The man in her dreams had long, blond hair. It could only have been Bradley, and she felt a tinge of betrayal. How was it that she was dreaming of an ex-lover while lying next to her husband? She felt a deep sense of loss that she could not explain, an almost physical pain she could not understand.

'I'm here, Angel. I will always be here for you, I promise,' said the General, hugging her even tighter.

Angel smiled and felt the fear and restlessness of her dream vanish; her anxieties replaced by the General's closeness. She might not have loved him when they first got married, but she had grown to cherish him more and more every day.

The following morning she made sure she drank the juice; the General was monitoring her to make sure she was following the sangoma's instructions. The sangoma returned at the news of Angel's disturbing dream and was delighted by the outcome. They sat out on the patio, the sangoma stirring with her stick a bowl of clean water in a metallic dish in front of her.

'It's working,' she said to Angel. 'There is a spirit hovering over you that is inhibiting the General, but we shall defeat it!'

Angel shifted nervously, her eyes downcast. The sangoma continued peering into the water, shaking her head in disdain. Then she stood up and marched through the house, spraying water with her *itshoba*, calling out to the ancestors. When she returned, she quizzed Angel about her father.

'What about him?' replied Angel, stiffening.

'His spirit is troubled. Did you consult him when you got married?'

'My father died a long time ago.'

'You can still consult his spirit,' said the sangoma accusingly. 'Except that it was never fetched. His spirit continues to roam the earth aimlessly.'

The sangoma suddenly stopped talking and was gripped by a violent seizure, her *isitshoba* dropping to the floor. It was a bizarre sight as her convulsions took over, a series of uncoordinated spasms. Then the seizures stopped, just as quickly as they had started. Angel and the General looked on in shock at the unchoreographed performance.

'Her father is not happy,' the sangoma declared as she slowly regained her faculties.

'What do we need to do?' asked the General, anxiously.

The sangoma shook her head, her braids rattling in acquiescence.

'You need to stay out of it,' she said, pointing the *isitshoba* accusingly at him.

She let out a loud, strangled shriek that made Angel quiver.

'I have to go now,' she declared. 'Let me go.'

She quickly gathered her things and Angel followed her out to the car.

The sangoma hugged Angel and said, 'You need to get away from that man. He is blocking your blessings.'

She climbed into her car and reversed speedily out of the driveway. Angel was concerned that she might have lost control as their driveway was steep.

Perplexed, Angel made her way back into the house.

It was clear that the General was equally disturbed by the sangoma's revelation.

'She's probably a con artist,' he suggested.

Angel shrugged her shoulders. 'Where did you find her?'

'Someone recommended her to me.'

Because his trust issues meant that he didn't remain with one for too long, the General had his sangomas on rotation. Angel didn't have the answers, but she did have a lot of questions.

For the first time, she and her husband had a conversation about her father.

'His name was Douglas Nzima ... His war name was Jones Sibindi.'

The General looked at her with a puzzled expression on his face. 'How is he your father? I thought you were raised by the Williamses.'

'Yes, when my parents went to join the struggle, I was essentially orphaned. The Williamses took me in. No one knows what happened to my father after he joined the army.'

'I can look into it,' suggested the General.

Angel smiled and felt a flicker of hope. 'I don't have any pictures of him. They were destroyed when the house was burnt down.'

The General swallowed hard. He doesn't need any pictures – he remembered Private Sibindi very well. They had had several encounters in the army.

Later, he reported to her that his enquiries had revealed nothing about her father and that there was no record of him ever being in the military.

46

Homeless

Three years go by before Angel managed to fall pregnant, and she finally gave birth to a cherubic baby girl in 2005. They named her Anerudo, 'the one who is loved', which Melanie immediately shortened to Annie. When she was a month old, Melanie visited her third granddaughter, the fourth of her grandchildren. She had only one grandson, Michael. Luke and Adrienne had two adorable twin girls, Brianna and Bryony.

As the only member of the family who had any sort of relationship with Angel, Melanie was feeling slightly apprehensive ahead of her visit. She hasn't been back to Zimbabwe since the wedding, and now she would be returning to Belle Acres, where Angel and the General permanently resided. She hadn't been there since Paul's death and going back felt too much like picking the scab from a wound that hadn't healed.

Angel often came to South Africa to visit her – more to do her shopping and attend art and décor shows – and she always travelled alone. She never stayed long, insisting that the General hated being left alone for too long. Melanie, still wary of Angel's husband, thought it odd that a grown man needed a babysitter.

They had since renamed Belle Acres, the signpost now reading 'Ngozi Ruins'. Melanie rolled her eyes so hard when she heard the name that she feared they would disappear into their sockets. The place was far from a ruin of any sort. They had rebuilt the farmhouse, but it was nothing like the structure that had been there before. In its place was a rather imposing eight-bedroomed home, all with en-suite bathrooms, screed floors and underfloor heating. All the bedrooms overlooked a courtyard with olive trees and a swimming pool. The garden boasted numerous sculptures and water features, and Angel had replaced all the white wooden shutters that had been destroyed in the blaze with silver aluminium window frames. There were no curtains, the interiors entirely exposed. She said it brought light into their home, which was plagued with so much darkness.

'It's really beautiful,' said Melanie, intentionally omitting to mention 'expensive'.

Nothing about the new house was cheap; everything was opulent, excessively so when the rest of the country lay in tatters. Driving from the airport, Melanie had felt that the whole city needed a lick of paint.

The night of her arrival, they held a braai in the courtyard overlooking the swimming pool. Angel informed her that the General loved to entertain and that they hosted many parties. He felt safer entertaining at home, where he was always in full control of the situation. The General had retired from the army and now spent his time 'farming'. This meant that he constantly barked orders at his staff. They were only producing milk and little else because the machines needed to process the yoghurts and package the by-products had broke down and hadn't been replaced. The General said it was because they didn't have foreign currency to import the machinery they needed.

He sat immersed in one of the wooden Balau chairs imported from Malaysia, cradling his daughter in his lap. He was clearly besotted with her and, unlike at the wedding, when she had seen him last and had found him cold and aloof, Melanie thought he seemed more amiable. His hair was more silver-grey and, at age 57, was well preserved for a man of his years. He was wearing shorts, his legs strong and muscled.

'Because he runs on the farm every morning,' explained Angel.

'You need to join me,' the General insisted.

'I can't keep up with you,' replied Angel.

He slapped her buttocks playfully and they wiggled with the motion. Angel hadn't lost the baby weight and was plump, with lots of extra padding.

While waiting for the steaks to cooked on the gas braai by a chef, they chatted over a fruit-and-cheese platter.

'How are things here in Zimbabwe?' asked Melanie.

'Things are great,' replied the General. 'ZANU-PF has won the elections yet again and that Mickey Mouse of a party is falling apart.'

He doesn't look her in the eye, but he was surprised Melanie didn't remember him, suggesting there was some truth, he thought, in the cliché that for most white people, all blacks look the same. He clearly recalled her face that morning when they combed the farm looking for Private Sibindi. That was when he had fallen in love with the farm, every acre of it.

After its split, the MDC had a poor showing at the 2005 elections and a new party, MDC-M, led by Arthur Mutambara and Welshman Ncube, was formed.

'I used to tell Angel that nothing will come of it but now that she's back, she knows where her allegiances lie.'

'But what has ZANU-PF really done for the people?' contested Melanie.

'Well, we're here aren't we?' replied the General. 'I have a farm and my children will be able to farm here.'

He didn't say as much, of course, but Melanie knew that his position allowed him to access loans at concessionary rates and he was able to access foreign currency at the official bank rate. That is how Angel could afford to shop in South Africa now that Zimbabwe was on the sanctions list and she could no longer travel to America or Europe. The General did not feel bad about it; he felt he had earned the right. The way Melanie saw it, there had been no real change. Power had just been transferred from the white elite to the new black elite, and the poor remained just that: poor and desperate, just as they'd always been.

After the meal, Melanie and Angel cleared the table and took the plates to the kitchen. Melanie really didn't recognise the space. Angel had had it completely revamped, with black granite worktops, stainless-steel appliances and mirrored walls. Melanie felt that it looked almost surgical, with its metal shelving in black and matching appliances. Angel had removed all traces of the wooden cabinets and the teak free-standing butcher's block.

'I hate clutter,' insisted Angel.

'I don't suppose you sit around the table and eat your meals in the morning like we did when you were growing up?'

'No,' replied Angel. 'We sit out on the patio in summer and use the dining room when it's cold.'

'I wish you'd consulted me when you were doing the interiors – you know it's my thing.'

'I know,' replied Angel, 'but I wanted our home to reflect us, not you. This is about us.'

Melanie was slightly affronted by Angel's response, but she understood too that Angel was trying to carve out her own identity. But she's not sure how much of it was really Angel because the General appeared to be very domineering.

'Are you happy, Angel?' Melanie enquired.

'Very happy, Mom, and now with Ane here, we'll be even happier.'

It is during Melanie's stay that the family's former maid, Esther, showed up with her husband Munya and their four children. They drove up in a battered Mazda bakkie piled high with their meagre belongings. Melanie recognised Esther immediately and they hugged excitedly. Munya and Esther marvelled at how Angel had grown into a fine young woman. They had both aged considerably; Esther was close to 50 and had filled out considerably, and while Munya was in his fifties he looked a lot older. Their four children were sandwiched in the car, ranged in age from five to sixteen years old.

'We weren't sure if you would still be living here,' said Esther, relieved to see her former mum.

'I'm not,' replied Melanie. 'Angel lives here with her family.'

'Oh,' gasped Esther, unable to mask her surprise. She couldn't envisage Angel *living* in a house like this, let alone being the mistress of it. 'Things have changed so much for us too,' she added. 'We lost our home not too long ago.'

Munya stepped forward to explain that they had been casualties of Operation Murambatsvina. Esther had been selling fruit and vegetables on the side of the road while Munya had done odd electrical jobs, wiring new homes for those who needed the service. He had also run a small shop where he fixed dysfunctional electrical items. Both had been in the informal economy, simply trying to get through day by day, making just enough money to pay the children's school fees and put food on the table.

It had been an ordinary day when the clean-up began, as tough as any. But then, in an unprecedented turn of events, the police ambushed vendors and began to destroy their structures. They said they had been given orders to clean up the city. After they were done with the vendors, they destroyed homes that were considered illegal. CAT trucks bulldozed homes, destroying people's livelihoods in front of their eyes. Those who couldn't bear to see everything being destroyed, tore down their own homes and tried to salvage the material before it all went up in flames. Over a period of ten days, buildings were demolished without mercy or favour. Settlements were burnt to the ground. This had been a nationwide clean-up and – coming two months after the election in which the ruling party had lost in urban constituencies – felt like a reprisal for voting for the opposition.

Munya told Melanie and Angel how desperate they were and how they were both unemployed and their family of six needed at least Z\$10 million to survive every month. At the official exchange rate, one greenback was equal to Z\$24 000. They had been reduced to poor millionaires.

'It's Mugabe – he wants to punish us for voting MDC.'

'Let's not be quick to apportion blame,' said Melanie quickly, not wanting to encourage that rhetoric, especially as they were seeking refuge in the General's home.

However, it was too late. The General had heard Munya's assertions and whatever sympathy he had felt for them disappeared.

'I really need a job,' begged Esther. 'Can I have my old job back?'

'Unfortunately, that's no longer my decision to make,' replied Melanie, deferring to Angel.

'Sadly, we don't have a position for you, Esther,' replied Angel, feeling sorry for her, but unable to fit her in anywhere.

Ottilia is in high command in their home, and they already had a resident chef who did the cooking.

'Angel, you haven't found someone to take care of Annie yet. Why don't you let Esther be her nanny? She raised you, after all,' suggested Melanie.

'And I've raised my own four babies,' declared Esther, pointing to her children whose faces were stuck to the car window, trying to get an eyeful of the surroundings.

'Please, Angel, consider it,' beseeched Melanie.

'We've lost everything. Everything.'

They smelled of desperation, their sad eyes reflecting their helplessness. Angel knew it would be cruel to turn them away, but she also knew she could not make a decision without first consulting the General.

'I'll have to speak to my husband about it,' she said, 'but for now, you can stay in the servants' quarters.'

Angel knew, even before she spoke to the General, that he wouldn't buy into it. But she was merely buying some time.

47

Father figure

From the get-go, the General was dead set against the idea of Esther and her family being there, even though Angel tried to justify it by saying they needed a nanny for Ane.

'I still wouldn't have hired her,' replied the General.

Angel knew it was because Esther's political ideologies did not align with his.

'Why are you going behind my back? Why couldn't we just have conducted interviews?'

'Sweety, I *know* Esther – she literally raised me. I trust her implicitly with our daughter.'

'I'm under no obligation to accommodate Esther's family, Angel. None. You decided to employ her, which is fine, but that troop of hers must go.'

'Sweety,' said Angel, trying to placate him, 'Esther's family is like my own. She raised all of us.'

'Angel, I can also bring the village who raised me into this home if you want to be like that. Our home is our home.'

Angel knew she would have to have an uncomfortable conversation with Esther. It was one she really didn't want to have, so she put it off for as long as she could. This served only to frustrate the General. And he was not alone; Ottilia's feathers were also ruffled by Esther's presence. She resented having to make space for the family of six and disliked their noisy children on sight. She resented the loss of her space, but mostly the loss of autonomy in the Ngozi household. It felt like a power-sharing agreement.

Ottilia tried to pull rank by virtue of the fact that she'd been in the job for a long time while Esther played the seniority card. Ottilia felt that her position as Angel's confidante has been usurped and Esther ranted about 'Angel and I go a long way back'.

Esther reminded Angel about her childhood antics, comparing her to Ane. She also made poignant observations about how Angel loved to sleep on her tummy or how she also used to suck on her thumb the same way Ane did. Angel enjoyed these insights and tidbits about her childhood, stories that Melanie never shared with her.

'I see you also married a soldier, just like your father,' said Esther.

Angel had never thought of it that way before. She had a vague recollection of her father but now that Esther had raised it, she started to see it in a different way.

'You were probably three or four when he came to visit you here on the farm,' continued Esther.

Angel searched her mind, fishing for that memory. She was horrified that she remembered nothing of it and it was at times like these that she wished she was still on talking terms with Adrienne and Bradley. They would have been there too and could have corroborated some of these stories. But she was more fascinated that Esther remembered so much of it.

'So you knew my father?'

'Oh yes,' replied Esther. 'I knew him very well. We grew up together.'

Angel was intrigued and wanted to hear more. Esther obliged and went on to regale her with stories about her father and growing up in the compound.

'Duggie was kind and generous. He went to fight in the war … The last time I saw him was when he came to see you when he was already in the army.'

Angel was saddened to hear this. In all the recollections she'd been told about her father, they end with his last visit to Belle Acres and never returning. Nobody seemed to know what happened to him after that.

Esther was ashamed of the role she had played in Duggie's disappearance and had never told anyone that she had been the one who had called the army that morning to report him. She had been bitter about the way he had beaten her, humiliating her in the streets. Of course, she couldn't say any of this to Angel, who was now her benefactor, having given her and her family a roof over their heads.

'He might have died during Gukurahundi,' suggested Esther. 'Many of our brothers died then.'

Angel, ashamed that she knew so very little of that part of history, tried to probe Esther about it.

'Ask the General,' replied Esther. 'He knows.'

'And my mother? What was she like?'

'Simphiwe was much younger than the rest of us, so we didn't really play together. We weren't allowed to play with her.'

Angel was puzzled. 'Why?'

'People said things about your gogo. They said she was a witch. My parents wouldn't let us play near her house. Simphiwe didn't have many friends. Except your father … '

Angel, crestfallen, crossed her hands over her chest. To think she had spent her whole life burdened by the shame of her grannies being domestic workers, and yet they had to shoulder the indignity of being labelled witches.

'I refuse to believe that about them,' said Angel indignantly.

'Well, the community believed it. A boy was found with his ears cut off and they blamed it on Mabusi. They burnt her house down because of it.'

'What proof did they have?' asked Angel. 'Or were they acting on some hunch?'

Esther shrugged her shoulders. 'I don't know what to say.'

'It's okay to say nothing,' said Angel sadly.

When it came to her family, Angel had an incomplete puzzle in her head. From time to time, someone would give her a piece to add to the puzzle.

After her disturbing conversation with Esther, Angel called her mother. Melanie corroborated the untruthfulness of the assertions levelled against her grandmothers and told her the story of why things happened the way they had.

Angel was appalled. 'So Uncle Graham got away with murder?'

Melanie was quiet for a minute, reflective.

'I don't think he did. He was punished in a different way.'

The year was 1982. Melanie remembered it distinctly because the case had hogged the international news in how it was handled. The Thornhill Air Base near Gweru had been bombed, destroying the air force's capacity, and Graham had been arrested as part of the saboteurs for colluding with the Recce Commandos in the sabotage. She recalled that he had been detained for six weeks and she and Paul had tried desperately to get him out. During his incarceration, he had been severely tortured and when he was finally released had walked with a limp and his hand had a twitch. He was not one of the six officers who faced trial for the crime, but refused to speak about his ordeal and resigned from the air force, emigrating to South Africa soon after his release.

Angel was intrigued and wanted to know more.

'Ask your husband, Angel. He probably knows more about it than I do,' said Melanie.

She did ask the General and he explained that 1982 had been a difficult year in Zimbabwean history. In February of that year, the prime minister announced that an arms cache had been discovered on Joshua Nkomo's farms in Ascot, Hampton Ranch and Woodville. These were followed by spurious allegations that ZAPU, in cahoots with South Africa, was involved in a plot to overthrow the government. The General said that, following the Entumbane wars, there had been instability in the country.

This was followed in July of the same year by the abduction of six tourists on the road between Bulawayo and Victoria Falls in the Lupane area. The abductors demanded the release of ZIPRA commanders Lookout Masuku and Dumiso Dabengwa and the return of ZAPU property that had been confiscated. While the demands were signed 'ZIPRA forces', the veracity was never substantiated. The following day, the government enacted its emergency powers and a dusk-to-dawn curfew was slapped over the Tsholotsho communal area, spreading all the way to Lupane and Nyamandlovu. The demands were never met and the tourists were murdered three days later. After that the government lashed out at ZAPU because they felt they were behind it.

'But why all this interest in the past, my darling?' the General asked Angel.

'I've been speaking to Esther,' Angel replied. 'We've been trying to figure out what happened to my father.'

The General's face tightened.

'I told you, I could find no information about your father. After the war, many men left and many didn't join the army.'

Angel was adamant. 'But he did join the army. Esther says she met him after the war.'

'What are you implying, Angel? That Esther knows more than me? I was the one in the army!'

Angel was silenced by his response, biting down her frustration.

There was a war of another kind being fought on the domestic front. Matters eventually came to a head between Esther and Ottilia, and Esther quietly approached Angel, seeking some sort of solution.

'Don't you think it would be better if Ottilia moves into one of the rooms in the main house and we take over the entire servants' quarters? We're really squashed in there with the four kids and you have a lot of space in this house. Some of the rooms are empty.'

Angel raised an eyebrow. 'Are you telling me how to run my home, Esther?'

Esther looked down at her feet, embarrassed at being dressed down by a woman less than half her age. A woman she had raised.

She started to stammer her response.

'No, erm, no. I was just trying, uh ... hmm ... I was only suggesting ...'

Out of respect, Angel decided to accommodate Esther and suggested that Ottilia move into the main house, leaving the quarters to Esther. The General didn't like the idea.

'I don't like having the hired help in our space. I'm no longer free in my own home. She must return to her quarters.'

Ottilia agreed with the General; she wasn't comfortable sharing the space with him either. There was something off about the General that made her uncomfortable.

The General refused to pussyfoot around the issue and that evening he gave Munya a directive that he had 24 hours to vacate the premises.

'There is only one person employed here and that's your wife. We're under no obligation to accommodate you here.'

'But, sir ... ' replied Munya.

'It's General.'

'Sorry, General, but we've lost our home and have nowhere to go. You have everything. We are not asking for much, just a little bit of space ... '

The General backhanded him. Munya stumbled back, stunned by the assault. It was swift and sharp, but humiliating nonetheless.

'I don't like repeating myself.' The General turned and walked away, leaving Munya rubbing his aching cheek.

The following day, they all left – including Esther. She came to Angel to offer her goodbyes.

'It wouldn't be right for me to stay under the circumstances.'

Angel hugged her and put some money into her hand. Esther

was touched by the gesture, tears welling up in her eyes.

'You really married your father,' she said as a parting shot.

The irony was lost on Angel.

48

The persecuted

For most of 1982, Douglas lived in the bush, camouflaged by his surroundings. He slept in trees to escape the snakes that slithered on the ground, recalling how Mugabe had likened Joshua Nkomo to a cobra.

'Nkomo is like a cobra in a house. The only way to deal effectively with a snake is to strike and destroy its head,' declared Mugabe.

Except Nkomo had slithered away, slippery and wily, evading arrest in March 1983 and exiled in the United Kingdom until 1986.

Douglas had become accustomed to snakes in the grass. They often crossed paths when he trekked through the bush during the day, the sun burning his back. He had lived in the bush long enough to know, however, that snakes only struck when they were attacked.

Camp life had prepared Douglas well for the rigours of bush life. But that had been voluntary. He had signed up for that life, not this one. It seemed unfair that he was running from his life, running from false allegations. He knew he was not alone, that many comrades had fled to neighbouring countries like Botswana and South Africa. He was now following that same path.

He avoided killing animals as much as he could, but when hunger set in he sacrificed the odd rabbit and braaied it over a small open fire. He tried to avoid making fires as the smoke would certainly give him away. As much as possible he survived on chewing berries like *ubhunzu* or *umbumbulu*. He drank from the rivers and, in the heat of the summer months, washed himself there too. Sometimes he got caught in the rain, cold and sopping wet until the sun came out and dried him. The rain was sporadic and fitful and came in short bursts. Rain or shine, Douglas continued on his path, forging his way. From time to time, he came across a small village. The villagers were always friendly and accommodating, especially once they realised that he meant them no harm. They would feed him and offer him a place to sleep. This was the only time he ever came into contact with others and could find out what was happening on the ground. There were many soldiers who had demobilised and were living in the rural countryside; they were all the same, disillusioned and desperate. Douglas eventually made his way home.

It was Christmas of 1982 when he finally arrived. He had no idea how much time had elapsed, but he felt that it had been enough time in exile to get the army off his back. There were collective cries of disbelief when he arrived in his village as it was thought that he had perished in the war of Entumbane. His mother told him how many mothers in the village had lost their sons and she had counted herself among them.

His mother was not alone but flanking her were Tabitha and Theresa.

'Your wives are here,' she said. 'Your wives and your children.'

Both women had babies strapped to their backs. Douglas's mind quickly circled back to the lascivious encounter he'd had with the young cousins, shocked that it had led to the conception of children. Two healthy boys, who would soon be toddling towards two years. One was named Velempini and the other Vusisizwe.

While it hadn't been his intention to remain in the village, Douglas knew there was no way he could abandon his growing family. He had already shirked the responsibility of one child; he couldn't do that to two more. He decided to stay and try to build them all a home.

He presented himself to Nkala and made a pledge to *lobola* his daughters once he was able to. Nkala gave him a disparaging look before dismissing him. This made Douglas even more determined to make right by him.

As the year crawled to an end, Douglas began ploughing the fallow fields. His wives helped, but the seedlings died in the fields when the rains didn't come. The land was so dry that it cracked and even Douglas's tears of despair couldn't wet it. And so Douglas made the decision to leave. He boarded a bus to Plumtree, but when it was stopped at a roadblock in Figtree, the passengers were told to disembark, and the men instructed to stand in one line, the women in another. The men's clothing was stripped from their bodies with bayonets, their skin scraped off in the process. They were then killed execution-style. Douglas held his hands to his ears as the gunfire rang and the men fell like dominoes.

Those killings marked the beginning of Gukurahundi, referring to the September rain that washes away the chaff, signalling the start of spring. But the 5th Brigade was deployed in January, long before any rains fell.

The men came wearing red berets. Their mandate was to quell the activities of the dissidents, to thwart any counter-insurgency from ZIPRA who they believed would front a civil war if left unchallenged. They had a list of names and Douglas's name was on that list. Even his mother was beaten for giving birth to a dissident, and she eventually died of concussion exerted by the heavy blows from the butt of a gun. Theresa and Thabitha were not spared either. They were bludgeoned to death for cavorting with a dissident. Douglas's boys were axed to death for being children of a dissident. The villagers were not immune either, and were beaten on suspicion of harbouring dissidents. Of feeding dissidents. Some were bludgeoned simply because they looked like dissidents. Others were beaten for withholding information they did not have. Soldiers danced on their bodies, making them confess to things they had no knowledge of.

For six months they caused carnage and chaos in the villages. The soldiers burnt homes they suspected had housed dissidents. They bayoneted the pregnant wives of the dissidents. They forced villagers to attend all-night *pungwes* and made them sing and dance and denounce dissidents. ZAPU was the dissident party, they said.

Dead bodies were left in the wake of the violent campaign. Villagers were not permitted to bury their loved ones, corpses left to rot and fester in the heat or become fodder for scavenging animals. In July 1983, the 5th Brigade finally withdrew from Matabeleland, signalling a lull in the Gukurahundi storm. General Ngozi had been part of that first deployment. The second deployment happened in September of that year, but Ngozi did not return, opting instead for a transfer.

The second campaign was characterised by mass beatings and mass torture. Mass executions were common as villagers were rounded up and frogmarched to schools and later to camps. Victims were forced to lie down in rows and endure beatings for hours on end. Those who survived were left with disabilities, permanent reminders of the trauma they had endured.

But at the beginning of 1984, the 5th Brigade changed its strategy. People were picked up in the middle of the night, their ankles entwined in barbed wire and transported in truckloads and delivered to detention camps like Bhalagwe. Here they were interrogated and beaten until they were black and blue, until their flesh tore under the repeated assaults. They cried until they could cry no more. Until they were only hiccupping in pain. Bodies were disposed of in mass graves and thrown down mine shafts.

The climate was hostile too; 1982, 1983 and 1984 were drought-stricken years and, with food aid suspended, many villagers starved to death. Many areas in Matabeleland remained under curfew and could not be accessed, with those living there could not leave. Bicycles, buses and cars were not permitted. The justification was that, in cutting off food supplies, they would cut off a lifeline to the dissidents. Not only was there a food embargo, but an information one too. Nobody was allowed into Matabeleland, the flow of news curtailed. The genocide happened in a silo of silence, and only those who survived were able to tell their stories. For those who died, their stories died with them. Their souls lingering, restless and disturbed. Their blood still crying, a permanent blemish on the landscape.

49

A fallen angel

The year was April 2008 and Bradley was part of a contingent of law firms representing disgruntled white farmers suing the government for unlawful expropriation, asserting that they had been wrongfully targeted by virtue of the colour of their skin. The farmers were demanding compensation for the improvements they had made on the farms. The suit had been instituted in 2007 and involved a delegation of 76 farmers challenging the unfairness of the land reform programme. Bradley had taken up the case pro bono simply for his father's sake. Like the other farmers, he wanted to see justice done.

'This is bullshit,' barked the General at the television.

Anerudo was sitting at her father's feet, playing with the remote control. Angel had tried to have more children, but it had been one miscarriage after another so she'd stopped trying.

'What's the matter?' asked Angel, as she drifted into the living room, followed by a waft of her signature Giorgio Armani scent.

The story was being covered by the BBC and her heart stopped when she spotted Bradley on the screen.

'These white boys are arrogant,' thundered the General. 'This is fucking nonsense! What improvements am I paying for? When I took over this farm, there was no farmhouse. It was in ruins.'

'Sweetheart,' said Angel, 'you took over a fully functional dairy farm. Everything was working.'

He eyed her askance. 'Whose side are you on?'

'Yours of course,' replied Angel. 'But if we're being honest ... '

'I'll call you if I want to have an honest conversation,' responded the General acidly.

Angel ignored him and continued to watch the broadcast, shaking her head. Bradley was wasting his time and she needed to tell him to abandon the case before he ended up in a shitstorm of trouble. The judiciary in Zimbabwe had long since been captured since the infamous November 2000 ruling when Chief Justice Gubbay proclaimed that the fast-track land reform programme was illegal. This was how he and his remaining cohorts were removed from the Supreme Court bench.

Bradley had reached out to her two days earlier in a text message.

I'm staying at the Meikles Hotel. Here till Sunday. Come and see me if you can.

She had been debating about whether she should see him or not, but after seeing the footage on TV, she decided she needed to. She couldn't allow Bradley to endanger his life; he was going to upset a lot of big people at the top.

Angel swept out of the living room, looking forward to getting out the house for a while. Things had been tense of late with the uncertainty surrounding the latest election results. The results had come out in dribs and drabs and the General had contested those in their area. He had made a decision to throw his hat into the political ring, but had been beaten at the polls. Even after they'd tried to stuff additional ballot boxes, he'd still been beaten. Angel didn't dare to say it out loud, but she was glad he had been defeated at the polls, glad that the circus was over. She'd been on the campaign trail with him, handing out T-shirts and food parcels to the masses. The acrid smell of unwashed armpits as desperate people reached for handouts still lingered.

The General hadn't taken the loss well. His libido had nosedived and he could no longer maintain an erection. He attributed this to witchcraft rather than the stress he'd been drowning in. Angel had to walk on eggshells around him. His drinking and weed smoking had become excessive and one of his doctors had prescribed hallucinogens that often lead to psychotic episodes. He'd gone off on a gun-toting and shooting frenzy one day, claiming he was under attack. This had all put a huge strain on their marriage.

It had been over two months since they had voted but the final results were still not out. The South African president, Thabo Mbeki, had been called on to mediate the crisis in Zimbabwe, but he had asserted on national television that there was no crisis.

'Mbeki is right – there is no crisis here!'

Angel was tired of living in denial, existing in a microcosm, cut off from the real world. The country was in crisis – how could he or anyone else not see that? Her marriage was in crisis too, but she was probably the only one who could see that. She poured herself a glass of orange juice and added champagne. Between her and the General, she'd started to wonder who drank more. The chef was making breakfast and she told him she was on her way out and wouldn't be having any.

As she was leaving, the General stopped her. He wanted to know whether the driver was taking her.

'No, I was going to drive myself,' replied Angel.

'It's not safe,' countered the General. 'Benson will drive you.'

There was a certain finality to his tone. He still didn't trust her. Not after she tried to leave with Anerudo on one of her shopping trips to South Africa. She had forged his signature on an affidavit, giving herself permission to travel with their daughter. Of course, the officials at the airport had called him straight away; he had his minions posted everywhere.

'I just want to travel with my daughter, for fuck's sake!'

'No child of mine gets on a plane,' he replied indignantly.

'Why are you burdening our child with your phobias?'

'Angel, I mean what I said. No child of mine flies.'

His control was a reminder that their marriage was just as oppressive as the country's politics. Angel had been looking forward to taking her Mercedes-Benz C-Class coupé on the four-hour drive to Harare and had already cued all her CDs and was relishing the time alone. But she decided not to argue and slid into the passenger seat of their Discovery Land Rover. The security detail sat in the front with the driver. The General came out to kiss her goodbye.

'Be good.'

'I'm always good,' replied Angel.

'What did you say you were doing?'

'Going to town to meet a friend for lunch.'

'See you later,' said the General.

They drove off, but he called twice before they reached Harare. Angel wondered why he was being so clingy. It was so unlike him.

On arrival at the hotel, Angel sent the driver and security to do whatever errands they needed to do. She didn't want the security detail hovering over her. Besides, she didn't consider herself worth killing.

She walked into the hotel reception, asked for Bradley Williams and was directed to his room. She was hesitant at first, but thought it was probably better that way. He was on the sixth floor and already waiting for her in the doorway of his suite. Her heart fluttered when she saw him. He was so handsome with his hair ruffled and eyes sparkling in the midday sun. His shirtsleeves were rolled up, exposing his strong arms. He leaned forward and kissed her chastely, first on one cheek then the other. They hadn't seen each other in six years, the duration of her marriage.

When Bradley saw her, it felt like he'd put his feelings for Angel in a box and shoved them in a dark room, but someone had found the key and set all those emotions free. He was heady with glee, felt so alive and so happy to see Angel. As he ushered her into the suite, she expected Mariska to come bounding into view.

'Don't worry, we're alone,' said Bradley. 'I thought it would be best to meet here because a few journos have been hounding me.'

'Where's Mariska? Is she not joining us?' asked Angel.

'Mom didn't tell you? We're going through a divorce. It just wasn't working. We tried, but it just wasn't there,' replied Bradley.

Angel swallowed hard; to say she was sorry wouldn't be entirely sincere, but she did feel sorry for him.

'It's not easy,' he said. 'Ten years of my life with her.'

His voice faltered. She comfortingly put her hand on his.

'And you? How's the General?'

Angel smiled. 'He's generally okay.'

They both laughed and Bradley promptly swept her into his embrace again.

'I've missed you,' he said longingly.

'And I you,' replied Angel.

It was good to be in his warm embrace. She felt safe with him; he was her safe space. With great reluctance she extricated herself from him. She sat across from him in the lounge area where he'd been working on depositions. The desk was piled high with journals and other case precedents, papers strewn all over the surface.

'I hope I'm not disturbing you,' said Angel, settling into the empty chair. She removed her shoes and sat with her legs outstretched.

'I want to be disturbed,' replied Brad. 'You can disturb me all you like,' he teased, pushing the papers aside.

He led Angel to the patio and they sat on the balcony overlooking the city below.

'Harare always looks great from a distance,' remarked Brad.

'Yes. It's a pretty skyline, but it's hell down there.'

He puts his hand on hers. 'How is it that you can be so breathtaking?' he said. 'Since I arrived in the country I haven't been able to sleep. I've just been dreaming about you.'

'Brad, please,' sighed Angel, 'let's not go there.'

'Okay, okay,' he said despairingly, passing her the room-service menu.

They ordered their meal and ate out on the patio. It was cosy and intimate and they finished a bottle of Chardonnay, the sun painting an epic backdrop behind them. Bradley coaxed her to dance. He just wanted to hold her, to cling to the moment. Angel suddenly became aware of the time and realised it was already after 7pm.

'I have to leave, Brad. I have a husband and a daughter who need me.'

'*I* need you, Gel!'

How could she tell him that there was no room for him in her life any more?

'Angel, please don't leave. *Please*, Gel.'

'Brad, I can't stay.'

If he only knew what she would give to be with him. But there was no way she could get involved with him again.

'Gel, don't go … Not just as we've finally found each other again.'

'Brad, we lead different lives now. I'm a married woman.'

'Do you love him, Gel? Do you truly love him – *that* man?'

She wasn't sure any more. Things were different somehow.

'It doesn't matter, Brad. He needs me.'

He grabbed her by the shoulders.

'I need you too, dammit! Why is it that everyone always seems to ruin it for us? First it was my father and now *him*. Dammit, Gel, will I ever have you?'

'Brad, I can't. I have to go.'

He looked into her eyes, but there was no dissuading her. She had made up her mind about leaving and she was about to walk out of his life forever. He watched helplessly as she slipped on her shoes, picked up her clutch bag and headed to the door. They were both torn by their circumstances.

Angel stopped at the door, hesitated briefly and turned around. Bradley knew that this was his last chance and quickly moved towards her before she could change her mind. Their lips locked in a searing kiss.

They tore at each other's clothes with a burning urgency. They were sucked in by an all-consuming passion so that nothing or no one mattered in that moment. Groping and groaning, they had given in to their mutual longing for each other. Wrestling towards that climactic release of years of pent-up passions. Afterwards, they lay slumped on the desk, physically and emotionally spent. Suddenly there was a loud rapping on the door, their naked bodies still wet and slick from their lovemaking. The raw smell of sex permeated the air.

'Who's that?' asks Bradley.

'Housekeeping?' suggested Angel. 'To turn down the bed?'

The knocking became louder.

'Angel, open the door! I know you're in there.'

The General.

50

Angels of death

A guard appeared and shone a bright light into recesses of the cell. Angel was cowering in the corner like a frightened animal. A hand roughly shrugged her awake.

'Get up. It's time to go.'

The jangling of keys heralded her freedom. The chains fell from Angel's wrists and ankles. She was free. Free at last. Her lawyer, Beather, was there to escort her and Angel could not hold back the tears.

'The charges have been dropped. You can go home.'

Angel wasn't sure she'd heard correctly and dragged her feet along the corridor. She could not believe she was free ... She wanted to pinch herself to make sure she was not dreaming.

'They were all trumped-up charges. The state didn't have a solid case,' said Beather.

Waiting for Angel was a woman in a starched white dress. She held out one hand, the other hanging limply at her side.

'We're going home, Angel,' said the woman. 'Come, my Angel.'

'Mum? Is that you?'

Simphiwe nodded.

At first, Angel thought she really must be dead, that she was in heaven, but then she was shoved brusquely aside by a barrage of men jostling to get out the prison gates. She started to run, fearing she might be trapped inside again. Her mother ran towards her and they embraced.

'Stop that,' said the guard sternly, jabbing at them with his baton. 'You can hug and kiss outside.'

When they were finally in the car park, Angel allowed herself to relax and bask in the glorious moment. She threw her arms around her mother, hugging her fiercely and sobbing into her chest. The space between them was filled by Angel's burgeoning baby bump. Her pregnancy had come as a surprise, but in the end that was what kept her going in prison in the last few months. After asking mother and daughter if they were going to be okay, Beather left quietly.

'Let's go home,' said Simphiwe. 'We have a funeral to plan.'

'Whose funeral?' asked Angel, shocked.

'Your husband's. He's dead. That's why the charges were dropped.'

'Oh God,' gasped Angel.

The General was dead.

Murder investigations into the General's death began with the taking of statements. Before the enquiry had begun, the commonly upheld view was that thieves had broken into the farmhouse, but the theory was debunked because it appeared that nothing of value had been stolen. Angel's jewellery collection had remained untouched. Her clothes and handbag collection worth millions lay undisturbed in her walk-in closets. The General's built-in safe with a stash of foreign currency had not been tampered with.

Secondly, it was suspicious as to how the thieves managed to get past security – if there was one thing the General had invested a lot of money in it was being secure. The farm was surrounded by stretches and stretches of electric fencing that sparked off any intruders, both real and imagined. The area around the farmhouse itself was walled and gated, crowned with barbed wire. Lastly, there were security cameras all over the house that beamed any activity to the sentry at the gate. Armed guards patrolled the farm at night just to stem off cattle rustlers.

The police finally whittled it down to a break-in, an 'inside job', concluding that whoever attacked the General lived on the farm. The intruders had intimate knowledge of the farm and the security detail and this meant that the list of suspects was extensive.

The guard on duty that night, Ernest Tembo, claimed that he had seen two women leaving the house at the time of the attack at around 3am. He couldn't see their faces, he said, but they had been dressed in long black gowns that swept the floor. Their gowns had been blood-stained and he claimed that he had shot at them, but the bullets had just gone through them. The women continued running into the dark until they appeared to float seamlessly in the air. The commanding officer taking the statement from Tembo stopped writing mid-sentence, scrunched up the paper and threw it away.

'Are you sure you were sober? You were not drinking on duty?'

Tembo nodded furiously. 'I saw them,' he insisted. 'I was watching the activity in the house on the camera and I saw the General run downstairs, shooting. I couldn't see who he was shooting at, so that's when I decided to drive up to the house.'

'We're talking about an ex-army man who knows how to handle a firearm. Why would he fire at someone and miss?'

The guard shrugged his shoulders. He was equally perplexed, but remained adamant: 'I know what I saw!'

The two officers inspected the footage and the guard wasn't lying. The General was indeed caught on camera rushing down the staircase, shooting aimlessly into the air. He was definitely shooting at someone – or more than one person, as the guard seemed to imply.

'There is no evidence of anyone breaking into the house, so are you saying the General knew these women?'

'Possibly,' replied the guard. 'After Missus Ngozi was arrested, the General brought a lot of women to the house.'

'But these women you speak of don't appear on the camera?'

'No,' replied the guard. 'Just the General. Unless they knew where the cameras were and avoided them. When I got to the door, they were leaving and their dresses were soaked with blood.'

'And then they disappeared into thin air?'

The guard nodded. 'I chased them for a while and then they disappeared. I thought maybe they had gone to the compound so I radioed for help. We got to the compound and searched everywhere, but the women weren't there. When the sun came up we searched the fields, thinking they might have abandoned the clothes somewhere on the farm but we found nothing.'

'Let's just stick to the breaking-and-entering story. This one makes no sense,' replied the officer, not sure how he could explain this 'disappearing into thin air' to the station commander.

The General was laid to rest at Heroes' Acre. Angel mourned behind her fascinator, regal in a black Prada dress. In a show of solidarity, both her mothers were present and she was flanked by Melanie on one side and Simphiwe on the other. Ottilia was there too, holding Anerudo's hand as she jumped up and down, oblivious to the proceedings. Angel remembered that she was about the same age when she lost her father and how history has an uncanny way of repeating itself. Or maybe it only repeats itself because we don't learn the lessons. That, in spite of hindsight, we continue to make the same mistakes over and over again.

Her mother's story of surviving the war was intriguing. She had crawled through the bushes, nursing herself with herbs and other concoctions before she was finally rescued by villagers. She was later transported to a hospital where her physical healing process began. By the time she had recovered, the war was over.

'I was sceptical about going back. I heard about what was happening at the assembly points and got scared. I heard what they had done to your father and I knew I could never come back.'

'What about me? You didn't think to come back for me?' asked

Angel in a small voice.

'I did,' replied Simphiwe, 'but Melanie and Paul had adopted you by then and I knew you would have a better life than the one I could possibly give you. I had nothing, Angel. Nothing.'

Simphiwe went on to explain that she had enrolled at the United Teaching Hospital in Zambia and later rose up the nurses' ranks. She married a man by the name of Thabo Molefe, a disillusioned ANC cadre who had been maimed in one of the camps. He had since died of liver cirrhosis. They never had children because his injuries hadn't allowed him to.

'So what made you decide to come back *now*?'

'I saw your story in the newspaper and I knew I couldn't stay away any longer. I couldn't stand the thought of you being alone and going through this on your own. Of course, the police wouldn't let me see you, but I just needed to be close to you. I was praying for you, Angel, every day I was praying.'

Angel smiled. 'I wasn't entirely alone. My grandmothers were with me.'

Simphiwe smiled knowingly. 'They were with me too … In my darkest times, they were there.'

As she squeezed her mother's hand, Angel wondered where the two matriarchs were. Since her release from prison, they hadn't appeared to her again. It wasn't like she could summon them; they come at their own will. Maybe they were finally resting in peace now that their work was done.

She hosted the After Tears at the farm, more for the General than herself. It was well attended by family, friends and relatives. A lot of greedy family members had been eyeing the farm, wanting to institute a land grab of sorts, but Angel wouldn't entertain the possibility. She had asked the army to provide reinforcement and they obliged. The General hadn't been in the ground long before other generals started making sexual overtures towards her.

'If you need any help, any assistance,' said one, stroking the palm of her hand suggestively with his finger.

'We take care of our own,' said another, rubbing her shoulder, hinting at more than just pure benevolence in his motivation.

'There is life after death,' another whispered in her ear. 'Especially for a beautiful woman like you.'

Angel smiled drily.

Yes, there was indeed life after death, or near-death. She looked to where Bradley was parked in his wheelchair, looking out of the bay window. She walked over to him and put an arm around him.

'I can't thank you enough for being here.'

He hugged her, his face resting on her protruding belly. 'I had to come,' he said. 'To make sure that bastard really is six feet under.'

He whispered, because the house still teemed with army personnel, friends of the General. After the General and his aides had thrown Bradley out of the hotel window, naked, he knew all too well the extent of their wrath. That he survived the fall was a miracle in itself. It did, however, cost him his mobility.

Angel knew they would rise above this, that it was their time now. After everyone had left, Angel removed the sign from the gate and in its place, *Belle Acres* returned.

ACKNOWLEDGEMENTS

Writing this book has been an arduous and consuming journey that began when I was fifteen years old with a manuscript I wrote entitled *Skeletons in the Closet*. I had the skeleton then, but I have spent the past two years fleshing it out and it has metamorphosed and transformed into the book you are holding in your hands. I had to consult critically, read extensively, research rigorously and write voraciously. I also made extensive use of archival interviews and videos, news reports, books and theses on the historical aspects of this story. Thank you to everyone who contributed to this book, whether through recollections and stories, or simply responding to my probing questions.

I would like to express my profound gratitude to Dr Bongani Ngqulunga and the Johannesburg Institute of Advanced Studies (JIAS), under the auspices of which I was able to refine and redefine this novel. Not only did you provide a comfortable work space, but you nourished me with soul food while I was cooking up this book.

Thanks to my fave fellows: Dr Yolande Bouka, Siya Khumalo, Professor Premilla Nadasen, Dr Maria Suriano and Professor Tendayi Sithole for the insightful and thought-provoking discussions and above all, the encouragement.

Thank you to my parents and proprietors of Little Rose Leaf Lodge for accommodating me for an entire month while I worked on the edits of this book. Not only did you provide a conducive workspace, but you played a great role in grandparenting Sabelo while I worked.

As always, the book wouldn't be in your hands if it were not for the Pan Macmillan team, headed by the formidable Terry Morris. Thanks to my patient publisher, Andrea Nattrass, and the editorial prowess of Jane Bowman. Three novels later and it still doesn't get easier. Thanks to the Pan publicists, Eileen Bezemer and Veronica Napier for putting me out there! And not forgetting everyone behind the scenes who works tirelessly to ensure that you can take this book to bed.

To the bookclubs, who will consume this book with mirth and wine, thank you once more for continuing to buy into my stories: Afrokulcha, Bafati Bebumbene, Between the Covers, Black Women Read, Books and Wine, Bubbles and Books, Chapters Between Friends, Dinaledi Bookclub, Divine Goddess Bookclub, EmpowerHer Bookclub, Kopano Odyssey Bookclub, Lire Bookclub, Mathapelo Bookclub, Oshun Goddesses, Palesa Bookclub, Reading Between the Covers, Reading Between the Wines, Sakura Book Club, Sinenhlanhla Bookclub, The Book Club with No Name, The Book Revue, The Bookwormers GP, The Bulawayo Bookclub, The Fat Cats, The Harare Bookclub, The Interesting Bookclub, The Read Soul Lit Bookclub, The Real Housewives of Serengeti Book Club, The Sisterhood Book Club, The Womanist Bookclub, Tusome Bookclub, WeCan SA Chapter Bookclub, When African Women Read Bookclub, Yehru Book Club and Zuri Bookclub.

My acknowledgements would be incomplete without God, the author of it all. You placed me in this path and helped me find my purpose.

Yours writefully!

FURTHER READING

Acting out the Myths: The Power of Narrative Discourse in Shaping the Zimbabwe Conflict of Matabeleland, 1980–1987 by Carl Swarr Stauffer

Architects of Poverty: Why African Capitalism Needs Changing by Moeletsi Mbeki

The Army and Politics in Zimbabwe: Mujuru, the Liberation Fighter and Kingmaker by Blessing-Miles Tendi

Becoming Zimbabwe: A History from the Pre-colonial Period to 2008 edited by Brian Raftopoulos and Alois Mlambo

Dinner with Mugabe: The Untold Story of a Freedom Fighter Who Became a Tyrant by Heidi Holland

The Elite: The Story of the Rhodesian Special Air Service by Barbara Cole

The Fear: The Last Days of Robert Mugabe by Peter Godwin

Guerrilla Veterans in Post-War Zimbabwe: Symbolic and Violent Politics 1980–1987 by Norma Kriger

Gukurahundi in Zimbabwe: A Report on the Disturbances in Matabeleland and the Midlands 1980–1988 by the Catholic Commission for Justice and Peace and the Legal Resources Foundation in Harare

House of Stone: The True Story of a Family Divided in War-Torn Zimbabwe by Christina Lamb

Joshua Mqabuko Nkomo of Zimbabwe: Politics Power, and Memory edited by Sabelo J Ndlovu Gatsheni

Power Politics in Zimbabwe by Michael Bratton

Re-living the Second Chimurenga: Memories from Zimbabwe's Liberation Struggle by Fay Chung

Rhodesia: Last Outpost of the British Empire, 1890–1980 by Peter Baxter

The Struggle Continues: 50 Years of Tyranny in Zimbabwe by David Coltart

Uprooting the Weeds: Power, Ethnicity and Violence in the Matabeleland Conflict by K Yap

War Stories: Guerrilla Narratives of Zimbabwe's Liberation War by Jocelyn Alexander and JoAnn McGregor

Women and Racial Discrimination in Rhodesia by AKH Weinrich

Yithi Laba: Diaries of the Role of ZAPU-ZIPRA Women Combatants in the Liberation Struggle of Zimbabwe, Volume 1 by Methembe Hillary Hadebe

Zimbabwe Takes Back its Land by Joseph Hanlon, Jeannette Manjengwa and Teresa Smart

HISTORICAL TIMELINE

1884/5   Berlin Conference puts in motion the 'Scramble for Africa'.

Sept 1870   Cecil John Rhodes arrived in Durban, South Africa, as an immigrant.

1885   Chief Kgosi Khama III of Bechuanaland (Botswana) signed a protectorate agreement that afforded him protection from the British Crown.

Feb 1888   King Lobengula signed the Moffat Treaty that he believed was a protectorate agreement from the British Crown.

1888   Rhodes registered De Beers Consolidated in partnership with Barney Barnato and Alfred Beit.

Oct 1888   King Lobengula signed the fraudulent Rudd Concession giving Cecil John Rhodes the exclusive mining rights to prospect in Mashonaland and Matabeleland.

Oct 1889   Queen Victoria granted Cecil John Rhodes a royal charter to form the British South Africa Company to administer the territories of Mashonaland and Matabeleland.

1890   The first pioneers arrived in Mashonaland and hoisted the Union Flag in Fort Salisbury.

Oct 1893   Leander Starr Jameson led an attack against the Matabele known as the Jameson Raid. King Lobengula fled and is believed to have committed suicide or crossed into Zambia.

1894	In the absence of King Lobengula and his heir, Prince Njube, Queen Lozikeyi became Queen Regent.
1895	Mashonaland and Matabeleland renamed Rhodesia.
March 1896	The Red Axe Rebellion – a Ndebele uprising against white settlers – led by Queen Lozikeyi in cahoots with her brother, Muntuwani Dlodlo.
June 1896	A Shona uprising against white settlers led by Mbuya Nehanda and Sekuru Kaguvi.
1898	Rhodesia recognised as a British colony.
March 1902	Cecil John Rhodes died in his home in Muizenberg and buried at Matopos World's View, known as Malindidzimu, the haunt of the ancestral spirits.
June 1917	Joshua Mqabuko Nkomo born in the Semukwe Reserve in the Matopo District.
1923	Southern Rhodesia annexed as a British colony and belonged to the Crown with internal self-government.
Feb 1924	Robert Gabriel Mugabe born at the Jesuit mission station of Kutama.
1947	Joshua Mqabuko Nkomo returned to Rhodesia after matriculating in South Africa and was employed by the Rhodesia Railways as a social worker.
1949	Joshua Mqabuko Nkomo graduated with a degree from the University of South Africa.
1951	Joshua Mqabuko Nkomo became the secretary general of the Rhodesia Railways African Employees' Association.
1957	Joshua Mqabuko Nkomo launched the African National

Congress (ANC), Rhodesia's first black national party. It was soon banned and rebranded as the National Democratic Party (NDP).

1957	Ghana became independent and Kwame Nkrumah became the first president.
1960	Mugabe joined the NDP and became public secretary.
1961	The Zimbabwe African People's Union (ZAPU) was formed with Joshua Nkomo, Reverend Ndabaningi Sithole and Herbert Chitepo.
1961	Tanzania became independent from Britain and Julius Nyerere became the first president.
1962	ZAPU banned.
1963	ZAPU splits and a new party formed – the Zimbabwe African National Union (ZANU), under the leadership of Reverend Ndabaningi Sithole.
1963	Nkomo, Sithole and Mugabe arrested.
1964	Ian Douglas Smith became prime minister and leader of the Rhodesian Front.
1964	Nyasaland (Malawi) became independent and Hastings Banda became the first prime minister.
1964	Northern Rhodesia (Zambia) became independent from Britain and Kenneth Kaunda became the first president.
1965	Smith announced the unilateral declaration of independence (UDI) from Britain.
1967	Three-day battle in Morogoro in Tanzania led to a split in ZIPRA and ZANLA armed forces.

1967	ANC and ZIPRA involved in the Battle of Wankie against Rhodesians. South African police dispatched to quell the fighting.
1974	Mugabe took over leadership of ZANU while Sithole remained in prison.
March 1975	Herbert Chitepo assassinated in Lusaka. This precipitated ZANLA migrating from Zambia to Mozambique.
1976	ZANLA resumed the armed struggle on three fronts: Gaza, Manica and Tete.
April 1976	The Geneva Conference held to discuss the issue of majority rule for Rhodesia.
March 1978	Ian Smith and three black leaders signed an agreement to institute a transitional government.
Sept 1978	ZIPRA shot down the Air Rhodesia Viscount. Martial law enacted in certain areas in Rhodesia.
Nov 1978	The transitional government decided to form a government of national unity, but was not endorsed by the Organisation of African Unity (OAU) because it excluded the Patriotic Front.
Feb 1979	Second Air Rhodesia Viscount shot down by ZIPRA. There were no survivors.
March 1979	Bishop Muzorewa won the elections and became prime minister-designate of the transitional government.
May 1979	Margaret Thatcher became the prime minister of the United Kingdom and leader of the Conservative Party.
Aug 1979	Commonwealth summit held in Lusaka and Nigeria nationalised British BP interests in the country. Thatcher

forced to convene the Lancaster talks on Rhodesia.

Sept 1979   The Lancaster House conference began in London.
             ZANU and ZAPU attended as the Patriotic Front in a
             show of solidarity.

Dec 1979   A ceasefire declared, effectively ending the war.

Feb 1980   Second elections held with ZANU winning a majority.
             Robert Mugabe became prime minister.

Nov 1980   First Battle of Entumbane.

Feb 1981   Second Battle of Entumbane.

1982   Nkomo sacked from government under suspicion of
             attempting a coup d'état. He fled to Britain.

1983–87   Mugabe deployed the 5th Brigade in Matabeleland,
             killing more than 20 000 civilians in the Matabeleland
             and Midlands region.

1987   The signing of the Unity Accord merged ZAPU with
             ZANU and effectively annihilated ZAPU and opposition
             politics in Zimbabwe and led to the formation of a one-
             party state.

1989   Edgar Tekere formed the Zimbabwe Unity Movement
             (ZUM) but it failed to make a mark in the 1990 elections
             due to voter intimidation and violence.

April 1990   Expiry of the Lancaster House Agreement.

1991   Zimbabwe adopted the Economic Structural Adjustment
             Programme (ESAP), with the World Bank's support to
             liberalise the economy.

1997   National Constitutional Assembly (NCA) raised

awareness on the need to replace the 1980 constitution.

1997	The Zimbabwe National Liberation War Veterans Association (ZNLWVA), led by Chenjerai 'Hitler' Hunzvi, challenged ZANU-PF.
July 1999	Joshua Mqabuko Nkomo died.
1999	The launch of the Movement for Democratic Change (MDC) under the leadership of Morgan Tsvangirai.
Feb 2000	A referendum held to vote for a new constitution, but was rejected.
April 2000	The first white farmer murdered, marking the start of the fast-track land reform programme.
June 2000	MDC won 57/120 seats in parliament, becoming the official opposition party.
June 2000	The first list of farms to be compulsorily acquired was published.
2002	Zimbabwe suspended from the Commonwealth.
2005	MDC split into two factions, thereby weakening the opposition. The MDC-T was led by Tsvangirai and MDC-N by Welshman Ncube and Arthur Mutambara.
May 2005	Operation Murambatsvina resulted in the destruction of over 700 000 homes.
April 2007	South African President Thabo Mbeki mandated by the Southern African Development Community (SADC) to mediate in the Zimbabwean crisis.
May 2008	Contested presidential elections held in Zimbabwe with results withheld for many months.

Feb 2009   The Government of National Unity formed in Zimbabwe
                  with Robert Gabriel Mugabe as President and Morgan
                  Tsvangirai as Prime Minister.

*During the writing process, I accessed transcripts and recordings of some of
the historical events included in this book. Some of the scenes and dialogue
are reported as, or based on, the actual transcripts. Transcripts have been
used verbatim with no amendments.*